St. Martin's Paperbacks Titles
by LESLIE LaFOY

Her Scandalous Marriage
The Perfect Desire
The Perfect Temptation
The Perfect Seduction

THE Rogue's Bride

LESLIE LaFOY

St. Martin's Paperbacks

This is a work of fiction. All of the characters, organizations and events portrayed in this novel are either products of the author's imagination or are used fictitiously.

THE ROGUE'S BRIDE

ISBN: 0-312-34771-5
EAN: 978-0312-34771-0

Printed in the United States of America

St. Martin's Paperbacks edition / November 2006

St. Martin's Paperbacks are published by St. Martin's Press, 175 Fifth Avenue, New York, NY 10010.

10 9 8 7 6 5 4 3 2 1

PROLOGUE

San Francisco, California
December 1885

$\mathcal{T}$wo hundred and ninety-one days at sea. *Well, not all at sea,* Tristan amended as he made his way up from the dock. Out of that there had probably been twenty or so, all total, that he'd spent ashore. Which, when it came down to it, hadn't been often enough or long enough at any one time for his legs to remember how to walk on land with ease.

He smiled wearily. A hot bath, clothes he hadn't grown sick of, a meal—of fresh meat—prepared by a real chef, and a bed that didn't move all night . . . There was nothing like traveling forever and a day to make one appreciate the simple, heavenly pleasures of home. Pleasures he had every intention of wallowing in as soon as he delivered the manifest to his company clerk.

He passed between two buildings—a hotel and a boardinghouse—that hadn't been there when he'd left ten months ago climbed the wooden steps of Townsend Importers, Ltd., with considerably less élan than he would have preferred, and pushed the door open. The bell overhead jangled, the heat blasted toward him, and his clerk looked up from behind the desk.

"Hello, Gregory," he said, grinning as the young man's thick spectacles fogged over.

"Good afternoon, Mr. Townsend," he replied, lifting the glasses and squinting in Tristan's general direction. "And welcome home. How was your voyage?"

He wouldn't bore Gregory with the details. Advancing to the desk and removing the manifest from his coat pocket, he supplied, "Long, largely uneventful, and hopefully profitable. And how have you and the company been in my absence?"

"I'm well and the company is, assuredly, hugely profitable," Gregory answered, using a handkerchief to clear his lenses.

"I did notice that the warehouse was almost empty."

"And your accounts show it." He settled the glasses back on his face, quickly looked Tristan up and down, and then, as usual, got straight to business. "I saw you sail into the harbor this morning. Full steam as usual. I've placed the ledger on your desk with the mail beside it."

Tristan handed over the manifest, asking, "Is there any correspondence that might be construed as even remotely pressing?"

"There appear to be some personal letters, sir. I put them in a separate stack on top of the ledger. Other than that, they're the usual things. Employment and merchandise inquiries along with social invitations from people who couldn't seem to remember that you were on the other side of the world. I ordered it all by date with the most current on the top."

Ever organized. And honest to a fault. "You are the perfect employee," Tristan offered, heading toward his office. He stopped halfway there and turned back to add, "You might want to spend the next few minutes cleaning out your desk."

Gregory instantly went pale.

"I bought you a new one in Singapore," Tristan hurried to assure him. "An ornate teak monster with abalone inlay. It was being off-loaded when I left the dock and should be up shortly."

"Thank you, sir!"

He couldn't tell whether Gregory's thanks were for the new desk or for the fact that he was still gainfully employed. Either way . . . Tristan smiled. "Hold the thanks until it's in place in one piece. A heap of exotic kindling is nothing to be excited about or grateful for."

"It is when every time that door opens, a blast of cold damp crawls through my bones."

While his glasses fogged over. "I bought a folding screen in Shanghai thinking to give it to Miss Sheraton," Tristan mused aloud as he resumed the course to his office. "Maybe you'd appreciate it more."

"Ah . . . Um . . ."

He stopped and turned back again, this time with his brow cocked. "Yes?"

"About Miss Sheraton." Gregory cleared his throat. "I don't suppose there's any way to soften the blow."

Uh-oh. That didn't bode well. "She hasn't died, has she?"

"No," he drawled, sliding a finger under his starched collar. He swallowed, took a deep breath, and then said on a single rush of air, "She announced her engagement two months ago. To a Mr. George Baker of Seattle. His family is reportedly in sawmills."

Sawmills, huh? Sarah had always appreciated the things a good dollar would buy. The ol' lumber mill had better be a bottomless money pit if George was going to have even the slightest hope of keeping her happy for any length of time. "Well, I can't say that I'm terribly surprised that she moved on," Tristan offered to relieve his clerk's obvious distress at having to deliver the news. "I wish the couple every happiness."

"You're not upset?"

No, not really. "Maybe just a bit irritated that I'm going to have to spend some time cultivating another convenient relationship, but beyond that . . ." He shrugged. "When's the wedding?"

"Two weeks from this coming Friday."

He nodded, wondering if somewhere in the stack on his desk he'd find an invitation to the affair. Not that he had the slightest intention of going. Meeting the groom could be decidedly awkward. "Why don't you go through the manifest there and see what strikes you as being a suitable wedding gift from a former lover?" he suggested as he headed for his office a third time.

"Very good, sir."

"And then see that it's delivered with a brief note expressing my congratulations."

"Yes, sir."

Dropping down in the leather chair behind his desk, Tristan considered the neat paper piles Gregory had lain out for him. The business correspondence had been opened and dealt with—as indicated by Gregory's concisely written notes on each piece. Ah, a good clerk was so hard to find. And a good clerk who didn't blink when asked to handle the messier details of life . . . If the books were just half as solid as Gregory had implied, Tristan was going to give the man a big, fat pay raise.

Tristan's gaze went to the ledger, to the four letters stacked atop it. His heart tripped and his good mood evaporated. Dragging a deep breath into his lungs, he looked out the office window and willed himself to see the ships and the sunlight sparking off the water of the bay. His mind, however, refused to abandon the past and played for him the memories of a long ago and far distant life. The ivy-covered stone of Lockwood Manor on a clear spring day was the best of the images, but it was a fleeting thing, unable to stand the assault of broken china and hurtling silver, of his father bellowing and crashing through the dark, cold halls and half-stumbling, half-crawling midway up the central stairs before falling back and rolling down to lie in a snoring, drunken heap on the foyer floor.

"Gawd," Tristan growled, shaking his head. His attention back to the present, he focused his gaze on the letters again. The letters that were arranged with the most recent on top. "Get it over and done," he told himself as he reversed their order. Recognizing his stepmother's handwriting, he clenched his teeth and braced himself for bad news as he tore it open.

It was dated February. The week he'd sailed out for the Far East.

Dear Tristan,

It is with great regret and sadness that I write to inform you that your father and your eldest brother have passed together into the arms of our beloved Maker. I will spare you the apparent details of the tragedy at this moment, respecting your need to mourn their untimely if not altogether unexpected loss.

Your brother James will, of course, assume your father's title once the official inquest has been concluded. At that point, should you so desire and if it is acceptable custom in America, you may make yourself publicly known as the Viscount Steadham.

Emmaline and I are enduring the situation as well as may be expected.

With warm regards,
Lucinda

Not altogether unexpected . . . Lucinda certainly had a gift for the oblique statement. Tristan sighed and read the note again, wondering just how they'd met their demise. It was a toss-up between both of them drinking themselves blind and doing something stupid like falling off the roof or drinking themselves blind and finally killing each other. The real mystery was in how they'd managed to keep themselves alive for as long as they had.

Tristan laid the letter aside with a wry smile, noting that Lucinda hadn't asked him to return to England to wear the title on home soil. Apparently she'd taken his . . . romantic . . . rebuff to heart. Of course, his having fled to the farthest edge of the United States had probably helped in the cause, too. "Out of sight, out of mind, and all that," he muttered, selecting the next letter from the stack.

"Ah, here's the plea to come home," he said softly, tearing open the letter from James. Dear, sweet, utterly placid, quietly artistic James. Tristan noted the date and smiled. May. Almost three months. He wouldn't have thought it would take James that long to send for help.

Dear Tristan,

> *As we have long speculated, Father spent his every earthly effort ensuring that he left the estate in financial ruin. We did not, however, have the slightest inkling of just how deeply he had dug the hole. To say that the estate is teetering on the edge of bankruptcy is a gross understatement.*
>
> *You know that I have never wanted to be the marquis. We both know that I do not have the intelligence to discharge the responsibilities with any sort of competence. Neither do I have the temperament to bear the strain of such burdens.*
>
> *I am truly sorry to do this to you, but you are far better suited to the task than I. Please remember*

*the good years of our childhood and do not hold my
cowardice too strongly against me.*

> *Always your loving brother,*
> *James*

Tristan reread the last line, his hands shaking and his
heart thundering. No. No, it wasn't what it seemed. James
wouldn't do that. He tossed it aside and quickly opened
the next letter, another one from Lucinda.

Dear Tristan,

> *It is with deep regret and sadness that I must
> write yet again to inform you of a family tragedy.
> Yesterday morning your brother, James, was found
> drowned in the Thames.*

There was more, but Tristan didn't want—or need—to
read it. Throwing the letter down and wiping away tears,
he picked up the one from the family's solicitors. Expelling
a long, hard breath, he opened it. The salutation thudded
in his numbed brain. The expression of regret rippled cold
and hollow through his heart. And the grim details that followed finished knocking the last of his world from under
his feet.

CHAPTER I

London, England
March 1886

$\mathcal{I}$t was a simple choice: either smoke a cheroot or kill someone. Simone drew the flame into the end of the tightly twisted length of tobacco, puffed in utter relief, and shook out the match. Not, she silently mused, shoving the burnt match into the dirt and leaning back against the garden wall, that there weren't a few people whose death would make the world a better place. And not that anyone would think it appropriate to see it in that light or to thank her for the improvement.

She considered the open doors of the mansion through a moonlit haze of sweet smoke and shook her head.

Another night, another ball. The third night of her official first Season and she was already bored out of her mind. She arched a brow and watched Lord Puff and Fluff come out onto the balcony and make a beeline for the shadows. Where, as it turned out, the wife of Lord Tinkle happened to be taking a respite from the dizzying gaiety of the ball— and the pathologically possessive eye of her husband.

Ah, the not-so-secret lives of the peerage. Simone blew out a stream of smoke and smiled wryly. If she got caught smoking in the garden, the news would be all over London within the hour. No one would be surprised, of course. But they would be beyond delighted to have what they'd consider irrefutable proof of her low breeding. As though proof of any sort was required before they expressed their opinions.

Simone sighed and watched Lord Puff and Fluff bend Lady Tinkle backward over the balustrade while simultaneously trying to liberate her breasts and choke her to death with his tongue. If they got caught at it, there would be some clearing of throats, some hasty rearranging of clothing, and a thoroughly proper gentlemen's agreement that nothing would ever be said of the awkward moment.

Unless of course it was Lord Tinkle who caught them. That would be ugly. He'd rage over his wife's fickle and faithless nature, beat Puff and Fluff to a bloody pulp, and then drag Lady Tinkle home by her hair to lock her up for the next aeon or two. She'd contemplate throwing herself out an upper-story window and it would never occur to Lord Tinkle that there might be just a bit of hypocrisy in his continuing weekly visits to Whitechapel and the madam with the Indian rubber sheets.

And no one in Society would ever utter so much as a

word about any of it in public. "Why would they?" Simone whispered on a sigh as she jabbed the end of the cheroot into the dirt beside the used match. "When they have me to talk about?"

Fishing a peppermint from her beaded reticule, she stepped from behind the cover of a flowering shrub of some sort and made her way along the path leading back to the mansion. The tortures one accepted for the sake of appearances and in the name of family. . . . Cruelly uncomfortable clothes, stupid shoes, and inane conversation were bad enough, but having to deal with all that *and* stifling hot and perfume-cloyed ballrooms . . . She really deserved a medal of some sort.

Simone gathered her skirts and climbed the steps to the balcony, ignored the spectacle in the shadowed corner, and stopped two feet inside the brightly lit ballroom. Snapping open her fan, she did what she could to produce a cooling breeze while considering the entirely too bejeweled and oh so publicly circumspect crowd. The actual London Season was just a few months long, she reminded herself. She could endure it.

The question, really, was whether Society could endure her. She smiled and fluttered the fan faster, wondering what unspoken message she was sending with it this time and what ninny had come up with the entire convoluted system of signs. God forbid that people actually say what they thought or—horror of horrors!—clearly and honestly articulate what they wanted. No, if people did that, the world would come to some sudden, hideously crashing end.

Simone's smile widened. According to her older sister, the matrons were saying that Simone was far more interested in courting Armageddon than she was in letting any of the peerage's money-chasing bachelors catch her. It really was amazing how perceptive the old hens could be. *And how utterly overwhelmed some of the chicks are,* Simone added as she watched one of her fellow sufferers sneak a quick peek from behind a potted palm in the far corner. Poor Emmaline. Being pretty, petite, blond, blue-eyed, and the daughter of a marquis didn't seem to have done much for her confidence; she was considerably more mouse than girl.

Simone closed her fan and made her way along the edge of the crowd. Emmaline certainly wasn't what she considered a friend. No, not at all. They'd met only twice. The first time had been three days ago at St. James's Palace while they were both waiting—wearing ridiculous panniers and hideously tight corsets—for their formal presentation to the queen. Emmaline had nearly fainted from the strain. Bracing her had been an instinctive thing—which had led to an obligatory bit of conversation once the girl had recovered her breath and balance.

It was only because Emmaline hadn't been the least bit peerish in that first meeting that there'd been a second. At Lady Somebodyorother's ball the night before last. Neither Emmaline nor Simone had wanted to be there. And while they had vastly different reasons for their aversions, it was at least something they had in common. Which, Simone knew, was far more than could be said for her and anyone else at this evening's ordeal.

"Hello, Emmaline," she said, slipping behind the potted plant.

"Oh, Simone," the other gasped, throwing her arms around Simone's shoulders and giving her a hard hug, "I was *so* hoping you would be here."

"That makes you the only one," she replied, chuckling as she was released. She checked her arms to make sure that she hadn't been pierced by any of Emmaline's hundreds of pale pink sequins. "Are you hiding for a specific reason or is it more a precautionary measure?"

Emmaline sagged back against the wall and stared down at the floor. "I pled a headache last night and was allowed to stay home. Unfortunately, Mother wouldn't believe it could happen two nights in a row."

It wasn't an answer to the question, but Simone didn't press. Neither did she point out that a second evasion might have been possible if Emmaline had been creative enough to develop a different ailment. "My sister insisted that I had to be here, too," Simone supplied, watching the eddying crowd through a veil of palm fronds. "Why, I don't know. But then, I consider this entire coming-out process to be one of life's great mysteries. And torments."

"Has anyone asked you to dance?"

Simone grinned and stepped back to help Emmaline hold up the wall. "The trick is to keep moving, to look as though you have somewhere important to go, and that you'll knock them down if they get in your way."

"Oh, I couldn't possibly do that."

"Do what?"

"Knock them down," Emmaline clarified. "You could and would and they know it. It makes all the difference, you know."

Yes, she did. Just as she knew from their brief encounters that the girl didn't have the foggiest notion of how to hold her own in a crowd of strangers. How to go about angling a shoulder for proper impact would be completely beyond her. The things some people didn't teach their daughters. Someone really should take poor Emmaline under their—

"Would you like to learn how to do it?" Simone offered, buoyed by the prospect of a diversion that could well last for months. For the entire Season! "I'd be glad to teach you."

"I don't think I can—"

"Nonsense," Simone happily interrupted. "I'm living proof that anyone can learn to be and do anything."

Emmaline's smile was weak at best. "I appreciate the offer, Simone, but there is no hope of success and the effort would leave you no time for your own . . ." She glanced through the fronds and then made another pathetic attempt to smile. "Pursuits."

Dear God, the girl was her own worst enemy. Did she ever utter a sentence that didn't contain a version of "*not*"? "I like challenges. As for my pursuits . . ." Simone laughed softly and then leaned closer to confess, "I'm going through all of this just to make my sister and guardian happy. Well, that and I got the horse I wanted for being agreeable. I have absolutely no intention of ending the Season tied elbow, hip, and ankle to some man."

Emmaline stared at her wide-eyed for a long second. Eventually she blinked, swallowed, and said breathily, "Truly? I'm going to marry the first man who asks for me so I don't ever have to do this again."

That is desperate. "Well," Simone ventured, undeterred, "they have to know you exist before they can ask for you."

"I suppose you're right."

Simone ignored the plaintive sigh. "I'm always right, Emmaline," she assured her, coming off the wall. "Trust me."

Emmaline looked as though she were being asked to walk the plank, but she did take a deep breath, and that was close enough to consent for Simone. She extended her hands and held them there until Emmaline reluctantly put hers in them.

"Now lift your chin," Simone instructed once she had the girl planted squarely on her feet. Emmaline looked up at the ceiling. "Not that high. Unless you want a crick in your neck and people looking up your nose."

Emmaline brought her chin down to give her a horrified look.

"Remember how Victoria held hers during the presentation?" Simone suggested. She grinned as Emmaline mimicked it perfectly. "You've got it, my dear. Now square your shoulders."

Bless the girl, she really had no concept of a midpoint on anything. Considering her ample chest . . . "That's not square," Simone observed, trying desperately not to laugh. "That's my-breasts-arrive-in-a-room-five-minutes-before-the-rest-of-me-does."

Emmaline sighed and sagged. "See, Simone? I'm hopeless. I've spent all of my life being a good girl and trying very hard, as good girls should, not to be noticed. And now . . . Overnight . . ." She shook her head. "I don't know anything about how to go about being noticed properly."

Obviously. Where the hell has your mother been the last few years? "We're going to fix that," Simone assured her. "Move your shoulders back half as far as you did before."

So trainable. So there's no excuse for your awkwardness. "Very well done. And now that we've mastered basic presentation," she said, giving Emmaline's hands a gentle squeeze, "we're going to walk—no, *glide*—ever so regally, over to the punch bowl and get ourselves something too sweet but otherwise unnoteworthy to drink."

Emmaline's gaze darted in the direction of the serving table. Her eyes were huge when she looked back at Simone. "Please promise me you won't go off and leave me alone out there."

"Cross my heart and hope to die," she promised, releasing Emmaline's hands. "We step out of here, on three, owning the world and all we survey. Ready?" At the girl's swallow, Simone lifted her chin and squared her own shoulders, saying, "One, two, follow my lead, three."

To her amazement, Emmaline followed and then bravely stepped up to her side as they made their way along the edge of the ballroom. It was nice to know that six long, hideous years of never-ending deportment lessons were worth something after all. And who would have guessed that what little she'd bothered to absorb of it all would be so much more than someone else had? Poor Emmy. Leaving her to fend for herself would be incredibly cruel. Hopefully she'd be able to give Emmy a bit of confidence before Mother Neglectful heard the stories about her daughter's new friend. Once she did . . .

Of course there was the possibility that everyone would consider Emmy a desperately needed positive influence on *her*. Simone grinned. Not that it was bloody likely.

*T*ristan sipped his champagne, looked over the swirl of skirts for the thousandth time that evening, and concluded that wife hunting, while indisputably necessary, was a dreadfully dull thing to do. Not only was his mind numb from the attempt to remember names and faces he didn't care one whit about, but his face was close to paralyzed from the effort of keeping a wholly false smile in place.

He moved his gaze along the edges of the room and caught a glimpse of pink satin and blond curls. Extreme thirst must have driven his sister out from behind the palms, he mused, sipping his drink again.

Or maybe not, he amended, his attention slipping to the dark-haired young woman standing beside her and obviously carrying the bulk of the conversation. The teal-colored gown she was wearing was uncommonly plain, which somehow managed to make the shape it encased all that much more curvaceous. And her hair wasn't swept up to a fashionable pile atop her head, either. No, she'd pulled the sides back and pinned them into a soft little nest but let the rest of the lovely raven curls cascade down her back in defiance of fashion. *And social convention,* he added as an appreciative smile lifted the corners of his mouth.

"I take it that you've found someone of interest?"

He made a mental note to work on not being quite so transparent and then answered, "Over by the punch bowl, Noland. The woman with my sister. What do you know of her?"

His friend from their Eton days leaned slightly forward and to the side for a better view—looking something like a teetering bowling pin as he did. After a moment, he came back to center, took a sip of his champagne, and replied, "I do believe that's Lady Simone Turnbridge."

"Turnbridge," he mulled aloud. "It's not ringing any bells."

"Probably because you never paid so much as a sliver of attention to those sorts of things."

"Probably because I wasn't in line to inherit anything that made it worth my while to pay attention."

Noland gave him a chagrined smile and a brief salute with his glass. "She's one of the old Duke of Ryland's by-blow daughters," he supplied. "The middle one. According to the rumors, she's twenty and her first Season has been delayed until now because it's taken forever and a legion of etiquette masters to make her even marginally presentable."

A legion, huh? Given the hairstyle and the plainness of her gown, Lady Simone apparently had outlasted them all. "She's certainly a beauty."

Noland softly cleared his throat. "Yes, well . . ."

Whether it was the clear notes of Noland's disapproval or the way Lady Simone tipped her head back to laugh at that moment . . . His pulse quickening, Tristan cocked a brow and pressed, "There's a story to her?"

"Quite a few, actually."

"Such as?" There was no artifice to her that he could see from across the room. Odds were quite good that she'd be a delightfully unrestrained lover.

"Suffice it to say that marrying her would ensure that your life would be a living hell. She's an uncontrolled terror and every mother's worst fear."

Which put her in the running for being one of man's favorite fantasies. Hopefully she didn't have a voice that sounded like fingernails on a slate board. "Give me an example of her terrible behavior."

"She rides astride. Need I say more?"

"No," Tristan admitted, grinning as he headed across the ballroom toward his sister and the delectable morsel at her side.

• • •

*T*en minutes to dinner, Emmy," Simone announced as her friend took another sip of the syrupy punch. "Once the hostess dings the little bell, we're off the dance hook for a couple of—" Simone frowned and tilted her head, trying to catch again the discordant sound.

"Is something wrong?"

"I don't know," she admitted. "I thought I heard a strange sort of cracking."

"Perhaps—"

Whatever Emmy had been about to suggest was lost in the deafening roar as a huge fireball shot up the stairwell and exploded into the crowded ballroom. In a single heartbeat the flames expanded in every direction, turning gay laughter to the screams of panic. Simone stared, her feet glued to the floor, her mind calmly noting that the air was suddenly very hot and very thin. Strange, really, since aside from the draperies blazing like torches, there wasn't much actually on fire yet. If people would just calm down, they'd be much better off.

Although . . . Yes, there went the wallpaper behind the orchestra. It was going to be only a matter of minutes now before the whole room was engulfed. Obviously the fire had started on one of the lower floors. Which one? And how?

Emmy grabbed her hand and crying, "Help me find my brother!" pulled her into the mass of humanity storming toward the balcony doors.

Simone went along, her mind calmly collecting bits of information. Too many people, too small, too few doors . . . If they went with the rushing, pushing tide . . . Something deep inside her snapped and her brain began to function properly again. Digging in her heels, Simone used every ounce of her strength to yank Emmaline back. "No!" she shouted above the din. "We'll be crushed! We have to go another way!"

"I have to find Tristan!"

As she had to find Haywood. Who, she assured herself as she looked around the ballroom, was probably in the gardens with Lord Denton's wife. "We'll find your brother once we get out," she promised, dragging Emmy toward the men's gaming rooms and desperately hoping not only that they were all connected but also that the last one of them in the line had a window overlooking the yard. If they had to jump, they had to jump. The chances of surviving a fall were better than those in joining the stampede or in hoping they could find a corner the fire wouldn't touch.

With a stumbling Emmaline in tow, the smoke thickening with her every footstep and burning her lungs with each gasping breath, Simone led the way through the rooms and past hastily abandoned card tables. The gamers had taken the money before they'd fled, she noted, her brain once again slipping into its oddly detached observations. And thought to close the doors into the ballroom behind them. Or perhaps they'd had the same thought she had and gone the way she and Emmy were heading. Perhaps the gamers had already made a way out and all the two of them would have to do was follow them. That would be nice.

So much for nice possibilities, she silently allowed as they raced into a room with, not a door, but a tall, intact window on the far wall and not another soul in sight. Behind her, Emmy whimpered. Simone paused just long enough to gulp a breath of heavy, acrid air and let go of her friend's hand and then went to the window. As she frantically yanked at the sash, the reality of the world beyond it registered in her awareness. She'd turned the wrong direction. It wasn't the rear yard spreading out far below; it was the front drive.

There wasn't anyone down there to help her and Emmy. Just coachmen frantically trying to move their carriages and horses away from the burning mansion and out of harm's way. No one would think to look up. And even if they did, they wouldn't be inclined to abandon their vehicles and snarl things up even worse to effect a rescue of two stupid young women.

Simone pulled on the sash again, desperately aware that the smoke was growing thicker around them. The window refused to budge and she gave up trying to open it that way. Whirling around, she scanned the room, looking for something hefty she could pitch through the window. The desk in the room had only smallish things on it, nothing that would make an opening in an efficient way. The chairs were entirely too big to even think about moving, much less lifting and throwing. The mantel . . . She snatched up her skirts and dashed past a seemingly frozen Emmaline.

Simone was halfway back to the window with an iron fireplace poker firmly in hand and vaguely wondering what they were going to do once they had the glass broken when Emmy cried, "Tristan!"

Simone wheeled back just in time to see Emmy launch herself into the arms of a tall, dark-haired, incredibly broad-shouldered man. A shorter, blond, rather pear-shaped man was behind him, closing the door. Emmy got a quick hug before she was all but slammed back on her feet. "Stuff a rug against the lower edge of the door," her brother said curtly, his dark gaze locked with Simone's as he advanced on her, his hand outstretched. "Permit me, please."

"Glad to see that you've made it this far," she said, handing over the poker. "She was worried about you. I'm Simone."

"Pleasure," he replied. He jerked his head in the direction of his companion and added, "That's Noland," as he strode on to the window.

"Charmed and all that," she offered over the sound of shattering glass.

Noland nodded crisply and stepped past her to look out the opening Emmy's brother had created. "Dear God, Tris," he said, straightening. "It's three stories down. To stone pavers. We'll shatter every bone in our bodies."

As the two of them looked around the room, Simone darted to the curtains. Even as she grabbed a handful of fabric, the hope they offered withered. Still, she gave them a hard yank, pulling them, rods and all, from the window frames. A cloud of dust swirled into the smoke and sent her, choking and stumbling, back, tattered shreds of rotten damask still fisted in her hands. A steel band clamped around her waist and hauled her hard against a massive wall of worsted wool and muscle.

"Stand still," he commanded, planting her on her feet just as abruptly as he had his sister. Releasing Simone every bit as unceremoniously, he added, "I'm going to cut your skirt off at the bodice."

And make a rope of out it. Brilliant. "Rather forward, don't you think?" she offered, lifting her arms out of the way and watching him slice the brocade with a nastily pointed shard of glass. "We've only just met."

He turned his head to look up her, his grin wicked. "It'll give them something to talk about if they find us dead."

Simone laughed as Emmaline wailed from the door, "I don't want to die!"

"We don't, either, Em," he assured his sister, severing the last threads on Simone's dress. "And we're not going to. Noland, get a piece of glass and cut off Em's skirt."

As Noland rushed to obey, Simone stepped out of the teal fabric pooled at her feet and then snatched it up, turning it so that Tristan could slice the seam that gathered and held the length into the fashionably full bustling train. Part of her brain noting the ever-thickening smoke around them, they worked together silently and efficiently to open the seams and then divide the fabric into substantial strips.

The last of them created, he took two from the pile at their feet, found the ends, and whipped them around and about. Simone arched a brow and watched him add a third length to the makeshift rope. Yes, he was using the bowline knot. Quickly, easily, instinctively. "You're a sailor," she observed.

His hands still working, he glanced up and cocked a brow as he gave her a lopsided smile. "You know many?"

"It's been a while."

His smile widened. "That's not what I asked."

"Yes, but it's what I'm answering."

He laughed, the sound low and rumbling and somehow both exciting and soothing at the same time. She was spared from having to contemplate the significance of that by Noland dumping pink strips on the pile of teal ones.

"Shall we use the desk as an anchor?" the portly man asked. "And move it to the window?"

Tristan nodded while tying and testing knots. Simone left him to the important task, trusting his ability, and went to help his friend shove the huge piece of furniture into place. Emmaline joined them and together the three of them managed to get the huge mahogany beast lurching across the room. As they pushed it into place, Tristan dropped the coil of knotted fabric atop it, took a free end, and bent down to secure it around the nearest leg.

He quickly tested it, using all of his weight, and then flung the length out the open window, saying, "Noland, you go first."

"Why?" his friend asked even as he sat on the windowsill and took up the rope.

"One of us needs to be at the bottom to catch Em or Simone should the fabric or the knots give."

"Oh yes," he replied, looking down. "Of course."

"That," Tristan added, grinning wickedly, "and if it'll hold your weight, it'll hold the rest of us."

Noland's gaze snapped up from the ground below. "I've never quite trusted you completely, you know."

"And I can understand why," Tristan countered with a chuckle. "Down you go."

Noland took a deep breath and eased his weight from the sill to the rope. The fabric went taut and the desk skidded slightly toward the window, but the knots didn't shift so much as a millimeter. Simone joined Tristan and his sister at the window, holding her breath with them as they watched Noland lurch and jerk his way down to the safety of the drive.

As his feet touched the ground, Tristan turned away,

took his sister by the shoulders, and sat her down on the sill, saying, "You're next."

Emmaline's eyes went wide. She looked back and forth between them. "That would leave you and Simone alone, unchaperoned."

"Oh, for God's sake, Emmy!" Simone challenged, picking up the slackened rope and forcing it into her friend's hands. "Given the somewhat dire circumstances, I hardly think your brother is of a mind to ravage me. *Or* that maintaining appearances is at the top of anyone's list of concerns at the moment."

"I suppose you're right," she managed to squeak out as Tristan lifted her feet and swung them outside, effectively turning her entire body and preparing her for the descent.

"Yes, I am. Now go. It's getting thick in here."

"Not to mention more than comfortably warm," Tristan chimed in from beside her.

To her credit, Emmaline resolutely inched her behind off the sill and trusted her weight to the rope. She went no farther, though. Tristan leaned down, his hands on the sill, and patiently said, "Just hanging there doesn't do you any good, Em. You have to loosen your hold enough to slide down the rope."

She glanced down and then up at him again, her eyes even wider than before. "What if I can't hang on and fall?"

"Noland will dash under you in a great act of chivalrous sacrifice. Landing on him will be like falling into a feather mattress."

Emmy glanced down at Noland, then nodded, swallowed, and started the descent, one tightly grasping handhold at a time.

"Our rope has taken two down," Tristan said softly,

stepping back from the window as his sister neared Noland's outstretched arms. "It could come apart at any time."

Seeing Emmy safely on the ground, Simone sighed in relief and picked up the slackened line. "My," she said, chuckling as she sat on the sill, "aren't you the cheerful sort."

He grinned and shrugged. "I'm just mentioning possibilities in case you have anything you'd regret not doing before an untimely end."

"Other than getting out of a burning building in time," she offered, swinging her legs out, "nothing comes to mind right this second."

As she considered Noland standing below with his arms up, Tristan said from behind her, "Well, there's something I'd regret if I didn't get to do it."

Oh, God, of all the times for anyone to pour out the yearnings of his soul . . . "What would that be?" she asked dutifully, looking at him over her shoulder.

His eyes twinkled and his grin . . . Her heart lurched and her chest tightened. Her breath caught painfully in her throat as he took her face between the palms of his hands and bent his head. *He isn't— Oh, he is.*

And oh, he did. Thoroughly, bone-meltingly wonderfully. Her breath escaped on a sigh as her lips parted beneath his. *So* good. Never in her life . . .

She swayed and blinked as he released her. The devilish, knowing angle of his smile snapped her awareness back to the moment. And brought her sense of self-preservation to the fore. She arched a brow and announced regally, "That was most improper, you know."

"Absolutely," he admitted, his grin going wider. "Was

it enjoyable as well?"

"Marginally so," she allowed, easing off the sill. "Just barely."

He leaned out after her. "Oh, please! Just barely marginal?"

"Yes," she answered, choking back her laughter. "But you are very good at tying knots. I definitely appreciate that bit of competence on your part."

Tristan watched her descend with a speed and agility that suggested considerable experience at escaping upper stories in the middle of the night. Lord Almighty, she was an interesting woman. She had grit and gumption under fire. Literally. Add in beautiful and naturally wanton . . . "I haven't even begun to show you knots, dearest Simone."

CHAPTER 2

 rope made of knotted damask didn't lend itself well to a display of his true rig-climbing abilities, but Tristan did the best he could with the opportunity and descended hand over hand with far more finesse than any of the others had displayed. Letting go a couple of meters up, he dropped the last of the distance to land squarely on his feet. Both Emmaline and Noland looked at him in wide-eyed and appropriate wonder—the very the kind of wonder and appreciation he'd designed his descent to illicit from Lady Simone Turnbridge. Unfortunately . . .

Tristan looked around the immediate vicinity and then

farther. A flash of white moving toward the end of the flaming mansion caught his eye. "Where's Simone going?" he asked, his eyes narrowed against the smoke and drifting cinders as he considered her.

"To find Haywood," his sister supplied.

"Who?"

"Haywood," she repeated. "I don't know who he is. She didn't say."

"She just thanked us for the adventure," Noland chimed in, "wished us luck in finding our carriage, and headed off on her own."

"Independent thing," Tristan muttered through a smile. As the first of the fire brigade wagons came racing up the shelled drive, he turned back to the others. Abandoning both his smile and his original plan, he improvised a new plan and set it into motion. "Noland, would you see Emmaline home?" he asked. "Lady Simone shouldn't be left unescorted."

Noland blinked. "Your sister and I alone together in the coach? Are you sure?"

You wouldn't take a liberty if it were offered on a silver plate. "The circumstances being what they are tonight, I don't think anyone is going to notice. Or care if they do."

It took the man a minute to think about it, but eventually Noland nodded. "I suppose that makes sense."

It made perfect sense, but a lukewarm acceptance was good enough. Especially with Simone putting more distance between them with every heartbeat. Tristan leaned down, planted a quick, perfunctory kiss on his sister's cheek, and promised, "I'll call on you in the morning."

She smiled and looked up at him adoringly. "Thank you for saving us, Tristan."

"I did nothing more than follow Lady Simone's lead," he countered as he eased away. "She's a remarkably level-headed and resourceful woman."

Em brightened. "I take it that you would approve of a continuing friendship?"

"Absolutely." *In fact, I'm counting on it.*

"Thank you, Tristan!" she cried. "Please keep yourself safe and I'll see you in the morning!"

He smiled, waved jauntily, and strode off. He grinned as he saw that Simone had stopped and hiked up her pure white petticoats and was in the process of stripping off her stockings. God and females only knew why it was necessary to do so, but he was most appreciative of the show. Long and gorgeously shaped legs had always been a weakness of his. As well as pert breasts. And hourglass curves. And elegant shoulder sweeps. And silken napes. And mischievous, sparkling bright eyes. Add in accepting an advance with a laugh and a dare. . . . From what he could tell so far, Lady Simone Turnbridge was very close to being his idea of the perfect woman.

He timed his pace so that he arrived at her side just after she'd dropped her petticoat hems and resumed her trek toward the end of the house. "Hello, again."

"Hello." She glanced over her shoulder and then up at him. "Where are Emmy and Noland?"

Oh, he liked the way she tilted her head when she met his gaze. She had the most amazing cheekbones. High and finely carved. When the light traced over them, they practically begged for fingertips to follow. And her neck . . . Long but hardly spindly, it was the ideal length for effective seduction. By the time a man kissed his way from the lobe of her ear to the hollow at the base of her throat, she'd be melted into a most willing participant.

God, it was going to be difficult to take things slowly with her. And damn difficult to keep his mind on anything other than her. What had she asked him as she'd set his blood on fire? Oh yes. Why they were alone together. He wasn't about to be completely honest with her and confess his most basic motives. Not when a superficial one would do for the moment. He cleared his throat and very deliberately put away his fantasies.

"Em and Noland are searching for our carriage and then hopefully on their way home. Who's this Haywood fellow you're looking for?"

"My escort this evening."

Escort? Damn. "Oh?" he posed ever so casually. "Am I likely to have to meet him in some field at dawn for having cut your skirt off you?"

She laughed softly. "He's my brother-in-law's friend and old enough to be my father."

That was fairly reassuring news, but it was better to be certain. "Age is seldom a consideration in matchmaking, you know."

She rolled her eyes. "He's like a favorite uncle. A matching with Haywood would be perverted."

The angels didn't sing, but they did hum a few bars of a snappy tune. Tristan stripped off his jacket as they walked and draped it over her shoulders, saying, "You'd best wear this."

Again she tilted her head to look up at him. "I'm hardly chilled."

He wasn't, either, and the fire had nothing to do with it.

The angle of her chin was so incredibly come-hither that he stuffed his hands in his pockets and forced himself to look away. "I was thinking to protect you from the drifting cinders."

"Oh. Thank you. That's very considerate."

A woman with more carnal experience would know that it wasn't an entirely magnanimous gesture. Tristan felt a slight pang of guilt, but it was short-lived, snuffed out in the tide of appreciation. A woman instinctively and naturally seductive was such a rare thing. In fact, now that he thought about it, he couldn't remember ever having met one. The women of his world came in three varieties: completely clueless fawns like Emmaline, deliberate, predatory sharks like Sarah Sheraton and a hundred others whose names he couldn't remember, and icebergs like his stepmother.

Lady Simone Turnbridge was decidedly not fawnlike, hardly predatory, and most definitely no iceberg. God give him strength to resist the temptation of her in a measured, well-timed fashion. If he was *too* bold too soon and scared her off, he'd likely kick himself for several months.

They rounded the corner of the mansion together in silence and then froze in the same step. The heat struck hard against his face and he had to narrow his eyes to look into it. Flames rolled out the doors of the ballroom and up the manison's already-blacked stone walls. Those windows that hadn't yet shattered from the heat glowed in promise. Knowing there was nothing the fire brigade or anyone else could do to save the structure, he looked away, out into the yard and the gardens.

In the pulsing orange light of the fire and the rain of cinders, people were moving about like oddly jointed dolls.

There were knots of them here and there, some clustered around a form lying on the ground, others standing mute and clinging to each other. Still others were moving away as quickly as they could and damning the indignity of stumbling. It was eerily close to the images of hell Dante's book had conjured for him.

"My God," Simone whispered.

Tristan shook his head to dispel the trance and took command. "Perhaps you should describe this Haywood," he suggested firmly, "and let me go about the search for him while you wait over there with the ladies."

"I'm not a lady. The title notwithstanding," she declared, starting forward. "And three-quarters of the windbags under that tree will be happy to tell you so and why. In great detail."

Interesting. "What about the other quarter of them?" he asked as he took up his place beside her.

"They wouldn't say shit if they were buried up to their necks in it."

He blinked and his jaw sagged. He quickly recovered, making a mental note to ponder the wonder—and implications—of her language at a later time. At the current moment, there were more important considerations. The immediate need to effect rescues was obviously past and no one in need seemed unattended, but the injuries he could discern ran the full gamut of severity.

"If you keep going," he warned, "you're likely to see some grisly sights."

"As you may have heard," she countered, continuing her course and looking around the yard, "only the last six years of my life could be described as sheltered. Ridiculously so, actually. But my memory goes back a good bit further than that. I can promise you that I will not retch or cry or faint."

Yes, but she might have nightmares. And he wouldn't be in any position to garner her appreciation for offering comfort in the dark of the night. "I haven't heard much of anything about you," he confessed. "But I'm incredibly fascinated by what I've seen so far this evening."

"Is that so."

He ignored her sarcasm. "Of course. You're very different from all the other misses."

"I *have* been described as a true diamond in the rough. The windbags were in a kind mood that day."

"I think roughness, like beauty, is defined by the eye of the beholder. Personally, I think man rarely improves on Nature's creations."

She stopped and slowly turned to face him. Her chin came up. So did one beautifully wing-shaped raven brow. "Are you attempting to make my heart go pitter-pat with all this?"

Well, yes. He smiled. "Is it working?"

"No."

"What *would* make your heart go pitter-pat?" He leaned down slightly. "Just a hint will do."

"Why?"

"Why not?" he countered, thoroughly enjoying the game.

She rolled her eyes and walked off, saying, "I don't want my heart tripping and skittering, thank you very much."

Only because she'd probably never felt the thrill of it being done properly. Once again, as was rapidly becoming their pattern, he caught up with her. "This is why you're so fascinating. Most women dream of feeling the flutter of true love."

"Yes, well, most women are—" Whatever observation she'd been about to make was lost as she darted off, calling, "Haywood!"

The man—presumably Haywood—into whom she flung herself was tall and fair-haired going to gray and wearing what had undoubtedly been, at the start of the evening, an impeccable suit of high-quality fabric and fine tailoring. Now it was badly singed and either the left sleeve had been torn loose or the shoulder under it had.

"Oh, thank God you're all right," Haywood said, giving her a hard, one-armed hug. "Drayton and Caroline would have killed me if something had happened to you." He let go of her, quickly looked her up and down and then over to meet Tristan's gaze and ask, "Where is the rest of your dress and who is this man?"

"My dress is hanging in knotted strips out one of the front windows," she supplied happily. "And this is Tristan."

"Tristan who?"

She frowned, the expression clearly conveying that she didn't have the foggiest notion.

Ah, but he was good at being a White Knight of All Occasions. "Lord Tristan Townsend," he said, extending his hand. "The Marquis of Lockwood. Lady Simone is a recent friend of my sister, Lady Emmaline Townsend."

His gaze was hard and openly assessing, but he stuck out his hand, saying, "The Honorable Cyril Haywood."

"It's a pleasure, sir."

"Likewise."

The formalities attended to, Simone moved them on, asking, "How did you break your arm, Haywood?"

"It's not broken. Thank God."

Tristan nodded. "If I were to guess, I'd say that your shoulder has been dislocated."

"It is. Compliments of Lord Marthorpe. He let nothing and no one stand in the way of his saving his own fat arse," Haywood explained, looking around. "And if I find him, I'm going to do some dislocating of my own. Starting with his ever-so-patrician nose."

Simone cleared her throat. "Yes, but that can wait. Revenge, as they say, is a dish best served cold. Shall we take you directly to a surgeon or summon one to the house?"

Haywood, still looking for Marthorpe, didn't reply.

"If you're willing to take the chance," Tristan ventured, "I think I can probably put your shoulder back into place for you right here."

Simone looked at him, her eyes bright and that brow of hers arched in a way that said he'd suddenly become a bit more interesting than she'd expected. He hadn't intended that as a consequence of offering his help, but he was pleased by it nonetheless. Seduction was far easier, not to mention quicker, if the woman was intrigued enough to be willing to meet a man halfway.

Haywood's gaze came slowly to him. "You've trained as a physician?"

"It's more a case of having considerable experience at making do in the absence of one. If it helps any to know, I've never killed anyone with my efforts."

After a moment of apparent contemplation, the other narrowed his eyes and asked, "What about maiming?"

"I think they would have limped or worse if I hadn't tried," Tristan answered truthfully. He shrugged and added, just as honestly, "But I suppose there's no way of knowing for sure."

Haywood took his measure another time, then sighed. "All things considered . . . Let's have a go at it. It's beastly painful and I'd prefer to have it relieved as soon as possible."

"If you would lie down, please."

As Haywood carefully and somewhat awkwardly laid himself out on the lawn, Simone took a deep breath and asked, "Is there anything I can do to help?"

"Well, you don't have to," Tristan replied, "but I'd really appreciate it if you'd hold his good arm down and keep him from using it to take a swing at me."

For some reason he'd expected her to go a bit pale at the notion that setting her escort's shoulder might involve some violence. Which, he realized as she tipped her head back and laughed, had been a complete underestimation on his part. Lord Almighty, she was absolutely gorgeous. And so utterly, delightfully unpredictable.

"I'd appreciate it," Haywood offered from the ground at their feet, "if the two of you didn't seem quite so happy about this. Smiling and laughing at the prospect of another's pain is rather ghoulish, you know."

"Sorry, Haywood," Simone offered, dropping unceremoniously to her knees beside him. "I'll try to look properly horrified. How's this?"

Haywood rolled his eyes at her futile attempt to control her smile, looked up at Tristan, and said, "Please get on with it before she explodes and makes a complete mess of my new suit."

Kneeling on his other side, Tristan carefully took Haywood's arm in hand. "I don't think she can do any more damage to your suit, sir, than the fire's already done," he observed as he gingerly checked the position of the bones and then began to carefully rotate the arm.

He cast Simone a quick look. At her nod, he set his free hand on the shoulder and added breezily, "There are at least a dozen cinder holes in your lapels, you know. Satin is a pretty fabric and all, but it burns so easily. And the coat itself is torn from the right pocket almost to the hem. I seriously doubt that even—"

The timing was spot-on. The pop was audible, quick and clean.

"—the world's best tailor could make it whole again," Tristan went on over Haywood's accompanying groan.

"At least," Haywood said breathlessly as they released his arms and Simone sat back on her heels, "it's a different kind of pain."

Tristan nodded and took Haywood's good hand. As he eased the man to sitting, he counseled, "You're going to be quite sore for a few days, and until the muscles settle back, the joint will be easily popped out of place again. Assuming that you'd prefer to avoid that, I'd suggest that you try not to exert the joint or overuse your arm. In fact, you should probably use a sling to make regular activities impossible for the next week or so."

"We could fashion one here and now with a piece of my petticoat," Simone offered, reaching for the hems behind her.

"Unfortunately," Tristan said, wishing Haywood wasn't there so he could fully and truly appreciate the fine ankle Simone was so casually displaying, "we don't have anything with which to cut it."

She pulled something from her garter that looked like

a chopstick. He was pondering the oddity of that when she turned around. For the second time that evening, his jaw dropped. Firelight dancing along the blade of the stiletto in her hand, he shook his head in wonder. "Why didn't you haul that out when we were in the study?"

"We didn't need it. You were doing nicely enough with the glass shard and I didn't want to insult your masculine sense of mastery."

How very kind of her. "Do you usually come to Society events armed?"

She arched a brow. "You don't?"

"I didn't know there was a reason I should. Of course, I've been abroad for—"

"If I might say something?" Haywood interrupted, looking back and forth between them.

Simone smiled. "Certainly, Haywood. It's your arm."

"Yes, it is," he agreed, shifting his weight forward in an obvious beginning effort to gain his feet. Tristan scrambled to his and offered Haywood a hand. As he pulled him upright, he went on, saying, "You're sufficiently underdressed already and putting my arm in a sling right this moment is hardly a life-or-death matter. It can wait until we reach home. And speaking of home," he added without pause, "it's time we take ourselves in that direction."

Simone nodded and put her knife away and then simply sat there, her gaze in the flames shooting from the ballroom doors.

"There's nothing for us to do here," Tristan said softly, stepping over and extending his hands for her.

"How many do you think were trapped?" she asked, still watching the fire as she let him pull her to her feet. "How many do you suppose were trampled?"

"No more than a handful of either," Haywood assured her. "If that many. Westfield and his friends were tossing people off the balcony right and left to get them out of harm's way. There are a good number of twisted, sprained, and broken ankles as a result, but better those injuries than the alternatives."

"There's nothing anyone can do for those still inside," Tristan offered in consolation even as his brain was wondering why a lady would have calluses in the palms of her otherwise soft hands.

Haywood cleared his throat. Loudly and pointedly. "Except pray for their souls, of course."

"Of course," Tristan allowed, releasing Simone's hands and stepping away from her as Haywood had so eloquently, if wordlessly, demanded. "If you're the praying sort."

"Or the sort interested in being perceived as one," Simone added, turning from the destruction. She tilted her head back to smile up at him and his heartbeat quickened. "Since you've sent Emmy and Noland on in your carriage, may we offer you a ride to your house?"

He really should decline. Haywood wasn't blind or an idiot. "That would be most kind of you. Thank you."

CHAPTER 3

*S*imone considered the man walking on her right and wondered how it was that she hadn't noticed before now that he was so . . . well, "handsome" wasn't quite descriptive enough. And it really was more than just mere looks. There were any number of men in London with well-carved features and dark, dark eyes with thick lashes. And quite a few were tall and broad shouldered, too. But there was something about Tristan that wasn't at all common. At least not in her experience.

It was a sort of presence, a serene confidence, about him that was both comforting and disquieting at the same time, comforting in that she knew if someone were to charge out of the shrubbery at them, it would be the last time they ever thought to assault anyone. The unease about such capabilities, of course, came from the suspicion that in the absence of such challenges, Tristan would, out of sheer boredom, cast about for other diversions. Diversions of the seductive variety.

Actually, she amended, smiling down at the ground passing beneath her feet, *boredom isn't a prerequisite for Tristan's attention to wander.* A building blazing around him and an escape in progress hadn't been sufficient to keep him from seizing an opportunity to steal a kiss. Not that it had been really and truly *stolen.* He hadn't taken it at blade- or gunpoint. And she hadn't made much of an effort to evade it. Her smile widened. All right, she hadn't made any effort at all.

And if he ever looked like he might want to kiss her again, she certainly wasn't going to squeak in protest or flinch in fear as all good and virtuous misses should. No, not in the least. Who in her right mind wanted to be good and virtuous instead of thoroughly kissed? And God, Tristan Townsend really was a good kisser. She could still feel the softness of his lips on hers. And just remembering . . .

Simone looked up, thinking it would be best to fill her awareness with something other than the thick, liquid heat sliding ever so deliciously through her limbs. The garden gateway to the street was some twenty meters ahead, she noted. It stood open and she could see that the carriages had come around to wait there for the owners. She hoped Emmy and Noland had found Tristan's and were already home, safe and sound. Emmy had probably blanched at the idea of an unchaperoned ride and then packed herself into the corner to pray the whole way that no one ever found out. Emmy was such a good girl.

Which *she* clearly wasn't, Simone had to admit. If the chance of a carriage ride alone with Tristan presented itself . . . Given how her mind tended to flit through the possibilities with glee, it was probably a good thing that Haywood was along this evening.

She glanced at him on her left and decided that she'd never seen him quite so grumpy. His shoulder understandably pained him, but she doubted that it was entirely the reason for the depth of his frown. *No, scowl,* she amended, looking more closely. What on earth could have set him off? Having her skirt hacked away wasn't any great sin, considering the circumstances. Her bodice was still very much intact. Untouched, actually. She was still wearing every thread of the petticoats and other underclothes she'd had on when she'd left the house. And there was absolutely no way he could even suspect that she'd been kissed.

Was he angry about giving Tristan a ride to his home? she wondered as they passed through the gate. If he was, it was horribly uncharitable of him and she was going to ignore him, his foul mood, and his apparent determination to be rude.

Their driver stepped from the knot of others awaiting their employers, his smile one of utter relief and happiness. "You hadn't given up on us, had you, John?" she asked as he motioned them to follow him to the carriage he'd parked a short distance away.

"Not at all, Lady Simone," he called over his shoulder. "I was just telling the others that if there was a way out, you'd find it and bring a half dozen along with you."

"Just three," she laughingly replied as he popped open the door of their carriage. "Two of whom have already gone home. Leaving only Lord Lockwood in need of transportation."

He looked past her to ask, "Your townhouse on Park Street, sir?"

"You know it?"

"Your driver is my cousin, sir. On my mother's side."

He chuckled, the sound of it low and rumbling nicely over her as he assisted her inside. "It's a very small world these days."

"It is indeed," Haywood deigned to comment as he came in behind her. He dropped onto the rear-facing seat and deepened his scowl just before Tristan stepped in and took up the other half of his seat.

Be as disapproving as you want, she silently countered, pointedly pulling Tristan's coat closer around her. *I'm ignoring you.*

As the driver climbed into the box and they started on their way, Tristan considered the delightful morsel on the opposite seat. That a woman could look so positively at ease wearing only half her clothes in public was truly amazing. Would she be just as comfortable stripped out of them completely? If Haywood weren't there, he'd be doing his damnedest to find out. The way one corner of her mouth tipped invitingly upward . . . Did she know what he was thinking? Would she protest a bolder advance?

"I seem to recall, Lord Lockwood," Haywood said beside him, "that I interrupted you earlier. You were saying something about having been abroad recently."

Ah, the inquisition begins. "I've spent the last twelve years in America and returned to England only a month ago," Tristan replied, determined to handle the situation with all the grace he could muster.

"And what brought you back after such a long absence? I would have thought that in that time you would have made a life for yourself that you would have been loath to abandon. Or are you planning to return to it at some near date?"

Simone lowered her chin and shot her escort a dark look. "Haywood, that's prying."

"Oh, I don't mind at all, Lady Simone," Tristan assured her. "Better to be asked questions than to be ignored." He half-turned on the seat to meet Haywood's gaze and answered, "I had made myself a very nice life in America, Mr. Haywood. Not that I spent overly much time there on a regular basis. Most of the last twelve years have been spent aboard one of my ships, plying the waters, as they say, between San Francisco and various ports in the Far and Near East."

Haywood didn't react at all, but Simone sat up straighter and her beautiful dark eyes shone. "You're a ship's captain?"

"Captain, owner, and renowned importer," he corrected with a mock bow. He sobered as he again faced Haywood. "It was on my latest return that word reached me of having unexpectedly inherited my father's title. I came home immediately to see to matters of the estate. As for returning to America any time soon . . . It won't be necessary. I've moved my offices to London and will continue my import activities from here."

"A marquis in trade?" Haywood observed dryly.

"I prefer to think of it as being a marquis with an interesting hobby." He grinned. "That also happens, quite coincidentally, I assure you, to be obscenely profitable."

Haywood clearly wasn't amused. "I doubt that others in Society are likely to be as creative in their thinking on it."

"I don't much care what others think. I never have."

Haywood considered him with a cocked brow and a frown that deepened as Simone's smile turned to brilliantly dazzling. "Tell me about your travels," she said, her voice slightly breathless. "Have you been to China? Japan? To India?"

To hell with Haywood. "All of them," Tristan supplied, enjoying her enthusiasm. "My most recent voyage was to the Polynesian Islands and then on to India, making ports all along the way."

"What sorts of things do you bring back?"

"Mostly textiles, art, furniture, and foodstuffs native to the East. All of it exotic, of course. And most of it edging a bit toward decadent."

Her smile widened. "How many ships do you own?"

"Three."

Haywood muttered, "The *Niña*, the *Pinta*, and the *Santa Maria*?"

Tristan cast him a quick look, replied, "The *Constance*, the *Margaret*, and the *Bernadette*." Turning his full attention back to Simone, he went on, "*Connie*, *Maggie*, and *Bernie* for short. And before you ask, no, I have no idea for whom they were christened. They came with histories that they, being ladies of considerable discretion and pride, haven't shared with me. And being a gentleman, I haven't pried."

She laughed as he'd hoped she would and then asked, "Are any of them in port? Here in London, I mean?"

"*Maggie*'s in China. *Bernie*'s in India. But if *Connie* safely rounded the Cape of Good Hope, she'll be into London in the next few days with the cargo I acquired on my last trip."

"I would love to see her. And to see all the lovely things you brought back."

"I'd be delighted to give you a tour."

He could feel Haywood bristling, but before the man could lay down the Laws of Propriety, Simone asked excitedly, "Did you happen to buy any large, fancy birdcages?"

Birdcages? That was unexpected. "How large?"

She glanced around. "The size of the inside of this carriage would do perfectly."

"For what?" he asked, chuckling. "A pony?"

"My younger sister, Fiona," she explained, grinning, "rescues injured animals of all varieties. She has a considerable number of birds who, while healed, wouldn't be at all safe if she were to release them. She has little cages everywhere in the house and I've often thought that it would be ever so much easier for her to care for them if they were all in one large cage. Not to mention that she'd so enjoy being in the cage with them. She really is a wonder with animals. You'll have to meet her and all of her charges sometime. Anyway, her birthday is in a week and if you happen to have such a cage, I'd pay whatever you'd care to ask for it."

Whatever? Oh, that would be—

"Within reason, of course," Haywood intoned darkly.

"I wouldn't dream of accepting your money for anything," Tristan countered smoothly.

"But I can't accept gifts," Simone protested. "Especially from men I barely know. It would be viewed as unseemly. I've been lectured unconscious about that."

"Then," he posed, thinking fast, "we'll consider it a repayment for having saved my sister's life this evening."

She rolled her eyes and waved her hand in a tiny dismissive gesture. "I saved my own life and simply took her along. It was hardly a great act of bravery or self-sacrifice on my part."

Meet me halfway, Simone! "Whatever your perspective on it, I very much appreciate that you didn't let her run headlong into the crowd trying to get out onto the balcony."

She sighed and shook her head. "We would have been toward the back of it, and given how quickly the fire was catching in the ballroom, I didn't think much good would come of being anywhere in the melee."

"Ah, but you thought when so many others didn't."

"Where were you," Haywood asked dryly, "when the fire began, Lord Lockwood?"

Haywood, you're a pest. "On my way across the ballroom for a cup of punch," he supplied, deliberately omitting the other pertinent details. "Where were you when the fire began, Mr. Haywood?"

"I was strolling in the gardens, alone, smoking a cheroot."

"Oh, please, Haywood," Simone countered with the most adorable and unladylike snort. She leaned forward, giving Tristan a lovely view of her décolletage as she went on, saying, "You were with Lady Denton, and if anything was smoking at all, it was Lady Denton's pantaloons."

Tristan laughed outright while Haywood cried, "Simone!"

"Don't even try to pretend to be an innocent with me, Haywood. I know you."

"Be that as it may, I—"

"He's a notorious womanizer," Simone announced, settling back in the seat and meeting his gaze. "It's hardly a public secret."

Tristan did his best to rein in his amusement. "So I gathered."

"Is there a Lady Lockwood somewhere?"

Simone looked at his seatmate and shook her head. "That didn't even flirt with subtle, Haywood."

"It would appear to me," he countered testily, "that we've passed the point where subtlety and finesse are necessary, much less expected."

Tristan cleared his throat and answered, "At the present time, the only Lady Lockwood is my late father's third wife. My stepmother, Lucinda."

"She's Emmaline's mother?" Simone asked.

"Yes." Deciding that things would go better if he supplied the details rather than let Simone hear them from others, he added, "She's announced that she intends to follow Victoria's example and spend the rest of her life in mourning."

She nodded and looked a little sad. "She must have cared deeply for your father."

"Actually, it was one of those marriages made in haste to be regretted at once and resented at long leisure. They lived separately from the very beginning. Her public display of grief at his passing is largely for the purpose of garnering public sympathy. I give her another month, at the outside, to grow bored with it."

As Simone seemed to ponder the information, he turned his attention to Haywood and said, "If you are unattached, Mr. Haywood, consider yourself fairly warned of the impending hunt."

Haywood's smile was thin. "Your mother's—"

"My mother," he corrected firmly, "has been dead for nineteen years."

Haywood had the grace to wince; a point in his favor. "My sincerest apologies. And while the thought is appreciated, no warning is necessary, Lord Lockwood. Your *step*mother's reputation precedes her."

As the entire family's reputation preceded *him*. Tristan braced himself for the inevitable, knowing that Haywood was the sort to consider it his duty to inform Simone— and him, too—of just how terribly unsuitable he was.

Ever so predictably, Haywood cleared his throat and droned, "As—"

"Really? She's that improper?" Simone said, cutting Haywood off and looking back and forth between them. "Then how is it that Emmaline is so . . . well, shy?"

"We can be honest about it," Tristan said as the carriage began to slow. "My sister's not only shy; she's painfully awkward. Lucinda wanted a title and producing a child was her most certain means of attaining one. However, being a good mother, much less a doting one, was never one of her aspirations. Em has grown up in the care of nurses and tutors. Had Lucinda been willing to pay sufficient wages to attract higher-caliber, more refined individuals to employment, my sister would have had better instruction in the social graces. But Lucinda wasn't and so Emmaline didn't."

"Oh, poor Emmy."

"I appreciate your willingness to befriend her," he offered sincerely. The carriage stopped and he reached for the door handle, adding, "I don't think she's ever had a true confidante. And certainly never one her own age."

"I think she's a very nice girl," Simone said softly as he stepped out. "Would it be all right to call on her?"

It would be my fondest hope. "She would be utterly delighted and I would be incredibly grateful for your kindness." He gave her a short bow, said, "Good night, Lady Simone. It has been a pleasure to make your acquaintance," and then gave her unhappy escort a brief nod. "Mr. Haywood, thank you for the ride and I hope your shoulder improves quickly."

"Lord Lockwood."

"Good night, Tristan," Simone called as he closed the door and waved to the driver.

His hands stuffed in his trouser pockets, he watched the vehicle roll away and weighed the possibilities. On the one hand was the certainty that Haywood wouldn't waste a single moment in telling her all the salacious details of the Lockwood family history. On the other hand was the equal certainty that the man only knew about the public scandals. And unless Tristan had badly misjudged Simone's temperament, she wouldn't let any of it deter her for so much as a heartbeat.

Yes, he allowed, smiling as he made his way up the front walk of his town house, the odds were very good that she'd be with Emmaline, waiting for him, when he went to call in the morning.

◆ ◆ ◆

$\mathcal{T}$hat's a very dangerous man, you know, Simone."

Well, of course she did. If Tristan weren't dangerous she wouldn't have given him a passing glance. But since it wouldn't do to say that outright, she breezily replied instead, "Dangerous? Oh really, Haywood. Don't you think you're taking the Lord Protector role just a bit too seriously? For heaven sakes, the man is a peer."

"He wasn't expecting to be a marquis and he hasn't lived a soft life breathing rarefied English air. He's a man of considerable worldly experience."

So she'd concluded—quite ably—on her own.

"I'd wager a dozen horses," Haywood went on, "that he's seen more than his fair share of dark haunts and illegal business."

She'd concluded that as well. And been fascinated. "You worry too much. I can manage him just fine."

He leaned forward to say slowly and succinctly, "No, Simone, you can't. What you see on the surface isn't at all what he's like beneath. He's a seducer of the first order."

Says another seducer of the first order.

"And he's chosen you for a conquest."

It really was amazing that people considered her so naive; how, in the span of the last six years, everyone seemed to have forgotten where and how she'd lived the previous fourteen. "I'm terribly flattered that he might consider me worth the effort, but he's going to be disappointed."

"You need to stay away from him."

Knowing that all of her assurances were falling on deaf ears, she stifled a sigh of frustration and chose another course. "I'll do my best, Haywood. I promise."

Haywood smiled thinly. "I would have preferred to say nothing on the matter, but since I know full good and well that you haven't been the least dissuaded by my appeal to your common sense . . . Your Prince Charming is the last surviving male in the Lockwood family. They've been known for three generations as the Lunatic Lockwoods. Such a reference is hardly kind, I know, but it's been quite appropriate."

Lunatic? Oh, Haywood had stooped low. "Tristan seems perfectly sane to me. Did you notice any peculiarities in his behavior? Any twitching? Did I somehow miss his eyes pinwheeling?"

"His paternal grandfather," Haywood went on sternly, "was a devoutly religious man who, during the full moon, displayed a penchant for frolicking in public parks and fountains without a stitch of clothing and in the company of . . . strange women."

God save her from those seeking to spare her. "Whores," she clarified.

"Well, yes." He cleared his throat. "Three or four at a time, actually."

"I'll allow that it was odd, but calling it lunatic is going too far, Haywood. The only difference between Grandfather Lockwood and most peers is that the latter confine their naked group frolicking to the inside of a brothel or their town houses."

"He died of . . . diseases."

"Lots of men do," she pointed out. "And since we've never had an opportunity to discuss the matter, let me take this one—since it is so perfect—to express my sincerest hope that you're taking precautions in *your* frolicking to avoid that horrible fate."

His eyes widened and he sputtered, "Ladies don't—" He swallowed the rest of the decree, his lower lip caught between his teeth.

She refrained from pressing any further on the matter, smiled graciously, and snuggled deeper into Tristan's jacket. How convenient that she'd forgotten to offer it back to him as he'd left the carriage. As excuses went, the need to return it would serve as the perfect one for going to see Emmy in the morning. And if he happened to come by the house to check on Emmy in the aftermath of this evening's stresses . . . Well, she couldn't very well get up and run away at the sight of him. That would be unconscionably rude. Not to mention silly and embarrassing.

"The old man's son—Tristan's father—was a raging drunk."

Simone swallowed a groan and Haywood continued on, saying, "I don't think I ever saw the man anywhere near the edge of sober. And he was not a jovial tippler, either. He was mean and crude and given to public brawls. In the later years, most often with *his* eldest son, who had followed in his alcohol-drenched footsteps."

"A good many men drink to excess," she countered wearily. "On a regular basis."

"Yes, but very few drunkard peers of the realm are found dead with their eldest son, bullets through both their hearts."

"Unless they were the victims of a robbery gone terribly wrong."

"They were found in the study of their country house," Haywood persisted, the definite notes of triumph edging his voice, "and it was concluded at the inquest to be a murder and suicide. The title went to the next son, James, an artistic sort who threw himself in the Thames shortly thereafter."

"It's all very tragic," she allowed. "But to my mind, it doesn't so much suggest madness as it does a family who has always had more money than good sense."

"And the present Lord Lockwood is one of them."

Her patience near the end, Simone managed a smile and tiny laugh. "Well, Emmaline certainly isn't a lunatic and I've seen nothing in Tristan's conduct to suggest that he is, either."

"Still, I think—"

"That the mistakes and poor judgments of the parents," she suggested coolly, "are always carried on by their children?"

He cleared his throat and pulled at his starched collar before protesting, "That's not what I was saying at all."

"Yes," she insisted sadly, "that is exactly what you're saying, Haywood. However indirectly and obliquely."

"Simone," he began, looking acutely distressed.

"Lovely night, isn't it?" she said lightly, cutting him off as the carriage turned and began to roll up the drive. "The horrible fire aside, of course. Do you suppose I might be really lucky and they'll cancel the Season for a mourning period?"

"I don't know, but I sincerely hope not."

"Why's that? Have you been filling in dance cards in advance?"

Haywood sighed. "Lord Lockwood is not an acceptable suitor, Simone. You need to keep looking and settle on someone safer. The Season continuing on would serve that end."

Tristan wasn't a suitor; he was a seducer. They'd already

established the distinction. Unwilling to discuss the matter any further, she smiled prettily and said, "I doubt that the doyens will consult either one of us on the matter, so there's nothing we can do but accept their decree with as much grace as we can."

Haywood opened his mouth to reply, but the carriage stopped and the footman opened the door to save her. Clutching Tristan's coat around her shoulders, she vaulted out onto the portico pavers and then turned back to await Haywood.

"I hope your shoulder lets you sleep at least fairly well tonight," she said as he joined her in walking up the stone stairs and through the open doorway. "And I'm glad that you weren't any more seriously hurt than that."

"It's not altogether a bad thing," he assured her with his usual smile. "Especially if I put it in a sling. The ladies will be obliged to offer their sympathies and express their concerns."

Of course. And little wonder that he recognized Tristan Townsend's underlying motives. Wolves did tend to know when another was about. She paused in the foyer and gave him a kiss on the cheek. "Good night, Haywood. Sweet dreams."

"Don't you dream at all!" he called as she started up the stairs. "And certainly not about scurrilous men!"

"I won't," she promised, simply because she knew she was supposed to. That was the thing about her life, she mused while making her way down the hall toward her room. Every waking moment of it was wrapped up in the expectation to meet expectations, large and small. Do this, do that. And for godsakes *don't* do that. The list of don'ts was endless and everyone seemed to think that the fate of the British Empire depended on her ability to memorize and live by it.

Not that there weren't just as many rules for those who hadn't been elevated to the status of the daughter of a dead duke, she allowed as she closed her bedroom door behind her. It was just that the rules for them were considerably more practical. If you ignored them, you could well end up dead by any number of grisly means. Which, all in all, made the restrictions not only understandable but also considerably less chafing.

She sighed, kicked off her mules, and removed Tristan's coat from her shoulders. And then went slowly still as she savored the scent wafting around her. A hint of spice, a shadow of something deep and woodsy, the barest touch of sunlight. Lifting the coat to her face, she buried her face in the warm satin lining and breathed deeply the scent of Tristan Townsend.

Simone drew back and considered the black silk fabric, her brows knitted. There was no way to reasonably count the number of men who had crossed her path in the course of her twenty years, men of every social class and with every imaginable vice and virtue. Some had been handsome, some not. Some had been obviously depraved to the point of being a physical threat, while others had been merely interesting in a "Good Lord, he's actually allowed to run loose?" sort of way. Not once had any of them ever interested her in a personal sense, in a way that . . .

Simone smiled softly. None of them had ever made her heart go pitter-pat. At least not in a good sort of way. Not the way Tristan Townsend did. And not that she'd ever in a million years admit that to him. Giving Tristan even a dram of encouragement would only lead to bolder advances on his part.

The prospect of which, she had to admit as she laid aside his jacket, made her heart race faster and in the most delicious, thrilling way. It was in how much she liked the feeling that the danger lay. Logically, she knew that she should stay well away from him; he was a rogue and a scandal waiting to happen. Of course, logically, she shouldn't ride spirited horses, either. And she did. All the time. And wouldn't have it any other way.

Riding Tristan Townsend . . . Simone arched a brow and undid the buttons of her bodice, both amazed and intrigued by the clarity and detail of the images playing past her mind's eye. Having spent her childhood in brothels, she'd seen lovemaking in what had to be all of its forms and positions. Given the business nature of the exchanges, she'd always percieved sex as a rather mundane and largely boring fact of life. Of course, never, not once in all of her years, had she been able to even vaguely imagine herself having sex. To so suddenly and unexpectedly be able not only to envision it but also to see how wildly enjoyable it would be with Tristan Townsend . . .

Good girls and virtuous women didn't enjoy sex, though. Everyone knew that. And all of her deportment masters had gone to great lengths to be sure she understood that she was to marry for money and social position and then quietly fulfill her obligations in the marital bed. Since it was just easier to go with the tide of things sometimes, she'd always nodded, letting them think she actually intended to marry and that she'd behave as she should once she did. The idea of marriage still didn't appeal to her any more than it ever had, but the possibility of twisting the sheets tight with Tristan . . .

Simone flopped down on her bed and stared up at the ceiling, wondering just how big a scandal Caroline and Drayton could tolerate.

CHAPTER 4

Simone stood in the parlor, Tristan's jacket draped over her arm, and hoped it wouldn't take the butler long to find Emmy. As rooms went . . . At home, the parlor whispered a very refined but decidedly cheerful welcome to visitors. The Townsends' parlor, however, didn't whisper and it didn't say welcome. No, it practically shouted. And the message was very clearly, *We have have money. Great wads of it.*

It was probably all very impressive, Simone allowed, studying a pair of rather fragile-looking white chairs with gilded scrollwork and brightly upholstered seats.

Unfortunately, the effort that had gone into the acquisition and display was largely wasted on someone like her. Now, if Emmy's mother had thought to hang a Norman shield and a couple of Scottish claymores over the mantel . . . Different interests, different tastes, she supposed.

"Simone! What a wonderful surprise!"

She turned to the parlor door at Emmy's welcome. Emmy was smiling and seemingly oblivious to the giant splashes of bright red that cascaded down the front of her white smock. Simone did a quick appraisal and then nodded toward her friend's right hand, asking, "Have you cut yourself, Emmy?"

Emmaline held up her hand. "This? It's paint. I'm in the conservatory doing my best to develop the essential skills of a true lady. Thank you for rescuing me." Her smile broadened. "Again."

Simone chuckled and lifted her arm bearing Tristan's jacket and said, "Your brother lent me his coat last night and I thought perhaps you might see it returned to him with my thanks."

"Or you can return it and thank him yourself," his sister countered, beaming. "He promised to call this morning and I'm expecting him at any time."

If she were going to be sensible and ever so safe, now was the time to conjure an excuse and run. "Oh yes, that would be even better. What are you painting?"

"Come along and I'll show you." And with that cheery command, Emmy spun about and headed off into the rest of the house, leaving Simone to tag along in her wake, to alternately note the incredible amount of fancy furniture lining the hallways and marvel at what a very different person Emmaline Townsend was at home. No hiding. No peeking tentatively. Here she strode, her head up and her shoulders squared without the slightest bit of coaching. Why she hadn't been able to bring that sort of confidence and presence naturally into a ballroom . . .

"It's supposed to be a still life with roses, but it's not going very well," Emmy said as they entered the greenhouse and she made her way toward the easel standing amid a collection of well-cushioned wicker furniture. "My roses look more like mud pies than flowers. Would you care for some coffee? It's fairly fresh and still a bit warm."

"Coffee would be lovely. Thank you," Simone replied, eyeing the picture as Emmy puttered at the tea cart. Simone glanced over at the pedestal that was likely the model for the painting. God, "not going well" was a massive understatement.

"Do you paint, Simone?"

"Not if I can avoid it," she admitted, laying Tristan's coat over the back of a chair and accepting the cup and saucer from her friend. "My elder sister once hired an instructor who made a valiant attempt to bring out the artist in me. He finally had to admit that I don't have one."

"Mine has gone on a very long holiday and forgotten to return home." Emmy picked up her own cup and then stared at her picture as she added, "Which I think is really selfish of him. James could paint pictures that looked eerily real. And Tristan can do the most spectacular things with a simple piece of charcoal and just a flick or two of his wrist. It's hardly fair that they got all the talent and left none for me."

"None" was right. "I'm sure it's just a matter of wanting to badly enough," Simone offered diplomatically. "And setting aside the time to practice."

"Do you really think so?"

No, but saying so would be hurtful. "Perhaps it's more a matter of being uninspired by still lifes. Have you ever tried to paint something more interesting to you?"

Emmy nodded and sighed. "The cat won't sit still long enough."

"Yes, they do tend to have a mind of their own," she allowed. "When they've had enough, they've had enough."

"I could paint you!"

Simone couldn't think of anything to say. Well, anything that would be considered even marginally nice. If Emmaline couldn't paint a flower in any sort of recognizable way, the odds of her being able to faithfully render a face were—

"Would you sit for a portrait, Simone? Please say *yes*. You could give it to your sister and her husband for a present."

She was trapped by kindness and knew it. "Well . . ."

"Oh, thank you!" Emmy cried happily, putting her coffee cup back on the cart. "This will be ever so much more fun than empty wine bottles and wilting flowers on a silly pedestal. How would you like to pose?"

"It's not enough to sit in a chair and look important?"

"Of course not," Emmy assured her. "I need to capture the true essence of you. Your energy and your confidence. I want people to look at the painting and know that you're the most interesting person they could ever hope to meet."

Given Emmy's artistic ability, the only thing people were going to know was that Emmy should stick to embroidery. "Maybe we could offer the cat some fish and a little bowl of cream. Where is he?"

Emmy laughed and took the cup and saucer from her, saying, "Why don't you wander about the furniture and look for someplace you'd be comfortable posing and I'll get my canvas and paints ready? It won't take long. I always have several canvases prepared in case the muse suddenly strikes and I'm overcome with a flood tide of creative urges."

If that expectation weren't the very definition of groundless optimism . . . But, bless Emmaline's heart, she was so hopeful and confident that there wasn't anything to do but go along and let her make the attempt. As Emmy went to a storage cabinet in the far corner of the glass room, Simone removed her riding jacket and laid it over Tristan's coat on the back of the chair. By the time her friend had returned with a very large, very white new canvas, Simone had decided that the chaise had the thickest cushion and the best chance for being comfortable for a near eternity.

"How's this, Emmy?" she asked, sitting down and arranging her skirt so that the riding split in it wasn't glaringly apparent.

"Tilt your head a bit to the side, I think."

Simone did as asked, thinking that she had to look like one of Fiona's cats watching a bird through the window.

"No, I was wrong. Put it back the way you had it."

Simone gladly obeyed and tried not to sigh too loudly as Emmaline began tilting *her* head at various angles as she studied her from behind the easel. God, it was going to be a very long day. If it weren't for the promise of—

As though conjured by the very thought of him, Tristan strode into the conservatory. Simone smiled and let her gaze slowly skim him from his handsome head to his manly booted toes. It was such a pleasurable trip that she took it again in reverse. His dark eyes sparkled as she met his gaze and his smile tipped up knowingly.

"What are you two doing?"

Emmaline's eyes widened and she whipped around, grinning. "I'm going to paint Simone's portrait!"

He sucked in his cheeks and cocked a brow but kept his opinion to himself as he stepped to his sister's side and gave her a hug. Looking over the top of the canvas, he met Simone's gaze again and said softly, "Good morning, Simone."

Her heart raced and she would have sworn that she'd felt his fingertips grazing her lips. "Good morning, Tristan," she managed to say despite being decidedly breathless. "I forgot to return your coat to you last night and brought it over. Thank you for being so thoughtful."

"It was my pleasure." His knowing smile returned. "Are you comfortable sitting there like that?"

She wasn't comfortable at all, actually, but it had nothing to do with where and how she was sitting. Standing wouldn't be any better, either. Not unless it happened to be where he could wrap her in his arms and pull her against him. "I suppose so," she answered, wondering why he so filled her senses this morning when he hadn't the night before. Had the stresses of the fire clouded her perceptions that thickly? Good God, he was nothing short of . . . well, intoxicating.

Still holding her gaze, still smiling that certain smile of his, he asked, "If I might make a suggestion or two?"

Emmaline beamed up at him. "Oh yes, please do, Tristan. You're so very good at this sort of thing and I need all the help I can get."

"Squared-off or sharp angles don't make for very flattering portraits. Lady Simone, if you would be so kind as to leisurely and fully recline yourself on the chaise."

And wait for me there, her mind wantonly finished. She looked away from his gaze and shifted about as he'd asked, bringing her legs up and turning onto her side. Propped against the arm of the chaise, she asked, "Like this?"

Emmy peered around the side of the easel. "Oh yes. That's much better."

Tristan looked over the top of the canvas, considered her, and then slowly cocked a brow to ask, "Do you always wear a ribbon in your hair?"

"Very seldom, actually," she admitted, keeping to herself the fact that she'd decided to tie her hair back that morning in the hope that he'd like the style. So much for trying.

"Please feel free to remove it."

And anything else you'd care to.

"Where are your pencils, Em?" he asked as Simone brought her wayward mind under control, tugged the ribbon streamer, and undid the bow.

"Pencils?"

"Yes, to sketch in the basic lines."

"Oh. They're in my room. I'll be right back."

Simone absently reclined on the arm of the chaise and watched in amazement as Emmaline took off like a shot. Last night, in the midst of a fire, Emmy had been worried about leaving her brother and her alone together in a smoke-filled room. But today? Apparently, with the dawn of a new day, they could be trusted to behave themselves.

"You look very starched."

"Starched?" she repeated, bringing her gaze to Tristan's.

"Prim and proper and ever so respectable."

The look in his eyes was anything but. "Emmy plans to give the portrait to my sister and her husband," she explained, smiling. "They pray every night for prim and proper and ever so respectable. They'll be delighted to know I'm capable of at least looking that way."

He laughed, the sound deliciously low and rumbling. "With Em wielding the brush," he said, making his way toward her, "your portrait, when finished, is going to look like a mangled monkey on a battered cushion. It will never leave this house. There's no harm in relaxing and being yourself for the process. No one but us will ever know."

She had to tilt her head back to look up at him. "And just what would being myself entail?"

"Being a bit daring," he answered, easing down onto the very edge of the chaise beside her.

She was only vaguely aware that the ribbon slipped from her fingers and fluttered to the floor. She was acutely aware, though, of the scent of his cologne, of the cleanly chiseled line of his jaw, of how his dark eyes seemed to see right to the center of her soul. Her heart racing and her blood warming, she considered it nothing short of a miracle that she could coolly reply, "Really. Daring?"

He cocked his brow slightly higher and his eyes sparkled. "And a bit provocative."

She resisted the urge to swallow. "Oh?"

"Do you like being buttoned all the way up to your neck, Simone?"

Oh, dear. She knew where this was going. The proper response would be a very firm *Why, yes, I do.* "I hate it, actually. But the requirements of propriety and fashion dictate—" The rest of the words drifted away as he reached out and very slowly, very deliberately undid the uppermost button.

"When *I* paint your portrait," he said softly, holding her gaze as he boldly undid two more, "we'll unbutton them all."

When he painted . . . Her heart skittered as a heady mix of anticipation and dread surged through her body. "Tristan," she whispered, looking up at him.

"What?"

She was trying to remember what it was she'd been about to say when he leaned down and planted a slow kiss in the hollow at the base of her throat.

Her breath caught, her senses reeling, she more gasped than said, "Em . . . could . . ."

He made a humming sound that vibrated through every fiber of her being, murmured softly, "Yes, at any moment," and then leisurely trailed kisses up the length of her throat.

Her eyes closed, Simone savored the wicked sensations coursing through her. "Unfortunately," she whispered just before his lips feathered over hers.

He drew back and smiled down at her, then let his gaze wander down the length of her, the look in his eyes bright and appreciative. "*Most* unfortunately," he said softly as he drew a fingertip over the damask-covered swell of her breast to tease the hardened peak pushing up from beneath.

A wondrous, pulsing heat shot to her core. Swallowing down a moan of pleasure, she eased away from his touch and breathlessly said, "This is the point where I should protest the boldness of your advance, isn't it?"

His smile went wide and he rose to his feet saying, "I think it comes a little late to be of much effect, but if it makes you feel better to offer one, by all means, please feel free."

As he walked over to a chair near the easel, she moistened her lower lip and drew a deep, steadying breath. "Doing and saying things only for the sake of appearances has always struck me as being the sign of a shallow person," she began as he settled himself on the arm. "What would you say to dispensing with the notion and agreeing to be honest with each other?"

He shrugged and grinned. "You go first."

"I enjoy your advances. Far more than is seemly and ladylike. Or safe." His smile fading by slow degrees, she added brightly, "Your turn."

"I want to make love to you."

Well, that was far more direct than she'd expected. "I'm flattered. And intrigued."

"Have you ever lain with a man?"

"No," she answered, wondering if perhaps honesty wasn't the best idea after all. But since she'd begun, she had no choice but to go on. "And I've never wrapped my legs around one, either. I've never wanted to."

"Until now?"

She gave him a shrug. "I'm mulling the notion. It's a decided first for me."

"I'm honored."

A quick movement behind him caught her attention. "Did you find the pencils, Emmy?"

"I found some," her friend announced as she sailed into the room, her cheeks flushed, "but I don't know if they're the kind Tristan wants."

He rose from the chair and stepped to Emmy's side at the easel. "If you're planning to do a charcoal portrait, they're perfect," he said, examining what she'd brought. "If you plan to paint in oils, though, they'll smudge your colors."

"Oh, I want to do oils. I know you prefer the shades of gray, but I think they wouldn't do Simone justice. So I need a simple lead pencil, don't I?"

"A very hard one that will give you the faintest, lightest gray line and disappear completely under the paint."

"I'll be back shortly," she declared, gliding out just as swiftly as she'd entered only a moment before.

Simone chuckled. "How long do you think she thinks 'shortly' is?"

"Not nearly long enough."

Why every word out of his mouth felt like a caress . . . "Are you hiding over there?"

"I'm not hiding," he clarified, taking up his place on the arm of the chair again. "But given my inclinations and the realities of limited time and no French letter . . ." He shrugged and gave her a lopsided smile. "At the moment, distance is the better part of discretion."

But if they had time and a French letter . . . The mental image was breathtaking in its detail. "True," she allowed, tamping down the swirl of heated desire. "But rather than waste this time we have alone . . ." She quietly cleared her throat. "I want you to know that I'm not engaged in a campaign to find myself a husband. My interest in you is purely physical and most definitely temporary."

He tilted his head to consider her. "Do you have any idea of how utterly refreshing you are?"

Laughing, she propped her head in her hand and

countered, "I believe the more commonly used term is 'outrageous.' Are you looking for a wife?"

"I'm supposed to be. Producing an heir and a spare with all due speed and all that. It's vitally important, you know. The queen lies awake nights worrying that I might croak off before there's another generation of male Townsends to inherit the title."

"I'm sure you won't have any problems finding a suitable mate. Marquises are considered quite the catch, you know. Add in that you're handsome and dashing . . . They'll line up to submit their pedigrees for your consideration."

"And all of them terribly perfect and cold and boring," he pointed out. "Why aren't you interested in marrying?"

"It's much more fun coming and going as I please, wreaking havoc hither and yon. I have no interest in keeping a household or in committing my life to any of the other things in which women are supposed to take great pride. I hate to embroider. My cooking could kill. And I positively loathe having to dress up and play at being a lady. I'd make a terrible wife."

"But you've come out for a Season," he posed.

"Only because I was offered a horse if I would."

He laughed, the sound rippling over her and warming her senses yet another degree.

"What are you going to do if someone makes an offer for you?" he asked. "Daughters of dukes are considered quite the catch, you know. Add in 'beautiful' and 'spirited' . . ."

"This daughter isn't considered a catch by anyone," she assured him. "They'd have to be truly desperate to ask for me."

"Why's that?"

"Found one!" Emmy exclaimed from the doorway. With a gasp, she froze two feet into the conservatory. "Oh, Simone, you're stunning. Don't move at all. Not so much as a twitch."

"She's right," Tristan said, his gaze sweeping her up and down. "Whatever it is that you're thinking, keep thinking it."

What had she been thinking? she wondered as the brother and sister stepped behind the easel and conversed in low tones. Oh yes. Tristan had asked why someone would have to be desperate to want to marry her. And she'd instantly felt the familiar pang of anger and the twist of resentment. But there had been a new emotion in the mixture, too, a potent wave of regret, of wishing that her past were different. Simone stared at the far wall of plants and wondered why, after all the years of her life, being the daughter of a whore was suddenly something she would undo if she could.

It wasn't as though she really wanted to marry and her mother's choices stood in the way. No, she really and truly believed that marriage was for women who didn't have anything better to do with their lives. Well, except for her sister Caroline. Carrie seemed to approach her marriage to Drayton the same way she did her decorating and fashioning of wardrobes; it was a creative endeavor that delighted her. But Carrie was Carrie and unique.

Simone sighed quietly and looked over at the easel. Tristan had stepped slightly to the side and was instructing Emmaline on the proper placement of her sketching lines. What was it about the thought of explaining her past to Tristan that made such a difference?

My mother was a prostitute. A simple statement of fact. And it wasn't as though it were a great secret; everyone in London knew it. In fact, odds were he already knew the truth and there was no need for her to make any sort of announcement of it. Then again, maybe he didn't know. Most people in Society treated her with a distant kind of stoniness, as though she had some dreadful disease they might catch if the space between them had the slightest bit of warmth. Since Tristan was anything but distant and cool, either he didn't know he was at mortal risk or he didn't care.

If he didn't know, then telling him the truth could change everything. It would be incredibly sad to lose the delightful, easy banter with him. Not to mention, she allowed in the name of honesty, the delicious way he made her feel. But if it was a matter of his knowing and not caring . . .

Or perhaps, she suddenly realized, her heart sinking, it was a case of his knowing and believing that the daughter was as willing to offer her body every bit as casually as her mother had been. And if that was the situation . . .

So far she hadn't done anything to disabuse him of the notion. Did she want to be nothing more than a casual romp in the sheets for any man inclined to ask for one? Most of the men in the world were . . . She shuddered and looked back to the easel.

No, only Tristan. She wasn't her mother any more than he was his father or grandfather. There was something about Tristan that she found absolutely compelling. It was part physical; there could be no denying that he was a handsome, assured man. The other part was harder to define but no less important: an irresistible mix of magnetism and curiosity and delight. It was special.

Special? She quietly snorted. How incredibly fairy-tale and juvenile. No, "special" wasn't within the realm of possible. He needed a wife and not only didn't she want to be one, but also her past made her a completely unsuitable candidate. Even the Lunatic Lockwoods had standards, and the bastard daughter of a duke and a prostitute didn't come anywhere close to meeting them. Yes, whatever physical relationship she and Tristan had was going to be, by practical reality, brief.

Of course, the surest and safest thing to do would be to avoid the temptation of Tristan Townsend entirely. There would be no need to explain her convoluted rise to the peerage. There wouldn't be any risk of scandal, either. Not that she cared about such things for herself, but Drayton was a member of the House of Lords and Carrie, when she wasn't confined to the house by pregnancy, was active in charity work; they could well live without the ugly whispers and nasty looks that a scandal would inspire.

Sure and safe were on the one hand, though. On the other . . . Her gaze slid up and down the length of Tristan's body and then across the width of his chest and shoulders, mentally stripping him ever so deliberately out of his well-tailored suit. If he looked even half as good as she imagined . . .

Yes, on the other hand was Tristan Townsend and a curiosity that she'd never in her life faced. And, truth be told, had never expected to face. What was it about him that stirred so strongly a desire thousands of other men hadn't even been able to awaken?

"Ah, your man Gregory was right. Here you are."

She looked to the doorway to see Noland advancing on Emmy and Tristan. Actually, Noland was advancing on Emmy and rather like a speeding, overloaded wagon; Tristan just happened to be standing nearby. Simone grinned and hoped he'd be able to jump clear of the wreckage.

CHAPTER 5

$\mathcal{W}$ell, Tristan allowed, mumbling a welcome of sorts, at least Noland's arrival had eased the disconcerting furrow between Simone's brows.

"Lady Emmaline, you look lovely today," his friend said as Tristan watched the tension ease out of the rest of Simone's body. Her delectable, wondrously responsive, arranged-so-invitingly body.

"I'm wearing a smock covered with paint splotches."

"And no other woman in all the empire could do it such justice."

If he could have just thirty minutes alone with her, he

could easily— Tristan blinked and brought his attention back to the easel. Or, more accurately, to the fact that his friend was blatantly fawning over his sister. His young and completely innocent sister.

"I'm sure you say such things to all the young ladies," Em protested, her cheeks flushing bright pink.

"I assure you that I do not. You are the rarest of flowers. Beautiful and delicate and the very essence of femininity."

Oh, good God. He was going to be sick. Smiling thinly, he asked, "Noland, is there a particular reason you've been in search of me?"

Noland looked slightly stunned for a second and then started, replying, "Oh yes. I've heard the details of last evening's catastrophe and simply have to share them with someone." Before any of them could say whether or not they wanted to hear them, he began the tale, saying, "Seems it started in one of the bedrooms when a lamp was knocked to the floor accidentally. Those in the room failed to notice it immediately and—"

"How could they not notice a fire?" Em interrupted.

Yes, a complete innocent. Tristan chewed the inside of his lip, trying to think of a way to enlighten her without really *enlightening* her. Noland—damn him—wasn't any help. He just stood there tugging at his collar and studying the glass roof over their heads.

"They were otherwise engaged, Emmy," Simone offered from her chaise. She laughed softly and added, "The expression is 'blinded by passion.' "

Emmaline's eyes went wide and the color in her cheeks deepened. "Oh," she said softly, quickly focusing on moving the paint around on the canvas before her. "I knew that, of course."

The silence was deafening. And rapidly progressing into the realm of awkward when Simone gently said, "Of course you did, Emmy. Your mind is just so wrapped up in your painting that anything beyond it is foreign and fuzzy at its first intrusion. It happens to me all the time." She grinned and added, "Not with painting, but other things. As you were saying, Lord Noland?"

While Tristan silently thanked her for her kindness and aplomb, Noland again took a few seconds to collect his wits. Again they returned with a start that launched him into a spirited telling. "The fire went quickly out of control and spread. As we well know. As of this morning, there are three dead and twenty-four known to be injured. Of those twenty-four, two are not expected to recover."

"It's just awful," Em said sadly.

"But," Tristan countered, "it could have been so much worse."

"True," Noland concurred. "And if it had been, we'd be packing away our dancing shoes for the Season. Instead, the revelry has been suspended only for the next two weeks. Time for paying respects and all. After that, the hunt's back on."

Simone sighed. "I suppose two weeks is better than nothing."

Noland—for the first time—actually turned to look at her. "You're not excited by the prospect of gala events and fabulous food?"

"I have a very low tolerance of boredom and pretension, Lord Noland."

That makes two of us, my dear.

Emmaline stopped painting and looked around the edge of the canvas. "And I suspect you've reached the limits of the former in posing for me this morning, haven't you?"

Simone grinned. "I'm not bored and no one has displayed the slightest bit of pretension, but I would appreciate it if I could stand and walk about a bit while I still remember how."

His sister looked up at him. "Are we at a good stopping point for the day, Tristan?" she asked, intruding on his appreciation of dark eyes bright with amusement.

He considered the painting and the basic, broad strokes that had been laid down. As progress went, it wasn't much. But there was an advantage in Em's lack of creative speed. "I'd say so. And as long as Lady Simone is willing to be a good sport again tomorrow morning."

"Certainly," she assured them from the chaise.

"Then we're done for the day," Emmaline declared as she swished her brush about in a tin of cleaner. "Would anyone care for a bite to eat? I can speak with Cook and see if we could have some of her bread and apricot preserves."

Watching Simone slowly stretch her back and shoulders, Tristan shrugged and replied, "I never pass up offered sweets."

"I'll see what I can do."

Noland was a darting blur at the edge of his vision. "Let me carry your paint pot for you, Lady Emmaline," Tristan heard him say.

Tristan looked over his shoulder just in time to see Noland wrest the tin away from Em as she protested, "It's not paint, Lord Noland. It's turpentine and it will destroy your suit if you spill any on yourself."

Together they headed for the doorway to the main house, Noland trying to hold the pot, turn the knob, push open the door, and step out of Em's way all while still flapping his gums. "I would gladly give up my entire wardrobe on your behalf, Lady Emmaline. No sacrifice would be too great to ask of me."

"I hope he's careful," Simone said, chuckling as she swung her legs over the edge of the chaise and rose to her feet. "I don't want to see Noland naked."

"None of us do."

"I think your friend is interested in your sister," she offered as she bent over and scooped her hair ribbon up from the floor.

God Almighty, even from the back, the woman had the most incredibly inviting curves. He moistened his lower lip and forced himself to swallow. "I'll have to make sure she gets out and about more."

"You don't approve of him?"

"Noland is nice enough and he comes from a respectable family," he explained, watching her amble toward him and wondering just how quickly he could push the seduction. "But he doesn't strike me as the sort who would make Em's heart race till death do they part."

"I can't help but notice, Lord Lockwood," she said softly, stopping before him and tilting her head up to boldly and brightly meet his gaze, "that you seem to have a fixation on racing and pitter-pattering hearts."

Well, yes. Largely because his had a tendency to do just that whenever she was around. And his heart wasn't the only part of him that found her stimulating. He casually shifted his stance to accommodate the growing tension while he stepped closer and placed his hands on her waist. "I like the way it feels," he murmured. "Don't you?"

Her eyes sparkled wickedly and the corners of her mouth tipped higher as she reached between them and toyed with the top button on his suit coat. "It is rather thrilling."

"Rather?"

"In a barely marginal sort of way."

"And what, precisely," he pressed, "is so marginal about it?"

She undid the button, sending his heartbeat racing. "It doesn't last nearly long enough."

If only they were lovers already. Five minutes was all it would take for him to lay her down on the chaise and see them both satisfied. But since they weren't and such a brusque—albeit efficient and masterful—performance wouldn't be at all appropriate for her first experience . . .

Very deliberately, he reached to her open neckline and began to mate the buttons with their holes, deliberately stroking the backs of his fingers lightly over the silken skin of her throat. "Choose the time and place, Simone," he murmured as he worked, "and I'll make the thrill last for as long as you can endure it."

Desire and temptation danced in the ebony depths of her eyes.

"Midnight tonight?" he offered before propriety and caution could stifle her impulses. "I'll wait for you in your family's garden."

Her gaze darted past him and then returned to his in the same second that she quietly cleared her throat and took a half step back. Wondering how Em had gotten Noland to shut up long enough for them to have arrived without making a sound, Tristan turned, letting his arms fall nonchalantly back to his sides. But it wasn't Emmaline. Nor was it Noland.

"Lucinda," he said tautly as his stepmother advanced toward them, dressed as always in black bombazine. As usual, she didn't respond to his greeting. And as was his custom, he first tamped down the resentment of her attempt to make him feel like an uninvited guest and then graciously refrained from reminding her that he owned the house.

Having successfully managed to delay a full-scale confrontation for another day, he turned slightly and drew Simone to his side, saying, "May I present Emmaline's friend, Lady Simone Turnbridge."

Well, he may all he liked, Simone thought, but the older, considerably stiffer version of Emmaline didn't really care whether he did or not. As Lucinda Townsend's gaze raked her top to bottom, her blue eyes cold and sharp, he went on with the necessary formalities. "Lady Simone, as you may well have surmised, this delightful creature is Emmaline's mother, the Dowager Lady Lockwood."

His sarcasm wasn't lost on Lucinda, either, and the woman's gaze snapped to his. "I remain Lady Lockwood until you wed, Tristan."

There wasn't the slightest bit of warmth in the smile he gave his stepmother. "Which could be before the month is out. Sooner, if I can manage it."

No loving family. Simone watched warily, her heart skittering and her mind chattering about finding a reason to leave so the two could do battle privately. Lucinda's jaw hardened for a second, and then, in the depth of her eyes, Simone saw a decision made. In the next second the woman shifted her attention to her. "You're the Duke of Ryland's ward. I've heard about you."

Yes, well, most of London had. And since it was too late to beat a timely retreat . . . Simone smiled. "It was nothing good, I'm sure."

"No, it wasn't."

"But I'm just as sure that it was wildly interesting."

Lady Lockwood blinked and rocked slightly backward. Tristan was still sucking in his cheeks and looking off to the far wall, his shoulders quivering with silent laughter, when Lucinda recovered from her shock and demanded, "Where is your sister?"

He cleared his throat and sobered. "She and Lord Noland left here mere moments ago, heading to the kitchen to beg bread and jam from Cook."

"Leaving you and Lady Simone alone?"

He cocked a brow. "You're not concerned about Em and Noland being alone together?"

"I'll wait here with you for their return," she announced, folding her arms across her clearly well-corseted midriff.

Simone was thinking that the woman's disposition might improve if she were to loosen her laces, when Tristan drawled, "So . . . How goes the mourning?" At his stepmother's glare he added brightly, "Any new furniture being delivered today?"

"No."

The chill in her voice only seemed to encourage him. "Oh, of course," he went on cheerily. "I should have remembered. Today is Wednesday. Jeweler day. Did he bring rubies or emeralds this time?"

"You are detestable."

"What can I say?" he rejoined, the warmth leaving his smile again. "You inspire me to great heights."

"Today was not jeweler day; it was solicitor day."

"Ah, that explains the knocked knickers."

The air between them crackled with icy fire. Simone

mustered a smile and stepped away from Tristan's side, saying, "I think I should be going."

"I can't say that I blame you," he said while she retrieved her jacket from the back of the chair.

"Please extend my thanks to Emmaline for her hospitality this morning, Tristan," she offered even as her mind suggested that the practice of good manners was a wasted effort in the situation. "Along with my regrets for not being able to stay longer." She turned to Lady Lockwood and finished her performance with an outright lie. "It has been a pleasure to meet you, Lady Lockwood."

"No, it hasn't. The butler will see you out."

Well, what did one say to that sort of dismissal? *I hope you fall down the stairs and break your nasty neck?*

"I'll see Lady Simone into the care of her waiting groomsman," Tristan announced, taking the jacket from her hands and holding it while she slipped her arms into the sleeves.

"I will remind you that while Lady Simone's reputation certainly isn't pristine," Lady Lockwood countered frostily, "there's no point in tarnishing it further by a casual disregard of propriety."

Simone wasn't the least surprised when he shrugged off the warning, took her by the elbow in open defiance of all-important propriety, and steered her toward the door. "You're welcome to tag along if you're so concerned," he said without looking back. "But you might want to lag a bit behind so you don't have to hear all the sordid details of our family story."

"Do you know any limits to low conduct?"

He paused just past the threshold to look over his

shoulder, smile thinly, and reply, "Certainly. And they're considerably higher than yours."

Simone didn't bother to peer around him to see Lady Lockwood's reaction. She'd seen quite enough already to well imagine the gleaming daggers in the woman's gaze. As Simone and Tristan moved down the hallway toward the front of the house, she decided that it was a very good thing Lucinda Townsend hadn't been much interested in mothering. From what Simone had seen so far, it appeared that the servants Lady Lockwood had hired to raise Emmaline had done a far better job of it than she could have.

"I'm sorry we placed you in the middle of that."

"It was a bit awkward," Simone allowed.

"Not to mention keenly unpleasant."

"Well, yes."

"Do you want to know the sordid details?"

She thought about it for a moment. One part of her was dying of a decidedly morbid curiosity. Another part, though . . . "I don't know," she admitted, looking up at him and noting his frown. "Would they make a difference in how I feel about my friendship with your sister? In how I feel about you?"

"Probably. And not for the better."

"I don't frighten or offend easily."

"I've noticed that," he said as a footman opened the front door for them.

Hearing the smile in Tristan's voice, she glanced up at him. Yes, the frown was most definitely gone. "Along with the fact that I'm easily enticed?" she teased as they made their way down the front steps and toward the street.

He grinned and answered quietly, "I consider you to be nothing short of a delightfully formidable challenge."

"Better that, I suppose, than to be thought of as wicked and wanton."

"Oh, I don't know," he drawled, his eyes sparkling. "I see the terms as wonderfully complimentary."

Out in the street, her groomsman, Alvin, waited for her, the reins of her mount and his in his hands. He snapped to attention at the sight of them and then quickly went about flipping the leather straps over the animals' heads. Another horse—presumably Tristan's, given the way the animal tossed his mane and snorted in greeting—stood there with the others, his reins tied off on the iron ring.

"That's because men and women are held to different standards," she pointed out. "Will you be back here in the morning to give Emmy another painting lesson?"

"Yes." Quietly he added, "But I'd prefer to see you alone at midnight."

Midnight. Alone. Her blood warmed and her pulse raced. She didn't dare give Tristan an answer, not with Alvin so close by. Given the speed at which news of her missteps always reached the dinner table, she'd long ago decided that Drayton or Haywood paid the man extra to report on her every breath. She didn't need to make any contributions to what was, in all probability, an already too interesting story.

Accepting the reins from Alvin, she said, "It's been a pleasure to see you again, Lord Lockwood," then placed her foot in the groomsman's cupped hands and swung neatly up—and quite impressively, she knew—across the saddle.

"Lady Simone," Tristan said with a wide smile and a brief bow.

She considered him from her elevated perch, her mind unexpectedly transforming reality into fantasy. Day became night and she straddled not the broad back of a horse but lean male hips. Her breath caught, and, her senses reeling, she wheeled the horse about, setting him into motion and her thoughts in a safer direction.

Tristan watched her ride away, narrowing his eyes to keep her in focus as the distance between them lengthened. Damn, she was a good rider. Anyone who could make a trot look comfortable and easy had been born to ride. At a canter . . . At a full gallop . . . A vision played across his mind: Simone half-standing in the stirrups, her body angled forward so she could stretch out over the animal's neck and laugh as the wind whipped her face and tangled through her streaming black hair. He smiled, truly appreciating her heart, her indomitable spirit.

She didn't frighten or offend easily? He'd bet the house behind him and everything in it that she didn't frighten at all. Strong, independent, fearless, and resourceful. Not to mention passionate.

He'd heard enough of the whispers about her to know that she wouldn't be the kind of wife he needed. No, he needed a wife of impeccable pedigree and spotless reputation to compensate for the decidedly tarnished one he'd inherited. But Lady Simone Turnbridge was so perfect in so many other ways that he'd be an utter fool to pass up the temptation of her. Of course getting her to agree to be his lover . . .

He pulled the reins of his mount from the ring and swung up into the saddle. How to go about convincing her? he wondered, setting out for the docks. Just laying the cards on the table would be the simplest approach.

She'd appreciate his honesty and directness. As for the risk of scandal involved . . . If she paused to consider it at all, it would likely be to appreciate the exciting edge it gave to the whole affair.

But if they were discovered . . .

His stomach tightened. Logically . . . As long as he didn't marry Simone, as long as she didn't end up carrying his child, Lucinda wouldn't consider her a threat of any sort. But, and as qualifiers went, it was a big but, Simone was the daughter of a duke, the ward of one, too. Riding astride and fencing were decidedly unconventional but within the realm of social tolerance. A wicked, deliberate affair was another matter entirely. If they were caught, her guardian would give him two choices, either marry her or stand there and allow himself to be run through. The first option would put Simone squarely in Lucinda's sights and could very well cost her her life. The second would leave her a complete social pariah. Given all of the unpleasant possibilities, banking on not being caught seemed a bit on the irresponsible and reckless side. He'd have to give his plan a bit more thought, iron out the wrinkles, as it were, before he moved ahead with the seduction of his wild lady. Where there was a will, there was always a way.

$\mathcal{T}$ristan was still mulling the possibilities and considering the angles when he swung down from the saddle and passed his horse into the care of the watchman. His steps ringing as hollow on the stairs as his ideas did in his brain, he lifted the latch and let himself into the office. The blast of warm air brought a smile to his face. A smile that became a grin as the man behind the desk looked up to peer at him from behind rapidly fogging glasses. San

Francisco or London, it didn't make much difference. It was nice to know that some things in his life were constant and predictable.

"Hello, Gregory," Tristan said, heading for the desk.

"Good afternoon, sir."

"Yes, I suppose it is so far," he allowed, settling himself on the corner of the mahogany monster. "What have you been able to find out about my lady Simone?"

Gregory removed his glasses and wiped them with a handkerchief as he answered, "Not much, I'm afraid. And what I have managed to scrounge in the way of information is more rumor and gossip than anything else."

"There's usually a small kernel of truth buried deep in the gossip. What are they saying?"

"She was born on the wrong side of the sheets and recognized by the Crown only after the passing of her father, the late Duke of Ryland, some six years ago. No one seems to know where she was before then. Speculation is that she was from the lower classes, though."

"And why do they think that?"

"They say she lacks social grace."

No, she lacked patience for the artificiality of it all. "What else do they say about her?"

Gregory softly cleared his throat and took a deep breath. "She apparently has a bit of a wild side, sir."

"Really?" he said, chuckling. "How so?"

"She's created several stirs by riding astride on Rotten Row."

Noland had told him the very same thing last night. Had it only been last night? It seemed like ages ago. "Because she defied convention or because she's a better rider than a good many of the men?"

Carefully settling his glasses back on his face, the secretary replied, "I didn't hear anything about her riding abilities, sir. Sorry. I did hear, though, that she has a penchant for arms."

Now there was a bit of information that didn't quite fit. "As in being wrapped in a manly pair of them?" he asked.

"No, sir!" Gregory said, his eyes widening. "I didn't mean to imply that at all. From all accounts Lady Simone is far more interested in slashing off buttons and ruining coat sleeves with sharp blades than she is in stepping into romantic embraces. From what I hear, she's considered too feral to risk even the most circumspect conversation. Touching her is regarded as beyond the bounds of sanity."

Interesting. He'd more than touched and she hadn't been the least bit unhappy about it. "What have you learned about her family?"

"Her Crown-appointed guardian, the current Duke of Ryland, is a former artillery officer who, like yourself, unexpectedly inherited the title. He married her older sister. Apparently in a cloud of minor scandal. He and the Duchess of Ryland have two small children and are reportedly expecting a third any day. There's a younger sister, but no one knows much about her."

"Her name's Fiona and she cares for injured animals," Tristan supplied. Which reminded him . . . "Did you manage to acquire that birdcage I asked about?"

Gregory snorted and pointed to the closed ledger lying in front of him. "Yes, along with everything else in the warehouse, just as you instructed. And it cost you a fortune."

Picking up the leather-bound book and flipping it open, he quipped, "What would I do without you, Gregory?"

"Your own work?"

Tristan looked up from the page, astounded and amused. "You've developed a mean streak."

"I've always had one," Gregory countered, cocking a brow and reaching for his pen. "You were never around long enough to notice it."

Tristan grabbed the pen to keep him from stabbing it into the inkwell. "You need a day off."

"To do what?"

"Go buy yourself a new suit. Tour a museum. Wander around a library or a bookstore. Dine in a fine establishment." Gregory looked at him over the top of his glasses. Tristan sighed and elaborated, "The new suit is to look wealthy when you tour the museum or wander among the books. If you do it right, you won't be dining alone."

Gregory let him have the pen and sagged back in his chair. "No respectable woman will accept a dinner invitation from a perfect stranger."

Good God. With that sort of attitude . . . "You're an American," Tristan pointed out. "A cultured, educated American. She'll put aside strict propriety out of sheer curiosity. Trust me."

Gregory—predictably—shook his head and reached for the ledger. "I have to go over the inventory."

"I'll do it," he countered, gaining his feet and heading for the door with the ledger in hand. He stopped, turned back, and tossed the pen to Gregory, adding, "Go buy yourself a good suit, then find a pretty skirt and smile at her. It will do wonders for your disposition."

"So says the voice of experience?" Gregory called after him.

"The voice of *considerable* experience," he corrected with a laugh as he headed out the door. He left it open behind him, figuring that if Gregory had to leave his desk to close it, he might actually take the advice and keep right on going. The man really was far too dedicated to his work; he made him feel guilty for enjoying life.

And enjoying life was the point of having spent a fortune to acquire a warehouse full of imported goods. Well, more accurately, enjoying Simone's delight and gratitude when he showed it to her. As for when he'd actually manage to get her there . . .

He let himself into the warehouse and paused to allow his eyes to adjust to the dim light of the interior. Since Simone hadn't agreed to meet him in the garden that night, he probably had at least another full day to wait, to prepare. Which was a good thing, he allowed, gazing over the crates and bundles; careful staging was so very important in any seduction. Almost as important as the sense of anticipation that drove the parties to it.

Tonight he'd see to setting a worthy stage so that he was free tomorrow to focus all of his efforts on making Simone breathless and bothered enough to willingly frolic with him on it. Chuckling and shaking his head, he wandered off into the maze of wooden boxes, trying to remember the last time he'd been so delighted by the mere prospect of an affair.

CHAPTER 6

$\mathcal{S}$imone let Jasper choose his own pace and smiled in appreciation as he proudly cantered down the Ladies' Mile. As always, heads turned as they passed the carriages. And as always, Simone pretended that she didn't notice the way the women scowled, how they quickly turned to their companions to comment on her passing. Or, as she suspected, to express their outrage at her daring to make an appearance in the park reserved for the public display of the socially anointed, circumspect female.

Yeah, well, Simone silently countered, whether the prissy misses and stuffy matrons liked it or not, whether they approved or not, she was anointed, too. By royal decree and sanctioned by the College of Heraldry even. Not a single one of them could say that. No, they'd either been born on the right side of the right sheets by sheer dumb luck or managed to marry into the peerage by hook or by crook. And still, despite their rather shallow claim to importance, they practiced disdain as a high art.

Unless they need money, she amended as one of the women waved to her. Simone nodded in polite acknowledgment while silently scrambling to recall the woman's name. No, it wasn't Lady Dammit. Lady . . . Lady . . . Danlea! Three daughters, a son, and a dead husband who had gambled the family into poverty long before finally being considerate enough to take a bullet in the heart at a faro table.

Lady Danlea waved again, adding a bright smile this time. Simone worked up a smile of her own in return and silently sighed as the deportment lessons trudged dutifully through her brain. Strictly speaking, since Lady Danlea was the wife of a baron, dead though he was, she shouldn't have initiated contact with the daughter of a duke. Waving and then calling her over was a clear and presumptive breach of the rules that were designed to keep everyone firmly in their social place. If abandoning good manners for the sake of protocol wouldn't reflect poorly on Drayton and Caroline . . .

Angling Jasper toward the Danlea carriage, Simone slowed his pace and allowed that it wasn't an entirely awful situation, that at least Lady Danlea had decided to go out and about today with only her eldest daughter in tow. God, she was going to have to stop naming people herself and make an effort to learn their real ones. Calling the daughter Neigh-Face wasn't going to go over well at all. Hopefully, she could get away with not using names. It was a damn good thing Lady Danlea had left Little Lord Lumpy at home or the possibility of an even larger social blunder would be only seconds away.

"Good morning, Lady Simone," the elder woman said as Simone sidled Jasper alongside the Danlea rig. "A beautiful day for a ride, isn't it?"

"It is indeed, Lady Danlea."

"You've met my eldest daughter, Diana, haven't you?"

Diana. Bless Lady Danlea. "Once," Simone answered, recalling the day and how Diana had curled her lip at their introduction. "Very briefly at one of Caroline's charity events. Earlier this year, I think." She nodded at the younger woman and lied, saying ever so properly, "It's lovely to see you again, Diana."

"And you, Lady Simone," Diana replied, looking—to Simone's thinking, anyway—as though she were trying to swallow a huge gulp of cod-liver oil. "We were wondering if you had made plans for luncheon yet."

They were asking her to join them for a meal? It had to be frosty in hell. But since it would have to be frozen solid before she accepted the invitation . . . "Unfortunately, yes," she said with what she hoped passed for a regretful smile. "Caroline's expecting me at the table within the next half hour. Being confined as she is until this baby arrives, she looks so forward to having company at meals. I'm sure you can understand."

"Of course," Diana allowed with what sounded suspiciously like a sigh of relief. "We wouldn't dream of depriving the dear duchess of her small joys."

Small joys? Well, there were two ways to take the

comment, one an expression of kindness and compassion, the other as a velvet-wrapped backhanded slap. Given that it was Diana . . . Jasper shifted under Simone, pulling at the reins. She wheeled him about and brought him back along the rig, countering sweetly, "Well, Diana, I suspect that if anyone knows about small—"

"Perhaps luncheon some other time then?" Lady Danlea quickly interjected.

"I'd be delighted," Simone lied. And then, because Lady Danlea looked as though she were consulting some great mental calendar for an official date, she added, "The doctor says that the baby should be here in another two weeks or so. After that, Carrie will be able to get out of the house. Maybe the four of us could plan for an occasion together."

"That would be perfectly lovely," Lady Danlea cooed. "You will speak with her about the possibility?"

"As soon as I get home."

"We would be honored by an invitation from the duchess."

The wrangling of which, Simone knew, had been largely the point of the entire encounter. She nodded to both of them as Jasper sidestepped away, then turned him and set him on the path back to the house.

The things some people did in the effort to climb the social ladder, she mused as she went. *Or, in the case of Lady Danlea and her progeny, the things people were willing to do to keep from falling off the ladder altogether.* Since barons couldn't pass their title on, Lumpy had to marry one or return to the gentry class from which the Danleas had come. No more parties. No more galas. And stripped of his courtesy title in the process, Little

Lord Lumpy would have to go through the rest of his life as Little Lumpy. The ignobility of it all.

Simone smiled and slowed Jasper to a cooling walk as they turned off the street and started up the family drive. But if Lumpy could manage to marry a title . . . And, while he was at it, money . . . Well, all would be right in the world of the Danleas. Lumpy could go on being a peer, his sisters would have better odds of snagging a peer of their very own, and while money wouldn't exactly flow like the fountains in Hyde Park, they'd have considerably more of it than they did today.

Now why they thought she might be willing to be the sacrificial bride in their grand plan for social survival . . . Somewhere in England there might be a titled woman desperate to wed and bed— Simone shuddered. Bed Lumpy? No, she took it back; there wasn't any woman *anywhere* desperate enough to marry a short, fat, bald man with a perpetually running nose and an eye that twiched to three-four time. God, if for some reason she was forced to marry him . . .

"Hey ho!"

Simone blinked away the vision of tossing Lumpy out the window of the bridal bower and focused on the rear yard. Ah, Haywood. Of course he was waiting for her. In almost the exact same spot he'd been standing in when she'd ignored his protests and ridden away.

"Hey ho yourself," she answered, reining in Jasper and swinging down from the saddle. "You haven't been standing there the whole time I've been gone, have you?"

Ignoring the question—and the groomsman dashing toward them—Haywood caught Jasper's bridle and asked, "Did you get Lord Lockwood's coat returned to his sister?"

"Actually," she replied as the groomsman politely jostled Haywood aside and led Jasper off to the stable, "I returned it to Lord Lockwood himself."

"You went to his home?" Haywood gasped, taking a half step back.

What? Of all . . . "And up to his bedroom," she supplied, with wholly feigned sweetness. "You may be right about that Lunatic Lockwood thing. A decor wholly dedicated to debauchery." As Haywood stared at her agog, she added, "Fur whips. Leather swings. I'm sure it was nothing you, being a man about town, would consider shocking. And come to think of—"

"Where is Alvin?" he asked, leaning to the side to look past her and down the drive.

"I sold him to a ship's captain bound for Shanghai." Haywood straightened to stare at her, his eyes wide. "Oh, for godsakes," she said, shaking her head. "He's somewhere behind me. And when he gets here, he'll tell you, ever so dutifully and faithfully and honestly, that I went to Lady Lockwood's home, not Tristan's."

"So you didn't actually see Lord Lockwood."

Sweet Jesus. Such hopefulness. "I didn't say that," Simone countered, desperately holding on to her patience. "He came by to visit with his sister while I was there."

"You left immediately, of course."

"Oh yes," she assured him dryly. "I squeaked like a little mouse, blushed furiously while babbling something inane, and then, wringing my trembling hands, ran out the door as fast as my quaking knees and delicate little feet would carry me."

He considered her with narrowed eyes. "You did not."

Well, at *last* he'd found his brain. "Then why'd you bother to ask if I did?"

"I was hoping that, just once, you'd surprise me by acting as a lady is supposed to."

And then he'd let it slip away again. "And just why would I want to behave ridiculously?"

"For the sake of your repu . . . ta . . ." He cleared his throat, looked down at his boots, and mumbled, "Never mind."

How, after six long years, the man could still harbor illusions . . . "Hark," she drawled as the sound of hoofbeats drifted faintly up the drive. "Alvin approaches. Just out of curiosity, do you and Drayton pay him to rat on me?"

Haywood drew himself up and squared his shoulders. "He does not *rat*. He offers reports when necessary, when he thinks there might be consequences for which Drayton or I might need to prepare ourselves."

"And he offers these reports freely?"

Haywood's blush was answer enough and every bit as telling as his muttered, "Well . . ."

"Just as freely as you two offer him tokens of your appreciation and gratitude, right?"

"It is a world based on exchange, Simone."

"Well, shatter my fantasies," she quipped, and then walked off, leaving him standing there looking confused. An accomplishment that wasn't all that difficult to achieve, she had to admit as, grinning, she vaulted up the back stairs and entered the kitchen. And that she could do it to him three, four times a day was just the most amazing thing. He was forever forgetting where she'd come from and the kinds of things that she knew.

Of course exchange made the world go round. She'd had that figured out by the age of five. Bits plucked from rubbish bins and gutters and the mud of the Thames could be traded for any number of things. A slab of bread, a chunk of cheese, a pint of ale. And once the body was fed, you traded your baubles for other baubles, eventually getting yourself a pair of shoes with a few more miles left in the soles, or a shirt, maybe even a pair of pants, that hadn't been worn too thin. Then, fed and clothed, you traded your labor for the roof over your head.

Making her way up the servants' stairs, she allowed that the whole matter of exchange was considerably less refined on the street than it was in the peerage. People of privilege didn't barter for their suppers. They wouldn't be caught dead laboring in any physical sort of way for anything. But trade they did. Carrie had given up her dressmaking shop to silence the wagging tongues when she'd been sucked into the peerage. Drayton had given up his military career because, as a duke, he was expected to be a prominent politician.

And the things she'd traded for a life of easy meals and a fancy roof . . . Pants for split skirts. Blunt honesty for deportment lessons and family reputation. For godsakes, she was even polite to obvious and desperate social climbers who wanted to use her.

All right, so her trades weren't great sacrifices, certainly not in the same league as the ones Caroline and Drayton had made, but still . . . In the final analysis, everyone was pretty much a whore. Not in that they were renting their bodies to strangers by the hour, but in that everyone traded away parts of themselves to get what they wanted and needed.

Well, all except Tristan. He didn't seem to be making any trades for his title. He wasn't giving up his shipping and import company. A peer *in trade*. Gasp! The horror! Simone grinned and slipped into her bedroom. Maybe his refusal to whore himself was part of why she found him so interesting. That and the fact that his interest in her was way beyond the bounds of socially acceptable exchanges.

A proper miss was supposed to trade sex for a spouse with a house. To give it away without getting a ring and long-term financial security in return was considered a sign of not only low morals, but also a lack of common good sense. How trading sex for marriage was all that different from trading sex for a few coins . . . A whore was a whore, unless she was a member of the peerage, and then she was a prudent lady.

What a farce. And how very typical of the pretentious, two-faced world she lived in.

$\mathcal{S}$imone stopped just inside the dining-room doorway. Fiona looked up from her book and arched a brow in silent question.

"Isn't Carrie coming down for lunch today?" Simone asked, continuing on to the table.

Fiona marked her page, closed the leather-bound volume, and set it aside while answering, "She says that food isn't sitting well—too much baby in the way—and she'd rather not make herself miserable. She's upstairs, knitting another set of booties."

"Better her than us, I guess," Simone countered, dropping into her usual seat.

"Neither one of us can knit."

Simone grinned. "Not well, anyway." As Fiona picked

up the bell and rang for the meal, Simone nodded toward the book. "What are you reading?"

"*Advanced Principles of Mammalian Anatomy.*"

"Sounds titillating."

"Hardly," her younger sister countered, tucking an errant lock of blond hair back under her headband. "But it is fascinating. And considering that they won't let me into the medical theaters to watch a live dissection, it's the closest I can come to a formal education on the matter."

Shortsighted men, Simone thought as the kitchen staff brought out a platter of sliced breads, cold meats, and cheeses and another platter of fresh fruits. Fiona could be just as good a doctor as any of them. And far better than most, actually. She was keenly intelligent and compassionate almost to a fault. Unfortunately, the only requirement for admission to medical school was an attached penis, and that Fiona didn't have.

"If push came to shove," Simone asked as the staff left them to their repast, "do you think you could actually do surgery on one of your furry little friends?"

"I don't know," her sister admitted, buttering a slice of bread. "I suppose it would depend on the likely outcome of cowardice. If they'd die if I didn't . . . Yes, I think I could. I would have to, wouldn't I?"

Simone nodded and shrugged. "Or live with the guilt forever."

"Could you do it?"

She grinned. "Live with the guilt? Sure. Guilt and I go way back together." She lifted her right hand, her first and middle finger held side by side. "Me and guilt, we're this close."

Fiona rolled her eyes and shook her head. "I meant would you be able to perform surgery if necessary?"

Now there was something to think about as you slapped a piece of cold, rare beef on your plate. "Well, I could open up something efficiently enough, but after that . . . Fluffy-kins had better be able to point to the problem and give me detailed instructions on how to fix it. Otherwise, it's not going to end well for ol' Fluff."

Fiona tilted her head to the side and arched a pale brow. "You have a secret."

"What?"

"You have a secret," Fiona repeated. "I saw it in your eyes when you were talking about being so comfortable with guilt."

Truth be told, she had a lot of secrets, but she couldn't think of any that she felt particularly guilty about. Tristan troubled her a bit, but she hadn't gone far enough with him to have earned any *real* guilt. "What kind of secret is it?"

"If I knew," Fiona countered, "it wouldn't be a secret, now would it?"

"What does it look like to you?"

"Well, judging by the fact that you're aware of it, I'd guess that you've done something so spectacularly outrageous that you hope Caroline and Drayton never find out about it."

Simone considered the merits of confiding in her younger sister. She did want to talk to someone about what she was feeling, what she was thinking, someone who wouldn't be duty bound to remind her of the rules of propriety. And while Fiona was very good at guessing secrets, she was every bit as good at keeping them. "Oh," Simone drawled, "I don't know that I'd describe it as spectacular."

"Oh, please, Simone," her sister said with a soft laugh. "You commit small outrages every day of your life and without the slightest bit of thought. It would have to be a considerable wrong for you to even remember that you'd done it. It would have to be spectacular for you to think it would drop Caroline's and Drayton's jaws after six years of dealing with your misadventures."

"True," she allowed. "But it really wasn't *that* bad."

"What wasn't?"

"How to put this delicately," Simone began.

"If you have to frame it that way," Fiona observed, "you must have achieved new heights. Is it going to be in tomorrow's paper?"

"No."

"There's a blessing."

Ignoring her sister's sarcasm, Simone shrugged and simply said, "I let a man kiss me."

"Why?"

She thought about it for a moment, remembering. The first kiss—the one Tristan had given her as they escaped the fire last night—could be explained as a consequence of the dire situation. Today, though . . . He hadn't actually kissed her. Not in the traditional sense. It had been more like a nibble. A long, delicious nibble. She reached up and skimmed her fingers along the length of her throat. "I suppose," she mused aloud, her pulse skittering, "I let him because I like the way he makes me feel."

"Well," Fiona said, "as long as you had sense enough to be somewhere private when it happened and he's not the sort to go running all over London telling people about it, I don't see that there's much chance in a little kiss being a horrid scandal."

Simone nodded. Fiona settled back in her chair and sighed softly before saying, "And since there's no scandal in the kiss, what's worrying you must be what came after it. Did it lead to more than a kiss right there on the spot?"

What a gift Fiona had for guiding a confession. She would make a great priest. If only she had a penis, of course. "In a matter of speaking, I suppose it did," Simone answered. "He asked me to meet him in the garden at midnight tonight."

Fiona considered her for a long moment. Finally, she said, "And you're seriously considering it."

Simone looked over at her. "You don't sound at all surprised."

"Part of me isn't at all," her sister admitted. "You've always done fairly well as you pleased, how and when you pleased, and without being the least bit concerned about what people outside of the family thought of you. Why should sneaking out to meet a man be any different?"

"But on the other hand?" Simone pressed.

"Well, I suppose that I've always thought that you would be harder to tame," Fiona answered with a shrug of her delicate shoulders. "I'm stunned that it's barely a week into your Season—the Season you fought tooth and nail to avoid, I might add—and you're willing to sit on a man's lap and purr for him."

Purr? Like some lap cat delighting over a tidbit of leftover fish? "I am *not* purring," she protested.

"Well, just as a point of information and generally speaking," Fiona countered calmly, "people don't take growling, snarling, and snapping things to bed with them."

It was a little late to profess complete innocence, but still . . . "I didn't say anything at all about being lovers."

"What?" Fiona asked on a breathy snort. "You've challenged him to a game of lawn croquet and that's the only time he could fit it into his schedule?"

And to think that Fiona had once been silent and shy. What a difference six years made. Simone shook her head and ate a bite of cheese. Abandoning pretenses, she said, "I haven't made a decision on his invitation."

"What seems to be the sticking point?"

"I don't know," she admitted. "Part of me is utterly fascinated while another part is frantically whispering, *Uh-oh, uh-oh.*"

"You know what Drayton always says. When in doubt, don't."

"Yes, I know," she allowed, suddenly very tired of having to think so hard. "But doesn't it strike you as being a terribly cautious and stodgy way to go through life?"

"No. But if you don't find that perspective useful as you mull your grand decision, you might want to consider the old saying 'curiosity killed the cat.'"

Lord save her from timid, overly rational people. "In the first place, I'm not a cat," she countered brightly, laying aside her napkin and gaining her feet. "And in the second place, it doesn't always kill them or there would be dead cats on every rooftop and hanging from the limbs of every tree."

Fiona looked horrified for a second and then rallied to say, "True. But sometimes it leaves them crippled or scarred for life."

"And sometimes they get away with it," Simone asserted with a wink as she snagged an apple from the tray and stepped away from the table.

"When was the last time you *didn't* get caught?" Fiona

didn't give her a chance to reply before adding, "You always get caught, Simone. You enjoy getting caught. That's nine-tenths of the reason you misbehave."

"No," she corrected, pausing and turning back. "I don't *always* get caught. And the thrill of having Drayton chew me up one side and down the other isn't quite the motivation you think it is."

Fiona tilted her head and considered her with somber green eyes. "Then what's the attraction in it?"

With a grin, Simone answered, "Boredom is a terrible, *terrible* thing."

Fiona clearly wasn't amused. "Please don't do anything that will overly and forever embarrass Caroline and Drayton. They've been so good to us."

"I won't," Simone promised. "Of course, it would be much—"

"No," Fiona interrupted, her curls bouncing as she shook her head. "I'm not going to help you."

How she'd known . . . "You're spooky sometimes."

"I'm not spooky," Fiona laughingly shot back. "You're predictable. And let's be honest, Simone. No amount of help from me is going to make the least little bit of difference to how it goes in the end, anyway. You'll be caught, Drayton will bellow for an hour and threaten to send you to Ryland Castle in chains, you'll shrug and walk away, Caroline will plead in your behalf, and—"

"Drayton will relent," Simone finished blithely as she headed back toward the door. "And that will be that until I do something else outrageous and everyone goes through the same thing again. You have to admit that I keep life interesting around here."

"That you do."

"And I make you look positively angelic in comparison. You should thank me for that."

"I *am* angelic."

"If a bit eccentric."

"By some standards, yes," Fiona allowed. "But still . . .
My behavior isn't giving anyone gray hairs or keeping
them awake at night with worry."

On the threshold, Simone paused again to look back,
smile, and say, "Ever the Good Sister."

"You don't have to be the Bad Sister," Fiona countered
softly, almost sadly. "Everyone would still be able to tell
us apart."

Timid. Overly rational. And now maudlin. "But I'm so
very good at being bad," she said on a laugh. "And when
we come right down to it, it's my only true talent."

She walked away before Fiona could ever-so-predictably
argue otherwise. Bad? She wasn't bad. Now if someone
were to suggest that she was a bit wild . . . Yes, she'd have
to admit that was true. But it certainly wasn't by conscious
choice. She never hurt people deliberately. She didn't sit
around putting concerted effort into thinking of ways to
shock or offend people. It simply happened. Rather like
the sun rising in the east every morning.

Well, except for Tristan Townsend, she allowed as she
climbed the stairs. She hadn't exactly planned the escala-
tion of their relationship, but she had deliberately put herself in his path to see what would happen. The decision
had produced results that weren't entirely surprising. Results, she had to admit, that she'd done nothing to stem.

Since she hadn't made any promises, she doubted that
he'd be waiting in the garden at midnight tonight, so it
wasn't as though she had to make a decision immediately.

But she had told Emmy that she'd sit for the portrait again tomorrow morning, and, given what she knew about Tristan so far, it was a sure bet he'd be there, too, waiting to see if she was brave enough to accept his dare.

She'd never in her life backed down from a challenge of any sort. She'd never *purred* for any man, either, and she didn't intend to begin doing so on mere command. Hopefully, between now and tomorrow morning she'd figure out how to balance her inclinations. Yes, she needed to find a middle ground, as it were, that her pride wouldn't mind sharing with Tristan. For just an hour or two. Maybe three if it all felt as good as that long, delicious nibble had.

CHAPTER 7

Tristan waved off formality and Lucinda's footman and made his way through the house toward the greenhouse on his own. Bless his sister's heart, she couldn't paint a picket fence, but her artistic illusions gave him the perfect opportunity to be with Simone. An opportunity he had every intention of taking as far as he could, for as long as he could.

And, he added as he slipped into the glass-enclosed jungle, whenever and wherever and however he could, too. God Almighty, when Simone smiled in that slow, easy, knowing way of hers, his blood went hot and his mind's eye served up a decadent feast of carnal delights. Pure, wondrous, never-ending . . . Yes, Simone Turnbridge . . . in a split skirt. If Em hadn't been there—

"Good morning, Tristan!" his sister called as though on cue.

He softly cleared his throat and dragged his mind back to the reality of the moment. "Good morning, ladies," he offered, joining them at the tea cart.

"And to you, Tristan," Simone said serenely while handing him a cup of steaming coffee. "Are you ready to paint?"

He could be. If they were alone. And both naked. And to think he'd spent his entire life thinking of finger painting as a child's pastime. How very shortsighted— and unimaginative—he'd been.

"Tristan?"

He blinked and looked back and forth between his sister and Simone, uncertain of which of them had called his attention back to the mundane and boringly circumspect.

"Simone asked if you were ready to paint on her portrait."

Judging by the bright, mischievous light dancing in Simone's dark eyes, she knew full good and well that he didn't give a damn about the picture Em was working on. In fact, if he had to guess, he'd say that her mind was racing along the very same course as his. "I'm ready whenever you are," he supplied, boldly holding her gaze.

"Then let's be on with it, shall we?" Emmaline suggested cheerily, cluelessly. "Unless, of course, there's some reason you'd prefer to wait until Lord Noland arrives."

Noland. Oh yes. Tristan took a quick sip of his coffee and watched Simone take a slow one. "I'm afraid I have some bad news, Em," he managed to say as Simone leisurely trailed the tip of her tongue along the rim of the china cup.

"What sort of bad news?"

Simone took pity on him, putting down her cup and gazing off toward the chaise she'd occupied during yesterday's sitting. Tristan dragged in a deep breath, willed his brain to forget about what she might be thinking they could do on it, and turned to face his sister squarely.

"Lord Noland sent word around before I left the house. He regrets that he has other obligations today and won't be able to join us for the painting session. He asked me to convey his deepest regrets and to assure you that he'll personally beg your forgiveness the very next time he sees you."

Em rolled her eyes. "I hope you'll tell him that begging really isn't necessary."

"Yes, but it would be nice if you'd humor him. He so enjoys playing the ever gallant gentleman."

His sister snorted and put down her coffee cup, saying dryly, "I don't think he's playing at it, Tristan. And yes," she added, walking over to the easel, "I'll be nice to him. He is your friend." She stopped and looked around, her pale brows knitted. After a second, she sighed and shook her head. Heading for the door, she explained, "I forgot that I wore my paint smock upstairs yesterday afternoon. I swear, if my head weren't attached . . . I think I remember where I left it. I'll be right back."

"Is it just me," Simone asked quietly from behind him, "or do you think she deliberately left that smock elsewhere?"

He turned and set aside his own coffee cup, asking, "Does it matter?"

"Only in how long she's likely to be looking for it."

Simone's smile was an invitation if he'd ever seen one. "I suggest," he said quietly, closing the distance between them to wrap his arms around her waist, "that we not waste a single second of it."

She twined her arms around his neck. "I agree," she whispered, her breasts brushing against his shirtfront. "What do you have in mind?"

He bent his head and trailed a line of light kisses to her ear. "If you were wearing a regular skirt," he whispered against it, "I'd lift it and make love to you standing right where we are."

She made a little humming sound, shivered, and then ever-so-lusciously arched her back to press her breasts harder into his chest. He slid his hands down over the dark velvet to cup her and draw her fully against the length of him. "But since you aren't and we don't have the time to remove it, we'll have to think of something else."

"For instance?" she asked on a ragged breath as he slowly moved his hips against hers.

"I'm willing to consider anything you might have in mind. Except," he added, moving against her again, "kissing you. Bruised lips are difficult to ignore and impossible to explain away."

"So is crushed velvet."

She had a point. To a point. Tristan eased back, sweeping the nap down over her backside as he released her. Her hands slid down his chest and then fell away as she took a half step back and skimmed smooth the fabric over her abdomen.

"But where it's crushed from riding," he said, catching her hands and drawing her toward the chaise.

"It's crushed and no one thinks anything of it," she finished as he dropped down onto the edge of the cushion. To his delight, she placed her hands on his shoulders and straddled his lap. Not as closely as he would have liked, but . . .

"Linen is another matter entirely, too," he pointed out. He lightly cupped her breasts and dragged the pads of his thumbs over the hardened peaks. "It wrinkles at the first look. After that, it's very forgiving."

"Speaking of forgiving," she said, holding his gaze and threading her fingers through the hair at his nape. "You weren't waiting in the garden all night for me, were you?"

He shook his head and shifted one hand to deftly open a pair of buttons on her blouse. "You didn't accept my invitation. And a gentleman never presumes a lady's consent."

"Of course not," she agreed, her voice low and soft, her gaze dark with desire. "He just keeps pressing ever so deliciously until he gets it."

"Deliciously? That implies that you're enjoying my advances."

She smiled slowly and reached between them to open a third button on her shirtfront, asking, "Has there ever been a woman who didn't enjoy your touch?"

He slipped his hand inside her shirt and beneath the silk of her chemise, his breath catching at the feel of soft hot satin in the palm of his hand. "There are no other women in the world."

She laughed softly and tugged at his hair. "Liar."

Caught, he grinned at her. "All right, there are other women. I just don't give a damn about any of them."

"At this particular moment, anyway."

"There haven't been any others since I met you."

"Two whole days?"

"And two nights, too," he countered, catching a peak between his fingers and gently squeezing. "Nights matter more than days, you know."

"The strain must be unbearable," she allowed on a held breath. Shifting on his lap, she asked with a faltering nonchalance, "How on earth have you endured it?"

He squeezed and then slowly pulled, answering, "The hope of being with you is the only thing that sustains me."

Smiling, she closed her eyes, arched her back. "Do women generally gobble up this sort of pablum?"

"You'd be absolutely amazed."

"I am." Letting her head drift back, she grinned blindly up at the ceiling. "On so many delightful levels."

If she thought he was good with his hands . . . He leaned forward and slowly trailed his tongue up the valley between her breasts. "God," she moaned, squirming on his lap. "We need to stop."

"True. In another minute or two, I'm going to turn and put you on this chaise on your back."

She shifted again, bringing her head back to center and opening her eyes. She arched a dark brow and twined his hair tightly around her fingers. "You wouldn't."

"Yes, I would," he assured her, pulling on her peak again. As her breath caught, he smiled and taunted softly, "And you would enjoy it, wouldn't you?"

"Tristan, be sensible."

He continued the delightful torture, saying, "Only if you promise to meet me tonight."

"You're a rogue."

"To your complete and utter delight. Promise? I won't

stop unless you promise." He grinned at her and cocked a brow as he squeezed her tender peak. "Emmy could be back at any moment."

With a quiet chuckle, she caught his wrist and met his gaze. "I promise to try. Would that be good enough?"

"Good enough," he declared happily, releasing his prize and sliding his hand out of her blouse. Placing his hands on her waist, he steadied her as she found her feet and stepped back. Rising himself, he noted the shaking of her fingers as she tried to button her blouse. Without a word, he eased her hands aside and undertook the task himself. And when it was done, he leaned down and feathered a kiss over her lips.

"Yes, a true rogue," she said, smiling and following him back to the tea cart.

"A gentleman rogue," he corrected, handing her her coffee cup. "It makes a difference, you know."

"Oh? How's that?"

"I swear that I'll take the wonder of your passion and willingness to my grave."

She nodded and smiled up at him. "That's nice. And as long as we're reassuring here . . . Just so you know, Tristan . . . If you *don't* take it to your grave, I'll put you there."

Well, that was a first, a woman threatening him with violence. By her own hand. Sweetly, calmly said, earnestly meant. What a delightfully refreshing change from the usual, from the viciously unspoken *I'll tell my father and then you'll be sorry*.

"Duly noted, my lady," he said, lifting his cup in salute. "In fact, it's carved forever on my heart."

She arched a brow and took another sip of her coffee.

"Let's leave our hearts out of this, all right? Keep things as simple and straightforward as we can?"

He lifted his cup in salute again, this time with a pang of regret. To have the most perfect woman in the entire world for a lover and not be able to tell anyone about it, much less shout his triumphant achievement from the rooftops of London . . . Damn. He couldn't think of all that many sacrifices he'd ever made for a female, and that this one should be so big . . . Of course, there had never been a woman more worth it, so all in all . . .

Emmaline chose that moment to return with her smock in hand and saved him from straining his brain and his conscience any further. Bless her little unartistic heart.

*S*imone followed Caroline into the parlor thinking that dinner had gone more smoothly than any she could remember. Drayton and Haywood had been preoccupied with upcoming Parliament business. Fiona had begged off to bottle-feed a litter of orphaned kittens someone had brought her late that afternoon. And Caroline . . . Poor Caroline was so terribly pregnant that breathing was a chore and eating required conscious effort.

Hovering close enough to help if she needed to, Simone held her breath and watched Carrie lower herself into a chair beside the hearth. The task accomplished without mishap, Simone sighed in relief and headed for the drink cart. She'd already poured herself a sherry and was adding lemon to Carrie's nightly cup of chamomile tea when her sister broke the pleasant silence.

"You're being rather quiet this evening, Simone. Is something troubling you?"

Uh-oh. "No," she answered brightly, carrying the drinks

over to the hearth. "I just don't have much to say. Nothing interesting, anyway."

Carrie nodded slowly and picked up her knitting. Looking down at it and threading the yarn through her fingers, she said, "Haywood tells us that you've met someone."

Here we go. "I'm sure Haywood said a great deal more than that," Simone countered, dropping into the facing chair and then turning about so that her legs dangled over the arm.

Carrie laughed softly and looked up from her knitting. "Well, of course he did. I was just leaving the conversation open for you to supply your side of the story."

"He's Lady Emmaline Townsend's brother," she began, choosing her words carefully. "He's a marquis. He's been in America for the last twelve years and he owns a shipping company. We met escaping the fire. And that's all there is to tell."

"Does he have a name?"

Well, at least it was Caroline asking the questions and not Drayton or Haywood. Carrie was a lot more understanding. "Tristan. Tristan Townsend, the Marquis of Lockwood."

"Haywood thinks his interest in you is improper."

Simone snorted. "That's because Haywood's interests in women are improper. He thinks all men are like him."

"They are," Carrie countered, going back to her knitting. "And you know that better than most young women."

"Even Drayton has improper interests?" she asked, thinking it was one of the smoothest changes in conversational direction she'd ever executed.

Carrie smiled as a pretty pink blush colored her cheeks.

"They most definitely were at one time. Even now he's a bit single-minded."

Well, this was interesting. Her sister *never* talked about her physical relationship with Drayton. "I can't believe you're actually admitting it."

Carrie sighed, laid the knitting on her belly, and looked at her. "With three babies in six years, it would be rather hard to deny it, don't you think?"

"Well, yes," Simone allowed with a chuckle, liking this uncommon frankness. She took a sip of her sherry and asked, "How are you feeling?"

"Fat."

Simone grinned. "Aside from that."

"And ugly."

Simone laughed. "You're not fat and you're not ugly. Although I must say that you're not making motherhood look all that attractive."

"There are parts of it that are rewarding," Carrie allowed, between sips of her tea. She sighed and looked down at her stomach. "But getting to them is something of a trial."

And not without its dangers, too. Simone lifted the glass of sherry and studied the firelight through it. "Is this your roundabout way of reminding me of the consequences of cavorting with rutting men?"

"Yes."

Roundabout but utterly honest. Always. Simone smiled and took a sip of the sherry. "To be really effective, you should probably tell me stories about young women who were caught being less than virtuous. You know, reputations destroyed, their families scarred forever by the embarrassment of the scandal, and all of that."

At Carrie's half smile and arched brow she added, "Oh, and don't forget the horrible marriages that had to be made and then endured because a girl couldn't remember how to say no to a man who didn't have a farthing to his name and even fewer strands of moral fiber. You need to tell me about those, too. In great gory detail."

"I would if I thought it would make one bit of difference in your thinking." Carrie set aside her cup and picked up the knitting again. "But it wouldn't, so I'm not going to waste the effort."

Well, as long as they were being honest . . . "Your own past having nothing to do with that decision, of course," Simone pointed out, thinking that she'd managed to resist Tristan for a good forty-eight hours longer than Carrie had resisted Drayton.

"There is a difference," Carrie said very carefully, "between having an affair with a guardian your own age and having one with a complete and—considerably older— stranger."

"A very small difference."

"But an important one."

"Not that it matters, since I'm not having an affair with Tristan Townsend."

"Yet."

Out of sisterly love, and a good bit of prudence, Simone ignored the bait. "And even if I were, he's not considerably older." *I think. I'll have to ask him.*

"Simone . . ."

Oh, no. Not a lecture. Please, Carrie.

"Being married isn't the prison you think it is." The needles clicked, punctuating her advice. "Honestly. Please don't do anything that might jeopardize your chance to choose that path, to be happy with life."

"I am happy with life," Simone countered, determined to keep the conversation from sliding into a gloom. "Well, aside from being forced into enduring a Season. That part's wretchedly awful and I hate it."

"There's more to life and being happy than horses and swords and the satisfaction of making people gasp and tsk."

"True." She lifted her sherry glass in salute and grinned. "There's making them faint."

Carrie glanced up to give her a censoring look that fell a bit short of the mark and then went back to knitting. "So what is it about Lord Lockwood that appeals to you?"

Always persistent Carrie. "I didn't say that he does."

"Is he handsome?"

Simone shrugged. "Passably so, I guess."

"Is he tall? Broad shouldered?"

Time to turn the conversation again. "Are you thinking about replacing Drayton?"

Carrie laughed. "Of course not. I'm simply trying to see if our taste in men is a shared, sisterly characteristic."

It clearly was, but Simone wasn't going to admit it. There was honest and then there was *honest.* "I suppose so," she allowed. "But then, maybe not. I haven't looked that closely at him."

Once again the knitting was laid down. "Simone," her sister said earnestly on a tiny sigh, "please be honest with me. Talk to me. I'm not clueless when it comes to matters of the heart."

That honest she could be. "If my heart ever becomes involved with a man, you'll be the first to know, Carrie. I promise."

"I'm not clueless in matters of attraction, either. I understand temptation and how instant and irresistible it can be."

"Yes, I know. And it's obvious," Simone quipped, grinning and pointedly looking at Carrie's belly.

Carrie chuckled. "You're deliberately muddying the waters."

"Of course I am. You'd be disappointed if I didn't."

"And would society be disappointed," she asked, her brow aching, "if you didn't have a torrid, illicit affair?"

"Oh, please, Carrie," she countered with a snort. "They'd be disappointed in me if I gave them anything less than a fully public, broad-daylight, buck-naked performance on the steps of St. Paul's Cathedral."

"You're not going to do that, are you?"

Oh, God. The look on her sister's face. Part horror, part delight. Simone laughed outright. "I do have some standards," she assured her. And then, just because she couldn't resist, she added, "Although I must say, given what Haywood was telling me about the Lunatic Lockwoods, that it might be something Tristan would seriously consider. I'll have to ask him the next time I see him."

"And when would that be?"

Ah, the crux of the entire conversation. And arrived at so smoothly and casually. Carrie really was good at this sort of thing. "Whenever he happens to attend the same party I do and we cross paths somewhere in the course of the evening," Simone answered just as smoothly. "With all the parties there are to choose among every night, who knows when that might be? It can't possibly happen until the week after next at the earliest, though. Everyone's making a show of being respectful of the dead for the next fortnight."

"I'll remind you that for some it will be a genuine expression of grief and regret. You need to leave your natural irreverence at home."

Yes, she did. And she would. "You're such a nice person, Carrie," she offered sincerely. "And a far better soul than I can ever hope to be."

"What I am is a very tired soul," Carrie countered, placing the knitting on the side table. "I think I'll say good night and lumber upstairs to bed."

Simone vaulted out of the chair and quickly set her sherry aside to offer her hands. Carrie took them with a smile of gratitude and allowed her to pull her to her feet.

"Sleep well and easy," Simone said as Carrie moved toward the parlor door.

Her sister stopped and turned back. "You are a good person, Simone. You're just very young and highly spirited. All that I ask is that you behave yourself for the next few weeks. Until this baby comes, I haven't the energy to stand between you and Drayton if something goes wrong."

Simone crossed the room and wrapped her arms around Carrie's shoulders. "Nothing's going to go wrong," she assured her with a hug. "I promise."

With a soft laugh, Carrie let go of her and, shaking her head, headed for the stairs, saying, "Napoleon said the same thing at Waterloo, you know."

"Except in French."

"Behave yourself!"

Yes, well . . . Simone went back to the side table, picked up the glass of sherry, and drained it. Returning it and Carrie's almost full teacup to the beverage cart, she considered her dilemma and how she might deal with it. Not meeting Tristan simply wasn't possible. She couldn't hide in the house like a mouse. But considering the promise she'd just made Caroline . . .

Hopefully Tristan would understand. But if he didn't . . . It would have been nice to be able to say that there were plenty of other interesting men in the world, but she'd seen the possibilities already and knew precisely how dismal they were. If Tristan decided to be ugly about her hesitation tonight, then it was going to be the longest, most torturously boring Season any woman had ever had.

If he did understand, though . . . If he was a real gentleman about it all . . . Of course a true gentleman didn't ask a lady to meet him in a garden at midnight. And a true lady didn't even entertain the idea. She most certainly didn't let her blood run hot at the possibility.

CHAPTER 8

He was insane. Certifiably insane. Tristan shook his head but kept his gaze firmly fixed on the darkened windows at the back of the Ryland town house. Not that the Duke of Ryland was likely to come out any of the rear doors. That would give his quarry a sporting chance of getting away. No, the odds were the duke would go out the front and circle around from behind. At least that's what *he'd* do if he knew there was a bastard waiting in the gardens, hoping to seduce his ward.

Tristan glanced over his shoulder. The horse was still tethered to the ring just outside the open gate. His calm assured Tristan that—for the moment, anyway—no one was on their way to see virtue defended and justice done.

Expelling a long, silent breath, he went back to watching the house and questioning his judgment. How pathetic it was to be sitting in the dark, waiting for a young woman. Actually, it was well beyond pathetic. It wasn't as though she was the only woman who would meet him. There were plenty of other beautiful women in London, and the vast majority could be had for an evening without all the risks that went with dallying with Lady Simone Turnbridge.

Of course, in that vast sea of available females there weren't any that intrigued him the way Simone did. Obvious beauty, apparent intelligence, a refreshingly direct honesty, a bold sense of daring, a willingness to be just as open about desire as he was . . . The characteristics of all accomplished courtesans. But with Simone—unlike courtesans—there was no underlying expectation of a businesslike exchange. There was no "if I do this for you, you'll do this for me" sort of thing—spoken or unspoken—in her acceptance of his advances. Which made Simone unique in his experience. She was carnal delight and wicked possibility wrapped up in a wondrously sultry innocence, a combination that he found not only fascinating but also irresistible.

Irresistible to the point of stupidity, actually. A man of his age, his experience . . . And his circumstances. Tristan shook his head and turned toward the gate, finally giving in to the tired voice of common sense. If Simone ever pressed him on why he hadn't met her as he'd promised, his only hope would be trying to explain his larger concerns. Maybe, with a bit of luck, she'd consider him slightly more noble than spineless.

The rustle was quiet but stopped him in his tracks. Holding his breath, he strained to hear as he turned to face the direction from which it had come. A shadow within the shadows of the house moved and he squinted into the darkness, straining to make out the details. Tall, slender, long legged. Dark from head to toe. His gaze skimmed the length of it. Part of his mind whimpered with relief. The other part . . .

Good God Almighty. Simone. Wearing pants. And he'd thought she had enticing curves in a split skirt? His heart hammered and his loins heated and tightened as he watched her saunter across the garden toward him. It was going to be damn difficult to get her stripped out of those trousers with any sort of efficiency. A skirt was certainly less inspiring, but it required considerably less effort to get under.

"You weren't about to give up on me, were you?"

He blinked, moistened his lips, and forced his brain to think in the moment. Not that the moment was all that conducive to cogent thought or intelligent repartee. She was dressed so simply—black trousers, black shirt, black boots, black jacket—but every inch of it all was so beautifully tailored that his only thought was of how badly he wanted to wrap his arms around her and pull those luscious curves against his body again. She was so warm, so delicious.

She stopped a circumspect distance from him. "I intended to be waiting for you when you arrived, but I was delayed by a brief crisis of conscience."

Conscience. The gears of his brain slowly ground to a semblance of normal functioning. "Apparently you overcame its nagging."

She smiled and shrugged. "To some degree."

"I know the feeling," he admitted.

"You do?"

"Intellect seldom approves of impulse, and the battle between the two can be especially ugly."

"If only intellect weren't so dreadfully dull and ever so predictable," she observed with a small laugh that ignited his senses. "Impulse has considerably more fun."

"Until the piper has to be paid," he countered, thinking that the tension in this moment was the payment for having run so freely with an impulse that morning. If his brain and conscience had been working then, he would have seen the pitfall of pressing her for this meeting. But no, they'd decided to stay home this morning and snooze most of the day away, leaving him with nothing but a penis for guidance.

"Yes, the piper," Simone said, interrupting his silent tirade. "It would be nice, wouldn't it, if he were to announce at the start just what the price might be? It would make decisions so much easier to make."

"I gather that you're here to officially and ever so politely decline my invitation."

She considered him for a long moment, her lower lip caught between her teeth. Finally she sighed, shook her head, and answered, "Intellect and impulse aren't quite done battering each other."

That he heard a reason to hope in her words . . . He was well beyond pathetic. "Oh, I don't know. The fact that you're standing a good arm's distance away tells me the contest is fairly well done and I've come out the loser."

"I'm sorry."

"There's no need to be," he assured her. "Truth be told,

while I've been waiting here for you, I've been sorting the pros and cons myself and coming to the same sort of hesitation."

Her smile was weak. "But probably not for the same reasons."

He had two options: assure her that social expectations actually mattered to him and walk away, or tell her the whole sordid, unappealing truth and hope to hell he could find some sort of balance between nobility and lust.

"There are some things you should know about me," he said, choosing. "About what's going on around me, before you make any decisions that involve spending time in my company."

Her smile instantly went from ear to ear and, even in the darkness, he could see the light dancing in her eyes when she asked, "Are you a wanted felon?"

"Sorry to disappoint you."

"Damn," she replied, chuckling. "That would have been exciting. So tell me what's so horribly troubling."

Now that he was to the point of having to put it all into words . . . She was going to think he'd lost his mind. "You might want to have a seat," he said, gesturing to the garden bench near the back gate as he considered the dilemma he'd created for himself. "This is going to take a while."

"All right." She walked off, leaving him to trail in her wake and try to keep his mind focused on framing his explanation. He arrived at the bench moments behind her, certain only of the fact that he'd never in his life seen a more cuppable, more perfectly shaped derriere.

"I'm now sitting."

Thank God. Tristan cleared his throat and began with

the first noncarnal thought that staggered through his awareness. "I always suspected that my father lived life larger than his financial resources really could allow." She looked up at him soberly and nodded. Tristan drew a deep breath and went on, saying, "Not that I had any proof of it, mind you. Confirmation of my suspicions came only recently and in a letter from my brother James. He inherited the estate after my father and eldest brother were killed.

"When James died and I was summoned home, I found the estate to be just as impoverished as he'd led me to believe. If I hadn't had a personal fortune available to pay the debts, everything would have been on the auction block the day after my arrival in London."

"Considering the way Lucinda is living," she posed, "you must have been very generous with your fortune."

"I haven't given Lucinda so much as a tuppence."

"Well, that rather begs the question of who has, doesn't it?" she asked brightly. "If the estate is teetering on the edge, she certainly couldn't be drawing an allowance from it that would let her live as she does and give Emmy a Season, too."

"I had the very same thoughts."

"And have you found an answer?"

"Not one I like," he supplied. "It seems that Lucinda received substantial sums of money following the deaths of my father and brothers."

"From who?" She frowned. "Or is it whom?"

He grinned. "The *whom* is various insurance companies. Apparently she had the incredible foresight to take out substantial policies on their lives just weeks before their unexpected demises."

"That's not foresight," she countered. "Once, yes, but three times? Three times adds up to a motive for murder."

"You have a wonderfully suspicious mind."

She grinned up at him. "Thank you for noticing. Has she taken out a policy on you?"

"And quick, too," he offered, dropping down beside her on the bench. The scent of cloves and sandalwood wafted around him and strummed tauntingly over his senses. "I haven't been able to find out. Confidentiality and all that. It stands to reason, though, that she would have. She does like her money."

"Well, money would certainly be a part of it, but I think it's more likely to be her secondary motive. I'd think she'd be far more interested in eliminating someone who suspects what she's done and might bring the authorities down on her."

Tristan shook his head, knowing that Simone's logic, while perfectly sound, was following the wrong course. "I don't have any proof. And the deaths of my father and brothers have cleared the inquests. There are no official suspicions surrounding her."

"Did they investigate her finances before reaching their conclusions?"

"Apparently it didn't even cross their minds that she might be anything more than the grieving widow and step-mother."

"That and that being around her could be fatal and the sooner they got her gone from their courtroom the better. If you were to provide the financial information, might they be willing to reinvestigate?"

He gave her a slight shrug and leaned his back against

the fence as he answered, "They found the suspicion intriguing, but of insufficient weight to spend the Crown's money on an official investigation."

"But they do know what you suspect. And they've made note of it somewhere?"

"They do and they have."

"Does Lucinda know that you've spoken with them?"

"No."

She turned on the bench, drawing her leg up to tuck her booted foot behind her knee. Her other knee pressed against his upper thigh as she leaned forward and asked, "How can you be sure?"

Sure of what? How easily he could wrap her in his arms? How little effort it would take to draw her closer? Seconds. He could have her straddling his lap in mere seconds. She'd be perfectly positioned for his hands to explore that invitingly curved backside of hers, and there wasn't any velvet to worrry about cru—

"Tristan?"

He cocked a brow and forced himself to breathe and swallow.

"I asked how you could be sure that Lucinda doesn't know that you've talked to the authorities."

Who the hell cared about Lucinda? He cleared his throat and willed the fantasy from the front of his brain. "I came into harbor, disembarked, and went straight to the solicitor's office. From there I went to find Noland. All of it was done within the first two hours I was back on English soil and well before word reached Lucinda that I'd returned."

"Why did you go see Noland?"

"He dabbles a bit at Scotland Yard."

"Well how about that," she said softly, shaking her head. "He looks so harmless."

"And he is. He specializes in puzzles and paper crimes. When his investigations come down to the use of muscle and grit, he merely points the way for those so inclined."

"I never would have guessed."

Tristan smiled. "And neither has Lucinda."

The nymph beside him nodded slowly. "So she's thinking that she needs to be sure that you don't live long enough to give them a nudge. Do you think she does her own dirty work or is she more likely to hire it done?" She didn't give him a chance to answer. "Probably more likely to do it herself. Hiring it done would leave her open to blackmail. Unless of course she dispatches her hirelings once they've served their purpose. But timing and luck would be crucial if she went that way. One slip, one miscalculation, and she'd be in trouble." She shook her head. "No, she does it herself."

"I agree."

"Given that three men in your family have already died under . . ." She cleared her throat softly. "Um . . ."

"Yes?"

She cleared her throat again and offered him a clearly apologetic smile before saying, "Haywood felt compelled to tell me stories of the Lunatic Lockwoods that first night."

Of course. It was nice, though, that she felt awkward about it all. "Not to worry, Simone. I expected that he would the second I was out of the carriage. It's all public knowledge."

"Well then, given that your father and eldest brother died in what everyone considers a murder-suicide, and your other brother ended up in the Thames, Lucinda has to be thinking that her luck might be running a little thin. I mean, with you it would be four deaths. . . . A fourth one by foul play would raise even normally naive eyebrows. So would a third by suicide. Seems to me that making your death look like an accident is the way she'd have to be thinking of doing you in."

"Absolutely fascinating."

She knitted her brows. "What are you talking about?"

"Your mind," he explained, willing to be only half-honest. "It works in the most amazing and unexpected way." *And I find it incredibly sensual.*

"How's that?" She smiled and the light in her eyes danced as she considered him.

God, he wanted to make love to her. Right here, right now. He expelled a long, slow breath to settle his impulses and collect his wits. "Has it occurred to you yet that being anywhere near me might—however inadvertently—place you in danger?"

"No." She pursed her lips, looked up at the night sky for a second or two, and then brought her gaze down to meet his as she brightly announced, "There, I considered it. Where was Lucinda the night the party went up in flames?"

Did Simone have even the slightest idea of how she was torturing him? "Presumably at home," he managed to say. "I don't know that for certain, though. She might have gone out after Em and I left for the party. You're thinking that she might have started the fire in an attempt to do me in?"

"It's a possibility," she answered, shrugging one delectable shoulder. "It wouldn't be at all suspicious to the authorities. Just another tragic loss for England's Black Widow."

"I don't know. I think Lucinda would want it to be more personal." He smiled at the mental image. "You know, to actually see my face as she runs me down with her town coach."

"You're too quick to run down with any sort of efficiency."

Tristan cocked a brow and met her gaze. "And how do you know that?"

"I watched you come down the rope that night. You're impressively strong and agile."

Virile, too, he silently added. "I didn't know you were watching."

"But you were hoping that I was," she laughingly countered, leaning sideways to crash her shoulder into his in just the way that he and his friends had jostled each other in their youth. He was still puzzling the gesture when she asked, "How are you going to draw Lucinda out and expose her?"

He considered her, his brows knitted. "Did I say that was my plan?"

"Well, if it's not, you're a dead man, and considering how much you like having your heart go pitter-pat, I figure you're thinking about how to keep it pumping right along."

It wasn't his heart that was interested in pumping at the moment. "And what would you suggest as a tactic to force her hand?" he asked, desperately trying to distract himself.

"I don't know. But I presume that you've given it some thought. What have you come up with?"

That I don't give a damn about Lucinda and that I'm

tired of talking. Once again he expelled a long breath and tamped down his impulses. "I tend to think that Lucinda is more interested in deepening her pockets than she is worried about being caught at it."

"Greed does make people a bit blind. And over-confident."

As does lust, he reminded himself. "So if simple greed is her motive, then it stands to reason that she'd want as much money as could be had from my death, right?"

"A logical assumption."

"So let's say that I'm found flattened on the street."

"She'd clutch her handkerchief and cry in a dignified way as she took the insurance money."

"Absolutely. And then she'd leave the offices of the insurance company and go directly to the office of my solicitor to cry some more as she listens to the reading of my will."

"Oh my God," Simone whispered, her eyes widening.

"Precisely. Without a wife and heirs, I have no one to leave my personal fortune except my sister."

"And with Emmy being a minor . . ."

Yes, an amazingly quick mind. "I'm sure Em would live very well. For a while, anyway."

"Until she met a tragic end, too. And then Lucinda, her grief-stricken mother, would inherit your personal estate as the only next of kin."

Tristan nodded. "It would require some patience, but not a great deal of luck. She could be a very, very wealthy woman before a year was out."

"But only if you die before you marry," Simone countered. "After you marry, your wife and any heirs would inherit your personal estate, not Emmy."

"Yes."

"In that case," she said, slowly, contemplatively, "announcing your engagement would send Lucinda into a panic. You'd have to die before you got to the 'I do' or she'd get nothing."

"Forcing her hand quite effectively," he allowed. "Unfortunately, I don't think she'd be all that put off by disposing of my beloved in the process of eliminating me. Which, all in all, makes it rather difficult on my conscience to consider actually inviting a young woman to step blindly into what amounts to a deadly trap. And I'd think that explaining the circumstances would tend to dampen the interest most women might have in accepting my proposal."

She grinned. "What you need is a young woman with some pluck and a set of eyes in the back of her head. A bit of ruthlessness to her wouldn't hurt, either."

Yes. Yes. And yes. Being a breathtakingly bold lover would be appreciated, too.

"Just out of curiosity, Tristan . . . When did you first think of me as the answer to all your prayers?"

She was assuming. Accurately. He could pretend to be a gentleman and deny it or face it squarely. "It depends on which prayers we're talking about," he answered. "If it's my prayers for a beautiful, passionate lover, then you were the answer the moment I saw you standing beside Em at the punch bowl the other night. But if it's my prayers for an accomplice in intrigue . . ."

He sighed. "Honestly, that didn't occur to me until I watched you ride away yesterday morning. In the hours between then and now lust has been battling my conscience over the notion. There's considerable danger involved and—"

"No one is going to believe that I'm willing to agree to marry. Not just out of the blue. Which, of course, I'm not. This would be purely for appearances and only for as long as it takes to draw Lucinda into making a move against you in Noland's presence. Once that's done, we'll call off the whole thing and go our separate ways."

"I haven't agreed to this, you know."

"I'd have to be forced into an engagement," she went on, apparently ignoring his noble intent. "Otherwise it's going to set tongues loose all over town. Well, they're going to talk regardless, but, if I'm not forced into it, it will be in a way we don't want. Lucinda may not know me, but she does listen to the tales. Our plan would come off ever so much better, not to mention quickly, if she doesn't suspect that *she's* being drawn into a trap."

"Simone, I—"

"Obviously we need a scandal that would force us to marry. And marry quickly. I mean, there's no sense in having a year-long engagement, is there? The faster we have to marry, the faster Lucinda has to act. We could have this whole affair over and done before the week is out."

Well, yes, in a perfect world. But the world wasn't perfect. "At which point," Tristan observed, "assuming we survive it all, your guardian will want to kill me for having endangered you and put your family in the midst of a horrible scandal. And, to my thinking, have every right to do so on both counts."

"Actually, that's the silver lining in it all," she blithely countered. "Not that Drayton would want to kill you. He wouldn't. Not seriously. He'd be furious with me. And for once he'd make good on his threat to send me to the country house in chains. I'd get out of having to go through with the Season."

"Your reputation would be destroyed."

She grinned. "Thoroughly. Spectacularly."

"You'd never have another chance at a Season."

"Proof that God is indeed benevolent," she rejoined, laughing softly.

"We'd be manipulating your family. Most unkindly."

She sobered instantly. "There is that," she admitted on a soft sigh.

"Let's think on the course, Simone," he suggested, feeling both virtuous and keenly disappointed. "We don't have to make a decision tonight. Tomorrow or the day after or even six months from now will be soon enough. Lucinda isn't going to act until she's forced to by circumstance. It's in her best interests to wait as long as possible. The longer the situation goes along as it is, the fewer suspicions that will be raised if something happens to me. I brought up the subject simply because I thought it only fair that you know that there are risks involved in being in my company."

She nodded slowly and stared down at his legs. "Then I suppose that we're to the time when I should wish you a good night and say that I'll see you with Emmy in the morning."

"I believe we are."

Neither one of them moved to stand. Tristan watched the rise and fall of her breasts, battling the desire to reach out for her, to suggest that perhaps prudence was an overrated virtue.

Slowly she lifted her gaze to meet his. The light of

desire flickered in the depths of her eyes and shimmered in her voice as she whispered, "Would it be all right to ask for a good-night kiss?"

A good man would kindly and politely decline the invitation outright. A cad would answer by taking her in his arms and pushing her mindlessly over the brink. Tristan forced himself to swallow. "That could be dangerous."

She arched a brow and one corner of her mouth rose in the smallest, most deliciously wicked smile. "There are so few edges in my life these days."

His sense of honor whimpered, but he ignored it and reached for her, slipping his arms around her waist and drawing her closer as he bent his head. She met his advance with a sigh of sweet sanction, twining her arms about his neck and melting against him. Her breasts pressing warm against his chest, her lips parted at the first touch of his tongue and she opened for him, willing and hot and delicious. Fire poured through his veins, arrowing into a hard, throbbing desire. He moaned at the sudden intensity of the need, and even as reason flitted through his awareness, he lifted her and drew her closer still.

She sighed and shifted in his arms, then tripped his heart as she seized control of their kiss and settled herself across his lap. God, for as long as he lived . . . He slipped his hands down her hips and then back to cup her and firmly hold her against the hardness of his desire. She went still and then tore her lips from his with a gasp. Regret flooded over him and he opened his eyes as his brain stumbled through scattered words in the hope of finding some that would make an apology. The light in her eyes caught his breath and sent his mind reeling.

"I don't want to say good night," she murmured,

rolling her hips and sending a wave of exquisite pleasure through him. "Not yet."

As he gasped for air and self-control, she moved against him again, slower and harder. "Simone," he groaned, grabbing her hips and trying desperately to still her. "This is—"

"An intelligent impulse," she declared, lifting her arms from his neck to open the buttons on her shirt.

Intelligent? No, it wasn't; it was reckless in the extreme. But what the hell, he didn't care. He'd just make damn sure they didn't get caught and then all the ifs, maybes, shoulds, and oughts wouldn't amount to a hill of beans. As for it being an impulse . . . It certainly could be; he was ready enough. But she deserved a better bed for their first mating than a cold wooden garden bench.

Tristan caught her hands and brought them to his shoulders. "You win, my sweet," he said softly as he slipped his hands under her legs. She grinned wickedly as he lifted her up and gained his feet.

It wasn't until he stepped to his horse outside the gate and slid her gently to her feet that she asked, "Where are you taking me?"

"To my bed."

Her smile was slow but so lusciously wicked that it took every measure of his self-control to pull the reins from the ring and swing up across the saddle.

CHAPTER 9

$\mathcal{S}$imone stood, her heart racing, and watched him settle into the saddle. God, if she was ever going to get caught being bad, there wasn't another man on earth she'd rather be caught with. There had to be credit awarded for picking someone so handsome, so strong. And a man who could turn reason to ash with just a touch . . . He looked down at her and slowly smiled.

"You sit a horse very well," she observed as her pulse quickened.

"Thank you. So do you." He moved back on the smooth leather seat. "Come sit it with me."

How exactly one did that . . . "I've never shared a mount before," she admitted with a grin. "And I definitely recall several of my many deportment masters saying that ladies shouldn't. Ever."

"Did they say why?"

She chuckled, remembering. "No, they just looked horrified when I asked."

He laughed softly. "Hop up on that mounting block, turn your back to me, and I'll show you why they were so adamant."

She'd long ago surmised the danger, but the prospect of actually experiencing it . . . She vaulted up on the stone and obediently turned to face the fence. No sooner had she done so than Tristan's arm slid around her waist. She folded her arms across it, tucking her fingers beneath the steel band as he lifted her up and drew her across his lap.

Oh yes. Why ladies shouldn't share a horse was obvious. Hard, pressing, and hotly obvious. She shifted, settling her hips between his thighs. His breath caught in a delightful way.

"Comfortable?"

She looked up at him and grinned. "Comfortable is what one is when sitting in a well-upholstered chair in the morning room, sipping coffee, and chatting with your sister. My sister's not here and you're not the least bit well upholstered. In fact." She deliberately wiggled her hips, rubbing against his hardness. "Yes, you're decidedly lumpy."

"I'm sure you can smooth me out with no effort at all."

"Right here?"

"God," he groaned, and turned the horse about.

As they eased out of the shadows and made their way

onto the dew-damp cobblestones of the street, his jaw tightened and his fingers tightened on the reins. She thought about easing slightly forward to ease the friction and his suffering, but even as the thought occurred to her, he laid his free hand on her thigh and began to draw heated circles with his palm. Circles that ever so slowly and deliberately moved inward and up.

"Where are we going?" she asked on a ragged breath.

"It's a surprise."

No one had ever touched her so intimately. The heat of his hand and the friction of her trousers against sensitive nerves set her on fire. She closed her eyes and tried to control the pulsing of her womb. "Generally speaking, I've never cared much for surprises."

"You'll like this one."

"I am so far," she admitted, shifting to allow him freer access.

He bent his head and feathered a kiss to her temple, asking, "Are you impatient, Simone?" as the heel of his hand came to rest on the lowest button of her pants. And stopped.

"I hope you don't consider that too brazen," she answered tightly as she squirmed, trying to get his hand to move again. "Not that I care if you do."

"In private," he whispered into her hair, "there's no such thing as too anything."

"Then could we possibly ride any faster?"

"But it's dark," he murmured, slowly pressing his hand into her and rubbing. "And the streets are deserted."

"Oh, Tristan," she whimpered as the exquisite heat and throbbing returned, instant and more intense for its momentary absence. "That's heav—" She gasped at the sudden jolt of pleasure. Even as she smiled in satisfaction another shot through her, deeper and hotter and more compelling. Then another even more urgent. And another. She arched up and turned into him, desperately trying to pull away, to trap his hand—anything to keep her wits above the flood of too keen sensation.

He didn't relent. Neither did the pleasure. In a heartbeat, it shattered her control, and delight quaked through every fiber of her body, melting her bones and wondrously overfilling her senses.

As he pressed kisses into her hair, her mind drifted slowly back to earth. "Dear God," she whispered, amazed.

He laughed, the sound rolling gently through her and deepening her contentment. She smiled, thinking that, yes, if there was ever a man worth a scandal, it was Tristan Townsend. She leaned into him, nestling her cheek against the heated plane of his chest. Listening to the strong, steady beat of his heart, she closed her eyes and surrendered to the lullaby.

𝒮imone stood in the shadows as Tristan had instructed and watched him lead the horse toward the dimly lit guard shack at the farthest corner of the warehouse. Part of her brain dully mulled the fact that she was serenely obeying what amounted to an imperial command. Another part was really quite impressed with his attempt to protect both her reputation and his horse. And yet another part of her brain was dutifully recording the sights and sounds and smells of the world around her. A world she hadn't seen since the day she'd been sold into the peerage.

The corners of her mouth twitched and her awareness roused from its deep and pleasant stupor. The river. She was back to the river. She could smell it, could hear it. To her left and behind. She turned and walked deeper into the shadows, rounded the near corner, and then stopped, her heart swelling. The Thames. The tide was high tonight. And the water was warm.

"Simone!"

Oh, how sweet. She wasn't where he'd left her and he was worried. "I'm over here," she called softly.

At the edge of her vision she saw him come around the building. His stride faltered for a second. But only for a second. "What are you doing?" he asked quietly as he stepped to her back and wrapped his arms around her midriff.

Home. She was home. Settling into him, she laid her arms over his and sighed dreamily. "Watching the fog rise and roll along the Thames. It's been forever since I've seen it. Odd how it's the littlest things we miss, isn't it?"

She felt him ever so slightly shift his stance and draw a long, deep breath. "It's not safe for you to be down here alone, Simone."

"I'm not alone," she pointed out in a whisper. "I'm with you."

His chest softened against her back and the tension in his arms ebbed away. Tucking her head under his chin, he stood with her for a long moment before he asked, "When was the last time you were down to the river?"

The morning of the day that her world had been turned upside down. The tide had been low, but she hadn't found anything in the foul mud worth selling. Others had, though, and she'd gone back to the brothel thinking she was going to be hungry another day and resenting that others would get to eat. Essie had been furious that there was no larking money to supplement her madam's share and . . . Simone deliberately closed those moments away. "It was years ago," she supplied simply.

"Something unpleasant must have happened. Your heart's racing and your body's tight."

He didn't know the half of it. Or even a sliver. She willed her body to relax, reminding herself that the past was over and that Tristan wouldn't let harm come to her from anyone. "The better memories seem as though they're from another lifetime and they've become a little faint and fuzzy," she explained. "The bad ones, though . . . They're still as close as yesterday and I try very hard to pretend they aren't."

"Then I'm sorry I asked you to look back."

Regret rippled sincerely through his words and tugged strangely at her heart. "I was born down here, along the Thames," she said, feeling an inexplicable need to share her story with him. "Where, exactly, I don't know. I don't think anyone knows. Or much cares, for that matter."

"Why?"

"My mother was a prostitute."

"And your father?"

"The Duke of Ryland." She smiled and shrugged within the confines of his embrace. "Or so they say. I've never really believed it, but my opinion doesn't carry any weight. The queen declared it so, waved her scepter, and I was hauled away to a life of considerable wealth, comfort, and privilege."

"And your mother? Where is she these days? Do you know?"

"She was murdered when I was ten. Someone cut her throat in an alley."

He hugged her long and hard, tucked her closer under his chin. "Who took you in?"

"It was more a case of who was willing to hand me a bucket and a rag mop in exchange for a corner by the hearth. Who was willing to trade what I found larking for a few bits of food. For the next four years."

"Bless the queen for eventually waving her scepter."

"As mistakes go, I came out well on it," she admitted. "And Caroline and Drayton have been very understanding of how difficult it's been to become someone else."

"A person can't ask, or hope, for much more than that."

No, they couldn't. That Tristan knew that . . . "Tell me about your life, your family."

"There isn't much to tell," he answered easily, lightly. "It wasn't much of a family. My father was a drunk who married three times. My brother Giles was by his first wife. My brother James was by his second, my mother. And Emmaline by his third, Lucinda."

Simone frowned and quickly ran the words through her head again. "He wasn't your father?"

"By name and law and rights of inheritance, yes. But not by actual seed."

So they were both bastards. "Did he know that you weren't his?"

"Oh yes. And it was never forgiven or forgotten. The day I turned eighteen I sailed for America, and we never saw each other again. That I'm the one who inherited his title . . . He's spinning in his grave. Around and around and around."

"Do you know who your real father is?"

His chin brushed over her hair as he shook his head. "My mother refused to name him."

Possibility bloomed. Simone arched a brow. "God, I hope it wasn't the Duke of Ryland. Otherwise . . ." She shuddered and Tristan chuckled. "Let's not think about that," she suggested.

"I have an even better idea," he offered, nibbling her ear.

"Let's not think at all?" she guessed while shivers of delight rippled through her and her knees went weak.

He eased his arms from around her and took her hand. Saying, "It's damp. Let's go inside," he drew her toward the door of the warehouse.

She let him lead her, her brain dutifully, calmly, recording realizations as they went. She'd never in her life docilely let a man lead her anywhere. And considering why Tristan was guiding her into a dark warehouse . . . She really ought to be a great deal more nervous than she was. Or, at the least, a tad reluctant.

But then again, she knew the basic mechanics of love-making; growing up in brothels had been quite instructive. Not that she'd ever put all that knowledge to any sort of actual personal use until now. Hopefully there weren't any great secrets to impressive lovemaking that she'd failed to hear. It had all seemed fairly straightforward and relatively simple. Not that she'd been paying attention *that* closely. Although she might have found it all more interesting if there had ever been a man like Tristan involved.

Lord, he had the most incredible smile, the most expressive dark eyes. Just the sight of him made her warm all the way to the center of her bones. And his touch . . . Even now, her fingers laced through his was enough to make her pulse quicken in anticipation. Right or wrong didn't matter. And the costs be damned. Even if it was only for a few hours, tonight she was his. She was wanted.

Tristan resisted the urge to sweep her up into his arms and stopped just across the threshold of his warehouse. "Careful," he admonished, letting go of her hand. "There are crates everywhere. Let me light the lamp."

She waited in silence, a shapely shadow of clove-scented temptation as she carefully eased out of her jacket and laid it aside. Determined to hold his course, he found the match and struck it.

"Oh, Tristan," she whispered in reward.

Leaving her to fantasize amid the mountains of brightly colored silks and satins, he removed his jacket and tossed it aside as he made his way along the path he'd laid out. "It gets better as we go," he cajoled as the second lamp cast its light over stacks of gleaming brass and well-oiled wood.

"It's perfect right here," she called from behind him as he lit the third and final lamp. He smiled and, waving out the match, went back to see which of the treasures had captivated her attention. He stopped at the edge of the light, his heart tripping in the most surprising way. He'd put the sword where he was sure she'd see it as she passed. He'd hoped she'd be intrigued enough to pick it up and give him a chance to gift it to her. And with the exception of the final part, it had gone perfectly according to plan. But as he stood there, his brain refused to think beyond how marvelously unique Lady Simone Turnbridge truly was.

"The balance is incredible," she said, grinning and stepping forward to thrust the point toward an imaginary opponent. She jumped back, brought the blade up in a quick arc to parry, and then danced forward two steps, her grin broadening with each. "I've never wielded anything as finely made."

And he'd never had a woman so freely and naturally physical. He swallowed and desperately tamped down his anticipation. "The first time I held your hands, I wondered how a lady could have calluses in both her palms. The left are from reins, of course. The right, I see, are from a hilt. You've been formally trained. By someone very good at close arms combat."

She stopped and held the blade up to study the light gleaming off the finely honed edge. "That would be Haywood and Drayton." She looked past the weapon to meet his gaze. "Do you fence?"

He nodded slowly as a fantasy of a rough victory played through his mind. He cleared his throat softly and came off the crate, shifting his stance to accommodate his sudden hardness. "We'll have to have a match sometime."

Her gaze went slowly up and down the length of his body. "But not now," she said softly, the light in her eyes deepening.

"I didn't see any épées in the inventory," he offered, watching her reverently place the sword back into its carved box.

She closed the lid and turned to him, her smile easy and knowing. "And we have better ways to spend our time?"

"Yes." He held out his hand and she stepped to the edge of light and took it without hesitation. He gazed down into smoldering dark eyes and, with every measure of restraint he possessed, slowly led her to the last pool of light.

"It's lovely, Tristan," she whispered, easing her hand free and stepping past him. She stopped halfway between him and the canopied bed he'd fashioned of silk and satin pillows and lengths of gold-embroidered saris. "Truly . . ." She shook her head and then eased her hip against the crate on which he'd placed the lamp.

"Opulent?" he suggested as he watched her bend down.

"Oh yes," she agreed, pulling off her boot. "Decadent, too." She bent over again to remove the other boot. "And wonderfully inspirational."

"Ah, yes, inspiration." He surrendered to it and stepped behind her to place his hands on her hips and ever so lightly draw her backside against him. "It's so important, isn't it?"

"You're distracting me," she accused, her breath ragged as she tossed her boot aside and straightened.

He held her hips in place and bent his head to nip at her ear and murmur, "It's only fair. You've been distracting me since I saw you across the ballroom."

"Did you want to do this even then?"

"Yes." He released her hips to slide his hands boldly over her ribs and up to cup her breasts. "And at least a dozen times since," he admitted, scraping his thumbs over the hardened crests.

She shuddered slowly and deeply, then, with a satisfied sigh and sensuous wiggle, eased out of his loose embrace. She took only two steps, turned to face him, and began undoing the buttons of her shirt, saying, "I haven't made you wait very long for your dreams. Barely a full two days."

A full day too long as far as he was concerned. "Which makes you the most wonderful woman I've ever known."

And if he didn't get about the business of stripping off his clothes, he'd have no one but himself to blame for any more time wasted.

"Am I the most wanton, too?"

"The most honest, Simone," he assured her as he blindly pulled off his own boot and threw it aside. "I am in awe of your honesty."

She made a little humming sound and undid the last button on her shirt. Leaving it hanging open just enough to slacken his jaw in stunned realization, her fingers moved down the line of her trouser buttons. His head was already light and his boot was halfway off when her pants slipped down over her hips and pooled at her ankles. His breath caught when the shirt fluttered down atop the pants a second later.

No chemise. No corset. No pantaloons. No stockings. Just creamy satin skin and lusciously sweeping curves.

"Sweet Jesus," he moaned, his balance faltering as his hands tightened around his boot. He yanked it off and pitched it blindly off into the darkness as he planted both feet on the wooden floor and seized a steadying breath.

Even as he struggled for control, she stepped out of the fabric and advanced on him with a soft, delightfully wanton smile. "You've forgotten all about my honesty, haven't you?"

Honesty was nice, but at the moment he was far more appreciative of her high, perfectly shaped, perfectly sized, perfectly crested breasts. "You . . . are . . ."

"What?" she drawled, reaching out to open the buttons of his shirt.

"Every man's dream come true."

"Really," she said to his shirtfront. "I always thought

men's fantasies required a bit more of a woman than simply standing about. If I'd known satisfying them involved so little effort, I would have happily and thoroughly met yours yesterday morning in the conservatory. And again this morning."

Naked in the greenhouse? "Well, there's always tomorrow morning," he offered, grinning as she pushed his shirt off his shoulders.

She nodded and skimmed her hands down over his chest. "True. But only if I enjoy it enough tonight to want to do it again."

His breath caught painfully in the center of his chest as her fingers trailed down to the top button of his trousers. She was magnificent. Beyond all of his dreams. "The *if,* my brazen beauty, is in whether you're going to be able to want again that soon."

Her eyes sparkled and her grin was wide and bright as she looked up to meet his gaze. "Oh, you think you're *that* good, do you?"

"Want me to prove it?"

"Yes, please." She winked at him and then turned and walked off to the bed, saying, "I'll be waiting for you."

He stood there as though rooted to the planking, watching her, marveling at her grace, her aplomb, her sense of confidence. And her marvelous backside. She stepped carefully into the mass of pillows, stopped, turned, and then slowly sank to her knees and sat back on her heels.

Good God Almighty. He was the luckiest man in London. In England. Hell, in the whole damn British Empire. Or he would be once he got himself over to the bed. And shed of his clothing.

He looked down to see what degree of disrobing she'd

accomplished for him and grinned. What a quick and efficient little thing she was. Undoing the buttons on his shirt cuffs, he shrugged and sent it to the floor. His pants followed, one button and a scant second later. Stepping out of them, he paused only long enough to turn the lamp down slightly and then made his way to the makeshift bower.

Her heart skittering madly, her nerves tingling, Simone watched him walk toward her and willed herself to breathe, to keep from gaping. She'd hadn't seen a naked man in quite some time, but she had glimpsed a fair number of them over the course of her earlier years. They hadn't been all that impressive. And certainly not the least bit inspiring.

But Tristan . . . Dear God. Long legs, a narrow waist, and trim hips. Broad shoulders. Muscles and sinew that rippled when he moved . . . Never in her less than sheltered life had she seen a man so powerfully, so magnificently, built.

He stepped into the pillows and eased down onto his knees in front of her. Trailing his fingertips along her shoulders, he asked softly, "Are you nervous, Simone?"

He wanted her to think, to talk? She shook her head and closed her eyes, savoring the pleasure that flowed from his touch. It cascaded through her, deliciously warming and liquefying. To feel this alive, this perfect, all the time . . .

He leaned forward, his chest brushing lightly over her breasts as he slipped his arms around her and pressed a kiss to the shell of her ear. Warmth turned to heat and sent her senses reeling. "Tristan," she murmured, her hands skimming to his waist as she turned her face to his.

He obliged her desire, brushing her lips with his own and drawing her body along the length of his. "Tell me what you want," he whispered, laying a trail of slow kisses down her neck.

"You."

"How?"

"Slow and gentle," she answered, kissing his shoulder. "Fast and rough."

He laughed and slipped his hands lower to cup her bottom. Holding her hips hard against his, he slowly, deliberately, rotated his pelvis. "You can't have both at once," he said over her gasp of appreciation. "I'm good, but not that good. Choose."

She kissed the hot satin of his shoulder again, her mind buffeted by the swirl of heady sensation, her pulse pounding through every fiber of her body, and her core molten. "I'm not good," she admitted, turning her head to lightly nip his neck, "at patience. Are you?"

He drew back to look down into her eyes. "I can try."

"Please don't."

He cocked a brow and a smile slowly lifted the corners of his mouth. "There's a French letter under the pillow to your left. If you'd be so kind . . ."

"It would be my pleasure," she whispered, easing out of his embrace. Balancing on her knees and one hand, she pushed her hand beneath the pillow. And froze, her breath caught and her heart dancing as his hands went to her waist and he trailed his tongue languidly over the curve of her backside.

"Do you like that?" he asked, doing it again.

"Yes," she gasped, her body quivering with delight.

He shifted behind her, placing his knees between hers.

Her heart stopped in wondrous delight as he cradled himself snugly against her. Heated and hard, heated and wet. God, could you die from pure pleasure?

"Don't you have something for me?"

Oh yes, the French letter. She'd forgotten all about it. If she could breathe, she'd apologize. If she could move, she'd hand it to him.

"Permit me," he whispered against her ear, leaning over her and slipping his hand under the pillow. He drew back, the letter in his hand, his lips grazing her skin and making her whimper in anticipation.

Sheathed, Tristan held her hips tightly and sucked a deep breath, willing himself to go slowly, to give her time to accept and adjust to his invasion. She gasped as he pressed forward, raising her head as she dropped down onto both elbows. He pressed deeper, struggling against a too rapidly building desire.

She didn't cry out, didn't resist. Neither did she passively accept his halting advance. She pushed back against him with a hunger every bit as demanding as his own. The wonder and power of it quickly swept him past noble intentions and into the realm of ageless instincts. Simone went with him with a low moan of acceptance and pleasure. He held her hips and let her set the rhythm of their dance.

Nothing had ever felt as right, as destined, as this did. Nothing. He tightened his grip on her and drew back, willing himself from the edge.

"Tristan!" she cried, her voice strained as she struggled against his hold. "Don't stop! Please!"

God help him, he couldn't deny her. He slipped a hand down across her abdomen, and his fingers arrowed into the wet nest of curls and found the swollen nub at its heart. She moaned and bucked back, pulling him deep, and over the brilliant brink.

Her bones were gone. Every single one of them. She'd never move again. Not that she cared. Simone sighed and let Tristan ease her down into the pallet of pillows.

"Simone? Are you all right?" he asked, gathering her into his arms and rolling them onto their sides.

She managed to hum a response. And she thought she was smiling. It was hard to tell, though. Her mind was adrift in the most wonderful sea of contentment. If she never came back . . . As long as Tristan came along, that would be fine, too.

$\mathcal{W}$akefulness came slowly, her mind rousing first to note the smooth warmth of the silk brushing her breasts as she breathed. Simone smiled and shifted, stretching and sighing with lingering satisfaction, and opened her eyes. Tristan lay on his side beside her, his head propped in his hand and a length of silk draped haphazardly across his midsection.

"Hello," he said quietly, trailing a fingertip over her cheek and smiling. "Welcome back."

"I didn't mean to fall asleep and be such poor company."

He chuckled and his dark eyes twinkled. "I've enjoyed watching you. Did you know that you smile in your sleep? And that you have the most luscious way of whispering my name while you dream?"

No, she didn't. And neither did she know why his knowing that made her feel suddenly awkward and . . . caught. She moistened her lower lip and shifted beneath the silk sheeting, desperately searching for a diversion. Deliverance came from the very edge of the lantern light. She sat up and leaned half across him to get a better view. "Is that a birdcage over there?"

"Lady Fiona's birdcage, to be exact," he answered, rolling onto his back and drawing her onto his chest. "Is it what you had in mind?"

"It's perfect." Everything was perfect again. She stretched up to graze her lips across his chin. "Absolutely perfect."

"When's her birthday?"

"A week from today."

"I'll see that it's delivered that morning. Would you like it wrapped with a big bow?"

"Oh, that's not necessary. Fiona will be so excited about the cage that she won't even notice whether it's decorated or not." She wiggled closer so that she didn't have to stretch to feather her lips over his. "She'll love it, Tristan," she whispered, adoring his generous heart. "It'll be her best birthday ever. Thank you."

He cocked a brow and smiled. "There is the matter of payment for it, you know."

Her pulse quickened with delightful possibilities. "Of course. Whatever you ask, I'll pay."

"Within reason."

"No," she clarified, leaning down to gently nip at his lower lip. "Whatever you want. Name your price."

He made a humming sound and then ever so slowly rolled her over. His weight balanced on his elbow, he gazed down at her and, dragging a fingertip down the length of her throat, warned, "If given free rein, my wants might shock you."

"That's what I'm hoping."

Grinning, he rolled off the pallet, gained his feet, and then extended his hands for her. She took them, letting him pull her from their nest and to his side. Skin brushed skin, sending a ripple of delight through her. He feathered a kiss across her lips, then released one hand and reached down to snag a pillow. Even as she was puzzling the action, he drew her away from their bed and toward the lantern.

"Bring the light," he murmured.

She obeyed, intrigued, and let him lead her farther into the warehouse. God, what could he have in mind that required a lamp and a single pillow?

The answer came in the moment he rounded a corner and drew her into the space between two stacks of crates. A huge mirror sat on the floor, leaning against one side of the corridor. Its frame thick and ornately carved, its face reflecting the opposite wall of wooden boxes, it fairly shouted of decadent possibilities. He drew her forward until they were centered in the reflection.

"Still feeling brave?" he asked, grinning and dropping the pillow at his feet.

Simone smiled and set the lantern atop a crate. "More than brave," she whispered, placing her hands on his shoulders. "Wicked," she added as she leaned forward.

She heard him suck his breath through his teeth as she trailed her tongue boldly down the center of his chest and her breasts brushed over his abdomen. Her hands skimmed over his nipples and he threaded his fingers with hers, drawing their hands behind him as she knelt on the pillow. Making slow circles with the tip of her tongue, she moved lower still. His knees quaked. Reveling in the power she had over him, she slowed her descent to savor his shudders, his gasps of pleasure, letting them feed the quickly rising tide of her own desire.

"God," he moaned, releasing her hands to thread his fingers in her hair. He bent his knees ever so slightly and angled his hips forward, growling, "Please, Simone."

Please? Well, since he'd asked so nicely, so desperately . . . And since she was so very close to her own edge . . .

CHAPTER 10

$\mathcal{T}$ristan considered the situation with a frown. The city was still asleep. He had an incredibly luscious woman sitting across his lap. He'd spent the last four hours having truly wonderful sex. He was sated. Beyond sated, actually. Finding the wherewithal to get up and dressed had been nothing short of an act of supreme will. How the hell he could feel anything at all was a puzzle in itself. But that he felt so damn irritable . . .

Simone stirred in his arms and sat away from his chest. "You should put me down here, Tristan," she said softly.

"I'll go the rest of the way on foot. It'll lessen the chances that anyone will see you."

"If that concerned me, I'd have given you the horse at the warehouse and thanked you for the evening."

She looked up at him, her brows furrowed. "Is something wrong?"

Nothing. And everything. He kept his gaze fixed on the looming garden gate. If he looked at her . . . If he tried to be nice . . .

"Tristan?"

He clenched his teeth and swallowed down a swell of sadness. Why the hell that was swirling around under the anger . . . God, he needed a drink. Several of them. Actually, he needed to get sloshed. Odds were that by the time he sobered up, whatever was bothering him would have either gone away or resolved itself.

"Oh, damn."

He blinked and focused on the world around him. Or, more accurately, on the man standing at the now open garden gate. Tristan's irritation flared for an instant and then, as inexplicably as it had come over him, it was submerged under an equally unfathomable certainty and calm. "Mr. Haywood," he said, reining in his mount. "Good evening."

"It's morning."

Simone shifted again, arching her back and angling her legs to slide down the side of the horse. Tristan tightened his arm around her and hauled her back against him. "No," he said quietly while holding Haywood's gaze. "We're caught. We face the piper with dignity."

He could feel her heart thundering even as she asked breezily, "What are you doing out here, Haywood?"

"Waiting for you," he replied coolly. "In the event that you might be interested, you have a nephew."

Her heart jolted hard enough that Tristan felt it in his own. She pushed against his arm, and rather than make a scene fighting her, he let her go.

"Is Caroline all right?" she asked as she dropped neatly to her feet. "Is the baby all right? He's two weeks early."

"She's fine," Haywood assured her as Tristan swung down from the saddle. "The baby's fine. You, however, are in a great deal of trouble."

Simone looked at the house and shoved her hands in her trouser pockets. His mind rapidly sorting through the implications and possible outcomes, Tristan drew the reins down, saying, "I assume that His Grace is expecting to speak with us. We probably shouldn't keep him waiting any longer."

Haywood considered him in silence, then stepped aside and gestured toward the house with a sweeping motion of his arm. It was tantamount to an order and Tristan didn't like it, but he moved anyway, determined to maneuver through the situation with all the grace he could muster.

"Let me do the talking," Simone said quietly, falling in beside him, her hands still in her pockets.

"Thank you for the concern, but I'm perfectly capable of speaking for myself."

"You don't know Drayton. I do."

"Yes, well, in about two minutes I'm going to meet the man and, considering the circumstances, there isn't much chance that ol' Drayton will keep his thoughts and opinions a mystery. It's my task to talk with him, not yours."

She looked up at him as they reached the rear of the house. "I don't like imperious men."

He shrugged and dropped the reins over the newel post on the back stairs. "That really doesn't matter at this point," he informed her as he went up the stairs and pulled open the door. As he held it for her, he added, "I make the decisions and you abide by them."

She yanked her hands out of her pockets to march up the steps and past him. On the other side of the threshold she turned to face him. "What is wrong with you, Tristan?"

He didn't know and now wasn't the time or the place to enlist her aid in helping him figure it out. Especially with Haywood on their heels. Tristan glanced around them, noting they were in the winter kitchen. "Which way to whichever room your brother-in-law favors for inquisitions?"

Muttering, "It's a damn good thing this engagement is a sham," she whirled around and marched off.

Tristan followed, passing through a series of rooms while mentally sorting through an odd mix of emotions. This wasn't going well with Simone and he felt bad about it. He wasn't angry with her. What he was angry about, though . . . It was as much a puzzle as the sadness eddying just beneath it all.

Although, now that he took a closer look, he wasn't nearly as melancholy as he had been a few minutes ago. Apparently the approaching humiliation of contritely dancing for the piper had fairly well pushed the gloom aside. Of course, being berated and threatened and forced to admit that he was a complete cad was the best of the possible ways it could go. Hopefully Lord Ryland wouldn't come at him in a rage; he'd hate to have to punch in the nose of an old man.

But if the man was a bit more rational, only going so far as to point a gun at him and demand an immediate marriage . . . Well, marrying Simone wasn't the worst thing that could happen to a man. Not by a long shot. But Simone having to marry *him* was another matter entirely.

If the duke expected a marriage before noon, the only decent thing to do was lay all the cards on the table. He'd marry Simone as long as no one knew about their relationship until *after* he'd rendered Lucinda harmless. Surely if he and the duke could agree on anything, it would be the necessity of protecting Simone from unnecessary risk.

"Drayton!" Simone cried cheerily, abruptly bringing his attention back to the moment just as she strode across the last of the foyer and entered through the wide-open doorway of what looked like a study. "Congratulations! I hear you have a son and that Caroline's fine."

"I do and she is," replied a man leaning back against the desk, his arms folded across his chest. A man, Tristan noted, fairly close to his own age. A man who—thankfully—wasn't enraged. Not that he was at all happy. And his obvious displeasure wasn't the least bit softened by either Simone's casual manner or the kiss she quickly pressed to his cheek.

"Where have you been for at least the last four hours, Simone?"

"With me," Tristan answered from the doorway.

The Duke of Ryland stood and squarely met Tristan's gaze. Simone looked back and forth between them as they studied each other, then drew a long breath and opened her mouth. Her guardian cut her off, saying, "I presume that you are the infamous Lord Lockwood?"

Tristan nodded and stepped into the room. "Lord Tristan Townsend, the Marquis of Lockwood. I'd offer to shake your hand, but I think perhaps it would be better to save the gesture for a more harmonious time."

"Should there ever be one. My ward has been in your company tonight?"

"She has, Your Grace. All night."

"Excuse me, gentlemen," Simone said testily. "If I might say something?"

"No," he and the Duke of Ryland replied in unison.

The duke cocked a brow. "Go to your room, Simone," he instructed without looking at her. "I'll be up shortly to speak with you privately."

"Save the trip and your breath," she hotly countered, her arms akimbo. "I'm not ten years old, Drayton. This was all my—"

"Simone," Tristan interrupted crisply. She turned her head to meet his gaze. "Please," he said as gently, as firmly, as he could, "don't embarrass me any more than you already have. Go as you've been asked."

Her chin came up with an almost audible snap. She didn't say another word, didn't look at either one of them as she stormed out of the room. Tristan expelled a long, slow breath at her departure and resisted the urge to drag his fingers through his hair.

"You'll rue the day for that."

Was that just a touch of amusement he heard in the duke's voice? "I'm sure I will. But it did get her out of the room."

The duke nodded slowly and leaned back against his desk. "Do you have anything to say in your defense?"

And with that, they were to the dance. "No," Tristan answered. "I wanted her. I seduced her. I'll marry her."

The duke nodded and folded his arms across his chest. "Am I expected to believe that Simone resisted your efforts at every turn, that you, in essence, had to all but rape her and managed—somehow—to come out of the scuffle without so much as a mark on you?"

Oh, this wasn't going to go well. "Yes, Your Grace."

"Really? Simone was forced to do something against her will? Either pigs are flying or you think I'm stupid."

"Neither, Your Grace."

The duke took his measure for a moment and then ever so slightly tilted his head to the side to observe, "In case you haven't heard, Simone is renowned for being impetuous and headstrong."

"Headstrong I'll allow. But impetuous?" He shook his head. "Not to the degree that she'd like everyone to think."

The duke smiled. "We are talking about the same woman, aren't we? Simone? Lady Outrage and Disaster Waiting to Happen?"

And to think that Simone always spoke so highly of her brother-in-law. How dare he characterize her so—The course came in a sudden flash of realization, full and complete, the perfect solution to the dilemma. Yes, perfect. And so very, very simple. Tristan cleared his throat and answered, saying, "Simone is the most intelligent, levelheaded woman I've ever known. She deliberately creates outrageous situations simply because doing so is the most entertaining aspect of her life."

The duke seemed to consider that pronouncement for a

moment and cocked a brow. "You're suggesting that she planned this evening's debacle for the thrill of it?"

Well, yes. In a manner of speaking. But he wasn't about to regale her guardian with the details of their private conversations and most certainly not with those of their frolicking. "I'm responsible for convincing her to meet me this evening," Tristan said firmly. "We both went into it fully knowing the possible consequences."

"And is she willing to pay them?"

He recalled the way she'd stormed past him at the back of the house. "She assured me that she was. How she feels on the matter at this point, though, I can't say. You'll have to ask her when you speak privately. I'm sure she won't mince any words on the matter."

The duke looked both slightly pained at and amused by the prospect. "And are you still willing to pay them as well?"

"Yes, Your Grace. I am." What the duke found in the assertion worth knitting his brows over Tristan didn't know and couldn't guess.

"If I might make an observation?"

"Of course."

"Most men who want to marry a woman just come to the front door, knock, and simply ask for her."

Several possible explanations flashed through Tristan's mind. He offered the duke the easiest of the bunch. "Perhaps I'm not like most men."

"That's occurred to me. Several times in the last few minutes, actually." He unfolded his arms, stood, and walked off, asking, "Would you care for a brandy?"

This was an unexpected turn. In light of the situation, he should decline. And it wasn't as though he and the duke had the slightest chance of ever becoming amiable drinking companions. Still, the duke wasn't finished with him—or he with him—and if the man wanted to conduct the rest of the exchange over a drink . . . Good brandy was good brandy. "Yes, thank you."

"So tell me about yourself, Lockwood," the other man said, bringing him a generously filled snifter.

"What is it you'd like to know?"

"The usual things," the duke replied, shrugging and walking back over to his desk. "How old are you? What are the conditions of your estate? Do you have a stable income? Are you a Liberal or a Conservative?"

"I'm thirty," Tristan replied, swirling his drink and knowing full well that the duke didn't care one whit what the answers were. "The estate is solvent, but only because I've poured my personal fortune into it. My money comes from shipping, and while the amount of it varies by the seasons, the seas, and the weather, I want for nothing. I don't give a damn about politics."

The duke nodded and looked at the sunrise through his brandy while asking, "Do you give a damn about my sister-in-law? Beyond the obvious physical interest, of course."

Ah, this was what the duke really wanted to know. "I enjoy Simone's company," Tristan answered with easy honesty. "She's beautiful and bright, witty and spirited. She's also refreshingly honest and delightfully straightforward. I can't help but think that if all the women in the world were more like her, life would be considerably more cheerful and a lot less complicated."

A smile ever so slowly lifted the corners of the man's mouth. "Were it not for you having compromised my sister-in-law, I could like you. You're honest and certainly don't lack for confidence. Actually . . ."

Whatever else the man had been about to say faded away as he swirled his drink. His smile faded as one brow inched upward.

Tristan took a sip while he waited. It was very fine brandy. He took another and swirled his drink in the glass again. The silence growing a bit awkward, he finally asked, "Do I want to know what you're thinking, Your Grace?"

The duke looked up, a curious mixture of amusement and concern in Tristan's gaze. "Simone is almost twenty-one," he said, once again taking Tristan's measure. "She was fourteen when she came into my care. In the years between then and now, she's been considerably more cloistered than in her early years. Still, men have crossed her path with great regularity. You're the first to have turned her head and I'm wondering what it is about you that she finds so irresistibly attractive."

There was a good question. Not that he had an answer for it. "I'm reasonably good-looking and wealthy?" he guessed.

"You enjoy personally taking the helm during storms, don't you?" He didn't give him a chance to reply before nodding and going on, saying, "What Simone sees in you is a kindred spirit. Which, of course, means there are only two ways this affair can go. Either it will turn into a perfect matching or it will be a spectacularly ugly train wreck."

Tristan would bet on a perfect matching. Physically, at least. Their bodies fit together so well that it was not only breathtaking but also almost magical. Beyond the physical, though . . . He wouldn't put money on that. There hadn't been a woman yet he couldn't walk away from with a shrug. Invariably boredom set in and his attention wandered. Simone would undoubtedly intrigue him longer than any others had, but eventually . . .

"Understand something very clearly," the duke said. "Simone's early years were far more difficult to survive than either of us can ever imagine. She doesn't wound easily. But when she is hurt, the pain goes deep. This family has been formed by circumstances none of us expected, and our bonds are stronger for it. I will not allow you to hurt Simone and walk away unscathed."

"I wouldn't expect you to."

"Neither will you be allowed to ruin her public reputation," her brother-in-law went on. "You will marry her."

"Of course," Tristan agreed. "Under certain conditions."

It took the duke a very long second to recover from his shock. "Excuse me?"

"There are some family matters that I must deal with before there's any public announcement of our betrothal."

"What sort of family matters?"

Since there was no point in wasting time with family history, he cut to the quick of it, saying, "My stepmother murders for profit." The duke stared at him, clearly stunned speechless, and so Tristan went on, explaining, "She took out insurance policies on my father and both my brothers shortly before they met their ends. I think she killed them in order to collect on the policies."

The duke swallowed twice before he managed to ask, "Can you prove it?"

"No, Your Grace, I can't."

"But you're convinced she did."

Tristan nodded and sipped his brandy. "And I'm just as

convinced that she'll try to kill me before I marry so that she doesn't have to share my personal estate with my wife and any child."

"Dear God."

"Yes, well," Tristan allowed on a sigh. "We're not called the Lunatic Lockwoods without reason."

"And you've involved Simone in this mess."

A statement. Unflattering and, despite the complex reasoning and groundless hopes that had brought him to this moment, basically true. "Actually, my plan when we left here this evening was to not get caught. If that had gone well, there wouldn't be a wedding looming on the horizon and she wouldn't be involved at all. But since we were caught out . . . I'm fully prepared to do the right thing and marry her. All that I ask is that you give me a bit of time to deal with my stepmother so that Simone isn't caught in any web she might spin for me."

"And how long do you think justice might take?"

He could lie. It would be easy to pull a time from thin air and placate the man. "I have no idea, Your Grace."

"A week?" the duke pressed. "Two? A month?"

"I honestly don't know, Your Grace."

The duke stared down at the carpet between his feet for several long moments. Finally, he looked up and asked, "Who outside this family knows what happened tonight?"

"No one."

"Here's what we're going to do, Lockwood. You're going to stay well away from Simone. You're going to forget that you know who she is. Is that clear?"

Clear, yes, but not particularly honorable. "I asked for time, Your Grace, not an out."

The duke shrugged and, knowing that the decision had

been made, Tristan took a healthy sip of the brandy, hoping the liquid searing his throat would make everything else pale. Later, he promised himself, he'd drink enough to make everything disappear entirely.

The duke drained his snifter and set it down on his desk. "Now that we're concluded . . . ," he said, moving toward the door. "If you'll excuse me, I'm going to go hold my wife and son."

Tristan stepped aside, offering as the other passed, "Congratulations on his birth, Your Grace."

The duke paused in the foyer and looked over his shoulder. "Do you have any children, Lockwood?"

"Not that I'm aware of. I've taken every precaution to see that I don't."

"That's good to know. Do you want children?"

"Not at the moment."

"Eventually?"

Tristan summoned a smile of sorts. "When my stepmother's no longer a threat. I do have an obligation to produce an heir to the title."

The duke snorted. "You have no idea what obligations are until you have a child." With that pronouncement, he resumed his course, saying, "I trust that you can see yourself out once you've finished your brandy."

"Good night, Your Grace."

"It's morning," the man called back from the foot of the stairway.

Tristan looked down at the dark liquid in his glass, feeling an odd sort of numbness. Not that it affected his brain at all. No, that part of him was whipping right along, congratulating him on how well he'd handled the situation, how honorably—albeit belatedly—he'd conducted

himself. Ending the affair with Simone was the right thing
to do. For every single reason.

But knowing all that . . . Well, numb wasn't all that bad.
At least he wasn't angry at the moment. And the sense of
melancholy wasn't welling up anymore. He drained his
glass and carried it over to the desk. He had brandy at the
town house, brandy every bit as good as the duke's. And
he had enough of it that he could turn agreeably numb
into wonderfully oblivious within the hour. Which
sounded like a damn fine idea to him.

*S*imone made her way up the stairs, her heart hammering and her teeth clenched as she glared down at the carpet. *Men!* she silently railed. And they accused women of
having sudden, inexplicable shifts in temperament? The
hypocrites. One moment he'd been lovey and solicitous
and then—in the blink of an eye and for no apparent
reason—he'd turned into . . . into . . . a presumptive, con-
descending son of a bitch! If she'd known—had the
slightest inkling!—he could be that way, he would have
spent the night alone in his fricking silk tent. Which he
probably knew. Which was probably why he'd been so
wonderful until they'd started back to the house. Until after he'd gotten what he wanted from her. Of course. Next
time she saw him, she was going—

"I'm glad you're still alive."

Simone looked up from the carpet to find her younger
sister standing in the doorway of her bedroom. Fiona.
Looking positively angelic in her ruffled white night-
gown, her long blond hair neatly braided. God, were there
ever two sisters more opposite? "Did anyone consider my
death a serious possibility?"

"No," Fiona admitted, her smile looking a little weak. "But Drayton said that you should probably hope for it."

Yes, by the time he and Tristan were done with all their male huffing and puffing and posturing, she probably was going to wish she were dead. For about a minute. After that, they were in for a rude awakening. But until she had to deal with them and their inflated illusions, there were more important matters requiring her attention. "How's Carrie? And the baby?"

"Both are fine," Fiona assured her, her smile strengthening. "Drayton sent Haywood for the midwife just after one. She arrived at half past and Callen was born at ten minutes after two."

Callen Mackenzie. It was a good name. "Ten fingers, ten toes?"

"He's perfect in every way. And Carrie says he was so easy to bring into the world that she just might have a dozen more."

"A dozen?"

"I think it was the moment," Fiona explained, her green eyes bright and her smile wide. "She wants you to come talk to her. To see Callen."

"Now?"

"She said as soon as the cat dragged you in."

Damn. Drayton and his anger she could handle. Easily. But Carrie's compassion and understanding had a way of taking the wind out of her sails. "Surely she's tired and sleeping. I wouldn't want to wake her."

"The only ones sleeping are Tess and Angelina," Fiona countered. "The excitement of having a baby brother didn't last five minutes. When I left Carrie, they were curled up on Drayton's side of the bed. I'm sure he's carried them back to their own beds by now, though."

In other words, there weren't any excuses that were going to work. Just as Drayton had been waiting for Tristan, Carrie was waiting for her. And since there was no point in making matters any worse than they already were, Simone smiled at her sister, gave her a hopefully jaunty salute, and headed for the double doors at the end of the hall.

She knocked lightly and pushed open the door in the same movement. Poking her head around the edge to peek in at the bed, she tried not to sag in disappointment as Carrie's gaze instantly arrowed to hers.

"Are you up to receiving visitors?"

"Come in and tell me the story," Caroline answered, shifting the bundle in her arms and then trying to shift herself in the pillows. "I need to hear your side of it before I hear Drayton's."

Simone quickly crossed the room. "Oh, don't worry about me," she said, adjusting the mountain of down pillows at Caroline's back. "It'll be all right. How are you?"

"I'm fine," her sister replied with a contented sigh as she settled back. "Each baby gets easier and faster."

Simone settled herself on the edge of the mattress and held out her arms. Carrie passed Callen into her care with a serene smile.

Simone considered the pair of dark eyes gazing up at her. Oh, no drowsy, fuzzy-eyed ball of fluff, this one. Callen had clearly come into the world with a mission and was prepared to start this very moment. "He looks just like Drayton," she offered, thinking that it wasn't going to be too long before she wasn't the only one in the family responsible for gray hairs.

"I don't think he could deny him even if he wanted to."

Simone grinned and tickled the palm of Callen's hand. He instantly caught her finger and squeezed. "Oh, look at that, Carrie. Look how strong he is."

Carrie nodded. "I assume you were out with Tristan Townsend?"

She couldn't resist the temptation. "No, Little Lord Lumpy."

"What?"

Chuckling, she freed her finger and passed Callen back to his mother. "Just kidding."

"Simone, this is no joking matter."

"I know," she allowed, rising. Smoothing the bedcovers, she went on, saying, "Drayton and Tristan are downstairs glaring at each other. When they're done with that part, they'll undoubtedly move on to picking a wedding date."

"You don't seem particularly distressed by the possibility."

She might be if there was a chance of the engagement ever progressing as far as the church. But since it was all a sham, she could play the part of the reasonable and resigned maiden. "Caught's caught," she replied with a shrug. "I don't see that throwing a fit about it would accomplish all that much at this point."

"And when it comes right down to it," Carrie countered, "the thought of marrying Lord Lockwood isn't all that unpleasant, either?"

"I could do worse."

"Ah, but the question is whether you could do better."

Simone plopped down onto the bedside chair. "Honestly, Carrie? I don't think there is any better. And even if there is, I'm not sure I could survive it."

"Does he feel the same way?"

The answer depended on what part of the night they were talking about. And since the last part of it seemed to indicate that she'd made a huge mistake in the first part, she preferred not to talk about it at all. "I didn't ask him to formally rate me against his past lovers," she hedged. "That would have been entirely too . . ." She shrugged. "I can live with illusions."

Carrie apparently thought about that for a moment and then said, "If, for some reason, Drayton sees a marriage as unwise—"

"*If?*"

"Just for the sake of food for thought," she soothingly countered. "If he doesn't demand that the two of you marry, would you see Tristan again?"

Yes, just to kick him in the shins for being such a pompous ass. Yes, if he'd apologize and take her in his arms again. Yes, because they needed to be engaged so Lucinda would be forced to act. Simone dredged up a smile and hedged again. "Would you give up Drayton?"

"No. I love Drayton. Do you love Tristan?"

At last, a question with a simple, easy answer. "Of course not. I haven't known him long enough. But I do know that I love being with him."

"Why?"

So much for easy. She cast around in the swirl of her thoughts and emotions. "I suppose I feel more alive when we're together."

"How so?"

"Everything is so much more interesting than normal." At Caroline's arched brow she added, "And my heart is always racing and skittering. It feels good in a way that's just the right amount of scary. Rather like being in a good bit of danger, but not. If that makes any sort of sense at all."

"It does," her sister replied with a slow nod and a soft smile. "What are you going to do if he refuses to marry you and then decides that he'd rather not see you again?"

Her heart skipped a beat and her stomach twisted into a cold knot. She pasted a smile on her face and blithely replied, "Tracking him down and running him through would have a certain appeal to it."

"You wouldn't."

Probably not, but no one needed to know that. She had illusions to preserve. "And then I'd retire to Ryland Castle and live out my days pacing the parapets, shrieking at the sky and giving everyone something to talk about."

Carrie grinned. "There aren't any parapets at Ryland Castle. Not real ones."

"Well, that's true," she allowed, smiling. "But pacing and shrieking in the halls wouldn't have quite the same dramatic effect. Let me think on it for a while. I'm sure I can come up with something sufficiently pathetic."

Carrie laughed softly and then abruptly looked toward the door. "Hello, darling," she called, practically glowing with happiness.

Simone studied her brother-in-law as he came to the other side of the bed. He wasn't sporting any bruises or welts that she could see. And his mood seemed to be considerably lighter than when she'd last seen him. "Obviously you two didn't go to blows," she offered as he slipped onto the bed and wrapped his arms around Caroline.

"Our exchange was thoroughly civil," he said without looking at her. He gave Carrie a kiss and then smiled softly as he stroked Callen's cheek with a fingertip.

Simone looked away and swallowed down an unexpected wave of longing. *To be jealous of what Carrie has? How ridiculous. Men are idiots and babies smell good only some of the time. And not all of them are beautiful like Callen is. In fact, there are a lot of really ugly babies in the world. Not to mention men who were horrible husbands and even worse fathers.*

"Do I have a wedding gown to design?" she heard Caroline ask.

"Darling, your hands are full enough for the time being."

"I suppose she could wear mine," Caroline went on as Simone's heart pounded. "It would have to be taken in a bit, but otherwise it would—"

"Your wedding dress is *your* wedding dress," Drayton quietly interrupted. "Not Simone's."

Caroline murmured her assent and then fell silent. Simone stole a glance in their direction. Both seemed oblivious to anything but each other and Callen. Simone inwardly winced at another inexcusable wave of sentiment, drew a deep breath, and rose to her feet.

Her movement finally brought Drayton's attention to her. He cocked a brow in silent question and her patience evaporated. "All right, Drayton, enough of this. Am I engaged or not?"

"Do you want to be?"

Oh, of all the insufferable . . . He made Tristan look like a saint. "Just answer the question, Drayton. Yes or no."

"No."

Calm, cool, altogether indifferent. As though none of this mattered one whit. "Am I being sent off to Ryland Castle at first light?"

"No," he replied, going back to adoring his son.

"Am I forbidden to see Tristan?"

"Yes," he said around a smile as Callen hiccuped.

It wasn't a surprise. Not at all. Still, her heart skittered and sank. She wanted to ask if Tristan had protested but quickly decided against it. Asking would imply desperation. And ignorance. "Then I'll wish you both a good night," she said, walking away. "Rest well, Carrie."

"Simone?"

She paused on the threshold and looked back over her shoulder. Drayton didn't look up as he asked, "Do you know about Lord Lockwood's stepmother?"

Well, since Drayton did, Tristan had obviously spilled the beans. "Yes," she admitted. "Why?"

"When did he tell you?"

"Before we left the garden this evening. Why?"

"Just wondering."

"Anything else?"

Neither of them responded and Simone closed the door behind herself without looking back. She made her way to her room, stunned. She wasn't going to be forced to marry Tristan. She wasn't going to be sent into exile. Everyone was going to pretend she hadn't had an illicit, scandalous affair. God, had the world been turned upside down?

Flopping down on her bed, she cradled her head in her hands and stared up at the plaster ceiling medallion. What did Tristan think of it all? Given his attitude as he'd brought her home, he was probably relieved to have escaped a forced march to the altar. Still, there was the matter of Lucinda and the need to draw her out. That had been the starting point for tonight. Not having to marry . . .

Simone sighed and closed her eyes. She'd have to talk with Tristan about it in the morning—after he apologized for being so ill-tempered—and see what he thought they ought to do next. Assuming, of course, that he wasn't already on his way back to America and counting his lucky stars.

CHAPTER II

$\mathcal{T}$ristan reversed the path he'd taken through the house earlier and emerged onto the back steps to find his horse right where he'd left him, the sky lightening, and Cyril Haywood pacing a path at the base of the steps. *Not wearing a sling for his arm*, Tristan noted as he made his way down and took the reins from the newel post. *As I should have noticed the first time I saw him tonight.*

"Haywood," he said in acknowledgment as the other stopped and squared up to him. "Why am I not surprised to find you waiting for me?"

"His Grace can be entirely too calm and rational at times."

An affliction Haywood apparently didn't suffer, Tristan silently observed.

"I don't like you, Lockwood."

Well, at least he was an honest and plainspoken man. "With all due respect, Mr. Haywood, you don't know me. I'd suggest that what you don't like is my interest in Simone."

"She's very young."

"In some respects," Tristan allowed. "In others, she's wiser than either one of us will ever be."

Haywood considered him through narrowed eyes for a long moment and then finally said with a great deal of crispness, "She is not a whore."

And Haywood thought he considered her one? Anger flared and seared through his veins, white and hot. "And I'll beat bloody," Tristan warned through clenched teeth, "any man who suggests that she is."

"Hurt her and you'll be the one beaten bloody."

Said the man with one good arm? Telling himself that while going to blows over the matter might be satisfying, it wouldn't be anywhere near a fair contest, Tristan flicked the reins over the head of his mount, saying only, "Duly noted, Mr. Haywood."

The man stepped back and watched him swing up into the saddle. Even as Tristan was thinking that they weren't yet done, Haywood reached out and caught the bridle.

"Simone is like a daughter to me," he said in a tone that, while firm, eddied with angry desperation. "I care for her more than my own life. Can you say the same?"

The sense of melancholy welled up, fearsome in its sudden onslaught, wrenching in its depth. Tristan dragged in a breath and clenched his teeth until the initial swell passed. "As to placing myself between her and all danger," he answered tightly, "yes, I can."

Again Haywood considered him through slitted eyes. The horse shifted impatiently and Haywood released the bridle. Without another word, he turned on his heel, walked up the steps, and let himself into the house.

Tristan expelled a long breath, trying to bring the swirl of his emotions under control. His effort succeeded only in creating a hard knot low in the center of his chest. He absently rubbed the spot, shaking his head and remembering how wonderful the night had been until he and Simone had left the warehouse. If only they had stayed there, had said to hell with trying to maintain the illusions. If only there were no Lucinda, no reason to be the noblest of cads.

He blinked and frowned. Had he just, in a roundabout sort of way . . .

Growling in frustration, he wheeled the horse about and gave him his head to the garden gate. Once beyond the garden wall, he heeled the animal's flanks, setting him toward home and the promise of brandied oblivion.

The sky was starting to turn pink by the time Tristan came from the stables and vaulted up the front steps of his town house. Even as he reached into his pocket for his key, the door opened. He crossed the threshold, remembering quite clearly having told his butler and footman not to wait up for him.

Stripping off his coat and handing it to the footman,

Tristan asked, "Potter, is there some particular reason that you're up at this ungodly hour?"

"Lord Noland is in the study, Your Lordship."

Noland? Tristan pulled his watch from his coat pocket. Yes, a quarter to six. He put it away, asking, "What's he doing here? Aside from waiting, I mean."

"He didn't say, sir."

Of course not. Peers didn't explain to servants. And servants didn't ask. Tristan made his way down the hall and into the study to find his friend seated in one of the wing-back chairs beside the cheerfully blazing hearth. "Noland?" he began, noting the empty snifter sitting on the side table. "What's brought you out this early in the morning?"

"It's not early; it's late," Noland replied, stifling a yawn with the back of his hand. "I haven't been to bed yet, either."

Well, if there was a story to be told . . . "Is there any brandy left?"

"A bit."

Making his way to the sideboard and the decanters, Tristan asked, "Are you going to tell me why you're here at this hour or do we have to play Twenty Questions?"

"I worked quite late this evening on a report I wanted to have on the commissioner's desk first thing today," Noland supplied as Tristan poured himself a generous drink. "It was after midnight when I left my office and headed home. Still, it was by sheer fortuitous coincidence that I happened to be in a position to notice that you and Lady Simone Turnbridge slipped away for what I presume was a tryst in your warehouse."

Tristan froze, the glass halfway to his lips. "You followed us?"

"More accurately, I followed Lady Townsend, who was following you."

Lucinda? His heart sank to the soles of his feet and his brain went absolutely, utterly numb. "Jesus," he muttered.

"I didn't think you knew she was there."

He hadn't had so much as an inkling. The possibility had never even crossed his mind. Blind and foolish. Inexcusably lax. His blood running like ice, he brought the glass to his lips and took a full drink. "How long did she stay?"

"Not very," Noland assured him. "As you passed off your horse to the night watchman, her carriage rolled on."

Maybe . . . "Are you sure it was her?"

Noland nodded. "Her coachman had parked under a street lamp near the Duke of Ryland's town house, and when you and Lady Simone passed, she drew back the curtain to watch you. I saw her face quite clearly."

Damnation. He took another drink and dropped into the facing chair. "Where were you?"

His friend gave him a chagrined smile. "Trying desperately to get smoothly out of sight before you saw me and assumed that I was there spying on you. Although, I must say that upon further observation, it became apparent that you weren't aware of anyone other than Lady Simone. I followed in the event that you needed assistance in fending off a surprise attack."

At least Noland had been in full possession of his faculties that night. It certainly wasn't anything *he* could claim. "Thank you."

"Four hours is a beastly length of time to spend on the docks at night, you know."

"It depends on what you're doing," Tristan offered dryly and with a half smile.

Noland chuckled. "I was playing cards with your night watchman. He's damn good at cribbage, by the way."

"I had no idea."

"In the interest of friendship and full disclosure," Noland went on, "I must mention that I followed you back to the duke's town house. Just in case Lady Townsend intended to instigate her mayhem on that leg of your outing. Once you were in the company of Mr. Haywood and others, I broke off my surveillance and came here to wait for you."

So Noland knew that he and Simone had been caught out together. And to think of how confidently he'd assured the duke that the affair was a secret. God, how a night that had been so good could go so bad. . . . Tristan took another drink, wondering how fast he could get drunk and how long he could afford to stay that way. "I owe you a great debt, Noland," he offered, hoping to move matters along. And Noland out the door.

Not that Noland took the hint. He laced his fingers, laid his hands on his considerable belly, grinned, and asked, "Am I to be offering you congratulations on an engagement?"

Tristan lifted the snifter and took a healthy swallow before he answered, "No. The duke was satisfied by my promise to keep the escapade secret and to break off the relationship."

Noland hummed a bit and cocked a brow. "Certainly not the typical or expected course of things," he observed.

Tristan shrugged. "He's not a typical peer."

"Considering that you aren't, either, it must have been an interesting meeting."

"Interesting" wasn't quite the term he would have used. "He was remarkably civil given the circumstances," he supplied. "Christ on a crutch," he whispered as his brain served up a startlingly clear and ugly realization.

"And the reason for your obvious agitation?"

"Lucinda knows about Simone."

"Well, yes," Noland agreed in an exceedingly patient tone. "But a tryst does not a marriage make. Lady Townsend doesn't know that you and Lady Simone were caught together. I can't see how she would think you might be contemplating matrimony. Forced or otherwise. She has no reason to believe that she needs to act against you."

"Or so you assume."

Noland, undaunted, countered, saying, "I didn't see her carriage anywhere along the return leg of the adventure. Undoubtedly she went home after seeing where you and Lady Simone were going."

His mind clicking through possibilities, Tristan nodded as though he accepted Noland's analysis. Why had Lucinda followed him and Simone to the warehouse? Wasn't knowing they were together sufficient? And if she'd actually been as dogged in her surveillance of them as Noland had been? If she'd seen Haywood waiting at the gate?

God, his brain was too tired to arrive at any sort of intelligent response to it all. The only thought that came to him—over and over again—was to keep as far away from Simone as he possibly could. And he needed to warn her, to let her know that Lucinda had found them out and that there was a chance that his stepmother would feel compelled to put her plan into action. Tomorrow, he'd . . . do something. Send Simone a note maybe. Or maybe not. There might be a better, more prudent course that he simply couldn't see through his fatigue.

At the moment, the wisest thing to do was go upstairs, fall into his bed, and get some sleep. He looked over at Noland and said, "I appreciate all you've done on my behalf this evening."

"Any time," his friend drawled, taking his cue this time and pushing himself to his feet. "But if you could see your way to having a daylight tryst next time, I'd be most appreciative."

"There aren't going to be any more trysts. At least not with Lady Simone."

"Ah, yes, your promise to the duke."

It was the very least of his reasons, but it would do for an easy explanation. Tristan nodded. "Speaking of promises, I trust that your knowledge of the affair won't be shared with anyone."

Noland nodded and then grinned. "Not unless you tell me that you really would like to marry her and need a way around the duke's objections. Then I'd be glad to tell everyone I know."

"You're a prince among men."

"A friend in need and all that," he said, grinning and heading for the hallway. "Good night, Lockwood."

"Noland."

Tristan stared down into his now almost empty snifter and listened to his friend's departure. If Lucinda had decided to act that night . . . He leaned his head back and closed his eyes, disgusted with himself. He and Simone were both alive and unharmed only by the grace of God and whatever motives had held his stepmother in check.

They'd been lucky. And it was up to him to make sure that at least Simone stayed that way.

The painting lessons were over. He'd have to think up a suitable excuse for Emmaline, of course. But he'd tell Simone the real reason that he couldn't see her anymore. She deserved to know that she might be in harm's way.

How to tell her that, though . . . Straight out would be the quickest. *I promised your brother-in-law that I wouldn't see you anymore in exchange for not having to marry you. Which I did to protect you from Lucinda. Which, as it turns out, was a rather empty sacrifice since she knows about our night together. So sorry. I don't know how seriously deranged she is and I don't think she'd consider you a threat, but still . . . You might want to keep an eye out over your shoulder for her. Just in case, you know.*

Tristan sighed and opened his eyes to lift and drain the snifter. And as long as he was being a total ass, he could just as well add something at the end along the lines of, *Oh, and thank you for a wonderful night. I thoroughly enjoyed you and would continue on with you if I thought there was any way I possibly could and get away with it.*

Yes, that ought to sufficiently lower her opinion of him. Not that it was going to be all that high once the duke informed her that her lover had taken all of a minute to agree to abandon her. God, what a mess he'd made of things. If only he'd listened to common sense and held to his principles in the garden.

Of course, he could just sail away and be done with the whole thing. He certainly didn't need the estate; actually, it was a drain on his personal fortune and he'd be considerably wealthier without it. And he didn't care one whit about taking his seat in the House of Lords. England wasn't exactly home anymore. Not that it had ever been much of one. In either case, there wasn't any great sense of duty to country that would keep him rooted to English soil.

Yes, sailing away would be the intelligent, rational thing to do. If Lucinda couldn't find him, she couldn't kill him for the insurance money. Most important, though, there wouldn't be any reason for her to harm Simone.

Still . . . Tristan sighed softly and leaned his head back again. He could justify and rationalize it a hundred different ways, but in the end leaving would amount to turning tail and running. Lucinda would not only get away with having killed three men, but there would be no one to stand in her way if she decided to insure Emmaline. And Simone's opinion of him . . . God, he didn't even want to think about how deeply and forever she'd loathe him.

He needed to find a way to force Lucinda's hand without endangering anyone but himself. Which was far easier said than done. Maybe if he closed his eyes for just a few minutes and thought about it, he could . . . come . . . up . . .

"Sir?"

Damn it all, he wasn't deaf.

"Sir?"

Or dead. He growled in protest, shifted his body from under the hand that was trying to shake his teeth loose, and opened his eyes. "Gregory?"

"Yes, sir. I'm sorry to disturb you, but I thought you'd like to know that the *Constance* is coming into berth."

He heard all the words, but putting meaning to them was a slow and foggy proposition. He was in the study.

Had apparently fallen asleep in the chair. The fire was still going. And somehow his brandy snifter had disappeared. Someone—probably his butler—had put the coffee service on the table beside him. Tristan scrubbed his hands over his face and then sat forward in the chair, asking, "What time is it?"

"Ten, sir."

Four hours of sleep. He could remember the days when two had been more than enough. Tristan scraped his fingers through his hair. "It's a bitch growing old."

"A rough night?" Gregory asked entirely too cheerily.

"A long one."

His clerk reached out and plucked something from Tristan's shoulder. Even as he was puzzling the motion, Gregory turned toward the window and held his hand into the light. "A long night with a brunette."

Simone. Tristan's brain didn't so much click into gear as it ground and squealed and lurched. "Do me a favor, Gregory."

"Aren't I always?"

Tristan looked up at his clerk. "You didn't find a dinner companion last night, did you?"

Gregory cocked a brow and asked dryly, "Your favor, sir?"

Chuckling, Tristan rose from the chair. "I'm supposed to be at my sister's this morning, helping her with a portrait she's painting of her friend."

"The travails of your life never end."

Actually, aside from the matter of Lucinda, he considered his life to be damn near charmed. Not that Lucinda didn't make a twisted knot of everything else. "I need you to go over to my sister's home and tell her that I have to be elsewhere this morning. Offer my apologies and all. While you do that, I'll make myself presentable. I'll meet you on the dock."

"And your sister lives where?"

"Go out to the livery—it's behind the house—and have the coachman take you to Em's and then down to the river."

Gregory nodded—a put-out gesture of acceptance if Tristan had ever seen one—and held out the strand of Simone's hair. "Do you want this back?"

"Thank you," he said, taking it and returning it to his shoulder just to see what Gregory would do.

He rolled his eyes. "And your sister's name? Just for the sake of not looking like a bumbling oaf on the front doorstep."

"Emmaline," Tristan provided as he left his clerk. "Lady Emmaline Townsend."

"Would you mind if I asked her out to dinner?"

The wholly innocent and the exceedingly circumspect? Tristan laughed and started up the stairs. "Not at all. Go right ahead."

Em and Gregory. Now there was a picture. With that pairing, there certainly wasn't going to be an early-morning scene like the one he'd had with the duke. Which, he decided as he closed his bedroom door behind him and crossed to his dressing room, wouldn't be a bad thing at all. And neither would a matching of the two, he realized as he stared at his reflection in the mirror. Both Emmaline and Gregory were even tempered, a bit reserved, and more than happy to stay within the bounds of social expectations.

Unlike . . . His gaze dropped to his shoulder. He drew the hair from the cloth of his jacket, then slowly wrapped

the silken thread around his finger. What was it about
her? he wondered. He could ably command ships and
crews. He was known throughout the East as a shrewd
trader. Through hard work and determined focus, he'd
amassed a personal fortune that most peers could only
dream about. He honestly couldn't remember the last
time any woman had seriously rebuffed a carnal invitation from him. All in all, he was a man with sharp wits
and the ability to keep them firmly directed toward a
well-considered goal.

So what was it about Simone that made him throw caution and good judgment to the wind? She wasn't the most
beautiful woman he'd ever met. And she most certainly
wasn't the first to surrender to a seduction. And she
wasn't the first woman whose seduction could have led to
a forced marriage, either. But she was the first woman for
whom he'd added up the potential costs, recognized that
they were too hefty, and then consciously decided to seduce her anyway.

What was it about her? The thrill of doing something
absolutely indefensible? Or perhaps it stemmed from the
fact that it had been months since he'd had a lover and Simone was the first willing female to cross his path. No,
that wasn't true. If he'd wanted just a warm body and release, then he could have had any one of a good dozen
married women who'd batted their eyes invitingly at parties. And where they'd failed to stir his interest, something about Simone had reached inside him and shaken
his mastery to the core.

Not, he told himself sternly as he unwound the hair,
that he was going to allow it to happen again. It had been
a onetime weakness, a momentary aberration. He'd send

her a word of warning about Lucinda and that would be that. He wouldn't see Simone again.

He laid the single strand of raven silk on the washstand, shrugged off his jacket, then filled the basin with water and forced his mind to mentally inventory the cargo that was coming into port.

Simone stood in the Townsend parlor, considering the furniture. The fragile white and gold-gilded chairs were gone. Nothing had been put in their place yet and so, for the moment anyway, the room felt a bit less overstuffed than it had the day before. Why she was noticing such things . . . The night had been as long as it had been wonderful and she was so very tired this morning that she could hardly stay awake, much less think straight. Simone shook her head and slowly dragged in a breath.

Since Tristan's horse hadn't been tethered outside, he likely was still on his way. If she'd had any more than a few hours of sleep, she'd have the energy to bounce with excitement. As it was, though, her anticipation coursed through her like warm honey. To find the opportunity to step into Tristan's arms and lay her head on his chest. To close her eyes and feel the beat of his heart against her cheek . . . It would be heaven.

"You look positively wretched."

Simone turned to the door and managed a smile. "Why, thank you, Emmy. You look absolutely radiant. If you weren't my friend, I'd have to hate you."

"Do you feel unwell?"

"I feel tired," she admitted as Emmaline studied her. "I didn't get much sleep last night. My sister had her baby. A boy they named Callen."

"How wonderful! You're an aunt!"

"For the third time. But he is my first nephew."

Emmy sobered slightly. "And everything went well? Your sister is all right?"

Simone nodded in assurance as the footman stepped into the parlor doorway.

"Pardon the intrusion, madam," he said with a slight bow. "There is a messenger from your brother at the door."

Emmy looked a bit startled but recovered quickly enough to practice good manners. "Please show him in."

The footman departed with another bow and Emmy turned to her. "A messenger? Something must have happened. He promised he'd be here to help me paint this morning."

Simone shrugged in noncommittal reply, thinking the odds were that Tristan was every bit as exhausted as she was and had chosen to stay home and sleep. A good decision that she had every intention of doing herself as soon as she could get away.

"Mr. Wade Gregory."

The footman backed away, clearing the doorway for a rather tall and decidedly bookish-looking young man. He certainly hadn't fallen out of the pages of any fashion magazine, Simone noted, deciding that it was a point in his favor. His gaze skimmed over her and then, with a slight smile, moved to consider Emmaline.

"Good morning, ma'am," he said, turning the bowler hat in his hand.

Was he actually blushing?

Emmy beamed. "You're an American!"

Yes, he was blushing. Even more so now that Emmy was eyeing him like a piece of Swiss chocolate.

He cleared his throat and lifted his chin. "Yes, ma'am. I'm your brother's clerk. He asked me to call and offer his apologies for not being able to join you and your friend for your painting session this morning. One of his ships has come into port and he needs to be at the docks."

"I've never been on a ship before."

Simone inwardly groaned, knowing what Emmy was about. God, she wanted to go home and back to bed, not play chaperone.

"I'm sure your brother will be more than happy to arrange a tour for you later this week."

"Wouldn't you like to see the ship, Simone?" She didn't give her a chance to answer. Instead, Emmy smiled brightly, said, "Let me get my hat and coat, Mr. Gregory, and you can escort us," and then swept out of the room.

Wade Gregory stood there, his hat frozen in his hand, his jaw sagging, and his gaze fixed on the doorway.

"She does that," Simone explained with a slight shrug. "Just decides and dashes, leaving everyone else to follow whether they really want to or not."

Mr. Gregory nodded slowly and then rallied to offer a weak smile. "As does her brother."

Yes. Tristan. Who was at the docks. It was a considerably more public place than she'd envisioned for their next meeting, but, now that she thought about it, that might be for the best. "I'm Lady Simone Turnbridge, by the way."

He gave her a polite bow. "A pleasure, ma'am."

Then he looked away, his cheeks coloring pink again and the corners of his mouth tipped ever so slightly upward. Thinking that he might be nervous and uncomfortable with the silence stretching between them, she dredged through the memories of her past lessons on appropriate parlor conversation and asked, "Have you been in Lord Lockwood's employ long?"

"Some days it feels like an eternity," he answered. "In actuality, it's been seven years. Since the day he founded the company."

She was nodding and trying to think of something else to talk about when Emmy sailed to the parlor doorway and saved them all.

"I'm ready! Simone? Mr. Gregory? Shall we?" And then she was gone, heading for the front door.

"Trotting right along, ma'am," Mr. Gregory muttered with a shake of his head.

"You're a terribly good sport."

"Not really, but I pretend well," he countered with a quiet chuckle. He motioned to the parlor door with his hat, saying, "After you, ma'am."

Simone followed after Emmy, hoping that no one expected her to be the ever vigilant doyenne of propriety during the carriage ride to the docks. Once her bottom hit the seat, she had every intention of taking a nap. Just in case Tristan was feeling hungry and daring. Yawning—however delicately—in the midst of a seduction had to be considered very poor form.

CHAPTER 12

$\mathcal{T}$ristan emerged from the hold and narrowed his eyes against the sudden brightness of sunlight. Dockside, the massive doors of the warehouses had been thrown open and carters stood ready with their handcarts and dollies. Behind him on the deck and down on the dock, crews worked the complicated rope-and-pulley crane system, making flawless work of lifting the first of the wooden crates from the bowels of the ship. Ahead, at midship . . . His gaze skipped forward, searching. Yes, and at the bow.

He made his way along the deck, wondering which of them had convinced Gregory to bring them along. Not that Tristan believed the old superstitions that women on board were bad luck. It was more a practical matter of the inexperienced getting in the way and inadvertently creating a disaster.

Not, he realized as he reached Gregory and Emmaline at mid-deck, that they were going to stay long enough to be a problem. "Em, you look a little green."

"I feel green," she admitted, pressing her hands against her midriff.

Gregory played the gentleman perfectly, taking her gently by the elbow and turning her toward the gangplank and saying, "Perhaps we should disembark, Lady Emmaline." As they moved away, Gregory glanced over his shoulder. "Sir, Lady Simone—"

"I see her," he said, already heading toward the shapely creature standing at the bow, her back to him. To know that those luscious curves owed nothing to laces, whalebone, or padding . . . And that satin skin, smooth and warm and so responsive to his touch. . . . God, he ached to have her in his arms again, to lose himself in her passion. Damn Lucinda. Damn the peerage and the fact that they both belonged to it. Why the hell couldn't he have met Simone in America?

Continuing to close the distance, he watched her lean out and look down at the water. And provide him with a most inspiring view of her backside. His blood heated and his groin tightened. Clenching his teeth, he reminded himself of all the reasons he couldn't touch her again. She eased back to her feet and then stepped sideways to stand perilously close to the coiled hawser lines. Tristan smiled tightly and decided that as excuses went, it would do.

He quickened his pace, reaching her to throw his arm around her waist. She squeaked in surprise and looked over her shoulder. Laughter bubbled up from her throat as he wheeled about and set her back on her feet.

"Never stand near a coil of anything on a ship's deck," he explained as he reluctantly released her and put a circumspect distance between them. "Unless, of course, you're hoping for a sudden death."

"I'm not," she replied, grinning up at him. "So thank you." Her gaze darted to midship and her smile was replaced by a frown. "Is Emmy leaving already?"

"I don't think so. It's just that she doesn't appear to have much tolerance for the movement of the deck."

"It's barely moving at all."

Tristan shrugged. "For some people even the slightest bit is too much."

"I like it," she declared, smiling up at him again. "I've never been on a ship before."

"I wouldn't have guessed," he countered, trying to affect a casual smile while fighting the impulse to wrap her in his arms and kiss her breathless. "I'd offer you the grand tour, but we really need to stay out of the way while they're unloading cargo."

"Understandable. Are your other two ships just like this one?"

Interesting. No other woman had ever asked him about his ships. "*Bernie*'s twelve feet longer and six feet wider," he supplied. "*Maggie*'s considerably smaller and has only two engines. But, of the three, she has the biggest heart. She'll ride any storm and laugh while she does it. Her draft is more shallow, too, and she'll go places other ships wouldn't even consider."

"How long are you going to be able to stand the life of a land-bound gentleman?"

Another interesting question no one had ever asked him. No wonder he found Simone so fascinating. "I haven't really given it much thought."

"I'd think you'd be very bored with it very quickly," she offered. Her smile faded a bit as she added, "Of course, there is the other side of always being away from family and not really having a home."

"Which doesn't matter if you don't have a family. Home is the ship and wherever you are at the moment."

Her smile disappeared as she nodded. "When I was younger, I lived that way," she said softly. "Not on a ship, of course. But still, I was unrooted."

"Would you go back to it now?"

"No." She brightened and looked up to meet his gaze. "Oh, sometimes I think it would be nice to come and go as I please without having to be accountable. But then there's a certain comfort in knowing that if anything horrible happened, someone would miss me and care enough to come looking. I suppose that having lived so long without that, having a home and family means a lot more to me than to most people."

Yes, she'd been very lucky. He hadn't. "A crew is like a family," he proposed, hoping it didn't sound as lame and desperate to her ears as it did to his.

"But they move from ship to ship."

"Some do. Not all."

She nodded and looked around the ship, asking, "So which of your three ships is your real home? Your real family? The *Maggie*?"

He never considered himself as having a home, on land

or sea. Rather than admit it and invite pity, he smiled, shrugged, and answered brightly, "I suppose so."

"When is she expected into port?"

"*Maggie* doesn't sail the open seas. She's too small. She runs the island routes and then meets the other two to transfer whatever she's collected along the way."

"So I'll never get to see the *Maggie*?" she asked, sounding genuinely disappointed.

"Not unless you sail out on one of the other two to meet her."

Rolling her eyes and chuckling softly, she countered, "I can't imagine Drayton being willing to give me *that* much free rein."

Since she'd brought up the matter . . . "Our affair is over, Simone." He bit his tongue, but it was too late to call the words back.

Her smile faltered, but she took a deep breath and bravely retrieved it. "Well, that certainly qualifies as an abrupt statement."

"And tactless, too," he admitted. "I'm sorry. I should have framed it better, more kindly."

"What about the plan to draw out Lucinda?"

God, his chest felt as though someone had plunged a knife into it and was twisting the hilt. "In the clear light of day and hindsight," he explained, "I can see that involving you wasn't a wise or caring thing to do. Lucinda is dangerous and if you were to come to even the least little bit of harm I'd never forgive myself." He shook his head. "I'll deal with her on my own."

"Alone," she said quietly.

"Yes."

"Of course. It's how you prefer to live your life."

"You make it sound as though it's a sad thing. It's not."

"I know. I remember. There is something to be said for going through life alone. It's certainly safer in some ways."

It was also cold and empty, but sharing that observation with her wasn't in the interest of being noble about ending their relationship. "Noland was waiting for me at the town house this morning," he said instead, moving matters forward. "He says Lucinda followed us last night."

"Well," she said, her gaze going to the dock below, "since no engagement is being announced, I doubt she considers her time limited. Brief and meaningless affairs being just that."

The pain in his chest deepened, catching his breath and weakening his knees. "It wasn't meaningless," he assured her. "And if I could manage a callous disregard for your safety, it wouldn't be brief."

The smile she gave him was soft and nothing more than polite. "Spoken like a true gentleman," she said with a tiny nod.

"Simone—"

"I think you have a lovely ship, Tristan. Thank you for letting me come aboard."

He watched her walk away, willing his lips sealed and his feet rooted to the deck. God, he couldn't remember when doing the right thing had ever been so hard, so soul-deep painful. If she had been just a bit unpleasant about it, he would feel better. But that stoic smile she'd summoned for him . . . Her quiet, dignified acceptance of having been cast aside . . . Tristan deliberately turned away so that he couldn't watch her make her way down the gangplank, knowing even as he did that it wasn't going to make the consequences any different; of all the women whom he'd left in his life, Simone was going to be the only one whose memory haunted him.

Don't look back. Pretend that nothing's happened. Keep moving. Keep smiling. If you run him through, you'll go to prison.

"Warehouse Three!"

Simone looked up from the ground and through the haze of her anger and humiliation. Emmy and Mr. Gregory stood side by side on the dock, he with a spyglass to his eye and she with a sheaf of papers in hand. As Simone drew nearer, Mr. Gregory trained the glass on a crate being lifted from the hold and called out a number. Emmy checked the papers and then looked over at the knot of waiting carters. "Warehouse One!"

"Enjoying yourself?" Simone asked needlessly, noting Emmy's wide smile and sparkling eyes.

"Yes! Do you know how nice it is to be able to do something that actually makes a difference to people?"

"Not really," she had to admit.

"Please don't tell me that you're ready to go."

Just because she was miserable didn't mean she had the right to ask others to share in it. "I can wait for as long as you can stand being useful," she replied. Looking around, she nodded toward a stack of barrels off to the side and added, "I'll just have a seat over there and watch."

"Is everything all right, Lady Simone?"

"Fine, Mr. Gregory," she lied, flashing him a smile as she eased away from the pair.

And fine she would be, she assured herself as she settled onto the stout wooden barrel. In time. Once she'd overcome the shock of having been used and tossed away like yesterday's newspaper. Actually, though, in their house, newspapers had a two-day life span; Fiona used them in her birdcages on the second day. It wasn't until the morning of the third that they were sent to the rubbish bin for burning.

One night. That's all Tristan had considered her worth his bother. Yes, he'd been kind in ending the relationship—although calling what had been between them a relationship implied that it was considerably more than it had turned out to be.

That he had looked distressed over declaring them done didn't mean much, she knew. She'd heard stories all of her life, had lost count of the number of discarded mistresses who had ended up in the streets or the brothels of her childhood. Men like Tristan Townsend were very skilled at getting shed of unwanted lovers. And part of their repertoire was making themselves look noble and genuinely regretful in the process.

Well, if nothing else, she'd certainly learned a valuable lesson about picking lovers of her own. Handsome, interesting, experienced, and wealthy men were off her list in the future. Simone frowned, realizing that that left her to choose among unattractive, boring, monkish, and poor men. Not that there was any scarcity of them. And not that she intended to ever again waste so much as a single moment of her life entertaining the attention of any man regardless of his attributes.

She sighed, stared blankly at her feet, and struggled against an unexpected surge of sorrow. She'd always known that she and Tristan weren't destined to be together for all eternity; she'd admitted that to him right at the start. But she had envisioned their affair lasting a bit longer than a single night. And, truth be told, she'd seen it ending on her terms, not Tristan's. She'd rather pictured him begging—in a dignified but heartfelt way—for her to change her mind, to give him just a few more weeks of heaven to remember for the rest of his wretchedly lonely days.

Now she was the one feeling lonely. Maybe just a bit wretched, too. Not because she missed Tristan all that much, of course. She hadn't known him all that long, barely three days. He'd hardly become an integral part of her life in that short of a time. And while there was no denying that she'd thoroughly enjoyed the time she'd spent in his bed, it wasn't as though she had a long list of lovers against whom she could compare him. He could have been a truly miserable lover for all she knew.

No, wretchedness was in the fact that everyone in the family knew she'd allowed herself to be seduced and then to have him promise Drayton that the affair was over after one night. . . . God, everyone knew she'd been found lacking and thrown over. There wasn't a hole deep enough to hide in.

"Yoo-hoo! Gregory!"

Yoo-hoo? Simone looked up. Gregory was blinking furiously, apparently unaware that his jaw was sagging and that the spyglass was going to fall out of his hands at any moment. Simone followed his stunned gaze. If ever there was a woman who wouldn't think twice about the idiocy of cooing *yoo-hoo* on the docks, it was the big-busted, big-bustled blonde advancing on him like a dog on a ham bone.

"Miss Sheraton?"

The woman tittered. *Tittered!* "Of course it's me, Gregory. You silly man." She paused to look around and then smiled coyly. "Where is Tristan? I want to surprise him, too."

Tristan? Of course she's looking for Tristan. The frigging rat. He probably met her on his way home this morning. Out with the old, in with the new. And an American at that.

"On board, ma'am," Gregory supplied, looking as though he desperately needed to cough up a fur ball. He tried to clear it, twice, but still sounded choked when he looked past her and said, "If I might be so bold as to ask . . . Where is your husband?"

"As it happens," the woman chirped, "I don't have one of those."

Gregory rocked back on his heels, went pale, and fumbled with the spyglass. He caught it just in time and then said on something of a last gasp, "The wedding has been delayed?"

"Permanently," she declared, sashaying past him with a sweep of her skirts and a rustle of her bustle. Simone watched her walk up the gangplank, fervently hoping she'd catch a heel and topple off into the Thames.

Emmy cleared her throat softly. "Is there a problem, Mr. Gregory?"

"Not one that I can do anything about," he said morosely. Then he sighed heavily, shook his head, and lifted the spyglass to his eye. "Crate Two-fifty-six. Which warehouse?"

"One!"

Simone sat where she was, battling the impulse to

stomp off for home. The last thing in the world she wanted to witness was Tristan courting his new lover, but if she ran away she'd give the impression that she was disturbed by the notion that she'd been so quickly and easily replaced. Better to brace up, continue the farce of not caring, and preserve what she could of her remaining dignity. While she did that and waited for Emmy to tire of being useful, she'd entertain herself with all the ways she could get even with Tristan Townsend, Lord of the Louses. Having decided her course, she turned her back to the ship and began to sort through some delightful possibilities.

Tristan lifted his head and listened. Yes, heels. Feminine heels on deck steel. He had no idea what he was going to say to her, but he'd start with an apology and go from there. If she let him. If she didn't . . . He turned, saying, "I need to say that I'm—"

Had he not had the gunnel at his back, he'd have fallen over. As it was, his stomach dropped to the vicinity of his knees and turned to ice.

"Hello, Tris. Are you surprised to see me?"

Surprised? Dear God, that didn't even begin to describe what he was feeling. "Sarah," he said numbly. "What are you doing here?"

"Throwing myself into your arms," she announced, stepping squarely into his chest.

He dragged a breath into his lungs, took her upper arms firmly in hand, and set her back a respectable distance, declaring, "We're in public."

"Does anyone here know us or care?" Sarah countered, laughing.

"Yes and yes."

"Who? Gregory and his mousy little assistant?"

He glanced down to the dock. Gregory and Em were still at their crate sorting. "His assistant is my sister, Lady Emmaline."

His heart lurched. Simone was still there. She sat on a barrel, watching the wagons and hacks come and go. Maybe she didn't know Sarah was here. If she did, it would be insult added to injury. Neither of which she deserved in the least. God, if they gave a prize to the man who could most severely mangle a relationship in the shortest amount of time, he was the winner, hands down.

"Oh, Tris," his former lover cooed, laying her hand on his arm and bringing his attention to her with a painful jolt. "That put us off on the wrong foot, didn't it? My apologies. I'm sure your sister has a sweet disposition and that we'll eventually be the best of friends."

His heart rolled over and sank to the bottom of his feet. "You're planning to stay for a while?"

"Of course I am, you silly man."

Silly man? God, he'd always detested that expression. His blood heated with irritation, buoying his stomach and centering his mind. "And what does your esteemed George think of living in London?"

"I wouldn't know. He's in Seattle."

"Obviously you had a change of heart about him," Tristan observed, his mind racing along the tracks of cause and consequence. "What happened?"

She batted her lashes at him and smiled. "It occurred to me that we didn't make a very good couple. That you and I are far better suited."

Oh yes. Of course. "When did you do all of this reflection? For poor George's sake, I hope it wasn't as you stood at the altar."

She laughed and waved her hand dismissively. "No, that would have been most unkind. It was ten days before."

Ten days, huh? "Was that before or after word had spread through town that I'd inherited the family title?"

She drew herself up, trying—and failing—to look wounded. "Do you think I threw George over for a title?"

"Yes."

More fluttering of eyelashes. "The title doesn't matter, Tris. It's you."

And I own the Crown Jewels. "I didn't matter enough to keep you from an engagement to poor George."

She took a half step back to consider him before saying, "You keep calling him poor George. He's really quite wealthy."

"He would have to be to have caught your eye. I mean poor as in suffering."

Her smile evaporated. "Being a British lord has changed you."

"And not for the good. You'd be far better off going back to Seattle and—"

"Nonsense!" she declared, obviously retrieving her confidence. "What we had in San Francisco we can have again. But it will be even better because you won't be sailing off for months and months at a time. We can be together day in and day out forever."

Dear God. He'd have to slit his wrists. "Sarah, I know you've come a long way on hope and—"

Anger momentarily flashed in the depths of her blue eyes. "Is there someone else? Are you expected to marry some pasty-faced English girl because you're a peer?"

"Yes," he supplied.

She blinked at him for a few moments and then slowly, regally, lifted her chin. "I've always heard that the British are more easily appalled by scandal than we Americans are. Is that true?"

Why wasn't he surprised that she'd stoop that low? "Don't," he said, his anger surging.

"Ah, Tristan," she purred. "Thank you for being reasonable. I promise to reward you well for it. Right now, if you'd like. Would you care to sweep me up into your arms and carry me off to your cabin?" She reached out to smooth his coat lapels and to smile in what he'd once considered an attractive, inviting way. "I'll do the ravaging once we get there."

"No," he declared, sidestepping out of her easy reach.

"Well, if you'd prefer to ravage, that's fine with—"

"No," he insisted, determined to be brutal if that's what it took to make her see her folly. "Neither of us is going to be ravaged. Not today. Not tomorrow. Not ever. I'm not going to marry you, Sarah. I'm sorry that you've come all this way only to be disappointed, but the truth is—"

"Very well, Tris," she interrupted with a dry laugh. She wheeled about and walked off, calling back, "Scandal it is."

"Sarah!"

She paused, looked over her shoulder, and smiled. "When you're ready to surrender, I'm staying at the inn on St. James's Street."

Tristan shook his head, but the gesture had no visible impact on Sarah's demeanor. She wiggled her fingers in farewell and smilingly went along her way. Tristan turned to look down at the dock. Simone was still watching the traffic, apparently oblivious to the nightmare he'd just endured.

"Thank you, Jesus," he muttered, raking his fingers through his hair as he headed for the captain's cabin and the brandy kept in the cabinet.

*Y*oo-hoo!"

God, she was back. Ignoring the voice of good judgment, Simone turned on the barrel to watch the blonde make her way across the dock toward Mr. Gregory and Emmy.

"Hello, Emmaline," the woman cooed, tilting her head and batting her lashes. "My name is Sarah Sheraton. Miss Sarah Sheraton. I'm a dear friend of your brother."

While Mr. Gregory turned ever-deepening shades of pink, Emmy coolly looked Miss Sheraton up and down.

"I was thinking," the woman went on, "that perhaps we could meet for luncheon one day this week and become acquainted. If you're not too busy with clerking, of course."

Simone watched in appreciative wonder as Emmy squared her shoulders perfectly and lifted her chin. "I'll have to consult with my secretary to see what my schedule will permit."

Oh, beautifully done, Emmy! Beautifully! My deportment masters would be so proud of you!

"Of course," Miss Sheraton allowed, pulling open her reticule and reaching inside. "My card," she added a second later, handing it over to Emmy. "Please let me know as soon as possible when getting together will work for you."

Emmy didn't even bother to look at the little piece of vellum before she stuck it under the papers in her hand and turned to Tristan's clerk, asking, "What crate number are we on? Have we missed one?"

Simone grinned and silently congratulated her friend for having held her own against the blonde tide of presumption.

"And you are?"

She looked up at Sarah Sheraton. "Lady Simone Turnbridge," she answered crisply as her anger flared again. "There's no need for us to become acquainted."

"I thought not." She walked off, calling over her shoulder, "Good-bye, Gregory!"

Simone was hoping for a speeding hack and a not so tragic accident when Mr. Gregory cleared his throat, looked between Sarah Sheraton, her, and the ship. Running a finger under his starched collar, his blush darkening, he managed to say, "Um . . ."

"No explanation is needed, Mr. Gregory," she assured him, rising from her makeshift seat. "None at all." And she didn't consider one necessary for her departure, either. Saying simply, "I'll see you tomorrow morning, Emmy," she stepped toward the traffic and raised her hand to hail a hack.

One rolled to a halt in front of her just as Emmaline called, "Simone, wait!"

She paused, her hand on the door handle, and waited until her friend came to her side to say, "There's no need for you to abandon Mr. Gregory."

"He can manage perfectly well without me for a few moments. And while you may not need an explanation, I would appreciate one. Who is that Sarah woman?"

Oh, for godsakes! "Just taking a wild guess, Emmy, I'd say that she's Tristan's lover."

"His *former* American lover," Emmy countered.

As opposed to her, his former *British* lover. Simone managed a smile, tight though it was. "I suspect that it's not former at all, Emmy. At least not now."

Emmy rolled her eyes. "Oh, please! I may not be the most worldly girl in the world, but I do know that if he had any intentions of having a relationship with her, he'd have brought her with him when he came back to England. Which was a little over a month ago. That she's appeared out of the blue for the first time today . . . She's chasing him."

Did it really matter if she was? As long as he was willing to be caught, Simone couldn't see that it did.

"You don't have anything to worry about, Simone. Tristan isn't going to start up with her again."

And pigs would someday walk on the moon. She shook her head, called the address up to the driver, and pulled open the door. "I don't care if he does, Emmy."

"You do, too. You're taken with him."

Simone froze on the step, her heart racing. "Excuse me?" she asked.

"And he's taken with you," Emmaline assured her with a beaming smile. "Just in case you were wondering."

No, she didn't wonder. She knew that she'd been thrown over. She pulled the hack door closed and sat on the edge of the seat so that she could look at her friend through the open window. "Emmy," she said kindly, "I appreciate your devotion to fairy tales and all, but there is absolutely nothing between your brother and me." *Not anymore.*

"Ha!"

"Really. Emmy. I wouldn't lie to you."

"Ha!"

And with that pronouncement, Emmaline turned on her heel and marched back to Wade Gregory's side. Simone leaned forward to knock on the wall of the carriage, signaling the driver to proceed. He did. So suddenly that she was pitched backward. She landed in an ignoble, awkward heap half on and half off the seat.

Gritting her teeth, she righted herself and swore that the next time she saw Tristan Townsend she was going to pretend that she didn't. He was taken with her? No, she'd been the one taken. And for one helluva ride. The bastard.

CHAPTER 13

$\mathcal{I}$t was the first of the funerals for those who had perished in the fire. Attendance was required, and Simone sat beside Fiona at the end of the row of mourners, dutifully still if not wholly attentive to the words being spoken. A big, fancy church, a hand-carved and brass-trimmed casket, the pews packed, and the clergy doing pomp and circumstance in their finest robes. Men standing to praise the life and heart and soul of whoever it was in the casket. Candles and flowers and more flowers. It was a fine funeral service, the kind of send-off that every member of the peerage hoped for. Even the weather was cooperating.

Sunlight streamed through the stained-glass windows, playing across the crowd and dappling the casket with a kind of holy light of approval.

It had been raining buckets the day they'd buried her mother. Simone had been doing her chores that morning when Harriet, the oldest and grayest—God, she could still see her wrinkled face and toothless smile—of Essie's girls, had said they should go to the services. That there would even be services had surprised Simone, and she remembered nodding and wishing that Harriet hadn't said anything.

They hadn't had fare for a hack and so they'd walked. And walked and walked. They'd been drenched to the bone and shivering with cold by the time they'd gotten to the little church with the graveyard behind it. In the midst of the rain and soot-blackened, lichened, and tilted headstones, they'd met the vicar. He'd stood frowning and hunch shouldered under his umbrella as Harriet told him who they were and why they'd come. With a great sigh of tried patience, he'd turned and led them to the farthest back corner of the cemetery and a pile of mud.

As they'd drawn near, two men had stopped shoveling and stepped back, removed their caps, and bowed their heads. The vicar stood off to the side and murmured something that Harriet had later told her was the Lord's Prayer. All she could really remember of those moments was looking down at the plain pine box and thinking how very uncomfortable her mother must be in such a short and narrow space. And that shoveling wasn't really all that necessary, not with the rain sluicing down the pile of mud, carving deep rivulets and pouring like black soup into the grave.

And then the vicar had walked off and left them. The shovelers had put their caps back on and hefted up their tools. It was then that Harriet had reached into her pocket and pulled out a crumpled, bedraggled daisy, handed it to her, and motioned for her to throw it into the hole.

It had landed on the top center, about where she imagined her mother's hands would have been crossed over her heart. One mangled, limp daisy. One tiny, wilted bit of color and hope in a world without either.

They had walked back to Essie's in silence and fading light. Two weeks after that, Simone had tossed a daisy into another hole and said good-bye to Harriet. Harriet, whose goodness had been willing to bear discomfort to remember the lost and whose aged body hadn't been able to recover from the effort.

It had been raining that day, too. The daisy hadn't been mangled, though. Simone had been very careful with it. And it hadn't made the least bit of difference in the end. Her mother was still gone. Harriet was gone. And the gift of a daisy, perfect or otherwise, didn't ease the pain or make the sun shine.

Unless, of course, you were a peer, Simone amended as the congregation rose and opened their hymnals. She stood silently beside her sister, her heart too heavy and angry to sing.

If you were a peer the sun shone and the choir sang; the world lamented your untimely passing and covered your expensive casket with lilies and roses. And when they buried you, there was a finely carved stone to mark your place, to record for all time that your life had been considered worthy and that you were worth remembering.

There wasn't a stone to mark her mother's grave. Or

Harriet's. Not even plain wooden crosses. Because they
were poor. Because they were prostitutes. Because those
who remembered and mourned them didn't even have
money for hack fare. To buy a headstone . . .

Simone started in realization. She could buy one! For
her mother. And one for Harriet, too. She had plenty of
money. Drayton would allow her all that she wanted. She
could have their names carved in an elegant script and
have the carver add some inspiring words about good
hearts and caring souls, about love and friendship. Maybe
some cherubs, too. Or angels. Or flowers.

God, why hadn't she thought of this before? All she
had to do was tell Drayton what she wanted to do, com-
mission a stone carver, and have him deliver the headstones to . . . to . . .

She blinked back a hot curtain of tears as brutal truth
twisted her heart. To not know where your mother was
buried . . .

𝒯ristan watched Simone slip out of the pew and move
quickly up the ambulatory. She passed him, tears coursing down her cheeks and fire blazing in her eyes. He
looked up the rows of pews to see if any of the family
were going to follow her out and offer her comfort. They
didn't. Closing the hymnal, he gave Noland a quick nod
and then went after her.

He found her on the walkway outside the cathedral,
looking up and down the street as though she wasn't sure
which way to go.

"Simone?" he called as he made his way down the
steps toward her. "Are you all right?"

She squared her shoulders, lifted her chin, and scrubbed

her hands over her cheeks before she turned to face him. "I'm fine."

Yes, he could see by her puffy eyes just how *fine* she was. He shoved his hands into his trouser pockets to keep from reaching for her and asked, "Did you know Lord Sandifer well?"

"Who?"

"Lord Sandifer," he said again, motioning with his head toward the church behind them. "Today's guest of honor."

"Oh." She sniffled and looked away. "I didn't know him at all."

"Aside from family and a handful of others, everyone inside could probably say the same thing if they were decent enough to be honest about it. Which explains why there aren't all that many weeping into handkerchiefs."

"I didn't notice."

"Since you didn't know Sandifer, it must be memories that brought you to tears. If you would like to ease the burden of them by sharing with me, I'd—"

Her dark eyes blazed as she looked up at him. "What I'd like, Tristan, is for you to go away," she said crisply, turning to study the roadway again.

Well, yes, and if he had a brain in his head he'd do just that. But he didn't. He stood there, the knife-in-his-chest feeling returning as he searched for something to say that would get her to turn around and talk to him again. About what, he didn't know and didn't care. He just wanted her to talk to him, to make him feel right about their ill-fated affair. Yes, it was shallow and selfish, but then, he was a shallow and selfish man. "Simone," he began softly as he eased toward her side.

"Yoo-hoo! Tristan!"

He froze as a shudder ran down the length of his spine.

"Tristan, sweetheart!"

He looked over his shoulder just as Sarah climbed out of a rented hack. "Goddamn it!"

Beside him, Simone sniffled and cleared her throat. "Pardon my language," he offered quickly. "And please give me a chance to explain about her."

"Oh," she said dryly, "I wouldn't miss it for the world."

And she wasn't going to make it easy for him. Not that he deserved it. He turned to face the oncoming woman, determined to be done with her as quickly as possible. "What are you doing here, Sarah?"

Sarah beamed up at him. "I happened to be passing by on my way back to the inn and saw you standing here. And I *had* to stop and tell you that I just shared the most *delicious* pot of tea and delightful hour of conversation with your mother."

Oh, he'd only thought things had gone badly before. "My mother's dead, Sarah. Long dead."

Sarah's smile faded. "Well, she *said* she was your mother."

"If you're talking about Lucinda, she's my stepmother."

Her smile suddenly as big and bright as before, she countered, "I don't think she sees the difference, sweetheart."

He unclenched his teeth. "And what, pray tell, did the two of you find to talk about for a delightful frigging hour?"

"You."

"And how you expect to marry me?" he added, his pulse beginning to pound behind his eyes.

"I really thought she ought to know that I'm carrying your child."

For a second his jaw dropped and his heart fell to his feet. And then reality slammed home. His mind racing furiously ahead, his blood coursing white-hot through his veins, he snarled, "You have to be kidding."

"The mother of the groom should not be the last to hear of such things, sweeting."

"Christ Almighty, Sarah!"

"Sweetheart, please," she cooed. "There's no reason to be upset. Your mother seemed quite pleased at the news."

Why his brain chose that precise moment to go absolutely numb . . . He stared at Sarah, dully thinking that he must have been damn desperate to have ever chosen her as a lover.

"You have a really interesting life."

He looked down to meet Simone's dark gaze. The corner of her mouth was tipped up and one raven brow was arched. God, she was beautiful. And intelligent. And as soon as he could deal with Lucinda, he was going to put their relationship back to rights. If he had to crawl through glass to grovel at her feet, he would. Well, maybe not crawl literally. Just because he was going to admit stupidity didn't mean he had to give up self-respect and pride.

"And you are?" he heard Sarah ask caustically.

Simone's smile went ever so slowly wide as she shifted her attention to his former lover. "Dredge your memory. We met on the dock two days ago."

Ah, yes. What a perfect response. How perfectly Simone.

"My, my," Sarah drawled, glaring up at him. "Haven't you been a busy boy."

He nodded and decided that there was no point in mincing words. "Sarah, I've tried to be kind and understanding, but we've now passed the point where I have the patience for it. Listen carefully. I am not going to marry you." As she looked at him aghast, he pointed to the rented carriage and went on, saying, "Put your arse back in that hack, have it take you to the inn, pack your bags, and be on the next ship sailing west."

"I'm afraid that I can't, sweetheart," she countered, her smile in stark contrast to the flint of her tone. "Your mother and I are having dinner this evening to discuss how to best make you accept your responsibility and do the *honorable* thing by me. If you'd like to spare us the effort, you could join us and we could spend the evening planning the wedding instead. It would be *ever* so much more enjoyable."

"I won't be there," he declared flatly, firmly. "I am *not* going to marry you, Sarah."

"We'll see about that, sweetheart." She wiggled her fingers at him, pivoted on her heel, and walked off toward the waiting hack, calling back, "Toodles!"

Toodles. Good God.

"Well, I've completely forgotten all of my problems."

He looked down at Simone. "If she is pregnant," he said, cutting to the core of the current matter, "it's not my child."

"Are you sure?"

He nodded. "It was over a year between the last time I saw her and the other day when she showed up on the dock. Yes, she was my lover when I left San Francisco for my last trading voyage. When I returned ten months later, it was to find both the news that I had inherited the family title and an invitation to her wedding to a man out of Seattle. I had Gregory send them a gift and I sailed for England three days later. I didn't see her in that time. I didn't talk to her. I sure as hell didn't bed her."

Simone seemed to consider it all for a moment and then shrugged. "All of which doesn't matter in terms of the scandal she can create with the accusation."

"I don't give a damn about scandal."

"But if Lucinda thinks you might—"

"She knows me better."

"No. Let me finish," she said softly. "If Sarah really were carrying your child, it would be a potential heir. If Lucinda thinks there's even a remote chance of Sarah forcing you to marry her in the next few months so that the child is born legitimate . . ."

The full scope of the consequences hit him square on. "Jesus," he muttered, raking his fingers through his hair. "Why is my brain not working?"

"I'd suggest you avoid going to dinner," Simone offered with a half smile. "A massive dose of arsenic slipped into your and Sarah's soup and all Lucinda's dreams come true."

"An accidental death by what everyone would assume was food poisoning."

"It's not a neat and tidy way to die, but I don't think Lucinda cares all that much about neat and tidy."

How very true. He sighed and looked off in the direction of the departing hack. "Sarah has no idea of the danger she's placed herself in with her lie."

"Yes, you have to warn her."

Oh, Jesus. Wasn't the whole situation ugly enough already? To go anywhere near her would simply escalate the woman's hopes even further. "I'll write her a letter and have Gregory deliver it."

"And if she thinks you're simply trying to scare her off?" Simone calmly posed. "If she takes that note to dinner with her this evening and shares it with Lucinda as proof of the extremes to which you're willing to go? The cat will be out of the proverbial bag and Lucinda will have to kill you as quickly as she can manage it."

Part of him was tempted to let her and be done with all of it. The stronger part of him rebelled at the notion of letting her win. "The results would be the same if I go in person to warn her. She'll simply tell Lucinda about it."

"Then the solution is to keep Sarah from going to dinner tonight."

"And tomorrow night," he countered, his brain finally—finally!—beginning to work in something approximating a normal manner. "And the night after that. And all the calling hours and teatimes between now and frigging eternity."

"And even that's no guarantee that Sarah will be safe. As long as Lucinda can find her, she's a heartbeat away from being the victim of a tragic accident."

"She has to go back to the States. Willing or not."

"Or anywhere as long as Lucinda can't find her," Simone offered with a tiny shrug. "At least until the baby's born."

True. But . . . "If there really is a baby," he growled. "I wouldn't put it past her to lie about it."

Behind them, the doors of the cathedral swung open and organ music spilled down the stone steps. Simone glanced over her shoulder and then looked up to somberly meet his gaze. "Just out of horrible curiosity, what is it about Sarah that appeals to you?"

"Not one damn thing," he assured her.

"Something must have at one time."

"I have no idea now what it was," he admitted. "I suppose it was that she was easy and willing."

He regretted the words the instant they left his tongue. He regretted them even more as Simone's eyes darkened with obvious pain. "Don't even think it, Simone," he hurried to say. "You're not at all like her."

Her laugh was shallow and brittle and she didn't turn away quickly enough to keep him from seeing the tears well along her lower lashes. Instinctively he reached out and laid his hand on her shoulder to stay her, saying gently, "You're not, Simone. Honestly."

She glanced at the church and then quickly stepped away from his touch. With a wholly false smile, she said, "Do stay safe, Tristan."

Of course. They were bringing the casket out. People were watching them. He couldn't expect her to say anything more personal than that. "Thank you for caring."

She laughed softly, the sound still a bit fragile, as she put more distance between them. "I don't care about *you*, Tristan. It's simply that the mayhem around you is the only interesting thing in my life. If you die, I'd have to find another entertainment, and that's such a bother."

And then she turned and walked away. No wiggling of her fingers, no threats, no stupid *toodles*. No, Simone was a woman of considerable substance. And pride. He'd done an excellent job of battering the latter over the course of the last few days. Odds were, when she got past the hurt of thinking of herself as being in the same class of throwaway women as Sarah Sheraton, she was going to be furious at him for putting her there.

"Is everything all right, Lockwood?"

He looked up from the walkway and into Noland's pale blue eyes. Actually, everything was as close to disastrous as Tristan ever wanted to get, but explaining it all wasn't something he was going to do as mourners streamed past him.

"I assume that Lady Simone recovered from her grief?"

It depended on what grief they were talking about. At the moment, he couldn't say that he'd done anything except add to her sad memories. And until he dealt with Sarah and then Lucinda . . . "We have a task to undertake, Noland."

"Oh? Could I hope that it's a matter of grave national concern?"

"Would you settle for a significant personal problem?"

"If I must." He grinned. "Does it have to do with a certain well-curved young brunette?"

"A blonde, actually."

Noland tsked and shook his head. "Damn, Lockwood. And here I thought you and Lady Simone made a rather attractive match."

"Really," he drawled, intrigued. "How so?"

"You have like temperaments and seemed—to my eyes, anyway—to share a certain . . . well, shall we say an unrestrained enthusiasm for life."

"That's putting it delicately."

Noland grinned. "I try."

"And it's deeply appreciated," Tristan assured him. "Now, about this blonde . . ."

How in the world, Simone silently groused as she waited for Fiona and the others to join her. How in the world she could be furious with him one minute, and not a heartbeat later fully and happily in league with him . . . For god-sakes, the man had seduced her, ended the affair in what had to be considered, even among rakes, to be record short order, then turned around and flaunted another of his lovers, and she couldn't seem to loathe him for any longer than it took for him to smile at her.

If she wasn't certifiably insane, then she was at least spineless. Weak. A complete idiot without a single shred of common sense or self-respect. She should have kept quiet and let him trot right off to dinner with Miss Yoo-hoo and slurp down a liter of poison. She'd have been doing the world a favor. But no, she'd piped right up and warned him of the possible danger. And then, as though that hadn't been enough, she'd told him that he had to warn his new old lover! Had to go off to her room at the inn and save her from the plotting of the evil Lucinda.

That was assuming, of course, that Lucinda really was the vicious killer Tristan claimed her to be. He might very well have made it all up to play on her sympathies and draw her more easily into the seduction. It had been the tipping point. Until then she'd decided against . . .

No, she amended, taking a deep breath, she had to be honest. When she'd gone out to meet him in the garden she had been willing to let him sweep her into an affair if he was so inclined. She'd decided that she didn't want to own the decision herself and put it all on Tristan's shoulders. He'd held to his course and she'd gone happily along. And she'd been more than content with the outcome, more than willing to continue on with him.

Then he'd ended the affair and she was left with . . . with . . . nothing. Well, nothing aside from the memories of one night of incredible pleasure. And the regret that she wasn't going to have any more.

God, men complicated life. But she'd learned her lesson and learned it well. Never again was she going to let a man disrupt the . . . boredom. The sheer, unrelenting, absolute boredom of her existence.

"Are you feeling better, Simone?"

Fiona. Soft, quiet, ever gentle Fiona. The sister who could see through false smiles and breezy lies. "Not really."

"Would you care to talk about it? Drayton and Haywood are discussing politics on the steps and I'm a very good listener."

Simone shrugged. "I don't know what to say or how to begin. Sometimes I think I know what's troubling me and then, even as I try to sort out a solution, I lose track of it as my mind flits off to consider something else." She laughed weakly. "And with just as much success."

"What were you thinking about as I walked up?"

"How utterly boring my life is."

"Boring in what way?"

"There isn't anything to it, Fiona. Nothing of consequence, anyway. I get up in the morning and have absolutely nothing to do with my day that means anything to anyone. When someone asks how my day has been and what I've done with it, there's nothing to tell them that's even remotely interesting. Honestly, if I didn't get up, if I decided to spend the rest of my life lying in bed and staring at the ceiling, it wouldn't affect a single person on earth."

"That's not—"

"Oh, Fiona, please. Your animals would perish if you weren't there to care for them. If something happened to

Drayton, the Liberals in the House of Lords would be staggered and Caroline would make Victoria look like a piker in terms of grieving. And if something happened to Caroline, all of our worlds would fall apart. But if I cocked up my toes in the next five minutes . . . Not one ripple."

Fiona considered her for a long moment and then smiled softly. "But it's different when you're with Lord Lockwood."

A statement, not a question. The truth, plain and simple and undeniable. "Which was inexcusable of me," Simone countered. "I know better. I know better than most women, actually. Caroline and Drayton were the only people I've ever known for whom a relationship is more than trading sex for money."

"And what's wrong with hoping that you can have the same kind of happiness as our sister's found?"

"There's nothing wrong with hoping," Simone admitted. "But it's absolutely pathetic to be disappointed when your luck isn't as good as someone else's."

"Are you sure it's over between you and Lord Lockwood?"

"Yes." On his side of it, anyway. On hers . . . Apparently her pride wasn't quite battered enough yet. "He promised Drayton that the affair was done."

"People often say things because they're expected to, not because they mean them."

"He means it, Fiona."

Her sister sighed and arched a pale brow. "So he promised Drayton. You make promises to Drayton all the time and have no intention whatsoever of keeping them."

"This is different. I was a temporary and obviously not

very interesting diversion. A former lover of his has arrived in London and—"

"He hasn't rekindled the romance."

Another statement of simple truth from Fiona's view of the world. If she weren't always spot-on . . . "How can you know that?"

"Lord Lockwood followed you out when you left the cathedral," she explained. "Whatever promises he made Drayton, he obviously still cares enough about you that your tears concerned him. If he was truly done and had moved on to another, he wouldn't have spent the service watching you and he certainly wouldn't have left his friend to go after you."

It would be nice to think of it that way, to believe that Tristan was being genuinely honorable, sincerely protective. "I suppose you could be right," she allowed, trying not to hope.

"Suppose?" Fiona countered with a chuckle, her green eyes sparkling. "If I were you, I'd be thinking about whether I wanted to be married in London or at Ryland Castle."

Simone snapped up her jaw and then laughed. "You think I'm going to marry Tristan?"

"Yes."

Oh, for the love of . . . "He has to ask," Simone countered. "And he's not going to."

"Since when have you waited for fortune to come to you?" Fiona didn't give her a chance to even mull the notion before adding, "If he makes life interesting, then go after him. Creating a scandal is better than lying in your bed, staring at the ceiling, and being miserably bored for the rest of your life."

"Caroline and Drayton would prefer—"

"That you be happy."

And they'd be happy for her as the family name was dragged through the muck and mud? Simone sighed and gave her sister the best smile she could muster. "I'll think about it," she offered.

"Sometimes," Fiona said softly, "it's best to not think but simply act on instinct."

"Oh yes. My instincts have served me so well on this already."

Her sister shrugged and looked past her. "Drayton and Haywood are coming this way. Are you going home with us? Or do you have other plans?"

"Other plans," she hastily decided, easing away. "If anyone needs me, I'll be at Lady Emmaline's lying through my teeth about her artistic ability."

She thought she heard Fiona mutter something about giving regards to Lockwood, but she didn't turn back and ask her to repeat it. If Tristan did turn up at his sister's . . . Simone didn't know what she was going to give him. A swift kick had appeal. So did a cold shoulder. And a good piece of her mind. Unfortunately, even more compelling was the hope that he'd give her one of his bone-melting smiles and then kiss her senseless.

"Lousy instincts," she groused, hailing a cab.

CHAPTER 14

$\mathcal{T}$he desk clerk, duly impressed with their titles and Noland's Yard credentials, dashed for the stairs, leaving Tristan and his friend to wait in the inn's quiet parlor. As Noland leaned against the mantel and considered his cuticles, Tristan paced and considered all that could go wrong with the meeting. If Sarah refused to be sensible or even moderately reasonable . . .

He stopped in front of Noland to grouse, "I'd rather take a sharp stick in the eye than do this, you know."

Noland clapped him on the shoulder and said cheerily, "But it is the right thing to do and the best way to do it.

You'd feel miserably guilty for the rest of your life if you didn't warn her."

"Are you sure there aren't any legal provisions for justifiable kidnapping?"

"Positive. If she refuses to act in the preservation of her own life, there's nothing you can do to force the issue. You'll simply have to be content in the knowledge that you made a good-faith effort to intervene."

"And if she trots right off to tell Lucinda that Scotland Yard has her under investigation?"

Noland shrugged. "It might be the easiest solution, Lockwood. Lucinda would undoubtedly flee the country and never look back."

"And never be brought to justice," Tristan pointed out.

"Justice, my friend, is like a diamond. It comes in many shapes, has complex facets, and is seldom found without a flaw of some sort or another."

Just what he needed, Tristan silently complained as he resumed his pacing. A damned philosopher.

"Sweetheart! I knew you'd come to your—" Her words stopped in the same instant that her feet did. Standing in the doorway of the parlor, she looked between him and Noland and frowned.

Tristan summoned his manners and a tight smile. "Sarah, may I present my friend, Lord Richard Henry, Viscount Noland. Noland, Miss Sarah Sheraton of San Francisco."

"*Formerly* of San Francisco," she corrected, gliding into the room. She gave Noland a nod and polite smile while saying, "It's a pleasure to make your acquaintance, Your Lordship."

Noland effected a real bow at the waist. "Madam."

Seeing no reason to let Sarah labor under the assumption that this was a social call, nor to prolong the inevitable ugliness, Tristan said simply, "Noland is an agent at Scotland Yard."

"How very interesting, Lord Noland. You must have a great many stories to tell."

Noland, God love him, practically preened. "Actually, Miss Sheraton, I do." At Tristan's scowl he cleared his throat and sobered to add, "But one in particular has brought me here today to speak with you."

"Oh?" She gestured toward a grouping of upholstered chairs near the hearth. "Would you care to have a seat for the telling?"

"Why, yes, I would. Thank you. After you, Miss Sheraton."

Tristan leaned his hip against the edge of the buffet, crossed his arms over his chest, and watched the two of them settle in as though tea were going to be served at any moment.

"Sweetheart, aren't you going to join us?"

Three ruined a game of patty-cake. He managed another smile. "I'm fine right here."

She shrugged and turned her attention to Noland. All gentility and social finesse, she smiled prettily and said, "Now, Lord Noland, if you would please tell me the story. Am I to assume that I am somehow involved in it?"

"You are, madam. Quite inadvertently, of course. However, that doesn't alter the fact that you are in considerable danger as a result."

"Danger?" she gasped, pressing her hand daintily to her chest and opening her eyes wide. "Good heavens. From what?"

A public that expects good acting.

"From whom, madam. And I regret to say that the source is none other than Lady Lockwood."

She sagged back into the chair for a second and then shot forward in it the next to glare in Tristan's direction. "You are completely and utterly despicable! Your mother warned me that you'd do anything to avoid accepting your responsibility."

He tamped down his anger and met her gaze squarely. "Sarah, enough of the games. If you are with child, it's not mine, and we both know it. Just as we both know that you've come to London because your latest great ambition is to be the next Lady Lockwood."

She gasped, quickly pressed her fingertips to her lips, and blinked in what he supposed was an effort to look as though she were holding tears at bay. It might have been more believable if there had actually been tears. "I'm here," she said softly, weakly, "because I've realized that I love you."

"No, you don't," he countered. "And I don't love you. I never have and I never will. We are done."

"How can you be so cruel?" She covered her mouth again, managed to make a little hiccuping sound, and then fumbled about in her skirt pocket. Producing a lace-edged handkerchief, she dabbed at her eyes and sniffled. "All I want is to spend the rest of my life with you, making you happy."

"Aw, Christ on a crutch," he snarled. "Noland, feel free to step into this charade at any point."

His friend started. "Ah, yes. That is why I'm along, isn't it?" He reached over and patted Sarah's hand. "Now see here, Miss Sheraton; while Lockwood is being decidedly brutal about the more personal aspects of the matter, he is also quite sincere in his concerns for your safety."

She shook her head and wrung the handkerchief. "Accusing his own mother."

"She's not my—"

"Miss Sheraton," Noland interrupted, shooting him a dark look, "I assure you that Lockwood isn't casting baseless aspersions. Lady Lockwood is under official investigation in the murder of her husband and two stepsons."

"No." Sarah lifted her chin in brave defiance. "I simply refuse to believe such a thing. She is a cultured and delightfully pleasant woman."

"You forgot," Tristan groused, "to mention wealthy."

"Lockwood," his friend chided, "I would deeply appreciate it if you would please refrain from escalating the tension in the situation."

He looked away, clenching and unclenching his teeth.

"Actually, Miss Sheraton," Noland went on, "Lockwood's observation concerning his stepmother's financial circumstances is of central importance. Lady Lockwood has profited greatly from the recent deaths of her male family members. Insurance and all that."

"Is insurance illegal in England?" she asked in a tiny, "I'm so wounded and helpless" voice. Tristan rolled his eyes. Simone would have been six jumps ahead of Noland by this point in the conversation. Hell, by now there wouldn't be any point to having a conversation; she'd have figured it out on her own and been well on her way to packing up her things and heading back to America.

Or maybe not, he admitted. Simone wasn't the sort to run from a contest. Or the sort to try to force a man to marry her.

"Insurance is perfectly lawful, Miss Sheraton. But insuring people and then killing them to collect on the policies most surely is not."

"I still can't believe it," she declared, obviously recovering a sliver of her strength. "If Lady Lockwood has done such horrible things, why haven't you arrested her?"

"We lack proof sufficient to please the Crown in court," Noland explained. "We are, however, developing a plan to force Her Ladyship's hand and reveal her as the cold-blooded murderess she is."

"And how is it, Lord Noland, that I'm endangered by all of this?"

God, she couldn't figure it out on her own?

"I'm afraid, my dear Miss Sheraton, that you have, without deliberate intention, of course, made something of a target of yourself in letting it be known to Lady Lockwood that you intend to wed Lockwood and that you are carrying his child."

"I'm not following your line of thinking. Exactly how does any of that endanger me?"

Tristan bit his tongue and kept his gaze fastened on the floor at his feet. How anyone could be so slow . . .

"Tristan is a wealthy man, Miss Sheraton. A wealthy man without heirs," Noland, the soul of patience, explained. "Well, direct heirs. He does have a minor-aged half sister who, by law in the absence of a will providing otherwise, would inherit his assets in the event of his death. Lady Lockwood, as her mother, would control the trust into which the inheritance would be placed."

"And I should care about all of this because . . . ?"

So incredibly self-centered . . .

"If you were to marry Tristan and produce a legitimate

heir," Noland supplied, "you and your child would inherit his considerable estate, not his half sister. Lady Lockwood would have no access to the fortune."

She blinked. Tristan cocked a brow, realizing that there was absolutely no artifice in the expression; Sarah was well and truly shocked.

Noland nodded. "It is in Lady Lockwood's interest to see that you do not marry Tristan."

"But she's been quite supportive of my situation. She's promised me that she'll make Tristan take the right and honorable course."

Damnation. And to think they'd been so close to acceptance. "What?" he scoffed. "You'd expect her to just come right out and announce that she's added you to her list of those who have to be killed?"

Noland frowned at him, sighed heavily, and patted Sarah's hand again. "However inflammatory his presentation, Miss Sheraton, Lockwood is right. His stepmother is devious enough to have killed three men and to have gotten away with it. For the moment, anyway. She is not being honest with you. She stands to lose a great deal of money if she furthers your plans to force Lockwood to the altar. It is not, I am sorry to say, in her nature to be altruistic."

She stared off into space for a moment and then snapped to attention as though she'd been bitten by some small bug. "Well, the solution's very simple. Tristan just needs to write a will that gives his fortune to anyone other than his sister."

"And leave her penniless?" Tristan countered. "And leave any wife and child of mine in the same condition? Plunge everyone around me that I care about into poverty so that Lucinda won't have a reason to kill them? Or me? What an astoundingly brilliant plan, Sarah. If only I'd thought of it myself."

Noland hung his head, stared at the carpet, and heaved a huge sigh of what was clearly exasperation.

"You're making up all of this," Sarah accused. "You've hired this . . ." she waved her hand in Noland's direction "*actor* to put on a play for me in the hope that I'll run away in fear for my life."

"No, Sarah. It's the truth. You've made yourself a target. And if you had a . . ." He bit back the caustic words just in time. Clearing his throat, he willed a calm into his voice that he didn't feel. "The intelligent thing to do is to remove yourself from the situation completely, Sarah. Tell Lucinda the truth, that you're really not expecting, and then return to San Francisco. If you don't pose a threat to her getting her hands on my money, she won't waste the time and effort to hurt you."

Her chin quivered and real tears welled along her lower lashes. "But I am expecting a child."

Oh, damn. "Then go to Seattle," Tristan suggested kindly, "and patch things up with good ol' George."

"It's not his baby."

Well, that explained a lot of things. And complicated the hell out of them, too. "Jesus, Sarah."

"I didn't throw him over," she cried into her handkerchief. "He broke the engagement when he found out I'd been having an affair."

"It would seem then," Noland said quietly, "that the logical course would be to inform the man, whoever he is and whatever his city of residence, of his impending fatherhood and demand that he step up to his responsibility."

"He's married. And his wife's family has all the money. He'll deny to his dying day that the affair ever happened."

The pit just got deeper and deeper. He suspected he knew the answer, but he had to ask anyway. "Does your family know the details of the situation?"

She nodded. "I've been disowned. Papa literally threw my things out onto the sidewalk for everyone to see. I've been trying to put a brave face on things, to hope for the best. But now . . . They've only gotten worse!"

God, what a mess. He met Noland's gaze and cocked a brow in silent question.

Noland nodded and reached out to pat Sarah's hand again and gently say, "If you would excuse Lockwood and me for a moment, Miss Sheraton, and let us see if we can perhaps come up with an acceptable solution for you."

Sarah nodded, then buried her face in her soggy handkerchief and sobbed. Tristan walked silently to the door of the parlor and waited for Noland to join him.

"Damn, Lockwood," his friend said in a hushed voice and casting a concerned look in her direction. "She obviously can't return to San Francisco and her family. Do you have any feelings for her at all?"

"None that I'd be willing to make a marriage on if that's what you're thinking. I'll gladly provide whatever financial support she needs in the months ahead, though. I'm not completely hard-hearted. At the moment, the most significant question seems to be where she can go."

"Well, she can't stay in London. That's obvious enough. Given the lies she's told Lucinda, she's not safe."

Tristan nodded. "Who's in residence at your country house?"

"No one but the servants at the moment. It's the Season. But come the end of it . . . My parents would laud my sense of Christian compassion and generosity. Then they'd kill me."

"And if Lucinda wanted to find her, any of your family homes would be the next logical places to look after she'd canvassed mine. But if Sarah were to take up residence at a comfortable inn some distance from London . . ."

"An inn chosen completely at random so that there's no following logic to her. . . ."

"Exactly. Perhaps something near the coast."

"Leave it to me, Lockwood. I'll choose the place and see her safely tucked into a hidey-hole."

"I'll have a letter of credit drawn up this afternoon and—"

"No," his friend said, shaking his head. "It's best to have no paper trail directly linking you and Miss Sheraton. I'll pay the expenses and you can reimburse me after a suitable period of time. The longer there is between expense and repayment, the more difficult it will be for anyone to follow the expenditures to Miss Sheraton."

"You really are amazing sometimes."

Noland grinned. "Thank you for noticing. And as long as you're in a mood to accede to my superior skills—"

Tristan chuckled. "Don't let it go to your head, Noland."

"Too late," he replied with a grin. "I'm seizing command of the situation from this moment on. That way, if you're asked where Miss Sheraton went, you can honestly reply that you don't know. Once I have her situated, I'll have her write a letter to Lucinda admitting the child isn't yours and that she's returned home to try to make the real father accountable."

It made sense. And it should wrap the ends up nicely enough. Tristan nodded and looked back into the parlor, hoping that Sarah wouldn't prove herself obstinate.

From beside him, Noland said quietly, "I think now would be the perfect time to let someone else step forward and play her White Knight. The sooner and more completely her ties to you are severed, the less complicated your life will be in the future. I can't imagine that Miss Sheraton and Lady Simone could ever find common ground for a friendship."

"They're not a bit alike," Tristan allowed.

"I've noticed that." Noland clapped him on the shoulder. "There were a few dicey moments in this, but I'd say your part's been done adequately. I'll manage it from here, Lockwood. I'm sure you have other things to do with what's left of the afternoon."

Tristan nodded, extended his hand and his thanks, and then left the inn. It was odd, he mused as he climbed into his waiting carriage, how he felt about the whole thing. He'd expected to feel a huge sense of deliverance in having Sarah no longer stirring the pot. And while he did feel some relief at that, it was only a part of the swirl of his emotions.

Part of the mix was a sadness for Sarah having placed herself in such a desperate situation that traveling to England to play a loathsome gamble was not only necessary but also her only real option. He had hope, though. Hope that, in the end, Sarah would be all right and maybe even happy with the turn her life had taken.

But mostly he felt as though he'd been handed a rare and unexpected opportunity to begin his own life over again, too. What exactly he was supposed to do with it, though . . . Not mucking it up was going to be a challenge that was already—just mere seconds into the realization—weighing on his shoulders.

If she followed Fiona's advice and acted on her instincts . . . Simone sat in the rear-facing seat of the Townsend family carriage and knew this was a mistake in the making; she could feel it in her bones. In hindsight, she could see that she really ought to have stopped the adventure in its tracks the moment Emmy had proposed it. But she hadn't. Largely because in the seconds when her opposition would have made a difference, she'd been thinking about the likelihood of meeting Tristan in the course of it. By the time Emmy had gotten her coat, hat, and gloves and sailed out the door, it was too late to voice the doubts that were niggling past her initial sense of anticipation.

"You are a dear and true friend, Simone."

Maybe it wasn't too late after all. "If that were the case, I'd have refused to go along with this. You're courting scandal."

"I know," Emmy admitted, grinning. "Isn't it fun?"

Hell's bells. What had happened to the shy little thing who preferred to hide behind potted palms? "You're not going to think it's all that much fun if your brother finds out."

Emmy snorted. "Oh, please, Simone," she said with a dismissive wave of her hand. "Mr. Gregory and I aren't going to do anything but talk about shipping and account ledgers. Tristan could walk in at any moment and not be the least bit outraged. In fact, I think he'd be pleased to find me taking an interest in his company."

"And you don't think he would eventually figure out that your interest really lies in his company clerk and that the books he keeps are just an excuse?"

"Never," Emmy blithely assured her. "Not in a million years. Tristan thinks I'm a complete innocent."

"That's because you *are* a complete innocent."

"I am not."

Knowing there was no point in arguing otherwise, Simone changed her tack. "What about Lord Noland?"

"What about him?"

"He thinks you're the most beautiful woman in the British Empire."

"I think he actually said that I was the fairest flower. No," she quickly amended, "it was *rarest* flower."

Taking it as a positive sign that her friend remembered the exchange in detail, Simone pressed on. "He could be considered a fine catch, Emmy."

Again Emmy snorted. "By whom?"

"Society." Deliberately adding a more upbeat note to her voice, she added, "He's titled. And a member of Scotland Yard. He's highly respectable."

"You're the last person on earth I would have ever expected to care about Society's dictums," Emmy charged. "I thought that if anyone would appreciate independent thinking, it would be you."

She could appreciate independence more than most, but she wasn't stupid about it, either. There were lines that she knew better than to cross. Lines that were vastly different for her than they were for Emmaline Townsend.

"I wasn't born into Society, Emmy," she began, hoping to make her friend understand. "You were. And that makes all the difference in the world. My presence is tolerated in its circles only because I'm the legal ward of a duke and they can't exclude me without insulting Drayton. People stand around and watch me, expecting me to make blunders of epic proportion. It's their greatest entertainment. And they allow my bad behavior only because they know that I'm, at heart, one of the great unwashed, untamed masses and that they can hold me up to their precious, perfect daughters as an example of how not to conduct themselves."

"How very small of them," Emmy said. The carriage rolled to a stop and she leaned forward, reaching for the door handle and saying, "I'd never do such a mean-spirited thing."

Simone caught her hand and stayed her. "Let me finish, Emmy," she said. "It's important and you have to understand." She didn't give her a chance to refuse. "You aren't accorded that sort of freedom, Emmy. No, it's not fair, but there it is. You were born and bred to obey the rules. You're one of the precious ones. You can't carry on with a man in trade, however nice and handsome he is, without toppling off your pedestal. And that you'd willingly, deliberately, choose to fall would be considered an indication of low moral character. They'd never forgive you for betraying them."

"Oh, pish," Emmy declared, pulling her hand away and climbing out of the carriage.

Simone sat in her seat, pondering a completely unexpected sympathy for Caroline and Drayton. At some point in her life she was going to have to apologize for putting them through hell.

"Pish?" she repeated, following Emmy out. "Contemplating social suicide is not *pish,* Emmy."

Her friend ignored her, lifted the hem of her skirt, and bounded up the steps of the Townsend Importers offices. Simone followed, stunned. "God," she muttered under her breath. "I can't believe I actually said that. I sounded just like Caroline."

"Lady Emmaline! What a wonderful surprise!"

Simone paused on the office threshold just as Wade Gregory's gaze skipped past Emmy to light on her. His smile faltered, but he managed to quickly and gallantly retrieve a bit of it to dip his chin and say politely, "Lady Simone. How nice to see you, too."

Oh, such a lie.

"Good afternoon, Mr. Gregory," Emmy said, bubbling and bright. "How are you today?"

"Considerably better than I was mere seconds ago, Lady Emmaline. To what do I owe the pleasure of your visit?"

"Unbridled curiosity. We were wondering if some of the crates had been unpacked yet."

We? We *didn't give a damn about what was in the crates.*

"They have indeed," Mr. Gregory answered. "And as a matter of fact, just as you arrived I was preparing to go back and check the contents against the manifest. Would you and Lady Simone care to accompany me?"

Simone's heart jolted. Into the warehouse? Had Tristan disassembled the silk bower? Had he packed it all away? What if he hadn't? Could she get away with pretending that she'd never seen it before? Oh, God, it could be even worse than that. Just how much did Wade Gregory know about his employer's private life?

Emmy intruded on her panic, saying, "We would love

nothing more, Mr. Gregory. Is there any way in which I can assist you with the process? I so enjoyed helping sort the crates as they were unloaded."

Mr. Gregory beamed, removed his spectacles, folded them, and slipped them into the breast pocket of his suit coat. "How kind of you, Lady Emmaline. A partner is always appreciated. This way, ladies," he said, taking up a portable desk and writing pen.

Simone went along. Slowly. Reluctantly. Wishing she were anywhere but there. Letting Emmy and Mr. Gregory forge ahead into the maze on their own, she paused and looked around. Soft afternoon light streamed in from windows high overhead, dust motes swirling and dancing in the shafts that fell onto the mountains of wooden boxes. The one great positive, she concluded, was that the addition of the newly arrived boxes and crates had necessitated the rearranging of the corridors between them. Not that she was very far into the space, but from what she could see so far, the warehouse only vaguely resembled the place Tristan had brought her that night.

Definitely a good thing, she decided, meandering along a line of unopened boxes labeled: FINE CHINA. Odds were the bed had been undone. The last thing in the world she wanted was to see it again. Hoping for something you couldn't have was so very pointless. Not to mention painful. Why the hope of seeing Tristan again kept springing up . . . Why she so enjoyed remembering the night they'd spent together . . .

"Because I'm a fool," she muttered, peering absently into the top of an opened crate as she wandered past. "A damn ninny without an ounce of—"

She stopped as realization filtered through the haze of

her self-disgust. Turning back, she looked down into the box again. Smiling, she brushed aside the wood shavings and fitted her hand through the guard.

"Oh," she whispered in appreciation as she lifted the weapon out. She snapped her wrist, grinning at the sound of the blade whipping through air. "Fine. Very, very fine."

She danced forward in pursuit of an imaginary and hapless opponent, then, pretending there was another at her back, pivoted to fend him off, too.

She froze, mid-stride, mid-parry, her silly heart skittering.

He smiled slowly, knowingly, making her knees go soft. "Hello, Simone."

CHAPTER 15

Oh, Sweet Mother-of-Pearl. He'd undone his tie and opened not only the buttons of his suit coat but also the one on his collar and the first two of his shirtfront. Leaning ever so casually against a crate, giving her that lopsided, bone-melting smile of his . . . Throwing herself into his arms occurred to her. So did slowly walking up to him and silently daring him not to reach for her. Pride saved her from acting on either impulse. Unfortunately, it didn't offer up any ideas of what she might do instead.

"I found a set of foils," she said lamely, lifting the weapon up in front of her face as though he might not have noticed her slashing and hacking the air with it a moment earlier.

"So I see."

Damn that smile of his. And the way his eyes twinkled when he was laughing on the inside . . . She really should hate him. Or at the very least be righteously indignant. "Would you care to have a match?"

"No."

So softly. So gently and sincerely. If she didn't find some way to work up an anger, she was going to make a cake of herself. "Are you afraid you'd lose?"

He shook his head. "I'd win. And you'd be angry with me for it."

So confident. "As opposed," she countered, arching a brow, "to my being angry at your presumption of superiority?"

He considered her for a moment and then his smile went full as he eased himself away from the crate. "Tipped or not?"

Oh, thank God he'd relented. If they were whaling away at each other with fencing foils, she wasn't likely to do or say anything remarkably stupid. "Tipped," she replied, reaching into the box to get the second épée. She tossed it to him, adding, "I don't want to hurt you."

He opened his mouth as though he was going to say something in response but closed it and laid the foil on a crate. She waited, watching him remove his suit jacket and roll up his shirtsleeves. If his intent was to be comfortable for their contest, she allowed that he probably was. If his intent was to distract her with a fine display of rippling muscle and sinew . . . Damn, he was good. Really good.

She stared down at the floor and focused on fitting the hilt in her hand, trying to ignore how fast and hard her heart was racing.

"Ready, Simone?"

She stepped back the required distance and set her feet. Lifting her chin and the foil, she met his gaze and formally, crisply, saluted him as a respected opponent. She sliced the air with the blade to end the salute and waited. His eyes twinkling, his smile quirked again, and he lifted the blade before his face with an easygoing, devil-may-care nonchalance that her rational mind said should be insulting. The rest of her, though . . . God Almighty, the man was positively delicious.

His blade sang through the air and in that second she realized that he had reason for his confidence and ease; Tristan Townsend was good. *Very good,* she allowed as he came at her in a low-line lateral attack. Septime? Nice. Aggressive. She parried instinctively, her body and blade moving in perfect coordination to execute a one-two disengagement. In the split second that his advance was checked, she initiated her own, taking the attack to the high line.

"You're very good," he allowed, neatly fending her off and advancing again.

She parried and advanced on him, bringing the line of attack low again. "Yes, I know."

"You're supposed to tell me how good *I* am," he said, grinning, turning her blade aside effortlessly, and stepping into an attack of his own. "How equally matched we are."

Parry-reposite. Advance. Low line. "You're already sufficiently impressed with yourself. A compliment would make you insufferable. As for being equally matched . . ." She parried and lunged. "We already know that."

He turned his body and stepped to the side to avoid her thrust. "That we do," he agreed calmly even as he swept his blade down in a swift, vicious arc.

Her point struck the floor and skidded forward, driven by the commitment of her lunge. The force he'd put into the blow vibrated up her arm and into her already-outraged brain.

"Foul!" she cried even as he stepped closer and increased the pressure on her blade, preventing her from lifting it to continue the match. "You can't—"

"Yes, I can," he murmured, slipping his free arm around her waist and hauling her against the length of his body. "I just did."

It wasn't right. It wasn't within the rules. But the power and heat of his body was radiating into hers, and her will to protest was melting right along with her bones. The look in his eyes . . . Dark and hungry and searching. Heat flared in her core, stealing her breath and tripping her heart. "Let me go, Tristan," she whispered.

"I seem to have a problem with doing that," he murmured, his gaze still caressing hers. "Deep down inside, I don't want to. What do you want, Simone? Deep down inside."

You.

One corner of his mouth lifted in a slow, certain smile. She closed her eyes in the face of it and waited, hoping with all her heart. The brush of his lips over hers was feather soft and she sighed as a tremor of anticipation cascaded slowly and deliciously through her. If he stopped now, if he released her and stepped back . . . She'd fall over. And cry.

His lips brushed over hers again, harder this time, more deliberately. "Tristan," she murmured against them, pressing her body into him and stretching up to keep him from withdrawing. "Tris—"

He moaned quietly in response, pulled her hard to his chest, and closed his mouth over hers. At the very edge of her awareness, for the barest fleeting moment, there was a clang of metal, and then there was only the taste of him, the feel of him. And the heady, driving swirl of heat and absolute need.

His tongue stabbed at the seam of her lips and she opened for him, grateful and greedy. He fed her desire, tasting her deep and boldly, exploring her body with deliberate hands. She was on fire, melting from the inside, pulsing and pouring out. Her knees quaked and she fisted the front of his shirt, frantic to keep herself from slipping away.

He growled low in his throat and cupped her behind, lifting her from her feet. The movement was quick and roughly deliberate, the end abrupt enough to startle her and break their kiss. Gasping for breath, she opened her eyes and met a gaze that was as burning and determined as she felt. Sitting on a crate, cradling his hips between her knees . . . Oh yes. It would work. "God, Tristan," she murmured, sliding her hands down his chest to the waistband of his trousers. "This is insanity."

"Yes, it is," he said, his voice raspy as he caught her hands and stilled them. "We have to stop."

Stop? Stop when satisfaction could be so easily had? "Do you have a French letter?"

He shivered and clenched his teeth. "Not here," he growled.

Doing without flitted through her mind. Begging did, too.

"It's for the best," he said on a ragged breath as he squeezed her hands and stepped back. "This is dangerous beyond excuse, Simone."

"I know," she admitted as desire began to cool and hope ebbed away. Disappointment rose up and sparked anger. "And I don't care."

"But we should. It could end very badly."

So calm. So goddamned rational. And chivalrous and in control of himself. "Yes, it could," she replied, pulling her hands from his and hopping down off the crate. She stood directly in front of him and tilted her chin up to meet his gaze. "Maybe. Perhaps. But I don't want to think about and plan for and anticipate only the bad things that *might* happen, Tristan. I enjoy being with you. And if given a choice in the matter, I'd much prefer to spend the hours of my day thinking about and planning the next time we can be together. I want to anticipate the thrill of making love to you. I don't want to give all that up for no more of a reason than there's a shadow in your life."

He cocked a brow and said, "That was certainly eloquent."

"And heartfelt, Tristan," she countered. "If you don't want to be my lover because I'm not good enough or you've found someone else, that's one thing. Just say so and I'll move on as well. But if you're pushing me away because you're worried Lucinda might come after me . . . I appreciate your protectiveness, but not nearly as much as I appreciate the extreme pleasure to be had in bedding you."

His eyes sparkled and the corners of his mouth twitched. "Extreme?"

She had him and she knew it. All that remained was to make the—

"Simone! Simone, where are you?"

Damn Emmy and her sense of timing! Simone looked off toward the front of the warehouse and called, "Stay where you are and keep talking so that I can work my way toward you!" Emmy did as she'd been bidden and as she rattled on, Simone met Tristan's gaze and said, "It would probably be easier for us if your sister and clerk don't know you're here and that we've spent the time together."

Furrowing his brows, he shook his head. "Don't you think they heard us fencing?"

"Frankly? No. I'll see you again soon, Tristan."

She could see misgiving in his smile, in the depth of his eyes. She stretched up on her toes to press a kiss to his lips, to trail the tip of her tongue along the soft seam. He moaned ever so softly and slipped his hands to her waist.

Grinning, certain of her course, she stepped back, whispered, "Trust me," and then left him standing there looking for all the world as though he'd been dragged through a knothole backward.

And, interestingly enough, she thought as she came out of the box maze, Mr. Gregory looked very much like he'd been pulled through the same hole. A couple of times more than Tristan had.

"Ah, there you are," Emmy said from his side. "We were afraid that you were lost, Simone."

"Lost in appreciation," she replied. "I found a foil in one of the crates. It's a very finely made weapon. How soon do you think Lord Lockwood would be willing to sell it, Mr. Gregory?"

He sighed in what looked to her like relief and then reached into his jacket pocket while he answered, "I'll have to ask him, madam."

Simone fought back a smile as Tristan's clerk considered the mangled mass of glass and wire he held in his hand. "What happened to your glasses?" she asked ever so innocently. "They look as though they've been crushed."

"They do, don't they?" He twisted one of the wires. "It probably happened when I reached into a crate to check the contents."

She nodded as though she believed the story, as though she didn't notice that he was blushing scarlet and that Emmy was grinning from one guilty ear to the other. There was a great deal of wisdom in the old adages. Especially the one about people who lived in glass houses.

Soon. Just exactly what was Simone's idea of soon? he wondered, staring up at his bedroom ceiling. Obviously, he admitted on a heavy sigh, it was different from his notion of soon. If it had been left to him to decide the time of their next tryst, it would have been within minutes of making the promise to have another. And Emmy and her sensibilities be damned.

Hell, if Emmy hadn't come along when she had, he'd have admitted to the French letter in his coat pocket, let Simone unbutton his trousers while he hiked her skirts, and they'd have had their pleasure right there. He smiled into the darkness. Their *extreme* pleasure.

The friction of the sheets against his growing hardness took the amusement from his smile. If she intended to make him wait for days, he decided, reaching down, then he had to do what he must to survive the tension.

The sound was sharp and quick and distracting. It came again, just as before. Sounding almost as though . . . He rolled out of bed and listened. Yes, someone was throwing pebbles against his bedroom window. He walked over, pushed the curtains aside, threw up the sash, and leaned out.

"Hello up there! Did I wake you?"

His heart raced and his grin was so wide it hurt his face. Good God Almighty, she couldn't be that reckless. "Simone?"

"Do you want me to climb up the trellis?" she asked blithely. "Or do you want to come downstairs and let me in?"

"You're insane!" And he was the luckiest fool on earth.

"Trellis or door?"

"Back door!" he called. She laughed, waved, and took off for the rear corner of the town house.

He snatched up his shirt and, shoving his arms into the sleeves, dashed out of his room and down the stairs hoping to hell that all the servants had gone to their part of the house for the night. If one of them happened to stumble into the pantry in search of a midnight glass of milk and a biscuit . . . The sooner he got Simone up to the privacy of his room, the— He grinned. The sooner he could make love to her.

He shoved the bolt free and jerked open the door. Simone stood on the step waiting for him, her hair tumbling over her shoulder and her smile wide and bright.

"Are you surprised?" she asked, slipping quickly across the threshold and past him.

"And delighted," he admitted, closing and locking the door behind her. "You are absolutely fearless, aren't you?"

"I believe in enjoying life with reckless abandon." She stepped into him and wrapped her arms around his neck. "How about you?"

Abandon, yes. But there were limits to his recklessness. He gently took her face in his hands and pressed a quick kiss to her lips. "If I had a letter in my pocket, my darling Simone, I'd gladly enjoy you right here on the spot."

"If you had any pockets, you mean," she corrected, wiggling her hips against his bare thighs. "Where do you keep your letters at this time of the night?"

Bless her for not wasting any time. "Allow me to show you," he offered happily. Bending down, he caught her around the knees and then hoisted her over his shoulder.

She laughed as he carried her out of the pantry. Midway through the dining room, she slid the palms of her hands down over the curves of his linen-covered cheeks and said, "This position has some distinct advantages."

"Yes, it does." And two could play the game. Holding her in place with one arm, he slid his hand under the hem of her skirt and up the back of her leg. His fingertips skimmed over the deadly little knife gartered to her calf and he smiled, glad that she'd had some way to defend herself as she'd come through the night to be with him, and making a mental note to put it on the nightstand before one of them found themselves accidentally stabbed. Having to compress a bloody wound wasn't at all conducive to romance.

She sighed. "That feels too good."

"There's no such thing as too good, darling."

"Well, in that case . . ." She shifted slightly on his shoulder to give him freer access. He was already taking advantage of the invitation and making his way to the inside of her thigh when she lifted the linen of his shirt and boldly stroked her hands over bare skin.

"Simone," he groaned in warning as he kicked his bedroom door closed behind them and headed for the bed.

"What?"

He bent again and rolled her off his shoulder, onto her back in the center of his bed. "Thank you for wearing a dress," he said, turning to pull open the drawer of the nightstand.

"Wouldn't you like for me to take it off?"

"Later," he allowed, removing the French letter from the packet.

"Could I at least raise the hems for you?"

Covering himself, he laughed and answered, "You can do anything for me you damn well please."

"Really?"

He froze as she bounded off the bed and onto her feet. "Where are you going?" God, he wasn't in the mood to chase her around the room. Maybe next time. But not this one. "Simone," he said, trying not to sound desperate. "What—"

"I've been so busy lately," she said, planting her hands on his chest and slowly pushing him back, "what with attending funerals and playing chaperone for your sister and all," she went on as he glanced back over his shoulder, "that I haven't had a chance to ride. I've missed it terribly."

Ah, no chasing at all. He dropped down on the chair and put his hands on her hips. "Have you now?"

"Yes," she replied with a sigh and a little pout. Gathering her skirts in her hands and lifting them, she added, "I think I may have forgotten how to do it. Do you think you could help me remember?"

"I'll do what I can," he promised, grinning and releasing her hips to slide his hands under the skirts and up the outsides of her legs until her hips were once again under his palms. "It may take several attempts, though."

"Practice does make perfect," she offered, her voice a sultry whisper as she stepped across his lap. "And I'm certainly willing if you are."

"Will—" Dear God. Nothing had ever felt this good. There had to be laws against it. He dragged a breath into his lungs, forced his jaw up and his eyes open. To gaze into sparkling ebony eyes. Oh, he couldn't surrender to her control. Not without putting up a fight. Even if he really didn't want to win.

He cleared his throat softly and cocked a brow. "You sit the saddle very well, Madam Rider."

"It does feel good." She rotated her hips ever so slowly. "And it's a lovely fit," she added as he swallowed down a groan of absolute appreciation and agreement.

If he didn't do something to slow this down . . . Releasing her hips, he brought his hands from under her dress and to the buttons on her bodice. "Proper attire is an important part of riding, you know."

"Oh?"

"And you are entirely too attired for it," he went on, efficiently working the buttons open. "I'm assuming, of course, that you want to fully enjoy your gallop."

"Oh, I do."

Breathy. And he could feel the little tremors rocking

through her. Willing his mind apart from sensation, he pushed the sides of her bodice aside and skimmed the palms of his hands lightly over the dark, hard peaks of her breasts. "You are so incredibly beautiful."

He watched her eyes drift closed and her breathing catch. He palmed over her breasts again, slower, harder.

"Tristan."

"What?" he whispered back.

"The reins are slipping."

"I know. I can feel you quivering." He caught a swollen peak between his thumb and forefinger and gently rolled. "You're so close to bolting. So . . ." He leaned forward and dragged his tongue over the other peak. "Very . . ."

Her fingers threaded through his hair and he obeyed the request, drawing her fully into his mouth and suckling. She whimpered and bucked and drove him over the edge and into the deep bliss of utter, soul-deep satisfaction.

*T*ristan opened his eyes and grinned. How the hell they'd gotten on the bed . . . He decided that it really didn't matter and rolled onto his side.

"That was the best ride I've ever had," Simone said dreamily, reaching up to brush the back of her hand along his jaw. "I'm going to sell all my horses, move you into the stable, and go riding three or four times a day."

"Don't you think that might raise a few eyebrows?"

"I hadn't thought of that," she admitted, her eyes sparkling and her smile widening. "I suppose I won't have much choice but to ride five or six times a day. I wouldn't want anyone to think you'd come up lame."

"Thanks."

"You're welcome."

Was there any more perfect lover in the world? he wondered, gazing down at her. Beautiful and spirited. And so honest in her wanting, so unstinted in her giving. If he lived to be a hundred, he was never going to find another woman like her. Ever.

"You're looking at me as though I might evaporate at any moment."

"I'm committing you to memory," he admitted before he realized how close he was to making a declaration he might mean at the moment but would likely regret at sunrise. He smiled and added an artful evasion. "So that I can draw your portrait later."

"With my dress unbuttoned."

It wasn't the body, the overt sexuality, that made Simone a work of art. "And the wanton happiness shimmering in your eyes. The wicked satisfaction radiating in your smile."

"Will you let me see it when it's done?"

"If you want."

She trailed the tip of her finger down the center of his chest. "Do you draw portraits of all your lovers?" she asked, not meeting his gaze.

"Just the ones I never want to forget."

"Would it be too prying to ask how many are in your portfolio?"

"I don't have a portfolio. But, if you'd like, I'll buy one to keep yours in. Although I'd much rather frame it and hang it on the wall."

Her gaze snapped up and she leaned back, putting space between them. "You wouldn't."

Even as he started to assure her that he was only teasing, she looked around his darkened room. Why her concern stabbed at his heart . . . "There aren't any other pictures, Simone."

"Please don't hang the one of me out where anyone might see it."

"Don't worry. I'll keep it a very private picture."

"Thank you," she murmured, the tension easing out of her body. She smiled up at him and trailed her finger over his lips. "Have you sufficiently memorized this moment?"

"Why?"

She trailed her finger down over his chin, down his throat, over his chest. "I was thinking," she drawled, following the thin line of hair lower, "that I might provide you with another inspiration or two before I have to go home."

"An artist without inspiration is a very sad thing," he allowed, hardening at her touch. "Might I help you out of that dress?"

$\mathcal{I}$f she could have thought of an excuse to stay, she'd have used it. There was something about walking away that just felt so terribly final. Even though it wasn't, of course. Tristan hadn't wanted to let her slide out of his arms and had made her promise she'd come back to him again before he'd been willing to let her go. And yet . . . She shook her head, called herself silly, and took her knife off the night table where Tristan had tossed it earlier.

She was tying it around her calf when he rolled off the other side of the bed. She looked over her shoulder just as he pulled on his shirt. "Why are you getting dressed?"

"So that I can see you home," he answered, picking his trousers up off the floor. "I'd prefer not to wander the streets naked."

She stood and picked up her dress, saying, "I managed to get here safely without an escort, didn't I?"

"Part of me sincerely hopes so. The other part is incredibly thankful nothing happened to you along the way."

Stepping into her dress, she drew it up over her hips. "Tristan," she began, putting her arms into the sleeves, "I appreciate the thought and the concern, but I'm perfectly capable of taking care of myself in the streets. I may be the daughter of a duke now, but I haven't forgotten how to scrap and scurry."

He dropped down on the chair and rammed his foot into a boot. "You shouldn't have to face the choice at all."

"All right, Lord Gallant, I'll be blunt about it," she countered, buttoning up. "If I go by myself and happen to meet Haywood at the gate, I can spin any story for him that I want. If you're with me, our goose is cooked. There won't be a second forgiveness."

He pulled on the other boot, saying, "It's not Haywood or your brother-in-law that concerns me."

"Lucinda."

He stood and smiled thinly. "You win the prize, darling."

Simone snorted and continued to work her way up the line of buttons. "She's too busy worrying about Miss Yoo-hoo to even think about me."

"Miss Yoo-hoo?"

"Sarah Sheraton," she clarified, shoving her feet into her mules.

"Oh," he drawled, coming across the carpet toward her. "Did I see a flash of green in those ebony eyes of yours, darling?"

Her heart was pounding so ridiculously fast. She

smoothed the front of her skirt and managed to sound breezily unconcerned as she answered, "Let's change the subject."

"Let's not." He tipped her chin up until her gaze met his. "In the first place, I have no feelings for her at all. You have no reason to be jealous of her. In the second, Noland has removed her from London and tucked her well out of harm's way. Where, precisely, I don't know and don't want to know."

She didn't want him to think that she cared one way or the other, but she had to know. "And her claims about a baby?"

He shrugged ever so slightly. "Apparently she is expecting. She told us that it's the child of a married man. Her fiancé broke off the engagement when he discovered the affair, and her family disowned her when they learned of the pregnancy."

"You don't feel sorry for her?"

"No, Simone, I don't," he said softly, gently. "She made her choices and righting the disaster isn't my responsibility. Keeping her safe from Lucinda . . . Yes, I'll own that one. But nothing else."

The thought that he might someday talk to another woman about her in the same way . . . Her heart aching, she turned away, saying, "I promise that I'll never be a burden for you to bear."

"That's not—"

"Which is why I'll get myself home without an escort," she went on, heading for his bedroom door.

"We're not going to argue about this."

She knew what he meant, but she pretended otherwise

on the slim hope that bluff might work. "I'm so glad you're willing to be reasonable," she replied, turning the doorknob. "Good night, Tristan. Sweet dreams."

She managed to get the door open all of a few millimeters before his hand landed flat on the inside edge and slammed it closed. So much for bluff. She looked up at him and arched a brow. "What are you doing? I have to go or I'll be caught."

"Darling, you either accept my company all the way to your brother-in-law's or don't leave here. It's as simple as that."

"You're being imperial."

He shrugged and nodded. "You might try being help-less and dependent for a little while. Just to humor me." He grinned and leaned close to whisper, "And to keep that portrait of you hidden away."

"Oh, that's low, Tristan."

"Better low than losing you."

"I ever see that picture anywhere but this bedroom, Tristan Townsend, you're a dead man."

Laughing, he opened the door. And then stayed her, taking one more long, deep kiss before they stepped out into the real world of another day.

CHAPTER 16

Simone closed the carriage door behind herself and leaned in the window. "Enjoy the lecture, Fiona. And thank you for the ride."

"If it's raining later, I'll stop by and give you a ride home." Her green eyes twinkled. "Perhaps you might even introduce me to Lord Lockwood."

Simone laughed. "As I've said repeatedly, I don't think he's going to be here today."

"Oh, who knows? He could be every bit as chipper as you are this morning."

Grinning, shaking her head at her sister's persistence,

Simone stepped back, waved good-bye, and turned toward the house. Yes, she was chipper, she had to admit as she skipped up the steps and knocked on the door. A mystery, since she couldn't have had more than a few hours of sleep at best last night. Thank goodness the feeling of wanting to cry had finally passed. It had taken long enough, though. The invitation from Emmy to call had apparently been just what she needed.

"Good morning, Lady Simone," the butler said, letting her into Lady Lockwood's home.

"Good morning, Baston. I'll await Lady Emmaline's whim in the parlor as usual."

"Very good, madam," he said with a short bow. "I'll inform her of your arrival."

And as usual, Simone stopped just across the parlor threshold to survey the room. The white and gilt chairs had disappeared first. A table and cut-crystal lamp in the corner had been the next to go. This morning the huge sideboard and all the folderol that had sat atop it were gone.

Simone cocked a brow and shook her head. Not that she'd ever be accused of being a domestic fashion maven, but even she knew that the purging had gone too far. The removal of the smaller pieces had made the space feel bigger and considerably less cluttered. All in all, a positive change. But without the sideboard, with the one wall absolutely bare, the whole room felt as if it might at any moment tilt in the direction of the remaining furniture.

It was silly and she knew it, but she wandered over to stand where the sideboard had been so that when the floor shifted, she'd be the last of the things to slide out into the foyer. Better to land atop the settee than under it.

Her brow inching higher, she surveyed the room from the new vantage point. It wasn't just the sideboard and little carvings and decanters from it that were gone. There had been a pair of large ornately carved, gold-leafed-framed pictures hanging on the walls on either side of the fireplace. They were gone this morning, where they'd hung marked by large rectangles of considerably whiter plaster.

Two possible explanations for the changes presented themselves. The first was that Lady Lockwood was redecorating the house on a massive scale. The second was that the allowance Tristan gave her wasn't sufficient to cover her taste in fine jewelry and she was selling off the furniture to pay for her baubles.

"Good morning, Simone. I'm sorry to keep you waiting so long."

She shrugged, thinking that it hadn't been long at all. "Emmy, where is all the furniture going?"

Emmaline looked around the room and then shook her head. "I have no idea. It's here when I leave the house, and when I come back, it's gone. Where Mother's moving it to I haven't the foggiest notion. There are parts of this house I haven't seen in years. I hope you don't mind posing for me this morning."

"What?" Simone teased. "You don't want to check the warehouse inventory again?"

Her smile was soft and not the least bit innocent. "Absence makes the heart grow fonder. At least that's what they say."

"I don't know, Emmy," she countered, chuckling. "There's another funeral tomorrow and one the day after that. They'll take all day. Are you sure you should be that absent from Mr. Gregory's mind? What if he has a short memory?"

Emmy grinned. "Oh, he's not likely to forget me for a very long time."

"Or at least until he has his glasses repaired."

Her friend laughed. "I've made a note to be more careful about that in the future." Motioning toward the parlor door, she added, "Shall we? I've had coffee and pastries sent back to the conservatory."

Together they made their way to the rear of the house, Emmy chattering away about painting and Simone silently noting the changes along the way. There was a lot of furniture missing. Either Lady Lockwood was furnishing a second house or she'd bought every damn jewel in London.

"I don't think Tristan will be joining us for any more painting sessions. I hope you're not too disappointed," Emmy said as they entered the greenhouse.

The hair on the back of her neck prickling, Simone dodged the personal aspects of the comment by replying, "I imagine that he's very busy with his business since the *Maggie* came into port. Painting couldn't be anywhere near the top of his list of daily priorities."

"Well, it might be partly that," Emmy allowed, heading for the tea cart beside her easel. "Mostly, I think, it's a matter of him not wanting to risk having an encounter with Mother."

Yes, considering how unpleasant the one encounter between them that Simone had witnessed had been . . .

Dear God, Tristan had been spot-on about Emmy's artistic abilities. She did look like a monkey on a mangled cushion. Actually, though, now that she looked closer, the cushion wasn't nearly as mangled as the monkey was. If Emmy insisted on gifting Drayton and Caroline with her masterpiece, *she'd* have to insist on a family gathering around the burn barrel.

"Did you know that that Sarah person came to see Mother the other morning? The day of Lord Sandifer's funeral."

Sarah? Caught by surprise, Simone slowly unbuttoned her pelisse and considered what she knew and what she could admit to knowing. Given that Tristan had said that he was trying to shelter his sister from as much of the ugliness as he could, she was very much obliged to do the same.

"She came to tell Mother that she's carrying Tristan's child."

"Really," Simone offered noncommittally, draping the pelisse over the back of the chair. She joined Emmy at the serving cart, casually asking, "And does your mother believe the story?"

"Mother always believes the worst when it comes to Tristan."

"Why? Hasn't he been kind to her since his return from America?"

"If I didn't exist, he wouldn't have given her so much as a bent farthing. He and Mother loathe each other."

Yes, she'd gathered that quite easily. But commenting on it was another matter entirely. Choosing her words carefully, she ventured, "They were made related by what must have been difficult circumstances for both of them. I'm sure they both had resentments that—"

"They didn't openly hate each other until Mother tried to seduce Tristan and he told Papa about it."

"Oh." God, what else was there to say? It had to have been a spectacularly ugly moment, an event well beyond the pale even by Lunatic Lockwood standards.

"Papa and Tristan had a horrific row over it and Tristan left for America. Mother's never forgiven him for turning her down and he's never forgiven her for driving him into exile."

"I have no idea what to say," Simone confessed. "It's all so awful, Emmy."

"It was. Papa accused Mother of all sorts of ugly things. He even said that I wasn't really his child."

"Oh, Emmy. How painful that must have been."

Emmy shrugged and handed her a cup of coffee. "He didn't live with us, so I didn't have to face him. That was good. But he cut our allowance to almost nothing, and that was terribly difficult. Every time we sat down to a meal of bread and butter, Mother would damn Tristan to hell and back for what he'd done to us."

"But it wasn't Tristan's fault," Simone protested.

"That's not the way Mother sees it," Emmy said with a dry, brittle laugh. She shuddered and then found a smile that struck Simone as being amazingly bright under the circumstances.

"Well, enough of depressing conversation," her friend said cheerily. "Would you care for a strawberry or an apricot pastry?"

"Strawberry, I suppose," Simone answered, her mind still reeling from all that Emmy had told her. A childhood spent in the streets and in brothels had been lean and hungry and at times mean, but at least it had been honest and consistent. To have been a child growing up in a fine house with all the genteel trappings of the peerage and have all of it be a cruel lie . . . It really was a wonder that Emmy could smile at all. She was a much stronger person than anyone would have guessed.

"Simone?"

She blinked and focused on her friend. "I'm sorry. I was lost in thought."

"I could tell," Emmy said softly. "Sad thoughts. Please don't let it all trouble you. Mother can insist all she likes, but Tristan is going to do as Tristan pleases. If he doesn't want to marry that Sarah woman, he won't. Scandal means nothing to Tristan."

She nodded, remembering what he'd told her about Sarah's circumstances and the solution he and Noland had found. Should she tell Emmy about it? Or would Tristan prefer that his sister be sheltered from the particulars of that situation, too? She sipped her coffee while trying to decide.

"Why don't you have a seat on the chaise, Simone? I'm afraid it's going to cloud over soon. We shouldn't waste good light while we have it."

Well, since Emmy didn't seem to expect her to comment on the matter of Sarah and Tristan . . . Carrying her cup and saucer and strawberry pastry to the chaise, Simone pondered the reason she didn't feel as relieved as she would have expected. There wasn't going to be a scandal where Sarah was concerned. Nor, thanks to Noland, was Sarah in any danger from Lucinda. Lucinda who had existed on the edge of poverty until she'd bought revenge in the form of insurance policies.

And who, according to Emmaline, still to this day blamed Tristan for her having had to resort to such cold-blooded ruthlessness. No wonder Tristan had said Lucinda would want to make his death a personal thing. It would have been nice if he'd considered it necessary to explain the reason, though. If he had, she wouldn't have been caught absolutely flat-footed this morning.

God, what a bizarre family Tristan came from. In comparison, hers seemed positively, boringly normal. No wonder he considered a ship his home and the crews his family. Lord knew they were more than he'd ever had outside of them. Running off to America had probably been the best thing he could have ever done for himself.

Why he'd bothered to come back, though . . . If she'd been in his shoes, she wouldn't have. She'd have left Lucinda to squander her ill-gotten fortune on furniture and jewelry and end up right back in poverty. And she certainly wouldn't have trotted home and made it easier for the woman to kill her for even more money.

Of course, factoring Emmy into the situation did make a difference. A considerable one. Emmy, completely innocent of any wrongdoing, had endured the hard years in Tristan's absence. And in the larger picture of her mother's scheming, Emmy stood a very good chance of ending up just as dead as the males of her family. If Tristan had returned for any logical reason at all, it had to have been to protect his sister.

Yes, Tristan was a very good man. Even if their affair eventually faded and they drifted away from each other, she'd at least have a wonderful standard against which to measure all the men who might ask for her consideration. Simone sighed. They were all going to fall so very, very short.

If only it were a perfect world. Their affair would never end. Tristan would realize that he loved her and get down on one knee, gaze adoringly up at her, pledge his undying devotion, and then beg her to marry him. They'd marry, have a houseful of babies, and be forever and always happy.

She chuckled and shook her head to dispel the ridiculous image. There was no such thing as perfect. No forever and always happy. People snored, passed gas, scratched, and burped. Well, ladies burped. Men belched. Rather proudly. Babies puked. And did all sorts of other, equally foul things.

God, she thought, setting her cup aside. *I must be more tired than I thought if all that sounds good. I wonder if Emmy would notice if I dozed off for a little while and collected my wits.*

*T*ristan shook the merchant's hand, thanked him again for the hefty purchase, and then watched him walk out the door. As it closed, Tristan turned to his clerk. "When you deposit that money into the account, make sure to hold enough out to have your glasses repaired."

Gregory slipped the check inside his lap desk, saying only, "Yes, sir."

"How did they get so badly bent? Were you in a brawl?"

He set aside his desk and removed the spectacles from his face. Making an attempt to straighten the wire earpieces, he replied, "I forgot I had them in my coat pocket yesterday when I leaned into a crate to check the contents against the manifest."

Well, as stories went, it was a good one. Not believable, but good. "So why are you blushing?"

"I'm not blushing, sir."

"Trust me, Gregory," he pressed, grinning. "I'm not

blind. And you're blushing beet red. What's the real story of how your glasses ended up bent double and twisted sideways?"

Gregory pulled at his collar and struggled to clear his throat. Looking out the office window, he finally managed to say, "They were in my pocket when I was caught unaware by a young lady."

Ah, closer to the truth, but not quite there yet. "Any young lady I might happen to know?"

Gregory groaned, "Oh, God, sir."

"Would it happen to have been my sister who assaulted you?"

"I'm sure it was entirely my fault," the man said on a single rush of air. "I must have done something to lead her to believe that I would be interested in—"

"Stop," Tristan said quietly, interrupting the torrent of guilt. "I've known you longer than I've known my sister. You couldn't invite a ravaging if you had written instructions to follow."

"Under different circumstances, I'd be insulted."

"Yes, well," Tristan said, chuckling. "Even under other circumstances, it'd still be the truth. You're every Society mother's dream come true. Handsome, well-spoken, respectable, and without a single predatory bone in your body."

"I beg to differ, sir. When properly inspired—"

The look of horror on the man's face . . . It took every bit of self-control Tristan possessed not to laugh. "Oh, the cat's out of the bag, Gregory. You might as well finish the thought."

"I'll marry her, sir," he said bravely. "It's the only decent thing to do."

Tristan sucked his lower lip into his mouth and caught it between his teeth. When he had his amusement under control, he cleared his throat and asked, "Were you an altar boy?"

"I'm a Methodist. We don't have altar boys. Just candlelighters."

"You were a candlelighter, weren't you?"

Gregory straightened his spine and squared his shoulders. "Sir, you're making this exceedingly difficult. I'm trying very hard to be honorable."

"And I appreciate the effort, Gregory," he assured him. "But unless you've fallen madly in love with Emmaline, I don't think marrying her is a particularly wise course of action."

"Why ever not? Your sister has been kissed!"

"Kissed?" he repeated, fighting back the bubble of laughter. "That's all? Just kissed?"

"Rather soundly!"

If he'd had to marry for a kiss, he'd have been at the altar at the ripe old age of twelve. "For godsakes, Gregory, a kiss does not a compromise make. Forget it happened. I'll speak with Em and make sure she understands that she needs to behave herself in the future."

"I feel just terrible, sir."

"I can tell. And it's a groundless—"

The bell over the door jangled and Tristan turned to see Noland coming across the threshold. All thoughts of his sister fled at the sight of the bandage wrapping his friend's head, the black eye, the mashed nose.

"Clearly you're not all right," Tristan said, looking him up and down for further damage. There wasn't much relief at seeing nothing more. "What happened?"

"We were waylaid on the post road. Just south of London."

"Sit down before you fall down," Tristan commanded, picking up an office chair and putting it in Noland's path. "When? And what happened to Sarah?"

"Very early this morning," he supplied, gingerly lowering himself to the seat. "We left London late yesterday afternoon and stayed overnight at an inn along the way. We'd gone only five miles or so this morning when the coach was attacked. My driver tried to outrun them, with disastrous consequences. The carriage overturned."

"Jesus."

"I was revived some time later by Good Samaritans who had found me sprawled in the ditch. My driver was some distance back along the road, an arm and a leg badly broken, but thankfully still alive. I couldn't find Miss Sheraton anywhere."

"Perhaps she wandered off in search of help," Gregory posed.

Tristan waited, knowing the answer wasn't going to be as simple or as hopeful.

"All of her baggage was gone," Noland supplied, confirming his worst expectations. "It was as though she had never been there at all. I made inquiries all along the way back to London. No one has seen her."

"I'll bet Lucinda has," Tristan declared, taking his coat off the wall peg. He was shoving his arms into the sleeves when Noland struggled to his feet. "Stay right there," Tristan ordered. "I'll do this on my own."

"No, you won't," Noland countered, wobbling a bit before finding his balance. "No matter what happens, you're best served by the presence of a witness."

"To keep me from killing her?"

"If it comes to that. . . . To swear that it was in self-defense."

"Sir, may I come along? If nothing else, I could catch Lord Noland when he falls over."

"An excellent idea, Gregory," he allowed, taking Noland by the arm. "Lock up and let's go."

The monkey was in the conservatory. And he was wearing boots. And limping. Poor mangled monkey.

Simone laughed and forced her eyes open. With the fuzzy vision of just waking, she could vaguely see Emmy peering around the edge of the canvas at her. "I'm afraid I fell asleep," she explained, stretching her shoulders. "And had a very odd dream. There was a limping monkey wearing boots."

"Where?"

"Here, in the conservatory."

Emmy stepped behind her painting, saying, "You have very strange dreams."

Not really, she silently countered. The past had a way of sneaking back on her while she slept. The more tired she was, the more vivid the dreams. Her mother was sometimes in them. Not very often, though. And as the years went by, her face became less and less distinct.

Still, no matter what was in her dreams and who traipsed through them, she usually knew where they'd come from and what had triggered their appearance. A limping monkey made perfect sense. All right, the fact that he was wearing boots didn't. Not at the moment anyway. It could be that her shoes were laced too tight. She wiggled her toes. Not altogether successfully. Ah, explanation found.

"Emmy," she said, pushing herself to her feet. "I have to walk about for a few minutes or my toes will fall off."

"If you must," Emmy said from behind her work. "But please don't take overly long. I'm at a critical point and need to have you sitting very still so that I get it right."

Simone smiled and shook her head as she walked toward the far wall. She could be dead-for-a-week still and it wouldn't make the slightest bit of difference; Emmy was the worst painter in the world. It would be a miracle if the portrait of her didn't have two heads and three hands.

Gravel? Yes. Shifting under boots. *It couldn't really be a monkey,* she silently chided, turning toward the back of the conservatory.

Her heart jolted up into her throat and fear shot through her veins. In the next heartbeat time staggered and then oddly stretched to a slow eternity of observation and horrible realization. No, not monkeys. Three men. Rough men who came from the darkest edges of the world she had once lived in. Men who would do anything for a pound.

She heard herself gasp. She called herself a ninny for being surprised and turned to run, screaming for Emmy to do the same. But Emmy didn't; she looked around the edge of the picture and just stood there, watching, her eyes wide and her mouth hanging open.

Simone moved toward her friend, her feet and legs frighteningly leaden, her mind methodically clicking through one crystalline thought after another. This was Lucinda's doing. She'd hired them. To kill her. To kill Emmy. God, she had to get out, get away. She had to warn Tristan.

The men were closing the distance. There wasn't much time. If she and Emmy could make the doorway and scream . . . If they could hold the door closed just long enough for her to get her knife . . .

Emmy stepped out from behind the painting, her eyes still wide, her jaw still hanging slack.

"Run!"

Emmy started and blinked and then looked around as though she didn't have the slightest idea of which way to go. Of all the times for her to revert back to the clueless, timid debutante . . .

"The door to the house!"

Emmy started to turn that way and then there was nothing but a blur in a world wheeling out of control. The impact came from behind, hard and ruthless and instantly driving Simone off her feet. The floor was there in a second, unyielding and rough, a force every bit as cruel as the weight that drove her down into it. Her breath caught, her lungs paralyzed, time crawled on. Her mind numbed, she dully noted the flash of Emmy's skirt hems.

God, no! Emmy was turning back, coming to help her. Simone tried to gather the breath to scream, to tell her not to, and was soundly crushed back into the floor to prevent it. One man went past her, after Emmy. The third man stopped beside her and the brutish beast who held her. Emmy squeaked.

Fight or die. Do you want to die?

Simone gasped, greedily consuming air, forcing her mind and body to work. She swore and thrashed against the steel bands encircling her upper body, kicking her feet and trying desperately to twist away. The arms around her tightened and a voice, raw and foul, rasped a warning in her ear. She ignored it and struggled harder, pouring all her strength and determination into the struggle to escape.

A second voice scraped across her awareness, a voice commanding that she stop fighting, that she breathe. Even as the command was issued, a hand twisted in her hair and yanked her head back. As she cried out in pain and anger, a wet rag was pressed over her face.

She tried to turn her face away, tried desperately to find air that didn't come through the cloth. She couldn't give up, couldn't die. She had to warn Tristan.

The rag tasted sweet and smelled like fruit. Almost like perfume, but not. Better, actually, in a way. She wasn't going to suffocate; she could breathe easily enough, but still . . . Damn, the arms around her were pulling her skin, making it burn. And the gravel of the floor had sharp points that pressed into her all along her body. The rock under her left hip was huge. And under her left knee, too. And the vicious laces of her shoes: she could feel every crisscross they made across her instep. They were cutting her, hurting just as much as the arms around her and the gravel under her.

Emmy wasn't exactly squeaking anymore. But Simone could hear the frantic pitch in her voice. She was begging them not to hurt her, to take the rag off her face and let her breathe. What a kind and true friend Emmy was. She had . . . to . . . to . . .

Escape. Fight. Emmy needed her. Tristan was going to die if she couldn't reach him. Warn him. Tristan. He didn't know that she . . . loved . . .

Sweet. But not too sweet. It smelled like a rosy, juicy pink.

CHAPTER 17

Tristan clenched and unclenched his teeth as Noland went on and on with an excruciatingly detailed account of his conversations with Sarah. Leaving Gregory to play the interested listener, Tristan glared at the traffic out the carriage window and silently railed at himself.

He should have had this confrontation with Lucinda the day he'd returned to England. He should have been straightforward and brutally thorough, should have demanded that she confess her crimes and surrender herself to the Crown for punishment. And when she refused to do that, he should have killed her. Right then. Right there. He should have just put a bullet through her black heart and been done with it.

But no. He'd opted for conducting himself within the requirements of civility and the expectations of the law. He'd taken the high and subtle road thinking that he could outmaneuver her and let the wheels of justice turn to a perfectly orchestrated, well-witnessed end. But the wheels were rusty and too slow moving to take into account the unexpected developments of life that went on outside its control.

Life such as meeting Simone. Beautiful, passionate, wickedly daring Simone. In hindsight he knew that he should have waited to pursue her, that he'd exhibited all the judgment of a sixteen-year-old in letting his desires control his decisions. Despite all his planning, all his rationalizations, he'd placed Simone in Lucinda's awareness and put her at risk.

And then Sarah had shown up out of the absolute blue. Sarah with her hopes and troubles and complete, utter ignorance about the dangerous pot she was stirring. And stir she had, putting herself into even greater danger than he'd put Simone. And, as it had turned out this morning, more imminent danger.

It was time, he silently declared as the carriage slowed and he reached for the door handle. Time for this to end. The wheels of formal justice be damned. Noland could witness and report whatever he liked. Gregory could do the same. But in the end all that mattered was that Lucinda would no longer be able to plot and scheme and kill. Between now and that end. . . .

Sarah was likely still alive. If the objective had been to kill her, it would have been done alongside the road and made to look like the consequence of the unfortunate accident. But that she and all of her belongings had been spirited away told him that Lucinda had a larger, more complicated end in mind. And before he wrung her vicious neck, she was going to tell him what it was and where Sarah had been taken.

The carriage stopped and Tristan threw open the door. Vaulting out in front of Lucinda's town house, he paused to wait for the other two men to join him on the walk. "Just so you know," he told them. "One way or the other, this is going to end in the next few minutes. Before Lucinda harms one more innocent."

Gregory frowned in confusion. Noland nodded and pulled his waistcoat down over his paunch, saying, "Seems like the only thing to do, to me. We're right behind you, Lockwood. Lead on."

He didn't bother to knock; he simply climbed the front steps with Noland and Gregory in tow, opened the front door, and walked in.

Baston stopped dead in his tracks beside the foyer reception table. "Lord Lockwood! I apologize most profusely for not hearing your summons to the door."

Tristan stopped only because he needed information from the man. Allowing a crisp nod in acknowledgment, he said, "It's not a problem, Baston," and then went straight to the reason for his presence. "Where is my stepmother?"

The butler was clearly startled by the lack of expected protocol. It took him a few seconds to recover. Finally, though, he replied, "At her sister's, Your Lordship."

If he hadn't been so angry, he'd have staggered back at the news. "What?"

Baston nodded. "Her Ladyship received a message from her sister shortly after breakfast this morning, packed a trunk, and departed saying she would be gone only a day. Two at the most."

"Her sister," Tristan repeated dumbly, wracking the closets of his memory, searching for information.

"Yes, Your Lordship. Apparently she has suffered a health decline and the family has been summoned to her bedside."

At the wedding to his father there had been three women—no, four—who Lucinda had said were her sisters. Which was utterly believable now that he looked back at the occasion with older eyes. There was a family resemblance in their faces, in their general bearing. But he remembered them as being considerably warmer and kinder than Lucinda had ever been.

They'd been older, too. It wasn't beyond belief that one of them was ill, perhaps dying. They would be of the age for that by now. But the timing of it . . . Lucinda hadn't left the house in almost a year, and the very day that Sarah was kidnapped she'd packed a bag and dashed out? An incredible, completely innocent coincidence was possible but not bloody likely.

"Did she say which sister?" Tristan asked the butler.

"No, Lord Lockwood. I'm afraid she didn't."

"Did she say where this sister lived?"

"No, sir. She was in a great hurry. I'm sorry. Is there a problem with which I might be of some assistance?"

"Did she happen to leave the note behind?" Noland asked.

Tristan frowned. Damned if he hadn't forgotten that he and the butler weren't alone.

"I'm not aware that she did, sir," the servant supplied. "But then, I have had no reason to enter her rooms since her departure."

"How long ago was that?" Tristan asked. "And did she go by her own carriage?" Maybe, if they were really lucky, they could dash out the door and see the carriage, could follow it, catch it, and extract both Lucinda and the answers they needed.

Baston calmly removed his pocket watch and flicked up the cover. "Her Ladyship left two hours and thirty-seven minutes ago, sir," he said, crushing Tristan's hopeful scenario. Snapping the timepiece closed and putting it back in his pocket, the butler added, "Which, as a point of additional information, was twenty minutes after Lady Simone arrived. And yes, sir, she did take her own carriage."

Simone? His heart jolted and his pulse raced. "Is Lady Simone still here?"

"Yes, Your Lordship. She and Lady Emmaline are in the conservatory. I believe the plan was for her to pose while Lady Emmaline continued work on the portrait."

If there was indeed a benevolent God . . . "Take Lord Noland and Mr. Gregory upstairs," he instructed the butler, "and help them search Lucinda's rooms for any evidence of where she might have gone. I'll check on Em and Lady Simone and then join you upstairs."

Tristan didn't wait to see what any of them thought of the assignments but strode off toward the rear of the house, his mind clicking through what he needed to do next. It was anyone's guess what Lucinda's plan entailed, but he'd rather err on the side of being too cautious than that of being too cavalier about his ability to find her before she could wreak further havoc. He'd already allowed her far more time and opportunity than he should have.

Of first importance, then, was to be sure that Simone and Emmaline were tucked away someplace where Lucinda couldn't get to them. And the quickest, surest course to that end was to take them to the Duke of Ryland's residence, explain the circumstances, and leave them in his care. Haywood would have Tristan's hide when it was all over, but he couldn't help but think he deserved to have a chunk removed for a thorough tanning.

Once Simone and Em were safe . . . How the hell was he going to track down Lucinda? She could be damn near anywhere. Especially with a two-and-a-half-hour head start. While he didn't believe the story of rushing to the bedside of the ailing sister for a single second, it was, at the moment, the only thread he had to follow. Maybe Emmaline knew where her aunts lived and could point him in their directions.

So that he could waste time on what was in all likelihood going to turn out to be nothing more than a wild-goose chase, he decided, yanking open the conservatory door. He was a good four steps into the greenhouse before his brain processed what his eyes were seeing. He froze, his heart hammering wildly in his chest.

"Jesus. No. Please, no."

The plea did nothing to alter the reality before him. The easel was overturned, the paint pots and brushes scattered around it, the portrait lying facedown, a hole punched through the center of the canvas. Simone's jacket lay, neatly folded, over the back of one of the chairs.

He swayed on his feet, his mind reeling and his throat

tightening with tears. He was too late. He'd blundered. He'd dawdled. He hadn't anticipated quickly enough. Emmaline. And Simone. God, his Simone. Gone. Taken just as Sarah had been. If anything happened . . .

Deep inside him, a dam suddenly gave way. Anger, white and molten, shot through his veins, turning his confusion and self-pity to ash and crystallizing his thoughts. Emmaline would have squeaked and stood by her easel petrified with fear and let herself be taken captive. But not Simone. He knew her, knew that it was in the battle with Simone that the easel had been overturned and the painting destroyed.

Two long strides took him to the jumble of paint pots. Squatting down in their midst, he snatched up the tin of turpentine and turned it upside down. A thin stream of spirits poured out to spatter on the rocks at his feet. Not long. It hadn't been overturned that long or it all would have evaporated. But how long? He pressed a fingertip into a puddle of raw sienna. The surface hazed for only a second and then gave way, pooling up around his nail. It had all been spilled no more than an hour ago. Maybe no more than thirty minutes. But even if it was the latter, it was too long ago for an effective pursuit; they were well gone.

Fighting off the anger and the frustration, Tristan rose and stepped out of the circle of debris. He moved forward, his gaze sweeping the furniture, the potted plants. Not one cushion or pillow was out of place. Not a single pot had been shoved askew, much less overturned. There wasn't a damn leaf broken or even twisted the wrong way. The gravel, though . . . There were small patches that had been turned and tossed slightly back. Given the pattern and length between them . . . Clearly a man had run along the path, toward the easel. Had Simone been standing beside Em when they'd been surprised?

Surprised . . . How the hell had that happened? Obviously whoever had taken them hadn't come in through the house or the servants would have seen them. Which meant they'd had to enter through the rear door of the greenhouse and come up on . . . It didn't make sense. Simone would have heard them enter, would have heard them moving.

Tristan strode along the gravel path that meandered through the foliage toward the rear of the structure. The door was in sight, closed and secure, when a slight glint off the path to the left caught his attention. He stopped and turned and bent to push aside the green and white leaves of some vining plant. Under them was a small glass bottle of the sort that apothecaries used for dispensing liquid medicines. He retrieved it, noting that only a drop or two of something clear remained to roll around the bottom edge. His heart sinking and his stomach twisting with certainty, he pulled the cork, lifted the opening to his nose, and cautiously sniffed.

"Lockwood!"

"I'm here, Noland," he called back, wheeling about and moving along the path toward the front of the greenhouse, the bottle clutched tightly in his hand.

"We didn't find anything in Lady Lockwood's rooms," his friend said the instant he rounded the bend in the path and came into sight. "Which is damn disappointing considering the other obvious concerns of the moment."

The man had always had a gift for understatement. The beauty of it was lost on Tristan's clerk, however. The man stood beside Noland, his gaze riveted to the scattered painting supplies, his skin growing more pallid by the second. "Gregory!"

As the young man lifted his gaze, Tristan tossed the bottle at him, saying, "Catch!"

"Chloroform?" Noland asked as it tumbled through the air.

"Yes."

"Let's hope that the bastard who used it on them knew what he was doing," his friend offered as something else caught Tristan's eye. "Otherwise . . ."

"Otherwise, what?" Gregory asked.

"Otherwise Em and Simone could have been easily overdosed," Tristan explained, moving toward the sidewall and the large, scuffed patch of gravel halfway between it and the main path.

"Overdosed! Do you mean they could be dead?"

"Only by accident," Noland supplied as Tristan studied the gravel. "But since I doubt very much that Lady Lockwood would be at all pleased to have corpses delivered, I'm sure that whoever took Lady Emmaline and Lady Simone would be most careful about applying the drug."

"Why would she care whether they're alive?"

"Because if she didn't need them alive," Noland answered, "she would have had them killed right here and been done with it. As she would have had done with Miss Sheraton this morning. Clearly she has some sort of larger plan."

"But how do we know they weren't killed and their bodies simply removed so that it appears to be only a kidnapping? What if they've been dumped out along a dark and rainy road, their—"

"Do get a grip on yourself, Mr. Gregory. It's mid-afternoon, the sky is reasonably sunny, and Lady Lock-wood is motivated by profit. Which isn't to be had in significant measure from any of the ladies' deaths. Now, of course Tristan's death is quite another matter entirely."

"Which means," Tristan said, leaning down to pluck several strands of long raven dark hair from the gravel, "that her plan likely involves using the ladies as bait to draw me into a vulnerable position."

"Wouldn't just one of them do for that? Why all three?"

"I don't know," he had to admit, slowly twining Simone's hair around his finger. "I honestly don't know and couldn't guess. Noland? Do you have any ideas on the matter?"

"I'm afraid not. Although," he added on a sigh, "I'm sure that once we see it unfold, we'll slap ourselves on the forehead, lament that it was painfully predictable, and then roundly chastise ourselves for blindness and complete stupidity."

"You're not making me feel very hopeful about a positive outcome, Lord Noland."

Noland said something in reply, but Tristan was too preoccupied with his own concerns and questions to worry overly much about a bit of tension between his friends. Judging by the way the gravel had been shoved and plowed and scraped, there had been a considerable struggle on the spot. And given that it was Simone's hair that he held . . . He bent down and looked the ground over carefully.

No blood. At least not any that he could see. That none of Simone's had been spilled was an incredible relief. And oddly enough, there was a bit of hope in knowing that none of her attackers' had been, either. If she'd managed to get that deadly little knife of hers unsheathed, there would have been plenty of evidence of that fact. That there wasn't . . . If they didn't think to search her, then she had the means to defend herself and Emmaline if they weren't caught unaware next time. How they'd been caught this time. . . .

He turned and looked back to where Em had had her easel, to the scattered paint pots and the torn canvas. The gravel was hardly disturbed under it all, though. Yes, several little spots where someone had walked, turning a few of the stones in the process, but beyond that . . .

Yes, it looked as though it was just as he'd surmised in the first moments. Simone had obviously put up one hell of a fight. And, just as obviously, Emmy hadn't. And while neither of their reactions was the least bit surprising, he had to admit that he was disappointed in his sister. She'd been making such wonderful progress in coming out of her shy and retiring shell. Of all the times to revert to timid mousedom . . .

"Lockwood, if I may make a suggestion?"

He looked up to meet Noland's gaze. "Any and all are welcome."

"It's apparent that we have no choice but to await Lady Lockwood's invitation to the end party. It would be best, don't you think, to place ourselves in a position to receive it and quickly act on it?"

"Agreed," he said, nodding, his mind working through the tangle of shoulds, coulds, oughts, and maybes. "Gregory, I want you to go back to the warehouse office and wait there. Noland—"

"I'm off to the Yard to advise them of the latest two

kidnappings. The more eyes and ears we have on the task of finding the ladies, the better our chances of actually doing so."

The man could read minds. Amazing. If only he could have read Lucinda's before all— Tristan left the thought unfinished and brought his brain back to the immediate tasks at hand. "I need to find the Duke of Ryland."

"Oh, damn," Noland said. "I hadn't thought of notification. Probably a good indication of why my superiors keep me assigned to a desk. Would you like us to go along with you? Moral support and all that?"

"Thank you for offering, but it's probably best if I dance alone on this one."

"If you're sure . . ."

Tristan nodded.

"If word comes to the warehouse," Gregory posed, "to where do I relay it?"

Good man, Gregory. Always thinking. "If it comes in the next two hours, I'm likely to be at His Grace's home. When I've taken the beating I'm due, I'll return to my town house. I think Lucinda's most likely to look for me there."

"Then I'll stop by your home on my way to the warehouse and advise your staff of your whereabouts for the time being. That way they can relay the message should it come more quickly than you seem to expect."

Yes, always thinking. "Remind me to give you a raise, Gregory."

"Assisting in the safe return of your ladies will be sufficient recompense, sir."

"I'll be to your house as quickly as I can, Lockwood."

He nodded his thanks to both men and then watched

them leave. *Your ladies.* God, how true. Emmaline. Sarah. Simone. The only three women in the world to whom he had any obligation. And to this point, he'd utterly and completely failed each of them. His only hope—their only hope—lay in everyone acting with some degree of rationality.

Not that that was likely to have a positive impact on the outcome as far as Sarah was concerned. She could recant her earlier claim of being with his child, but considering the circumstances under which she'd be singing a different tune . . . Lucinda, acting in a perfectly rational and logical sort of way, wouldn't believe her. The birth of a descendant, legitimate or not, would put one hell of a kink in Lucinda's long-range plan. She couldn't, wouldn't, let Sarah live long enough to give birth. So why hadn't Lucinda had her killed along the road this morning? . . . Quick, easy, the perfect accidental death. Why did Lucinda need Sarah alive for the moment?

Tristan expelled a long breath and scraped his fingers through his hair. Noland was undoubtedly right; when Lucinda's plot unfolded, he was going to kick himself for not seeing it sooner.

Whatever the plot, the odds of Emmaline emerging from the ordeal unscathed were the best. She was, after all, Lucinda's daughter. She posed no threat whatsoever to her mother's ambitions. In fact, if Em lived, Lucinda would have access to her trust fund monies without all that many eyebrows being raised in suspicion. So why she'd had Em kidnapped, too . . .

Most likely it hadn't been intentional, he reasoned. Em had been taken simply because she'd been with Simone at the wrong time.

Simone. He could see her so clearly in his mind's eye. The inviting way she tipped her head back to smile up at him, the sure and artful way she skimmed her hands over his body and sent his senses reeling. And God, how wonderful he felt when she sighed and nuzzled into him so contentedly in the aftermath of their lovemaking. Never in his life had he felt as he did when he was with Simone. Emotions ran deeper and stronger. And as ridiculous as it sounded, the sun really did shine brighter and life did offer more hope, more happiness. He actually counted the hours until they could be together again, looked for ways to put himself in her path just so that those hours could be fewer.

Jesus, how he enjoyed the way her eyes sparkled when he surprised her. He adored how she laughed when he teased her, how passionately she surrendered every time he tempted her. She never shied back. Never pleaded inexperience or modesty or used any one of the million other ploys women used to bend men to their whims. She made him hungry in a hundred different ways, happy in a thousand.

But Lucinda didn't know any of that, he assured himself. The only thing that she could surmise was that Simone was the latest Sarah in his life, that she was just another female whose company he enjoyed for the moment and who would soon be replaced by another. There was no logical reason for Lucinda to have taken Simone. None at all. She wasn't carrying his child. She wasn't hoping to marry him. And it was the illogic of her being swept into Lucinda's plot that frightened him the most.

He knew the odds of Sarah's survival. He knew the

odds of Emmaline's as well. But Simone's . . . She was a survivor, he reminded himself. She'd grown up in the streets and hadn't left her sensibilities behind when she'd moved into the peerage. She'd led them all out of the fire that night at the party. Simone had uncommon good sense and incredible instincts for survival. If she had just half a chance to fight or flee, she'd be all right. But if there wasn't that half chance . . .

If only he'd never met her. If he had had the patience to wait until after he'd dealt with Lucinda . . . But he had met Simone and he hadn't been able to resist the urging of his desires. And somewhere along the way, amid the lust and the danger and the knowing better, he'd also heard the whispers of his heart.

Tristan closed his eyes with a groan as realization and certainty cascaded through his soul. His days of running from the ugliness and disillusionment of his life were over. There would never again be a year spent at sea. Nor another night cavorting in the bed of a woman whose name he either didn't know or couldn't be bothered to remember. Amassing a fortune was no longer going to be the largest purpose of his days. Its extent wasn't ever again going to be the measure of his worth or the source of his greatest security. He was going to pray every day and for things he had never wanted or cared about until now.

If he died today . . . or tomorrow . . . or the next day . . . He wasn't going to lie down and let it happen. If he was going out, it was going to be in the fight to live the life he'd never thought he could have, never thought he'd deserved.

And if Lucinda thought she was going to cheat him out of all those rare and beautiful dreams when he was so very close to achieving them . . .

"Simone," he murmured, his chest tight, his heart aching as his blood ran cold. "Please, darling. Please don't tell her that I love you."

CHAPTER 18

$\mathcal{T}$he Duke of Ryland's butler announced him at the threshold to the man's study and then stepped aside, giving Tristan a clear view of the room and the two male occupants. The duke sat at his desk and the ever attendant Haywood leaned against the fireplace mantel looking none too happy to see Tristan. Neither had a weapon in hand. A definite positive in the situation. The desktop, however, was covered with any number of normally innocuous items that could be made lethal in an enraged heartbeat. Tristan advanced anyway, determined to get the matter done.

"From the looks of you," the duke said, leaning back in his chair, "I gather you're not here to invite us to play cards at your club."

"No, Your Grace, I'm not," he admitted, stopping between the pair of red leather chairs in front of the desk. And since there was no point in trying to dance up to the issue, he added, "I'm here to inform you that I believe Lady Simone has been kidnapped."

"What!" Haywood cried, taking a half step forward.

As the duke sat in silence, taking Tristan's measure, he went on, saying, "Along with my sister. It appears they were taken by force from the conservatory in my stepmother's house just over an hour ago."

"We have to notify the authorities, Dray. I'll go right—"

"An inspector with Scotland Yard was with me when we discovered the scene," Tristan assured them. "He is, as we speak, mobilizing what official resources can be brought to bear in finding Em and Simone."

"All right," the duke said crisply, leaning forward, his eyes hard and dark, "now that we've dispensed with the formal notification and conveyance of the most basic facts . . . Who has her and why?"

"The who is most likely my stepmother. The why . . ." Tristan shook his head. "I could make a couple of guesses, but that's all they'd be."

Haywood swore under his breath and then asked, "Do you have any idea of where she might be holding Simone? And your sister?"

Jesus. Of all the questions . . . "If I did, I'd have been there already."

Haywood took a step forward, his hands clenched into

fists at his sides. The duke held up his hand to stay his friend. "Of your couple of guesses for why," he said calmly, "give me the odds-on favorite."

"To use as bait," Tristan supplied, distilling the matter to its essence. "Lucinda wants me dead and she's using Em and Simone to lure me to wherever she's decided the deed needs to be done."

Haywood glared at him. "Drayton's told me about the latest chapter in the Lunatic Lockwood saga, and it seems to me that there's a great deal of conjecture in your accusations. You don't have a shred of hard evidence or physical proof against Lady Lockwood, do you?"

"And therein, Mr. Haywood, lies the reason that she hasn't been arrested and charged. Why she's free to commit further mayhem."

"It could be," the man went on, "that she simply recognized inevitabilities and had the prudence to invest accordingly."

"It could," Tristan allowed. "But, given Lucinda's basic inclinations, it's far more likely that she expedited the deaths to make her investments profitable on her timetable."

"Are you telling us," Haywood said slowly, "that you became involved with Simone while knowing that you could be your stepmother's next intended victim?"

It wasn't, Tristan reminded himself, that he hadn't anticipated the question, or never faced it before. No, the demoralizing aspect of it was that he hadn't thought of a very good answer yet. Which meant, now that he was on the spot, there was nothing to do but serve up the absolute truth and the humiliation be damned.

"I've discovered," he began, "a number of less than

sterling qualities about myself since having met Simone. The most troubling of them is that when I'm anywhere near her, my intellectual ability drops to that of a mud brick. And despite knowing that, I can't stay away from her."

Considering the circumstances that had required the confession, the duke's grin wasn't what he'd expected in the way of reaction. Haywood's grumble didn't disappoint, however. But grumbling while tossing a gold crown down on the desk in front of the duke . . . Clearly there'd been a wager on something and Haywood had lost.

Even as Tristan was pondering what to say next, the duke chuckled. "It's happened to the best of us, Lockwood. Welcome to the club. There's nothing to be done about it but muddle on as best you can."

He had no idea what *it* was, but he didn't like the notion of being viewed as a bumbler. When this entire debacle was over and done, when he had Simone and Emmaline safely back home . . . Being considered a muddler wasn't going to do much to help his petition for Simone's hand. "Despite what the present situation suggests, I'm quite competent. I'm a successful businessman. I've amassed a personal fortune. I'm—"

"In love with Simone," the duke supplied quietly.

Damnation. How had the man guessed that?

"And until you learn how to manage the rest of your life in light of that fact, you're going to feel as if your whole world has gone off the rails. It'll all come right at some point, but initially . . ." He shook his head. "Mudbrick stupid. What a perfect description. I remember it well. If not necessarily fondly."

"Yes, but the worst you did," Haywood observed, "was destroy the wall. You didn't get Caroline kidnapped."

"Actually, as I recall that whole time, I cruelly ended our affair and abandoned her to a horde of idiots and hangers-on. Neither of which was a particularly kind thing to do."

Tristan cocked a brow. "I'm sure there will come a time, Your Grace, when I'll appreciate knowing that I'm not the only clod in the world, but at the moment, it's of very little consolation. I'm more interested in bringing Simone and my sister safely home."

"And what is it, exactly," he asked, "that you think you can do at this juncture?"

"Be prepared to meet Lucinda's terms."

Haywood dryly added, "Throw yourself on the sword and all that."

"Yes," he replied, wondering why the man harbored such a deep disdain for him, "if that's what's required."

The duke half-smiled and shook his head, asking, "Has it occurred to you that Simone would make an incredibly *dangerous* hostage?"

"Yes."

"Frankly, Lockwood," the man went on, rising from his seat, "I'm more worried that I'm going to have to hire a barrister to defend her on a murder charge than I am with the possibility of having to effect her rescue."

In a perfect world . . . "I'd like to be as calm about the outcome, Your Grace, but—"

"Of course," he said, opening a desk drawer. "Understandable," he added, taking out a revolver. He tucked it into the waistband of his trousers and, buttoning his suit jacket to conceal it, came around the desk. "You haven't lived with Simone as long as we have. Assuming that Lady Lockwood would send her demands to your residence, I suggest we go there and wait for their arrival.

"Haywood?" he asked, pausing beside Tristan to look back at his friend. "On the off chance that she sends them here, would you be willing—"

"Certainly."

And with that promise, Simone's brother-in-law motioned toward the door of the study and smiled. "Shall we?"

Enlisting the man's help hadn't been the reason he'd come here, but knowing that he couldn't very well decline it, Tristan nodded and followed the man out the door, through the foyer, and down the front steps.

"A point of information, Lockwood," he said once they were in the carriage and on their way. "In the eyes of Cyril Haywood, no man is ever going to be good enough for Simone."

Well, it was good, he supposed, to know that it wasn't a purely personal animosity. "Does he love her?"

"Rather like an older, adoring, utterly-blind-to-her-faults brother. He'll come around in time. When he sees Simone happy in her life with you."

"You're assuming that she'll agree to marry me."

He shrugged and nodded. "I'm also assuming that you're going to ask for her."

And they were both assuming that Simone was going to come out of the misadventure alive and not furious with him for having gotten her tangled up in it. But if the gods of good fortune deigned to smile on him . . . "Would you be opposed to our marriage?"

The duke snorted and chuckled. "Would my opinion one way or the other make the least bit of difference to either one of you?"

"Probably not," Tristan admitted. "At least in the short run."

"Then I don't see much point in standing in the way. And since you've already had the wedding night and apparently found yourselves sufficiently compatible to pursue the honeymoon in the days since, I consider a wedding something of a mere formality at this point."

They'd already had their wedding night. It was an interesting notion. That first time with Simone certainly hadn't been anything like what he'd imagined a bridal night would be. Always in his visions there had been a great deal of awkwardness, coaxing, and no real satisfaction beyond that in getting the deed done so the marriage was official. And truth be told, he hadn't ever expected the days and years that came after it to be any more satisfying than that first night. A title, a wife, an appropriate number of children, a productive estate, all of his duties to Society perfunctorily, joylessly, fulfilled.

"What do you think, Tristan?"

"That until I met Simone my life was one of miserably low expectations."

The duke laughed softly. "I'd suggest that you keep some of your expectations low. She's a terrible cook. If left to her own devices, she'd simply wander about and call whatever she found to eat a meal."

Like the street child she had once been. Tristan considered the world outside the carriage and firmly put his hopes on the fact that grazing for food wasn't all that remained of her survival instincts.

• • •

$\mathcal{D}$amnation, her head hurt. She couldn't open her eyes. If she even tried, they'd pop out of her head, and then where would she be? *Blind,* she answered herself. Not that she wasn't blind with them closed, but at least this way it was a matter of choice and not a permanent crippling.

Jesus. Her brain was a wreck. As though her eyes really could pop out. And there were certainly more important things that she needed to be thinking about. Starting with . . . with . . . Well, her whole body ached. Especially her arms. Probably, her sluggish mind suggested, because they were tied behind her back. And her right one hurt worse than the left because she was lying on her side and it was underneath her.

Her feet . . . She focused on the sensations of her ankles. Well, there was one bright spot; her feet weren't bound at all. Oh! An even brighter spot! They hadn't searched her! Her knife was still in the gartered sheath. She could feel the hilt pressing into her calf.

Buoyed by hope, she went back to analyzing the world beyond her closed eyes. Only her hands were tied and she was lying on her side on . . .

A floor? Yes, it was hard, cold, bare. And, judging by how her nose tickled, dusty. But not bone-numbingly cold as stone usually was. So it was most likely a wooden floor. In the home of a bad housekeeper.

A bad housekeeper? As if that tidbit of observation mattered. Where the house was, was probably more important to know. Then again, it might not even be a house at all. It could be a warehouse. Or a nice stable.

No, it wasn't a stable. She didn't smell even a hint of

hay or horses or leather. Warehouse? If it was, they were far away from the docks, because she couldn't smell the river. And, now that she was noticing things a bit more clearly, she didn't feel the damp in her clothes, either. Other than that paltry amount of deduced information . . . There wasn't any other real choice about it all; she was going to have to chance an actual look. She lifted the lashes on her left eye the tiniest bit and just long enough to make her heart race.

She swallowed and instantly wished that she hadn't. Holding her breath as fire scraped raw skin all the way down to her lungs, Simone resisted the urge to whimper, refusing to give the woman on the other side of the bed so much as a dram of satisfaction.

How the hell one could feel dizzy lying on the floor? . . . She drew in a slow, steadying breath and willed her mind to work through the puzzle of her predicament. Her arms were tied and she was lying on the floor of what seemed to be a bedroom. Since there weren't any carpets on the floor that she could see, it was likely a bedroom of a poorer person or a room at a less than stellar inn.

And given the brightness of the sunlight she'd glimpsed in her quick peek, it was still fairly early in the day. Which wasn't all that important except to make her wonder if enough time had passed for anyone to even notice that she and . . .

Emmy! Her heart pounding, Simone opened her eye again and took a longer look. No, the dress hems that she could see on the other side of the bed weren't Emmy's. Emmy didn't wear black bombazine. Simone glanced up at the underside of the bed and then, relieved, went back to pretending that she was still unconscious.

She was on the floor. Emmy was on the bed. Lucinda was seated in a chair on the other side of the room. It had only been an hour or two since she and Emmy had been taken from the conservatory.

Now that she knew all that, what was she supposed to do about it? Wait for rescue? Yes, Tristan would come for them, no doubt kicking down the door in the process, but how long would it take for him to get there? And how would he know where they were and which door to kick in? Unless Lucinda was going to send him a note with directions . . .

Well, now that she thought about it, odds were that that might be just what the woman had in mind. An invitation of sorts. *The pleasure of your company is requested at . . . wherever . . . and if you don't show up, both your sister and your lover will die.*

As plans and plots went, she had to admit that it certainly had a nice theatrical quality. Why Lucinda would go to all the trouble, though . . . A bullet fired from a carriage racing past the warehouse offices would be just as effective and considerably easier. Tristan dead was Tristan dead.

And, Simone hurriedly assured herself as her heart sank into her stomach, Tristan was still very much alive. He had to be or Lucinda wouldn't have had any reason to kidnap her and Emmy in the first place. And there most definitely wouldn't be any reason for her and Emmy to still be alive.

"Waking up finally, are you?"

Simone's heart leaped and hammered against the walls of her chest.

"Why are you doing this?"

The relief that Lucinda wasn't talking to *her* was instant and full. It was followed in the same second by stunned realization. Sarah Sheraton? Lucinda was holding Sarah captive, too? Why? Simone strained to hear over the thundering of her heartbeat.

"Because," Lucinda said, "it's simply too perfect an opportunity to pass up."

God! If it wasn't Emmy on the bed . . . What had Lucinda done with Emmy?

"Opportunity for what?"

Good question, Sarah. But you almost cried while asking it. Buck it up a bit, girl.

"Tristan caught in a lovers' triangle. You have to admit that it's incredibly believable. The authorities won't have the slightest doubt as to what happened when the scene is discovered. Oh, the horror of it will shock, of course. It will be terribly messy. So messy, in fact, that they won't think to look past the obvious and ask any troublesome questions."

"Triangle?"

God, Sarah, don't cry! We're in this deep and it's—

"You, Tristan, and Lady Simone Turnbridge."

"Oh."

That's all you can muster? "Oh"?

"I'll allow you a choice of your role in the drama," Lucinda went on. "Would you prefer to be the body found in bed, wrapped in poor dead Tristan's arms? Or would you prefer to be the one found at the foot of the bed, the wronged woman who killed her lover and his mistress before tragically turning the gun on herself?"

Good plan. Interesting in a decidedly sick sort of way. It did answer the question of why she and Sarah were still alive. And it was a sure bet that Lucinda wouldn't kill anyone until Tristan arrived. Of course, the basic facts left quite a few questions unanswered, too. Gunshots tended to draw attention and crowds. How Lucinda intended to get everyone into position at just the right time to make three quick shots count just as she needed, though . . . Then there was the getting-away-afterward-without-being-seen part. That would be tricky. Especially when people would be running toward the sounds of the shots.

And how did Emmy fit into the grand scheme? Had Lucinda ever intended for her to be kidnapped? Had she been dumped out along the road somewhere when the mistake had been discovered? God, Simone hoped so. Emmy could be with Tristan now, telling him what had happened and . . . and what else? Precious little if she'd been tossed out like refuse before they'd reached the room.

"I'd prefer," Sarah said, an encouraging bit of steel of her voice, "to be the survivor only wounded in the assault and able to tell authorities what happened when the crazed Lady Simone burst into the room."

Oh, that's low! Trying to throw in with the bitch to save your own skin!

"It's an idea," Lucinda allowed. "And if I thought there was even the remotest chance that you wouldn't expect to be financially rewarded for your complicity, I might seriously entertain it. But since I don't like to share, and a surviving witness isn't at all necessary for the plan to work beautifully, I'll have to decline the kind offer."

There, take that, Sarah.

"I do very much appreciate," Lucinda went on, "how your mind works, though. You appear to be a woman after my own heart."

Which is another reason you really have to die.

"Which is probably the most important consideration, my dear Miss Sheraton, in why I cannot allow you to live to see another day."

Well, close enough anyway.

"Where are Tristan and Simone? Are you having them kidnapped, too?"

"Lady Simone is on the floor on the other side of the bed, neatly trussed and drugged unconscious with chloroform. Tristan will be along shortly to play the fair knight and attempt to rescue his damsel in distress."

I'm not in distress. I'm biding my time.

"Actually," Lucinda drawled over the rustle of bombazine, "now that I think on the matter, I'm afraid that I must withdraw my offer of letting you choose your role, Miss Sheraton." The floorboards creaked. "Tristan will be far easier to get to the bed if it's Lady Simone lying on it, waiting for him."

"Where are you going?"

Thank you for asking that, Sarah.

The doorknob squeaked as it was turned; the hinges groaned. "To secure the brawn necessary for switching your and Lady Simone's positions. Don't go away now. I'll be right back."

The door closed softly. As it did, Sarah sobbed.

"Oh, stop the blubbering," Simone snapped, rolling onto her back and sitting up. "We have two seconds to get the hell out of here."

"You're not unconscious!"

Awkwardly gaining her feet, Simone countered, "Was I supposed to have announced otherwise?"

"No, I guess not."

"And thanks for offering to sell me out to save your own damned hide."

"I was desperate. You would have done the same thing."

No, she wouldn't. "Lower your voice," Simone instructed as she wobbled around the end of the bed, "so the whole world doesn't hear us. And sit up."

Sarah obeyed, her movement supplying Simone with two bits of information. The first was that the curls atop the woman's head were a hairpiece that was in danger of sliding off at any moment. The second was that whoever had kidnapped her hadn't been very experienced at such things.

"God, I can't believe they tied your hands in the front," Simone said, stopping beside her. "Not that I'm ungrateful for it. Roll off the bed and then reach down and under my skirt hem. On the calf of my right leg is a knife. Get it and be careful with the blade. It's sharp."

Well, Sarah did deserve credit for following instructions well. She lost a bit of the regard when the hairpiece hit the floor and she choked back a sob, but, overall . . . When she managed to get the knife out without cutting either one of them, Simone turned her back and presented her bound wrists.

"Where are we going to go?" Sarah asked, sawing at the rags. "There's only the one door, and if we go that way, we're likely to meet Lady Lockwood coming back with her brawn."

"Given her larger plan," Simone countered as she pulled her hands from the binding and turned to take her knife, "there's probably a choice of exits right outside the door." Severing Sarah's bonds with a quick slash, she added, "In fact, I'll bet you ten pounds that one of them is less than two steps away and leads straight outside."

Sarah bent to retrieve her hairpiece. "And if there isn't?"

"There is," she assured her, leading the way to the door, her brain working both efficiently and well ahead of the moment. "Have you seen Emmy?"

"Who?"

"Lady Emmaline. Tristan's sister. We were taken from the conservatory together."

"No. But then, I've been asleep since the carriage overturned."

Carriage overturned? As curious as she was, the story would have to wait for a few moments. Pressing her finger across her lips, Simone listened at the door. Hearing nothing, she turned the handle, eased it open a crack, and peered into the hallway on the other side. There were quite a few doors, all of them alike and spaced evenly down the corridor.

An inn. And, with peeling and grimy paint, a not very reputable one. As though Tristan would take any woman to a place this shabby.

Simone pushed Sarah off her back and eased the door open just enough to poke her head out. Ah, it was so nice to be right. There were three doors that didn't lead to rooms. One at the far, far end of the hall that opened to the outside, one in the middle that obviously led into the main part of the structure, and one to her left.

"I win ten pounds," she whispered, pulling the door wide and moving quickly across the threshold. "C'mon."

There was no need to instruct Sarah twice. Nor was

there any need to check to see if the woman followed. In the short distance and time it took to reach the other door, she stepped on Simone's heels three times.

"For a halfpenny," she muttered as she wrenched open the door and vaulted outside. Sarah shot past her, the hairpiece in one hand and her skirts fisted in the other, holding her hems high above her ankles. Simone paused just long enough to quietly close the door behind them, then shifted the hilt of the knife in her hand, lifted her hems, and took off in Sarah's wake.

"I could leave you to fend for yourself," Simone finished, glaring at the woman's back and matching her pace. "And if we weren't in Whitechapel . . ."

The inn was out of sight and a good distance behind them when Sarah finally slowed, sagged against a deteriorating stucco wall, and gasped for breath. Simone trotted up and considered her. "You don't fence, do you?"

She ignored the hard look Sarah gave her and went on, saying, "You said the carriage overturned. Which carriage? Where? When? Who was with you?"

"On the road south of London," Sarah supplied, holding her hand against her side. "Early this morning. Lord Noland was with me."

"Is he all right?"

"He was alive when they dragged me out of the wreckage and slapped the rag over my face. What happened after that . . . I can't tell you."

Simone hoped Noland was not only still very much alive, but also that he'd come straight back to London and found Tristan. If he wasn't . . . If he hadn't . . . She glanced up at the sky, trying to judge the time and guess what might have happened in the hours since she and Emmaline had been taken from the conservatory. Had the servants heard the struggle and summoned the authorities? Had Emmy found her way home and relayed the story of what had happened?

Did Tristan have even the slightest inkling that Lucinda had set her plan in motion? If he didn't, where would he be at this time of the day? Where should she go to find him, to warn him? The warehouse? His town house? God, did he have a club?

There was so much about him that she didn't know, so many things that she thought she'd have forever to learn. Over toast and coffee and the morning paper in bed. Late at night in the garden, watching the moon rise with Tristan at her back, his arms wrapped around her and holding her close. On the carriage rides to and from the theater and the country houses and at parties and . . .

Simone seized a slow breath and swallowed down her fear. The rawness of her throat brought her mind fully back to the moment, back to the need to think clearly and rationally.

Tristan not knowing that the plot was afoot was one thing. That he did was another matter entirely; it changed everything. If he knew, what would he be doing and where would she be most likely to find him to let him know that she was safe? He could be anywhere. The warehouse, his town house, Lucinda's.

Lucinda.

Oh, dear God. What if Lucinda had already sent the invitation? Was Tristan even now on his way to the inn and about to walk into the deadly trap? What would Lucinda do once she discovered that the bait had slipped off the hook? Flee? Only in a world where there were no such things as greed, resentment, and revenge.

Her heart twisting and her stomach turning to lead, Simone squared up to Sarah and gambled for love.

CHAPTER 19

𝒯ristan paced back and forth across his study, silently railing at having absolutely nothing else to do in the situation. Waiting was something small children and the elderly did, not successful merchants and peers. He glanced over at the chair and wondered for at least the hundredth time how the duke could sit there and calmly read a book.

"Because I know Simone," the man said without looking up from the page. "If there's the slightest opportunity for her to turn the tables, she will."

"And if there isn't that slightest opportunity?"

"She'll make one out of nothing. Have faith in her. She's remarkably resourceful."

Tristan scrubbed his hands over his face and then raked his fingers through his hair.

At his exasperated sigh, the duke added, "And if not, you can amaze her with your resourcefulness when Lady Lockwood summons you to the scene."

"I'm not interested in amazing her, Your Grace. I just want her safe. Preferably in the next minute and a half."

"You know what they say about patience."

"It's for saints," he growled, pacing again. A saint he wasn't, had never been. And considering that he intended to kill his stepmother the first chance he had, the odds were stacked against his ever being one.

𝒮imone eased her shoulder off the crumbling plaster wall, pulled her hems to one side, and then looked away just long enough to kick the curious rat toward the rear of the alley. Ignoring the squeaking and scurrying, she turned her attention back to the front of the inn. There were the usual weekday-afternoon-in-Whitechapel people moving up and down the walkways, the usual traffic in the street.

It was what didn't belong there that interested her: the Townsend family carriage. It and two other vehicles—a rented hack with AT AT MARQUAT'S painted on the back and a battered open-bed delivery wagon—had already been parked along the walkway in front of the inn when she'd made her way back and into the shadows of the alley. There was no sign of the Townsend driver. No sign of Emmy, either. The reins of the delivery wagon were tied off, too. Only the hack had a driver in place and he was taking a nap in the box.

Jesus. How long was it going to take Lucinda to come bolting out the inn door and into her carriage? Surely by now the woman had discovered that she and Sarah had escaped. Without the two of them, the plan was ruined. Unless, Simone realized, her stomach twisting, Lucinda was willing to forgo the elaborate staging and be content with simply shooting Tristan the moment—

No, Simone hurriedly assured herself. Lucinda needed a carefully crafted scene. If she didn't have one, she'd be a certain suspect in Tristan's death and that would put the insurance money at risk. Not to mention the inheritance. Lucinda wanted all of it, free and easy; that was the main reason for all of this, for all the murders. No, she wasn't likely to give up and go running off to hide.

But without Tristan's lovers in hand . . . What did the woman have to work with? Her driver, maybe one of the working women at the inn, maybe a drunken customer . . . But getting them all into place without arousing suspicion, and so quickly . . . Surely Lucinda had to know that her time was running short, that she and Sarah would have headed straight to Tristan to warn him. Unless—

"No," she said firmly. "Stop making yourself crazy."

The sound was small but close and telltale. She yanked her skirt to the side, sent another rat flying back into the darker shadows of the alley, and then turned back to her vigil, muttering, "Filthy ro—"

Her heart hammering, she leaned closer to the wall, deeper into the protective shadows to watch as two men carried a rolled-up rug along the side of the inn and toward the street. A third man stepped out the door behind them, called out something, and then ducked back inside as they continued on their way.

A bit of dirty white cloth hung limply out the front end
of the roll. *A sheet?* she wondered, watching their progress.
A sheet inside a rug? The inn wasn't the sort of place
where housekeeping or decor mattered. Hell, the rugs
had probably never ever been taken out for so much as a
good beating. Why would they—

The men turned the corner of the building, clearly
heading toward the delivery wagon. And just as clearly,
now that she could see the full length of the roll, a sheet
wasn't the only thing wrapped up inside it. Lumpy and
bumpy, it was just the sort of odd shape a rug would take
if it were wrapped around a body.

The men stopped at the side of the wagon, shifted their
burden, and then rolled it off their shoulders to drop it unceremoniously into the bed. A cloud of dust rose as it hit
the wooden planks with a dull and heavy thud.

Even as the dust still swirled upward, one of the men
climbed into the box and took up the reins. The other
walked to the rented hack, paused at the door to speak to
someone inside, and then slapped the side to rouse the
driver before going on to the Townsends' carriage. As he
climbed up into the box, the driver of the wagon moved it
out of the line and into the traffic. The hack followed immediately in its wake.

Simone left the shadows, darting toward the alley en-
trance, her heart racing. For a second the light was blind-
ing, but she shielded her eyes from the worst of it just in
time to see the hack turn the corner. As it disappeared
from sight, the carriage rolled away from the inn as well.

Simone watched it make its way up the street, following not the hack but the delivery wagon with its gruesome

cargo. Who was dead? she wondered. The Townsends' driver? Her heart lurched at another possibility.

Slamming her eyes closed, Simone ignored the frantic hammering of her heart and summoned the image of the rug from her memory. No. Thank God, no. Tristan hadn't arrived in the time it had taken her to make her way back to the inn. It would have taken three, maybe four, men to carry his body out and dump it. And the dead man was the Townsends' driver only if he were a small man. A really small man, a man about the size of . . . Emmy.

Simone swallowed down her stomach, opened her eyes, and deliberately forced her mind in another direction. Lucinda had to have been the passenger in the hack. Where was she going? And why hadn't she taken the family carriage?

It didn't matter, Simone assured herself. What did matter was that, against all the odds, Lucinda had given up the game and fled. The danger was over. Maybe it would come again; maybe it wouldn't. But for now . . .

Simone swallowed down the thick lump in her throat and forced herself to breathe. The day wasn't done and there were difficult things yet to do. Sarah couldn't be that far ahead of her. If she hurried . . . Stepping into the street, Simone raised her hand.

A hack rolled to a stop up the block to let out its passengers and Simone sprinted for it, determined to get there before anyone else could claim it. She reached it just as the man inside stepped down onto the walkway. Grasping the door handle to claim the ride, she nodded to acknowledge his tip of the hat and caught the inside of her lower lip between her teeth to keep from smiling. His bowler hat was of cheap, thin felt, but brand-new, and his suit was the uniform of very respectable clerk in the world. She had to give him credit for trying to be fashionable. If only his tailor hadn't robbed some poor horse of its plaid blanket for the effort.

He turned and extended his hand into the cab. Simone swallowed back a groan of frustration. *C'mon, Madam Clerk,* she silently railed, *let's rustle a bustle. I'm in a hurry.*

The foot that emerged first from the dark interior of the hack . . . Simone arched a brow. High-heeled mules, huh? At midday in Whitechapel. No stockings. No petticoats and skirt of lace-covered lawn. Well, everyone had their uniforms on.

Staring down at the pavers, Simone gritted her teeth and resisted the temptation to shove the two of them out of her way. *Time is money, madam,* she silently reminded the woman practically snaking her way out of the cab. *And you're wasting both.*

The very second there was sufficient space between the woman's skirts and the cab, Simone slipped into it, vaulted onto the step, and looked up at the driver.

"Same time next week, Roger?"

Simone froze as the voice registered in her memory. She whipped back. "Diana? Diana Dalea?"

The eyes that looked back at her were heavily painted and kohl-lined. And wide with shocked recognition.

"Fancy meeting you here," Simone offered dryly. "I wish I had the time to visit, but . . ." She shrugged. "Do give my regards to your mother and tell her that since my sister's had her baby, we'll be able to have lunch sometime next week. Personally, I can't wait."

Diana didn't say a word. Not that there was much she could say, Simone allowed as she looked up at the driver again, supplied the address of Tristan's town house, and promised him a double fare if he flew. Diana—looking horrified—was still standing there with her customer, who was thumbing through his pocket calendar, when Simone popped inside the carriage, closed the door behind herself, and kicked the wall.

The hack rolled out instantly, carrying her away from a world gone entirely too ugly, too bizarre. She scrubbed her hands over her face, then leaned back into the seat to stare up at the roof. Kidnapping and murder, rats, and brothels and whores. A regular, not all that notable day in the world of London's poor streets. How far she'd come in only six years. If there was a God . . . No, even if there wasn't, she was never again in her life going to come back here.

$\mathcal{P}$ardon the intrusion, Your Lordship."

Tristan whirled about at the sound of his butler's voice to find the man standing in the study doorway, a scrap of paper in his gloved hand. "That just arrived?" Tristan asked, his heart hammering as he strode over to take it.

"Yes, Your Lordship," he supplied while surrendering it. "A messenger presented it at the kitchen door, saying that it was of great importance."

Tristan opened the folded scrap of paper to find an address scrawled in an unfamiliar hand. There were no instructions, no threats or promises. None were necessary. He unclenched his teeth and handed the note over to the duke. "Thank you, French," he said, his mind racing forward. "Please tell John that I'll be leaving within the moment."

The butler bowed and departed as Tristan crossed the room to his desk and the duke quietly observed, "It's in Whitechapel."

"Do you know the building?"

"Not from personal experience."

"No matter," he replied. Taking a revolver from the desk drawer and checking the cylinder, he added, "I'll find it. If you'd be so kind as to take that note to Lord Noland at Scotland Yard and ask him to meet me there, I'd appreciate it."

The duke folded the note closed. "One of your staff can do the running. I'm coming with you."

Tristan understood the man's motives. Were he in the duke's shoes, he wouldn't accept the role of messenger, either. But there was a great deal of difference between being a party to a rescue and being a party to vengeance. He tucked the revolver into the waistband of his trousers and retrieved his jacket from the back of the desk chair.

"My stepmother is going to be dead at the end of this," he announced matter-of-factly as he shoved his arms into the sleeves. "If you're there when it happens, you'll be considered an accessory, at best. At worst, an accomplice. A scandal is even more certain than a trial."

"Scandals fade and pass. As for the legal aspects . . . The sworn testimony of a duke carries considerable weight. If there's a trial at all, it will be a very short one."

Tristan nodded his acceptance, took the note from the duke, and went to the doorway. "French!"

Simone darted behind the trunk of an old oak tree and then carefully peered around it, blinking in disbelief. Even as she tried to deny the certainty of what she was seeing, her heart sank. Bits and pieces of conversation, fleeting expressions and gestures, careened from her memory, pushing the pieces of the dark, twisted puzzle into undeniably perfect place. Angry tears welled in her eyes, but she swiped them away and bent down to lift her hems.

The hilt of her knife palmed, the blade resting against the underside of her forearm, she made her way along the side of the house, looking for an open window. There was no other choice, no avoiding the truth. What had to be done, had to be done. And done right. She could be heartsick about it later.

$\mathcal{F}$rench!"

His summons was still reverberating down the hallway when the front door burst open. For a second he wondered why the hell his butler was outside; in the next his heart soared with relief.

"Em!" he cried, throwing open his arms. "Thank God!"

She started and looked up from the foyer floor, her eyes wide in surprise to see him waiting there for her. For a second only the hems of her skirts moved, and then her face scrunched up as she squeaked and flung herself into his arms, crying his name and burying her face in his chest. He hugged her tight and then took her upper arms in hand and put her out far enough that he could look up and down the length of her.

"You're all right?"

"Yes, yes, I'm fine," she breathlessly assured him. "But Mother has Simone. And that Sarah woman, too. I can't tell you where. I don't know the streets. But I can take you there."

"If I might intrude to ask . . . How did you get away?"

Em gasped and looked past him, the blood draining from her face. "This is the Duke of Ryland," Tristan hastily assured her, stepping aside so she could fully see the man. "He's Simone's brother-in-law and guardian."

"M-M-Mother let me go," Emmaline supplied haltingly, her breathing ragged and her gaze darting all over the foyer. "She put me in a hack and told me to go home and pretend that I didn't know anything or she'd kill me." Seizing a deep breath, she brought her attention squarely to Tristan and swallowed hard. "She's mad, Tristan. Stark raving mad. You have to stop her. You *have* to."

As though doing so was on his list of maybe things to do that day? He tamped down his irritation, reminding himself that his sister was delicate and that the strain of her ordeal had battered her sensibilities. "Are Simone and Sarah all right? Has she hurt them?"

"They were fine the last time I saw them. Tied up, but fine."

"Ah, French," he said as his butler rounded the corner. Tristan released his hold on Emmaline and went to meet his man halfway, handing the note to him and saying, "Have one of the staff run this directly to Lord Noland at the Yard. He'll know what to do. Also have them tell him that Lady Emmaline has been recovered safely."

As the butler left, Tristan heard Ryland ask, "How many men does Lady Lockwood have in hire?"

"I don't know," Em answered, an edge of frustration in her voice. "How could I know?"

Tristan went back to them, asking for the same information in a different way. "How many men took you from the conservatory, Em?"

She looked back and forth between them. "Two," she supplied, the pitch of her voice rising, her breathing suddenly quick and shallow. "And what does it matter? You're wasting time asking me all of these silly questions. We have to go—"

"You're staying here, Em," he said, taking her by the arm. The duke stepped aside and back to let him guide her into the study and toward one of the leather chairs. "Just sit down, take a deep breath, and collect your wits. I'll have the staff bring you a pot of tea and we'll be back with Simone before you're done with it."

She pulled her arm from his grasp, took two full steps back, and fisted the fabric of her skirt. "But I have to take you there."

"No, Lady Emmaline, you need not risk yourself any farther," the duke assured her, his voice calm and soothing as he leaned a hip against Tristan's desk. "We have the address. Your mother sent it. That's what's on its way to Noland."

"I didn't . . ." She gulped a breath and fisted her skirt tighter. "But . . ."

Deep in his brain, an alarm dully sounded. Why was Em on the verge of panic? Why was she insistent on holding to her course? They'd explained. They'd reassured. She was safe. He glanced over at the duke. All right, that made two of them puzzled.

"But what, Emmaline?" Tristan pressed gently. "You didn't what?"

"Give her a moment to think about it."

His heart skipped a beat in delight as his knees went weak in relief. "Simone!" he cried, his gaze arrowing to the slim, dark-clothed figure in the doorway. "Thank—"

He froze in mid-stride, his pulse racing and his blood suddenly as cold as the look in Simone's eyes.

"What she didn't know," Simone said softly, slowly advancing into the room, her gaze riveted on his sister's, "is that her mother had sent for you already and the *but* is to buy time."

He looked over at Emmaline. Her face was absolutely bloodless. Her gaze, fixed on Simone, sparked with feral panic.

"She's having to come up with a new plan on the spot," Simone went on, still moving toward them. "She didn't expect to find Drayton here, either, which has really complicated things. It's all falling apart and she's scrambling, trying to think of a way to salvage it."

Emmaline swayed on her feet. The movement startled her and in the blink of her eyes the panic was gone. For a second it was replaced by the gleam of calculation. In the next, her blue eyes clouded with innocent confusion. "Why are you being so mean?"

Oh, Em, he silently moaned, awash in the misery of certainty. *Stop. Just stop.*

Simone ignored her question. "Three men took us from the conservatory."

"So I miscounted in the melee," Emmaline shot back, her voice hard-edged with anger. "Given the confusion, that's hardly unexpected."

"There was no confusion for you," Simone countered with deadly calm. "You stood there by your easel and watched. I thought that you were just too frightened to move, but that wasn't it at all. You were only waiting for me to be taken down."

"That's not true."

Yes, it was and Tristan knew it. He'd looked at the spilled paint pots, at the ruined portrait, and been disappointed in his sister for not putting up the fight Simone had.

"And if Tristan and Drayton are only expecting to deal with two men, the third has a chance of catching them by surprise." She shrugged ever so slightly. "And they wouldn't put you in the count against them, either. Until it was too late."

"What?"

The duke shifted his stance and cleared his throat. Simone, her gaze never straying from Emmaline, stayed him with the barest movement of her hand.

"Who's wrapped up in the rug, Emmy?"

The feral glint flickered in his sister's eyes and then was gone, hidden once again behind the false cloud of confusion. "I don't know what you're talking about."

"It was too small to be the body of a man, so odds are it isn't your driver. I thought it was you. But since you're obviously standing here . . . Is it by any chance your mother?"

Lucinda was dead?

"You poor thing," Em cooed. "Your mind has—"

" 'At at Marquat's.' "

Emmaline's confusion wasn't any more feigned than his own. Or, apparently, given the "Huh?" he muttered, the duke's.

Simone nodded. "That's what was on the rear of the rented hack that pulled away from the inn after the body was dumped in the wagon. It was, at one time, I'm sure, *EAT* AT MARQUAT'S, but the paint on the *e* was somehow chipped away. What do you suppose the odds are that there would be two hacks in London with a missing *e*? And that I'd see both of them within a half hour of each other? One leaving the inn, the other rolling away as I arrived here."

Emmaline stared at her, alternately gasping and swallowing as the wild look in her eyes came and went and came again. She let go of her skirt and plucked mindlessly at the wrinkles.

"Emmaline?" Tristan called softly.

She jerked back as if his voice had been a physical blow. "She would have killed me, too," she snapped, tearing her gaze from Simone to glare at him. "Eventually. That makes it a case of self-defense."

"Yes," Simone allowed, calling Emmaline's attention back to her. "And if you'd gone back and checked to see if Sarah and I were still there before you came to get Tristan, you could have stopped there and been home free. A heroine, even. But you didn't, Emmy. You picked up your mother's plan and ran with it for yourself."

"Would either of you," the duke asked quietly, "care to tell us what that plan was?"

Emmaline's chest rose and fell as her breathing went quick and shallow. Simone answered, "It was supposed to look as though Tristan was killed in a lovers' triangle. Tristan, Sarah, and me. Just guessing as to the other part of it, I'd say that the bodies of Lucinda and her driver will be found in a wrecked carriage sometime later today."

Ryland nodded. "Leaving Lady Emmaline the sole survivor of the family."

"The sole inheritor," Tristan clarified, his heart and soul numb. "Just as Lucinda intended to be."

A smile spread slowly over Emmaline's face. "You can't

prove any of this," she said sweetly, brightly. "There's not one scrap of evidence against me."

He wanted to cry for the madness of generations, for the loss in this one of the only person he'd ever counted as family.

"Emmy, there's no honor among thieves," he heard Simone say. "All we have to do is find the men who hauled that rug out of the inn. By the time they're done trying to save their own necks, yours will be firmly in the noose."

She waved her hand and scoffed, "They'd take my word over that of a common thug's."

"Not when I add my word to theirs."

The smile faltered, reasserted itself, and then drained away. Emmaline swayed on her feet and looked around the room, her gaze unfocused. Tears welled along the rims of her lower lashes and then spilled to course in wide rivers down her cheeks.

"Em, it'll be all right," he said earnestly. "You won't go to the gallows. We'll get you a doctor. Someone who can make your mind right again."

She shook her head slowly and then straightened her back. She sniffled. "I don't have any choice, do I?" she asked, her voice weak and wet as she reached into her pocket.

"No, you don't," he agreed, watching her fumble about for a handkerchief that probably wasn't there. Pulling out his own, he stepped forward to offer it, adding, "The game is done, Em."

She looked blankly at the square of white linen and went still. Slowly, the haze of confusion left her eyes and her tears stopped welling. She lifted her gaze to meet his. "But I don't want to spend the rest of my life in Bedlam."

The calm, the cool certainty, in her voice prickled across his nape. "You won't," he promised warily, drawing back the handkerchief. "There are other places that—"

"But if I am, Tristan, then it's only fair that you spend the rest of yours," she said sweetly, shifting her gaze to Simone and pulling her hand from her pocket, "in hell."

The dull glint of blued metal and the clarity of mad intent turned his blood to ice. He threw himself at it in the very instant that the world exploded with the searing heat and deafening noise of unholy fire.

CHAPTER 20

$\mathcal{W}$ade Gregory stood at the door and looked back toward the bed, at Tristan propped up with pillows and oblivious to the world around him. "You're sure he'll be all right?"

Simone nodded. "The doctor said he'd be abed for no more than a week."

"If he's there that long," Gregory scoffed with a roll of his eyes and a snort, "will you be staying with him?"

She shrugged and tamped down her doubts. "Everyone seems to be assuming so. At least for a short while."

"When he wakes, please assure him that he needn't

hurry back to the office. That I can manage quite nicely without him for the next year or so." He cleared his throat and took a deep breath before adding, "And please tell him, as well, that I'm terribly sorry about Lady Emmaline and his stepmother."

"I will, Mr. Gregory. And thank you for all your help this evening."

"My pleasure, Lady Simone," he said with a slight bow. Turning, he stepped out of the room and then to the side, giving way for the housekeeper.

"Good evening, madam," the woman said, sweeping through the open doorway with the jangle of keys, the clink of china, and the *ting* of silver. "I thought that perhaps you might be ready for something to eat," she explained, carrying the laden tray to the skirted table on the far side of the room. "The lighter fare is for His Lordship should he be hungry when he awakens."

Six hours after the moment . . . At what point would it finally dawn on the staff that she wasn't the mistress of the house? "Thank you, Mrs. Davis."

"If you need anything else, madam," the woman said, pausing on the threshold, "you need only pull the bell cord."

"Thank you, again."

To Simone's amazement, the housekeeper closed the door behind herself. *Leaving the master and mistress in private.* Never in a million years would she have—

"Is a brass band coming through next?"

She grinned and turned to the bed, her heart happy and light. "Hello, Tristan," she said softly, sitting down beside him on the bed. She leaned forward and kissed him gently, then drew back to study his handsome beard-shadowed face. "I won't ask how you're feeling."

He looked her up and down. "Are you all right?"

"Not a scratch on me," she assured him brightly, holding her arms out so that he could see all of her. "Fiona says I have more lives than a cat."

"Thank God."

She let her arms fall into her lap. "I suppose you want the whole story from where you turned gallant?"

"Not if it's as ugly as I think it is."

"Emmy's still very much alive, if that's what you're worried about."

He closed his eyes and expelled a long breath.

"She's still just as crazy, though," Simone added, not wanting to raise his hopes. "And shrieking, claw-your-eyes-out furious for having been accused of being anything but perfectly proper and sweetly demure."

One corner of his mouth ticced slightly upward. "Is she locked up where she can't hurt herself or anyone else?"

Hearing the regret, the sorrow, in his voice, she squeezed his hands and quietly assured him, "Drayton is taking her to a private asylum outside Bath. Noland sent three officers along to be sure that she makes it there without any problems."

He nodded and opened his eyes. Staring at the far wall, he asked, "Lucinda?"

"Carriage crash outside London," Simone supplied. "They found the wreckage half-submerged under a bridge. Lucinda was inside. Her diver was found downstream." With a sigh and a shake of her head, she added,

"Sometimes I amaze even myself. I was just guessing when I tossed that one off. I was hoping Emmy would challenge it with the truth and give herself away. Not that she did, of course."

He reached out and took her hands in his. "You amaze me all the time," he said softly, stroking his thumbs over her knuckles. "You're the most incredible woman I've ever known."

Incredible? Only because he didn't know half of the story. "Yes, well . . ." she hedged.

"What?"

There was no avoiding the confession. But there wasn't any need to rush into it, either. "Where do you hurt?"

He chuckled and instantly caught his breath. "Well, definitely my left side," he admitted.

"That's where Emmy's bullet went into you. And out, too. The doctor said that if you hadn't been pressed against the muzzle it wouldn't have gone cleanly through and he'd have had to dig the bullet out of you. He was very glad that he didn't."

He snorted. "I'll bet his bill isn't any less for having the job be an easy one."

Probably not. "In case you're interested, there wasn't any serious internal damage done. Just some blasted and torn muscle. You're going to be sore for a while."

A smile lifted the corners of his mouth and his eyes sparkled with devilment. "Ah, but will I have a scar to show for it?" he asked as her heart, as always, melted. "I hear women find scars attractive."

Yes, he and Haywood were cut from the same bolt of cloth. "Where else do you hurt?" she asked, keeping to her course.

"My shoulder burns like the blazes," he allowed, shifting it slightly. "It was a two-shot derringer Em hauled out of her pocket?"

"Single-shot."

He blinked and softly cleared his throat. "Your brother-in-law shot me?"

"Of course not!" she laughingly answered. "Drayton was the one who pulled you off Emmy so she wasn't crushed when you fell on her. And he was the one who dealt with her while I was stanching your blood flow. Your carpet is ruined, by the way."

"What happened to my shoulder, Simone?"

There was no point in attempting to put a shine on it. "My knife got stuck in it."

His brow shot up. The expression ended abruptly and with a hearty, "Ow."

"Actually," she admitted, "I'm rather surprised that it wasn't the headache you noticed first. The bruise on your forehead is from where you hit the corner of the desk when you took Emmy down."

He released one of her hands to reach up and gingerly explore the bruise. "How did your knife get in my back?"

"I threw it at Emmy," she supplied, "and you jumped in front of it trying to take the gun away from her. The point didn't go very deep, though. The doctor said that you have shoulder muscles of steel. I didn't agree with him, of course. I just nodded and pretended that I was a lady and didn't know the first thing about your steely muscles. You're going to have a scar there, too. But just a little one. It took only five stitches to close it."

He looked up at the ceiling. Five stitches, a bullet hole, and a knot the size of a duck egg. "Well," he finally drawled, "I certainly acquitted myself well in this whole affair, didn't I?"

"I'm impressed," she assured him. "Really."

"With what?" he countered, bringing his gaze down to meet hers. "My ability to knock myself unconscious?"

"That was purely an accident," she cheerfully asserted. "I'm sure that you would have had the presence of mind to avoid the desk if you hadn't just had a hole blown in your side and a knife quivering in your back."

"Uh-huh."

"Tristan . . ." she cajoled, squeezing his hand.

"A man isn't supposed to be rescued by a woman."

"Oh, for heaven's— You did rescue me. You're the one with the bullet hole I was supposed to have. Presumably through my tender little heart."

He snorted. "Well, it was the least I could do, considering that I didn't figure out Lucinda's plan, didn't know where to go to find you so that you were forced to liberate yourself, and didn't know that Emmy had gone mad, killed her mother, and taken over the plot to kill us."

"I think you're being more than a tad bit hard on yourself," she countered. "I hadn't figured out that Emmy had gone over the edge until I got here and saw that hack rolling away. And I didn't know Lucinda's plan until she felt obliged to share it with Sarah."

He blinked and winced. "Damn. Sarah. I forgot all about her. Is she all right?"

With a shrug, Simone answered, "Apparently. At least she was well enough to sprint for her hotel room, throw her things in a trunk, and book passage on a ship sailing for Cádiz."

"*Cádiz?*"

"According to Noland's men, it was the first outbound ship she could find after we got away from Lucinda. She was *supposed* to come here and tell you that we'd gotten away and not to go when Lucinda sent for you."

"Yes, well," he said dryly, "she was supposed to marry George, too."

Simone softly cleared her throat and then slowly said, "Speaking of marriage . . ."

Which she was clearly reluctant to do. "Yes?" he pressed.

"We have a bit of a problem," she replied on a single rush of air. "Nothing," she hurried to add, "that we can't figure a way out of, I'm sure."

"What sort of problem?"

"I have no idea of how it happened or why he thinks so," she began. "But Drayton seems to be under the impression that we're going to marry each other."

It wasn't how he'd intended to go about it all, but since the duke had let the proverbial cat out of the bag. . . . "He thinks we're marrying, darling, because I asked him for his blessing."

She blinked and he felt her pulse quicken. "You didn't."

"Yes, I did," he assured her. "It was amid the running about right after you were kidnapped, but I distinctly remember the conversation. He felt compelled to warn me that you're a terrible cook and that you have a tendency to graze about the kitchen and call it a meal. After which he said he doubted that we gave a flying rat's ass what he thought and so he wouldn't waste his time opposing us."

Simone grinned, her heart soaring. Oh, life was good. Very, very good. And it was going to get even better. Not that she wanted to hurry through the process of getting there. "Drayton didn't say 'flying rat's ass.' "

"No, I was embellishing."

She smiled patiently, nodded, and then squeezed his hand. "Well, I'm sure that he won't hold you to it," she said softly. "That you can plead the strain of the crisis and all that."

She was playing at reluctance. But because the games with her always ended with her in his arms, he was perfectly willing to go along. "And why would I want to beg out?"

"Why would you want to marry me?" she countered. "Drayton's right. I'm the worst cook in the world."

"I have a cook and don't need another one."

"I can't sew or knit or embroider."

"So? I have a tailor and if I want knitted or embroidered goods, I go to a haberdashery."

"I'm a walking scandal, Tristan," she countered, a hint of true concern eddying beneath the lightly spoken words. London's already abuzz with the news that I stabbed you in the back. Literally."

He cocked a brow and grinned through a wince. "I hardly think they're terribly worked up over that. Not when they have the Lunatic Lockwoods' latest—and decidedly greatest—debacle to discuss and dissect. Darling, I'm sorry, but a crazy sister, a murdered stepmother and coachman, two kidnappings, and an assault on an officer of Scotland Yard outdoes a slight knife wound. By at least a league."

Ah, if ever there was a match made in heaven. . . . "Well, when you put it that way. . . . Why would I want to marry you?"

His grin went wicked. "I have steely muscles." He

pushed the bedcoverings lower on his hips, asking, "Would you like to see them?"

It was done, and they both knew it. Still . . . she undid the uppermost button of her blouse while saying, "You're not the only man in the world with marvelous muscles and imperfections, you know."

"True," he allowed, reaching out to take care of the buttons on her skirt. "Would it give me a leg up on the others to know that I love you?"

"It would," she admitted, softly, sincerely. She grinned. "But you have taken a blow to your head. Decency demands that you be given some time to regain your senses."

He hooked his fingers in her waistband and hauled her closer. She went without resisting, her heart singing, and let him wrap her in his arms. "You can give me forever and a day," he whispered, brushing his lips across hers, "and it's not going to make any difference, Simone. I love you. I've loved you since the moment you sat on that windowsill and dared me to chase you."

"And now that you've caught me?"

"Are you? Caught?"

"Well and truly, Tristan. Happily. And I have been from the beginning. I've loved you since that moment you grinned and ever-so-efficiently cut my dress off me."

"Really," he murmured, clearly pleased with himself.

"And your bowline knot . . . I almost swooned."

He laughed and eased his arms from around her. "It would appear that we've wasted a great deal of time," he said, nimbly opening the upper buttons on her shirt. "What do you say to not wasting any more?"

She leaned beyond his easy reach, countering, "I'd say

that physically taxing yourself isn't a particularly good idea right this moment."

He smiled, slowly, knowingly, fully aware of the effect on her. "Happy men heal quicker, you know."

The breath she drew was a shallow one, but she held to her resolve and lightly replied, "Not if they tear open their wounds and bleed to death."

Bleed to death? Not likely. "I'm not going to tear anything open. Well, maybe the front of your shirt if you don't move back here so I can undo the buttons." She didn't move. "You're not going to be one of those worrying, always fussing and doting wives, are you?"

"If that's what you're hoping for," she answered, chuckling and easing off the bed, "you're in for a bitter disappointment."

He wasn't bitter, but he was definitely heading toward disappointed. "Where are you going?"

"Over here," she answered, moving toward the skirted side table. "But I really ought to be going home. You know, reserve what's left of the illusions of propriety and all."

Propriety? If that mattered to anyone at this point, Haywood would be standing at the foot of the bed, a disapproving frown firmly in place. Tristan reined in his smile and asked, "Is your brother-in-law's faithful toady downstairs waiting to collect you?"

"Not that I know of."

"Darling, if Haywood doesn't care, no one does. Besides, it's way too late for us to even pretend that we care about propriety. As they say, that ship has sailed."

She looked over her shoulder and grinned at him. "Are you hungry?"

"Not for food."

Her eyes sparkling, she countered, "Would you like something to drink? Mrs. Davis brought up a pot of tea."

"Not tea," he answered, a brilliant plan unfolding in his brain. "In my writing desk is a bottle of brandy."

She crossed over to the ornately carved piece of mahogany and lowered the front. "With two glasses," she said, taking the flask and the small snifters from their slots. "How very forward-thinking of you."

She poured a generous amount into each glass and then put the stopper back. Leaving the flask on the desk, she brought him his drink, saying, "This is likely to make your head hurt worse, you know."

He lifted his glass in salute. "Or it could make me forget all about the pain."

The smile she gave him suggested that she was anticipating an "I told you so" opportunity in the very near future. "What else can I get for you?" she asked. "Are you sure you're not hungry?"

"I'm sure. In my armoire," he said, deliberately, patiently working through his scheme, "are my sketch pad and charcoals. Bottom drawer, right-hand side."

She considered him, a knowing smile playing at the corners of her mouth. He met her gaze squarely and silently dared her to refuse. And then, because she was Simone, she chuckled softly, took a sip of her brandy, set the snifter on the desk, and then walked over to the armoire. Tristan watched as she bent over and retrieved his supplies, his smile broadening and his blood warming in appreciation.

"And what is it you intend to draw?" she asked, heading back to him.

"You."

"Really," she drawled, arching a raven brow and handing him the pad and pencils.

"I promised that I would. Remember?"

"I do indeed." She touched the tip of her tongue to her lower lip, her eyes sparkling. Slowly undoing the buttons of her shirt front, she asked, "Where would you like me?"

Tristan grinned, victorious. Setting his brandy on the side table, he patted the empty space beside him on the bed.

Incorrigible. Persistent and reckless. The light of her life. "You are a rogue," Simone laughingly accused, accepting his hand and letting him help her climb onto the mattress.

"If you want, I could try to reform."

"Don't you dare," she countered, leaning across his lap and smiling at him. "Ever. I love you just the way you are."

He slowly trailed his fingertips down the length of her throat. "Your heart is going pitter-pat."

Yes, it was. In the most delightful way. "Should I go lock the door?"

He smoothed the linen off her breasts, his smile sinful and irresistible. "Let's be scandalous."

"All right," she agreed, shivering with anticipation. "But just this once."

"Of course," he offered, chuckling as he wrapped her in his arms and drew her close against him. "Just this once and then we'll be respectable for the rest of our lives."

She laughed and his heart soared, borne on the pureness of love and boundless hope, on the absolute certainty that he was the luckiest man who had ever lived.